The
STONE-COLD
HEART *of*
VALENTINE
BRISCOE

Center Point
Large Print

Also by Marcia Lynn McClure
and available from Center Point Large Print:

Dusty Britches
Weathered Too Young
The Windswept Flame
The Visions of Ransom Lake
The Heavenly Surrender
The Light of the Lovers' Moon
Beneath the Honeysuckle Vine
The Whispered Kiss

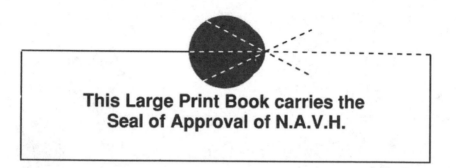

**This Large Print Book carries the
Seal of Approval of N.A.V.H.**

The STONE-COLD HEART *of* VALENTINE BRISCOE

Marcia Lynn McClure

CENTER POINT LARGE PRINT
THORNDIKE, MAINE

This Center Point Large Print edition
is published in the year 2018 by arrangement with
Distractions Ink.

The text of this Large Print edition is unabridged.
In other aspects, this book may vary
from the original edition.
Printed in the United States of America
on permanent paper.
Set in 16-point Times New Roman type.

ISBN: 978-1-68324-789-0

Library of Congress Cataloging-in-Publication Data

Names: McClure, Marcia Lynn, author.
Title: The stone-cold heart of Valentine Briscoe / Marcia Lynn McClure.
Description: Center Point Large Print edition. | Thorndike, Maine :
   Center Point Large Print, 2018.
Identifiers: LCCN 2018003803 | ISBN 9781683247890
   (hardcover : alk. paper)
Subjects: LCSH: Large type books.
Classification: LCC PS3613.C36 S76 2018 | DDC 813/.6—dc23
LC record available at https://lccn.loc.gov/2018003803

To Brette . . .
Who knew I'd go from changing your diapers
when you were a baby to being eternally grateful
for your friendship, willingness to hang in there
with me, encouragement, and support. I am
being literal when I say that I could never, never
have written this book without you. I hope you
know how true that is!

With all my love and sincerest gratitude.
This one is for you, Brette!

————*and*————

To my hero and inspiration . . .
Kevin from Heaven!

PROLOGUE

Haven stared at the letter in her hands. They were dead. Her mother, her father—her parents were dead. Her aunt's letter explained everything, even that by the time Haven received the letter—the letter that had traveled all the way from England before it was delivered to Haven in Covington, Georgia—her parents would have already long been buried in a cemetery on the outskirts of London.

"Here you go, sweet baby," Mipsie said, placing a glass of water on the table in front of Haven.

But Haven just continued to stare at the letter she held. She well recognized the handwriting, for her Aunt Alice (her father's sister) had been somewhat famous for her perfect script as a younger woman. Thus, Haven knew the information contained in the letter to be true, and acceptance began to soak into Haven's consciousness—into her mind and her heart.

Mipsie and Arabella sat silent in their seats at the table. Upon realizing what the contents of the letter entailed, Old Joe had excused himself to see to the horses. For long moments Haven was silent, tears drizzling over her cheeks.

Closing her eyes, Haven inhaled a deep breath,

exhaling slowly as she fought to maintain her composure. From the moment she had first read her aunt's account of the cholera epidemic in Egypt—the epidemic that had erupted while her parents had been touring there—Haven had somehow already known her parents had perished miserably at the hand of the wicked disease. She knew it even before she had read onward in the letter. She had known they were dead. And now, as she listened to the quiet of the night—the soothing songs of bug noise, the light, melodic tinkling of the lamp prisms throughout the house as the breeze wafted in through the open porch doors—she tried not to envision her mother and father as cold, lifeless corpses, buried in the soil of a foreign land. She determined to remember them as they had appeared when last she had seen them: bright and alive, her mother's cheeks flushed with the excitement of the trip she and Haven's father would be taking abroad, her father's proud smile in sharing his wife's pleasure in anticipation.

The heavenly sweet fragrance of the lilacs and wisteria blooms just outside the kitchen porch, so brilliant in their shades of lavender and amethyst, fluttered in on the coattails of the same breeze that was playing music on the lamp prisms, and Haven offered a silent prayer to heaven that the angels had greeted her mother with violet florettes and bouquets of lilac blossoms with fern fronds. Her mother so loved her purple flowers in the spring and her pink posies of sweet peas in the summer.

"Do they have flowers in heaven, do you think, Mipsie?" Haven whispered aloud. "Mother so loved her flowers here . . . and bein' that she will be missin' them this year, I . . . I . . ."

"Oh yes, my girl," Mipsie answered, her familiar voice ever so soothing to Haven's hurting heart. "You knows God made dem flowers out in da garden. So's I'm sho' he has dem growin' all about up dere."

Haven opened her eyes. Comforted by Mipsie's reassurance, she sighed with adoration as she glanced across the small table to the beautiful woman sitting across from her—the woman who truly loved Haven as her own. She felt guilt rise in her throat at the sudden relief welling in her bosom—the relief it had been her mother and father who had taken ill and died, and not Mipsie and Old Joe.

Haven's eyes filled with more tears as she gazed at Mipsie with gratitude and admiration. What a strong woman Mipsie Barnes was! Her life account was so full of misery and pain, of heartache and injustice, Haven could hardly think of it without feeling her own heart would tear itself in two. And yet there she sat; Mipsie, with everything she had endured, sat in comforting Haven. There too sat Arabella—

there, just at Haven's side, tears streaming down her own face as if it had been *her* parents that had died.

Haven's silky, sleek, obsidian-black hair, almond-shaped green eyes, and petite yet curvaceous figure mirrored Merial Abernathy's. And yet she thought not of Merial Abernathy first when she thought of the word "mother" but rather of Mipsie. Although Haven had inherited Felix Abernathy's sense of humor, compassion, and bright smile, it was Old Joe she secretly thought of as her true father. And as Haven mused lovingly over the three people she considered to be her truest family, her heart did begin to break, but not for the sake of the loss of her parents. In that moment, as it often did when contemplating their pasts, Haven's heart broke for Mipsie, Arabella, and Old Joe.

In 1846 Mipsie had been born into slavery. The daughter of a sixteen-year-old slave girl, Chloe, and the plantation farmer who owned her, William Jones, Mipsie had grown up oppressed, abused, and unfathomably afflicted in the rancid, vile stew of slavery. Naturally, everyone ignored the fact that the farmer had fathered Mipsie—especially the farmer's wife. And yet, though Mipsie's paternal parentage was never spoken of, William Jones sold Mipsie and Chloe to another plantation owner when Mipsie was just thirteen. Mipsie's mother had always believed they were sold because Mipsie so directly favored her natural father in appearance. It had become more and more difficult for Mrs. Jones to endure the whispers that followed in her wake concerning the beautiful mulatto slave girl her husband owned and so closely resembled.

Furthermore, as Mipsie blossomed into her own young womanhood, her beauty, so strikingly magnified by her ivory-brown complexion, drew attention and great admiration from men of all colors and means when they set eyes upon her. Therefore, sadly, the sale of Mipsie and her mother did not shelter Mipsie from suffering the same violent fate as her mother. And at the tender age of sixteen, Mipsie found herself expecting a baby conceived of her new white master, John Barnes.

Nevertheless, Mipsie, as her mother before her, did not hate the child she bore but loved her more than her own life. The babe, Arabella, born mere months before President Lincoln signed the document declaring "all persons held as slaves" should be free, must have touched the heart of John Barnes. For Barnes did indeed give both Mipsie and Arabella their freedom—even for the war still blazing on and many in the South refusing to hold to Lincoln's dictates. More even than that, John Barnes gifted Mipsie, Arabella, and Mipsie's new husband, Joe Barnes (whom he had owned since Joe was a child), a small sum of money, which he hoped they could use to make their way north.

But Mipsie, Joe, and Arabella were not able to flee any farther north than northeast of Louisiana to Georgia—pillaged, burned, Sherman-defeated Georgia. And it was there, in 1864, when Haven's own mother had just given birth to her, that Haven's father, Felix Abernathy, witnessed Joe working odd jobs. Seeing Joe was a fine, strong, able man, Felix approached him and inquired of the now-free man if he were interested in laboring for him in Covington for wages. Joe explained to Felix that he had a wife and young daughter to shelter and feed. To Joe's astonishment, Felix, now knowing Mipsie had a child of her own who was still at the breast (Arabella had not much to eat but her mother's milk, even for her being two years of age), then asked if Mipsie would be willing to serve as maid to Haven's mother and wet-nurse to his new daughter, Haven. The wage that Felix offered Joe for his family's labors was far beyond any wage Joe had ever imagined. And after discussing the opportunity with Mipsie, the family made its way to Covington to care for the Abernathys' farm and their new baby girl.

Consequently, it was Mipsie's lovely face Haven remembered seeing above her cradle, crib, and bed. It was Mipsie who had suckled Haven as a baby, cooled her forehead with a damp cloth when she was ill—Mipsie who had rocked her in the rocking chair at night, softly singing the beautiful, albeit haunting songs of the slaves, just as she had done for Arabella. Even it was Mipsie who taught Haven to walk, to talk; it was Mipsie who Haven first called "Mama." And, as ever it had been, it was still Mipsie who leapt to her mind when Haven heard the word "mother."

As for Joe—it had been he who had picked Haven up when she'd fallen and scraped her knee, kissed the wound quick, brushed the tears from her cheeks, and told her all was well.

"Ol' Joe'll keep you safe, chil'. Ol' Joe loves his girls, he do. Now you run on and play some mo'. Ol' Joe'll be right here," he would always assure her. Oh, how Haven loved Old Joe for treating her like his own. It was Old Joe who Haven thought of as "father."

Mipsie Mama and Papa Joe had never once abandoned Haven for travel, social gatherings, or business. Certainly Haven understood that Felix Abernathy provided the money that purchased Haven's clothing, food, and shelter. She understood that Merial Abernathy had given birth to her. Still, it was Mipsie who held her, rocked her, played with her, fed her, helped her dress. And it was Joe who bounced her on his knee, tumbled and ran with her about the farm, and protected her from anything that meant to harm her.

Once when Haven was but five years old, while Mipsie and Joe were tucking her and

Arabella into bed for the night, Haven asked when her own skin and Arabella's would begin to turn a bit darker to mirror that of Mipsie's soft chocolate skin, or even the richer coffee color of Joe's. Haven had ever to that point felt slighted by God somehow—as if she had not lived well enough to prove herself worthy of a darker flesh.

Haven remembered the manner in which Mipsie's eyes had filled with tears. "Oh, now don' you go wishin' after such nonsense, chil'," Mipsie had soothed, smiling. "You and Bella . . . yo' goin' to be happy yo' bofe white-skinned babies. And ol' Mipsie . . . I'z been prayin' yo' skin don' get no darker dan it is now, huny."

"Why, Mipsie Mama?" Haven had asked in her innocence. "I want to be beautiful like you. I don't wanna be plain ol' white. Nobody will ever marry me if I ain't beautiful like you!"

Again Mipsie smoothed Haven's hair back from her forehead, smiling as she said, "Don' you go worryin' on it no longer, chil'. You a beautiful baby. A beautiful baby! You go to sleep an' dream of fairies and bunnies now, you hear?"

Old Joe had chuckled and in his low, booming voice said, "You a good girl, Miss Havey. A mighty good girl."

Haven had been obedient, closed her eyes, and gone to sleep. Even still, it was some time before her innocence of childhood was lost to the knowledge of how cruel the world had been—how cruel it still was. And although Mipsie and Old Joe eventually convinced Haven that she could not be so affectionate with them when others were present, Haven had never treated Arabella as anything other than a sister—no matter who was about.

Arabella had been Haven's lifelong friend. Lovely Arabella was to Haven her sister—if not by birthright, then by their hearts being so interlaced together. Arabella had grown from a mesmerizingly lovely child into an exquisitely beautiful quadroon woman, and Haven oft wondered how it could be that Arabella was so stunning in her loveliness—with her blue eyes, black hair, and enthralling smile—and Haven of such average appearance. After all, as Arabella had one-quarter African slave blood to complement her magnificent complexion and features of face and form, Haven owned her own one-quarter of ethnic blood. And though Haven's secreted lineage was full as hated by others as was Arabella's, at least Arabella inherited beauty from hers.

"You should leave, Havey," Arabella stated quite unexpectedly, jostling Haven from her reveries.

Haven asked, "What?"

"You should leave," Arabella repeated. "You should leave Covin'ton and move west the way you've always talked about doin'. There's nothin' holdin' you here now."

New tears filled Haven's eyes. Reaching over, she took Arabella's hands in her own, frowning as she wept.

"What on earth are you talkin' about, Bellie?" she squeaked. "I have *you!* I have Mipsie Mama, Papa Joe . . . and you! Why would I ever leave my family?"

"Arabella's right, Havey," Mipsie agreed, however, even as Arabella brushed a tear from her cheek—a tear of not wanting to lose her sister. She smiled, her brown eyes alight with sudden excitement. "And Arabella can go witcha!" Mipsie suggested. "There ain't nothin' here for her, nothin' at all. But out west . . . folks have opportunity out west. I been readin' about it. In truth, it seems to me both ya'll should travel west," Mipsie continued. "Here theys only sadness, old wounds, and hatred for the likes of you two. It's well you know it, Havey." Mipsie paused, wagging a slender, brown finger at Haven. "Anybody ever finds out about yo' grandmama—yo' mama, fo' dat matter—well, yo'll be worse off dan me or Arabella."

Haven knew Mipsie was correct—and on both accounts. Going out west would be a liberation of sorts for Arabella too—an escape to a newer world where old hatreds might not be as thoroughly rooted, especially if they weren't

16

as recognizable. The fact was, the only reason anybody in Covington even knew Arabella was a quadroon was because they knew Mipsie was her mother—assumed Old Joe was her natural father. Why, Arabella's skin was as fair as Haven's, and Haven's was even fairer than her own mother's— an actuality she attributed to her father's being so thoroughly British. If folks out west only saw the white of Haven's lineage in her outward appearance, then how would they see anything else in Arabella's?

"Oh, that's a wonderful idea, Mipsie!" Haven exclaimed. Brushing the tears of mourning from her cheeks—for hope and exuberance had begun to well in her now—she turned to face Arabella directly. "Think of it, Bellie! You and I, two white girls from Georgia, moved west to . . . to . . . I don't know . . . to find adventure!"

But Arabella shrank in her chair. "Oh, Havey . . . no! I just could not do that. I couldn't! People would see right through me!"

"Why?" Haven asked, however. "You and I could be sisters, we're so much the same! I mean, maybe we don't look like twins, but our manners are the same—our speech, our strivin' to be proper ladies."

"Just 'cause you taught me everythin' you learned in that fancy finishin' school of yours doesn't mean I am the same as you, Havey," Arabella offered.

"Oh, fiddle-dee-dee, Bellie," Haven said, waving a graceful hand in the air as a gesture of dismissing Arabella's concerns. "If you and I stood up in front of a Sunday congregation and recited scripture, no one would guess *you* hadn't been the one sent off to finishin' school instead of me." Haven giggled a little. "Fact is, you're still better at walkin' and keepin' your bustle from bouncin' to Atlanta and back than I am."

"I don't know," Arabella whispered.

Haven could see Arabella was truly afraid—not just nervous but afraid. And why shouldn't she be? After all, the war had been over for twenty years, but it had not changed the hearts of many who still blamed the slaves for causing it. People with mixed blood were often treated even more poorly than those with dark skin were, and Arabella was all too familiar with the vile truth of it, just as Haven was.

Mipsie reached across the table, taking her daughter's hands in her own then. "What if Haven goes before you, huny, hmm?" she asked Arabella. "What if Havey goes and tests it all . . . sees if what folks is sayin' is true? Sees if folks ain't as sensitive to skin color out west as dey still is out here, hmmm?"

"Yes!" Haven agreed with excitement. "What if I do go first? What if I set up the millinery shop . . . in the buildin' the Misses Sandersan own, like they suggest in their letters? What if I go before you, get things all ready and the hat shops in Denver well on the hook for buyin' our hats—"

"*Your* hats," Arabella interrupted.

Haven shook her head and continued, "*Our* hats. With bein' closer to Denver the way we will be, the Misses Sandersan sisters assure me we will be busier than a one-armed paper hanger!"

Haven gasped, horrified that the news of her parents' deaths had raised some strange sense of hope and freedom in her. "Why, I am terrible! Here I am, still holdin' the letter informin' me of my parents' death and yet feelin' as tickled as a tick on a dirty dog! I should be overwrought this moment . . . not hopeful of change. And even so, how could I leave my family?"

But as always, Mipsie's soothing voice calmed Haven's guilt. "Oh, I'z sho' you gonna shed a river of tears once you reclize yo' parents is gone, Havey. Sho' nuf you gonna feel it. So don' you go wishin' for it to be worse dan it seems it gonna be right now." Mipsie stood up from her chair. "Fact is, I best be gettin' supper on so'z we can et 'fore the mournin' sets in somepin' furious."

"I'll help you, Mama," Arabella said, rising from her own chair.

"What *do* you really think, Bellie?" Haven asked in a quiet voice. "Do *you* think we should go out west and . . . and just see what it brings?"

Arabella paused, smiled her beautiful smile at Haven, and answered, "I think if you have the chance to escape what we both live in fear of every day of our lives . . . then you should go. Yes, I think you should go."

"But you *will* come with me, won't you?" Haven ventured.

Arabella's blue eyes filled with tears. "I don't think I could ever leave Mama and Daddy. Just abandon them here all alone."

Haven felt the same way about Mipsie and Old Joe; she didn't want to leave them either. And that's why she spoke her mind aloud to Arabella, yet softly enough that Mipsie could not hear from her place in the kitchen.

"Well, I never planned to leave them behind . . . at least not for very long," she confessed. "Just long enough to prepare a good place for them to live out their later years with us."

Arabella's tears escaped her lovely eyes to stream over her cheeks. "I figured you had mischief in mind, Havey," she said, bending down and hugging Haven.

"None of us has anything to stay here for, Bellie," Haven whispered into her sister's ear. "Not now. Mama and Daddy aren't even buried here on the farm, so what have any of us got holdin' us here, right?"

Arabella released Haven and stood straight once more. Brushing the tears from her eyes, she said, "I'll go help Mama. And you know she's right. The loss of your parents, it will come to

20

you very hard at some time here very soon." She paused, adding, "I'm so sorry, Havey. I know you feel like they didn't love you . . . but they did, you know. They did. And you love them too. So don't resist in mournin' them proper, all right?"

Haven nodded, even as the sense of deep mourning began to overwhelm hcr unexpectedly in that very moment.

"I know," she breathed as she began to weep. "I do know."

＊ ＊ ＊ ＊ ＊

Haven's eyes were so puffy, her nose so red and swollen from crying, she wondered if her face would cver return to normal. Furthermore, her head was pounding like there was a ghost of a drummer boy pent up inside it.

Mipsie, as always, had been correct. The news Aunt Alice's letter had brought had indeed begun to sink into Haven's heart. Shortly before supper, Haven had found herself lying on her bed, her body wracked with the pain of loss and the sobbing it brought with it.

For hours she had cried. For hours her heart ached so brutally she wondered if it would stop beating altogether. Haven had never experienced such pain—never imagined that the loss of loved ones could physically destroy a body. Nevertheless, her parents were gone, and Haven

21

now knew the agony death could inflict on those who lived on.

Finally, Haven was able to find a remnant of fortitude and resolved to distract her mind by writing to Wynifred and Merigold Sandersan, the two elderly sisters with whom she had been corresponding via post for near to a year.

Haven Abernathy fancied herself a somewhat talented milliner. Ever since childhood, Haven had adored the fabrication of hats. Oh, the hats she had made for her and Arabella when they were girls had been gaudy and tasteless in the very least. And although Haven's mother would not allow the girls to wear Haven's millinery creations while in public, Mipsie would don a gaudy hat here and there while going about her tasks just to please and encourage Haven's hatmaking.

Thus, several years previous while still in adolescence, Haven had made several quite lovely hats and shipped them off to a famous hat shop in Denver, Colorado. There, two "spinsterly sisters," as they referred to themselves, had contacted Haven via post, asking that she design more hats the likes of the kind they had purchased from the shop in Denver. Hence, Wynifred and Merigold Sandersan of Fletcher, Colorado, had become loyal admirers and patrons of Haven's work, as well as regular letter-writers with Haven herself.

Moreover, for the past two years, the two Sandersan sisters had been begging Haven to join them out west where she could be close to Denver and the shops that had begun to carry her hats on a regular basis. Wynifred and Merigold had once owned a dress shop in the small town of Fletcher and had explained that the building where their business once thrived now stood empty and useless. Being that the sisters owned the building, they had graciously offered to lease the space to Haven to set up her own millinery shop and workplace.

From the moment she had received her first letter from the Sandersan sisters suggesting Haven move west, Haven's heart had been set on one day doing so. Yet the desire to stay close to Mipsie, Old Joe, and Arabella kept Haven from acting upon her desires to spread her wings, as well as the fact that her parents did return to Georgia once or twice a year. She could not live without her family near to her—or so she thought.

But now her parents were gone—truly gone. The farm, and all other of her father's properties and investments, would fall to her, and Haven did not want the responsibility. Nor did she feel or wish to be tied to her Georgia roots. After all, with her mother and father gone, all that remained of her blood relations had quit Georgia long ago. Still, she wondered if she could find the courage to leave Mipsie, Joe, and Arabella behind for any length of time at all—even the short time she hoped it would take to set up her life in Fletcher, Colorado.

Nevertheless, as she sat in her bed—her tear-soaked pillow propped against the headboard as she leaned back against it reading Wynifred Sandersan's most recent letter—something deep inside Haven spoke to her, assuring her that she *could* find the courage to leave Covington, that she could and *should* endeavor to make a better life out west. And not just for herself but for those three she loved more than her own life: Arabella, Mipsie, and Old Joe, the family she still had living.

Folding the letter and laying it on the small night table next to her bed, Haven put out the flame of the lamp there as well and lay down in hopes of finding respite in slumber.

Haven closed her eyes and tried to steady her breathing, ragged still from hours of sobbing. She wondered what the Sandersan sisters looked like—wondered what the town of Fletcher was in appearance.

She heard a quiet buzzing and opened her eyes to see that a lightning bug had wandered in through the open window. The soft yellow blink of light from the insect that broke the darkness around her brought a slight smile to Haven's mouth.

"Candle bug, Candle bug . . . what are you about?" she whispered, quoting a sweet poem her mother had often recited to her when she was a little girl. *"Do you seek a dark haven? Or a lover, devout? Candle bug, Candle bug . . . why came you so near? Did you know I was lonesome, and wished you were here?"*

More tears escaped Haven's eyes to trickle over her temples and moisten her already dampish pillow. She did truly love her mother and father so! It was true that she did not even blame them for staying away almost all of the time, for she knew the secret her mother bore, the secret her father kept for her mother—and for Haven. Georgia and Haven herself were reminders of the past: the hurt, the wrongfulness and hatred that lingered still, even in lovely Covington.

So there, weeping over her lost parents, knowing heartache the likes she could never have imagined, Haven forgave her mother for the near abandonment of her daughter—and her father too. After all, they had made certain she was loved and cared for in the arms of Mipsie and Old Joe, even ensuring she had a perpetual friend and playmate—a sister—in Arabella. They had done well by Haven—they had.

Haven was quiet, watching the lightning bug slowly flit around her room and listening to the melody croaked out by the frogs down near the pond. She thought for a moment that it was amusing that such a creature as a frog, with such a harsh sound as a croak for a voice, could make such soft, soothing music at night. Haven smiled, imagining a chorus of frogs lining the pond bank and dressed in high collars and bow ties.

The fragrance of the night-blooming flowers in her mother's flower garden filled her senses and brought more quiet tears to her eyes. Her mother's flowers—the one thing she knew she would miss when she and the other remaining members of her family moved west.

"Candle bug, candle bug . . . the night was so dark! Yet your flame lights the night now, with steadfasted spark," Haven whispered in continuing the poem she had so loved to hear her mother softly speak. *"Candle bug, Candle bug . . . I am lonesome no more,"* she breathed as she wept for the flowers that would never again know her mother's touch. *"Incandescent companion . . . how thee I adore."*

CHAPTER ONE

Haven smiled as she descended the front porch steps. As she often did, she had to consciously remind herself not to skip. She was a lady, after all, born and raised in the graceful South, polished at one of the finest finishing schools in the East. And it certainly would not do for folks in Fletcher, Colorado, to see Haven skipping, her bustle bouncing about like a baby's ball at her backside—not when she had accepted their requests to teach their children decorum, etiquette, and even social dancing. No, indeed, it would not do at all!

Glancing over to the small cemetery just a ways away, Haven smiled, nodded, and softly called, "Good morning, everyone!" to the residents sleeping in eternal repose there—well, to their remains, at least. She was glad she'd decided to secure the little house near the graveyard as her own. Not only was it a quiet, peaceful setting and just a sniffle on the outskirts of town, but also it gave her the opportunity to delight on gazing out her kitchen window each day to the pansies and petunias she had planted at the base of each tombstone. Haven fancied the little burial ground didn't look quite so gray and gloomy now that pretty green-leafed flowers of cheery yellow, pink, and purple lingered there. The thought drifted through her mind that her mother would be pleased with the beauty Haven had attempted to add to the world by planting flowers in a place so many folks thought unpleasant. Tending to the graves here and there also afforded a bit of comfort to Haven. Though she knew that in all likelihood she would never have the opportunity to visit her own parents' graves in England, at least she could tend to the graves of those who were buried in Fletcher. And in that she did indeed find a measure of comfort.

Turning her face toward the sun for a moment, Haven closed her eyes and allowed the dry warmth of the day to fill her with gladness as she slowed her pace. Oh, certainly she had experienced rain since leaving Georgia and settling in Colorado. But the rain in Fletcher was fast and furious, invigorating, and often even cold—a very stark difference from the slow, hot, muggy, obstinate rain she had known growing up. But it was the sunshine that truly filled Haven's heart with joy. The Colorado sunshine was like nothing Haven had ever known before! And it wasn't just the sun that delighted Haven when it greeted her but the vast sapphire of the sky in which it dallied—the billowy, pearl-white clouds that slowly drifted overhead in accompaniment, like angelic sentinels of mammoth proportions watching over the world in silent visibility.

"Mornin', Miss Abernathy," Margie Shaffer greeted as she hurried past Haven.

Opening her eyes, Haven called, "Good mornin', Margie! Late for school again, I see."

"Yes, ma'am! Miss Neeley will have my hide if I don't make it before she rings the bell," Margie called over her shoulder. "I'll see you this afternoon at classes, Miss Abernathy! Bye now!"

Haven giggled, shaking her head at Margie Shaffer and her perpetual tardiness. As she heard the familiar clanging of Miss Neeley's school bell, Haven mused, "That Margie Shaffer could not be on time if her life depended on it."

Haven nodded, knowing that she would have to reiterate punctuality at her etiquette and decorum class that afternoon. Nevertheless, at the thought of yet another item of importance to be echoed, Haven exhaled a heavy sigh.

Twice a week, after Miss Neeley let out school, Haven met with ten or so children from the ages of nine to eleven. An hour and a half after that, she then held another class for the youngest adolescents of Fletcher between the ages of twelve and fourteen. There were only eight of the older children. Still, three hours twice a week after a full day's work at the millinery shop—it had turned out to be a bit more taxing than Haven had expected. Even so, it made Haven happy to see the children progress. With Denver so close to Fletcher, it was to be expected that many of the children of Fletcher would be thrust into city life or choose to join it and its social settings as they grew into adulthood. It was exactly why many of the parents of Fletcher had approached Haven only several weeks after she arrived, inquiring as to whether she would be willing to hold classes on social graces for their children. Haven had been more than delighted to help, as well as a bit flattered. That the townsfolk would think she was such a refined and proper lady worthy of emulation by their children was a great compliment indeed. Furthermore, she had quickly discovered that the children brought more joy to her than she ever could have imagined.

"Is it true, Haven?" Miss Wynifred Sandersan called as she hurried toward Haven from across the street.

Haven paused, not wanting the older woman to have to rush. She watched as the brown-eyed, gray-haired lady, donning one of Haven's own millinery creations, hurried toward her.

"Is what true, Miss Wynifred?" Haven asked as she approached.

"Merigold says Baby Doe Tabor herself purchased not one, not two, but three of your hats from Le Chapeau Argent in Denver!" Miss Wynifred exclaimed.

Haven could not keep the blush of pride from rising to her cheeks. Haven still had trouble believing that Elizabeth "Baby Doe" Tabor, wife of the famous silver baron and Bonanza King of Leadville, Mr. Horace Tabor, had purchased several of Haven's millinery creations. Certainly the Tabors, who had made an unfathomable fortune in Colorado silver mining, were the most famous and admired couple in Denver—in the entire state! Scandalous as their relationship had begun, Baby Doc Tabor was now legally Horace's wife and spent her husband's fortune on whatever thing might catch her fancy. Haven was nearly overwhelmed with delight in finding out that Mrs. Tabor was possibly, at that very moment, wearing one of her Abernathy and Barnes hats while strolling about in Denver.

Reaching out to take Miss Wynifred's hands in her own, Haven's excitement rose even further as she exclaimed, "Yes, it is true! I received Madame Lefebre's letter only last evenin', and Miss Merigold was indeed present when I opened it and read the news!" Inhaling a deep breath in an effort to calm her excitement, Haven continued, "Madame Lefebre said in her letter that Baby Doe Tabor herself came into her shop, Le Chapeau Argent—"

"The Silver Hat," Miss Wynifred translated quietly to herself. "Go on, dear!"

"Madame Lefebre wrote that Mrs. Tabor selected *three* of my hats to purchase then and there *and* requested that she be notified when more of my hats arrive in the shop!" Haven rambled. She frowned just a little, lowering her voice and adding, "Not that I approve at any length of the scandalous manner in which Mrs. Tabor came to be wed to Mr. Horace Tabor."

"Scandalous, indeed," Miss Wynifred agreed, shaking her head with disapproval.

"Yet I cannot regret Mrs. Tabor's patronage . . . not one whit! For indeed she is a woman that all in Denver looks to for an example of high fashion." Squeezing Miss Wynifred's hands with pure delight, Haven asked, "Can you believe such a thing as Baby Doe Tabor wearin' one of my hats . . . a true, labeled Abernathy and Barnes hat? And all around town in Denver?"

"I certainly *can* imagine it, Haven!" Miss Wynifred chuckled. The light in her faded brown eyes sparkled a bit brighter in that moment. "Why, I myself—and my sister too—we are ladies of grand taste in fashion, as you know, even though we did quit Denver for Fletcher years ago. And I knew it! Merigold and I both knew your hats would be the ones to strike gold in that big silver baron city! I'm just as tickled pink as a possum, Haven. Pink as a possum!"

Haven released Miss Wynifred's hands, throwing her arms around the woman in an embrace of thanks and endearment. Oh, how she adored Miss Wynifred Sandersan—Miss Merigold Sandersan, as well. The two spinsterly ladies had changed her life, in truth. Haven knew beyond a shadow of a doubt that had the Sandersan sisters not purchased her hats one day more than a year before, she would never have found her confidence in her true love of the millinery arts. And certainly she would not have found the success that had already come to her via her hats selling so well in the hat shops of Denver. Above all else even, Haven knew that without Wynifred and Merigold Sandersan, she never would have found the courage to leave Georgia to fulfill her dreams of living out west.

"I owe you and Miss Merigold my life, Miss Wynifred," Haven whispered as tears of gratitude filled her eyes.

"Nonsense!" Miss Wynifred said, squeezing Haven tight once more before releasing her. "It's your talent that set your path, honey. Your talent and your goodness and strength of character . . . all the things that are you, Haven Abernathy. You are what has made your life's path so lovely."

Haven felt her smile fade a little. As it was every time someone complimented Haven, the little secret in the back of her mind made itself consciously known and dampened her gladness just a bit—set a tiny flicker of doubt and fear to burning brighter for a while. Even in that moment, the thought nested in Haven's mind. *Would she think me so wonderful if she knew the truth?*

"Forgive me, dear," Miss Wynifred apologized then. "You seem to be on your way somewhere, and here I've stopped you dead in your tracks."

"Oh . . . uh . . . yes," Haven stammered, pushing her secrets and worries to the corner of her mind where they belonged. "I hope to post a letter to Arabella before Mr. Warner makes the post this morning," she explained.

"Oh, well then don't let me keep you, sweet pea!" Miss Wynifred exclaimed. "The faster we can coax your friend Arabella out to Fletcher to join you, the more delight we'll all have, won't we? You run along and post your letter, Haven. And stop in for some lemonade later, won't you? Merigold and I are just as curious as kittens about your new creations."

"Yes, ma'am," Haven promised.

She smiled as Miss Wynifred smoothed the hair up at the back of her neck. Tossing her head with pride in displaying the hat Haven had made just for her—a rather large, garish creation in Haven's mind, complete with a spray of pheasant feathers at the back and an orange ribbon at the front—she said, "And to think—if you hadn't made this just for me, Haven Abernathy . . . why, Mrs. Tabor herself might be wearin' it as we live and breathe!"

Haven giggled as Miss Wynifred rather sashayed away, stepping up on the boardwalk and greeting Doctor Perkins with a pleasant, "Good mornin', Doctor Perkins," as her bustle swished this way and that.

"Good morning, Miss Sandersan," Doctor Perkins returned, politely touching the brim of his black derby as he nodded.

Giggling with delight at Miss Wynifred's obvious pride in her Abernathy and Barnes original, Haven hurried to the other side of the street toward Crabtree's General Store.

"Oh, I hope I didn't miss the post already," Haven mumbled to herself.

Arabella had agreed to come to Fletcher, and Haven did not want to lose even one day in making certain she arrived as quickly as possible.

For the near to five months since she had quit Covington, Georgia, for dry air and blue skies in Fletcher, Colorado, Haven had spent nearly as much time writing letters to Arabella as she had in her millinery crafting and social etiquette instruction combined. At least, sometimes it felt that way.

Yet Haven's persistent reassurance to Arabella—her willingness to answer any and all of Arabella's questions truthfully and in detail—had finally worked to convince her sister to join her. Mipsie and Old Joe were uncertain yet as to whether they would join their girls. Sometimes Haven grew frustrated in their fearfulness of change. After all, it seemed to her the two former slaves would instantly embrace the chance of change. And yet she understood as well. Covington and Georgia were familiar; Old Joe and Mipsie's way of life was familiar. And they were not so young and fresh and hopeful as were Haven and Arabella.

Nonetheless, Haven was determined not to give up on her mission to provide an easier life for Joe and Mipsie. In her daydreams she often fancied Mipsie sitting in the Sandersan sisters' parlor, whirring away at doily making or playing cards as the three women laughed and shared friendship. Old Joe would know his own delight in caring for horses of his own—the four horses Haven had brought with her from Georgia in the hopes that Joe and Mipsie would follow their girls west so that she could make a gift of the animals to Joe. Oh, how she longed to give her father's horses to Joe! After all, it was Joe who had cared for them—raised them from foals. It was Joe who loved them and Joe whom they loved. Haven could sense the horses missed their Old Joe—and Haven understood, for she missed Joe and Mipsie and Arabella to the point of tears very often.

Nevertheless, Arabella had agreed to come to Fletcher, at last. And Haven hoped that Mipsie and Joe would follow very soon thereafter. With both of their daughters so far away, surely they could be convinced. It was what Haven prayed for each night.

"Good mornin', Miss Abernathy," Mr. Crabtree greeted in his familiar monotone.

"Good mornin', Mr. Crabtree!" Haven chimed in an attempt to affect him.

" 'Spose you got another letter to post, have ya?" Mr. Crabtree asked.

The man had the personality of a dishcloth! Haven often wondered how it was that Mr. Crabtree's son, Walter Crabtree, could be such a pleasant, friendly fellow, when his father was so very dull.

"Yes, sir, I do, Mr. Crabtree," Haven confirmed. "But this one is the most excitin' of all—for my friend Arabella has agreed to come to Fletcher to join me and help me with the millinery shop!"

"That's nice," Mr. Crabtree mumbled, peering at her over the rim of the set of spectacles perched low on his nose.

Handing him her letter, Haven watched Mr. Crabtree move as slow as molasses going uphill in January as he placed a postage stamp on the envelope of her letter and then marked the stamp with a penciled X before saying, "That'll be a penny."

Pressing a penny she'd been holding in her hand with the letter to Arabella onto the countertop, Haven asked, "Is there any news today, Mr. Crabtree? Walter Jr. tells me his daddy thinks his crop of apples will be especially sweet this year."

Making conversation with Mr. Crabtree was

37

like pulling hen's teeth. But Haven was determined to soften the man up, one way or the other.

"Yep. Walter Sr. says the trees are heavy . . . had a lot of blossoms in spring," Mr. Crabtree responded.

Haven smiled with triumph. When she'd first arrived in Fletcher, Haven had once asked Mr. Crabtree how his morning had gone. He'd looked at her like she had crawfish squirming out of her ears. Therefore, the fact that he was responding to her inquiries at all pleased her to her core—monotoned responses or not.

"How wonderful! I just love apples," Haven sighed.

"Oh, and the sheriff says there's a new feller in town," Mr. Crabtree offered.

Haven held her breath, hushed to astonishment at the fact that Mr. Crabtree was presenting more information—information that had not been prodded out of him, at that.

"Sheriff says some fellow named Briscoe bought the Vickers' farm just out west of your house," the man monotoned dryly.

"Oh, so I have a new neighbor then, hmm?" Haven pressed.

"It would seem that way," Mr. Crabtree confirmed. He raked a hand back through his graying hair, licked his index finger, and smoothed his right eyebrow with it. "Sheriff says he ain't much of the friendly sort though. And though I didn't know who he was yet when he come in yesterday for some flour, the way he just nodded and grunted at me would lead me to believe that what Sheriff Sterling said is true." Mr. Crabtree frowned. Looking up to make eye contact with Haven again (such a rare thing in itself that Haven still didn't dare inhale a breath), he continued, "That man's got a scowl heavier than a boardin' house biscuit." He paused to nod a moment. "Don't think you'll be doin' much neighborly socializin' with him."

Finally drawing a breath, Haven said, "Well, thank you for the information, Mr. Crabtree. It's always good to know when new folks are movin' in nearby."

Mr. Crabtree nodded once in agreement. Then he put Haven's letter to Arabella into the mail pouch under the countertop.

"You have a good mornin', Miss Abernathy," he said.

"And you, as well, Mr. Crabtree." Haven turned, having had quite enough of Mr. Crabtree's gray-cloud conversation for one day. She snapped her fingers and spun around, however, when she remembered the other purpose she'd had for visiting the store.

"I need about a quarter pound of your lemon drops, Mr. Crabtree," she said. "I plan to give the children a little treat after lessons today. They've been progressin' so well and all."

"Lemon drops. A quarter pound," the man mumbled as he turned and retrieved the large glass jar of sugarcoated lemon drops from a shelf behind him.

Haven watched as the man meticulously measured one small ladleful of lemon drops into a small paper sack. He placed the bag of candy on the same scale he used to weigh everything else of a small nature in the store.

"A quarter pound of lemon drops," he said. "That'll be two cents."

Reaching into the pocket of her skirt, Haven retrieved two more pennies, placing them on the counter before picking up the small bag of candy and turning to leave.

"Thank you, Mr. Crabtree," Haven called cheerfully as she exited the general store.

"You're welcome," she heard the man mumble in her wake.

Turning right onto the boardwalk, Haven couldn't keep herself from opening the bag of lemon drops and choosing one to enjoy on her way to the millinery shop.

Oh, how wonderful it would be to see Arabella again, to have her so close, the two of them working together! Haven wondered how on earth she would manage to wait two more weeks to see her dearest friend—her sister. Of course, she had no other venue but to wait. Hence, Haven determined she would simply work her fingers to the bone creating more hats for the shops in Denver to sell, as well as endeavoring to help the children and adolescents of Fletcher polish their manners and social graces.

Her mind flittered to the man Mr. Crabtree had mentioned—the one who had purchased the Vickers' farm just west of Haven's house. Sheriff Sterling seemed to think the man was unfriendly. Well, Haven would wait and see about that. After all, everyone knew Mr. Crabtree was . . . well, crabby. The children always referred to him as Crabby Ol' Crabtree whenever the subject came up during her time with them. Even his own grandson, Walter Jr., thought Mr. Crabtree was crabby.

Still, Haven had managed to soften up Crabby Ol' Crabtree a bit, so maybe she could soften up this Mr. Briscoe, as well—draw him into the wonderful little community that was Fletcher. And yet, if even Sheriff Sterling thought the new citizen of Fletcher unfriendly, then Mr. Briscoe must be as unfriendly as they came.

Haven smiled at the thought of the sheriff. Sheriff Dan Sterling—easily the handsomest bachelor in Fletcher, the handsomest man in Fletcher period, for that matter. Tall as a Colorado pine tree, with dark hair, blue eyes, and a smile that made any day seem brighter, Sheriff Sterling was as charming as the summer days were long. Haven giggled to herself, thinking that Sheriff

41

Sterling couldn't have been more the iconic ideal of a western town sheriff if he'd stepped right out of the pages of a dime novel!

She sucked hard on the lemon drop in her mouth, relishing the sweet taste of the granulated sugar encrusting it. The children would work extra hard at practicing the waltz and Virginia reel that afternoon if they knew a lemon drop each was at the end of it.

Glancing up at the beautiful blue of the sky overhead, Haven sighed in greeting the lovely white cloud sentinels watching over her. Oh, how she loved her new life out west. How she loved the people of Fletcher—the children, their parents, Sheriff Sterling, even Crabby Ol' Crabtree. After all, he was another character straight out of a dime novel.

Turning to gaze toward her lovely little white house, Haven let her attention wander beyond her home and the pretty little Fletcher cemetery for a moment.

Yes, she could see the very top of the red roof of the Vickers' barn just over the hill to the west, and she wondered aloud, "Maybe this unfriendly Mr. Briscoe will prove to have walked out of a dime novel as well."

Smiling as she returned to walking toward the millinery shop, her smile broadened. "After all, what would an ideal western town be without a mysterious, unfriendly stranger, hmmm?"

Exhaling a sigh of pure satisfied happiness, Haven pulled the key to her millinery shop from her pocket, unlocked the squeaking front door, and stepped in. Mipsie had been right, as she ever was: Fletcher was a better life for Haven. And one day, it would be a better life for her entire family, for Haven knew that with Arabella's arrival, not only would her own days be more delightful, but so would Arabella's—and eventually Mipsie's and Old Joe's too. She was certain of it!

CHAPTER TWO

The bell of the millinery shop's front door jingled.

"Good afternoon, Miss Abernathy," Andrew Henry greeted as he stepped through the front door of the Abernathy and Barnes Millinery shop.

"Good afternoon, Andrew," Haven returned with a smile of approval. In truth, she adored the fact that the boys and girls of Fletcher were polishing their social graces, for she knew it would prove to serve them well one day. "You're the first to arrive today," she added. "Why don't you just go ahead into the classroom and wait for the others while I finish up in here, all right?"

"Yes, ma'am," Andrew answered with a nod.

"Thank you, Andrew," Haven offered, as the tall, towheaded adolescent strode into the adjoining room.

Andrew Henry was a good-looking boy. All the girls in Fletcher thought so, and Haven understood why. At fourteen, Andrew already looked like a young man, and Haven knew that one day he would inadvertently leave a string of broken hearts in his wake. Andrew had been well mannered even before his parents enrolled him with the other twelve- to fourteen-year-olds in town in Haven's etiquette, decorum, and social

45

dance class for the older children of Fletcher. Haven suspected Andrew's two older sisters, Marian and Martha, were to thank for their brother's having a step up where social graces were concerned—for both had been tutored in such things by an aunt who was the proprietress of a charm school somewhere in Texas.

Still, even for Andrew's head start, as it were, Haven had been delightfully surprised at how even more polished and well-mannered Andrew had become under her instruction. Haven was proud and happy that Andrew had benefited from enduring her classes. Always prompt, always polite, and always courteous, the boy was also very masculine, a hard worker, and determined. Yes, Andrew Henry was well on his way to being a very balanced adult man one day.

Haven watched as Andrew strode into the next room. The companion room to the millinery shop, the "instruction room," as Haven had dubbed it, stood entirely empty, save lines of rather raggedy wooden chairs against two opposing walls of its perimeter and the piano on the far end of the room, opposite the large glass window that looked out on Fletcher's main street. Andrew selected the chair he most always did—the one nearest the piano—and sat down to wait.

The bell at the front door of the millinery shop jingled once more, and Haven looked over to see Margie Shaffer step into the shop.

Haven's smile broadened with understanding, for Margie had arrived a bit early, and Haven knew it was for the chance to sit next to Andrew. Perhaps she wouldn't have to repeat her lesson on the importance of being prompt after all—thanks to Margie's adoration of Andrew.

"Good afternoon, Miss Abernathy," Margie greeted, her smile bright and her cinnamon-colored hair perfectly pinned up, giving her the appearance of being older than her tender thirteen years.

"Good afternoon, Margie," Haven chimed, pleased with Margie's promptness. Margie had been perpetually late for every class during the first month Haven held classes. The fact that she was adhering to Haven's dictum of "better three hours early than one minute late" was very admirable indeed—even if it did have more to do with Andrew Henry's always being early than true devotion to studies in etiquette.

"Andrew is already in the classroom, if you'd like to join him in waiting for the others, Margie," Haven needlessly presented.

She giggled when Margie—eyes already affixed to Andrew's position—hurried toward the entrance of the other room, barely remembering her manners and dropping a quiet, "Thank you, Miss Abernathy," as she flittered away.

Placing the hat she had been working on in a large, round hatbox, Haven stood up from her chair, smoothing her hair before removing her apron. She had managed to make a good bit of progress on the project between the finish of class for the younger children earlier in the afternoon and the arrival of Andrew Henry, heralding the beginning of the older children's class. Thus, the day had been more productive than she had at first anticipated, and she smiled with satisfaction in a job well done as the front door bell heralded the arrival of Johnny McGhee, Edith Crabtree, and Oscar and Nancy Dalton.

"Good morning, everyone," Haven greeted.

Polite responses were given by the four youths as they headed for the instruction room. Haven could see Grover Lewis and Florence Ray just a ways down the street. Checking the small watch pendant hanging on the long chain around her neck, Haven nodded, satisfied to know that everyone would arrive promptly. She giggled, knowing Grover and Florence were sweet on one another. It was the reason they were always the last to arrive—for they enjoyed lingering privately in one another's company as often as they could.

Earlier in the afternoon, the younger children's class had been akin to herding cats for Haven. Robert and Ronald Henry, in stark contrast to their elder brother, Andrew, had been unusually chatty and rambunctious and had nearly worn Haven to a frazzle. Haven had wondered if all twin boys were as constant in their activity as were Robert and Ronald. On the other hand, shy little Addie Bernard had been so weepy and bashful, Haven had ended up holding her on her lap to comfort and soothe her while she instructed the other children.

Therefore, as she entered the instruction room, Haven smiled and sighed with relief—glad that the older children were so much more cooperative, less demanding, and less in need of redirection than the younger children always were, for she was already feeling a little more fatigued than she usually did on her instruction days.

Grover and Florence entered directly behind Haven, taking their seats.

"Good afternoon, ladies and gentlemen," Haven cheerily greeted as she nodded at each student in turn. "I hope you're all in the mood for dancin' today . . . because I thought we'd practice the waltz and Virginia reel a bit, before discussin' table manners once again."

Haven bit her lip to suppress a smile of amusement as she noted that the eyes of each girl in the room lit up like fireflies at sunset, while it took all the restraint every boy could muster not to groan with disappointment. She understood that young men—all men, in truth—felt a great weight of responsibility when it came to attempts to please the females of the human race. More than that, she knew the male gender more often than not hid a deep and thoroughgoing fear of rejection—that every time he must approach—or worse, *wanted* to approach—a lady, it took no less than the courage of a Templar knight to do so. Even though the young girls of Fletcher did not yet realize it, they held a certain power over their male counterparts—the power to soothe and build a tender male ego, as well as the power to crush it.

She mused in that moment how odd were the goings-on between men and women. Women for their part were romantic, nurturing, with loving hearts that could easily be broken by men. Men were brave, courageous, protectors and providers, with hearts that could just as easily be crushed by women. It was a conundrum, in truth—a real puzzle of life and living.

"Let's all stand . . . and I think we will begin without the piano accompaniment, all right?" Haven began. When not one boy moved toward one girl, Haven shook her head with understanding. "Very well, young men, if you won't choose a lovely dance partner for yourself, I will choose one for you." Resting an index finger against her chin and feigning ignorance to the fact that certain girls were sweet on certain boys and vice versa, Haven said, "Andrew . . . why don't you begin with Margie?" Haven again bit her lip to hide an empathetic smile as Margie stepped up to stand directly in front of Andrew. "And let's have . . . Johnny, why don't you partner with Florence for a bit today?" Haven again feigned naiveté as Grover scowled. Yes, he was sweet on Florence and Florence on him. Yet Haven knew there was wisdom in separating them here and there.

"Oscar, will you please partner with Edith? And Grover, you dance with Nancy, please."

Exhaling a rather obvious sigh of forfeit, Grover strode to Nancy Dalton, straightening his posture as he took a stance before her. The other young people were more obedient—less obstinate than Grover tended to be—yet Haven had seen such a marked improvement in the boy's temperament that she would not deny him the occasional sigh of stubborn disappointment.

"Now, gentlemen, take your lady, right hand at her waist, left hand cradling her right hand," Haven began.

"Your hand is sweaty, Johnny," Florence scolded.

"Florence," Haven interjected at once, "it is no small thing for a man to ask a woman to dance. It is a compliment to you and very unsettlin' for him. And once you have accepted his request, it is very ill-mannered indeed to comment upon any perspiration that might be about him, due to his nerves or physical exertion."

"But Johnny didn't ask me to dance, Miss

Abernathy," Florence pointed out. "You assigned him to."

Haven inhaled a long, calming breath. Of all the children in the older class, Florence was the least respectful of Haven—and it wore Haven's nerves at times.

"That doesn't matter, Florence," Haven stated. "Rudeness to a kind man like Johnny is never acceptable behavior."

Johnny looked pale, as if someone had beaten him over the back with a stick, and it fanned Haven's generally calm temperament. She knew that Florence wanted to dance with Grover, and because Florence had embarrassed Johnny in an attempt to get her wish, Haven would certainly make sure that Florence did *not* have the opportunity to dance with Grover at all that day. She was their teacher—an elder to them, no matter her own youth—and she would not be manipulated by a stinker like Florence Ray.

Johnny was, in fact, a very handsome boy. He owned very dark hair, deep brown eyes, and a chiseled jaw and cheekbones that would ordinarily belong to a much more mature man. Yet good-looking a boy as he was, Johnny lacked confidence, and it was Haven's secret hope that she could help the young man to unearth some within himself. Florence Ray certainly wasn't going to assist her in that.

Therefore, Haven instructed, "Oscar, will you

please exchange dance partners with Johnny?" Haven allowed her eyes to narrow a bit as she looked at Florence—an unspoken warning to Florence that she should mind her *p*'s and *q*'s for the rest of class time.

She watched as Johnny left Florence and moved to stand before Edith Crabtree. Edith, her heart sweet and kind, her character soft and encouraging, greeted Johnny with, "Good afternoon, Johnny. Thank you for bein' my waltzin' partner." Her dark brown eyes sparkled as she smiled at him.

A smidgen of color returned to Johnny's face as he took Edith's hand in his and placed his other at her waist.

"Now, before we commence," Haven began, "I do want to note to you all that when you are at a dance in the city—or here at home, I suppose—it is always best for each young man and each young woman to wear gloves. It is a sign of decorum and fashion—a way to elude the intimacy of touch with those of whom you are not familiar. And it also serves to keep excess moisture from your palms from soiling a lady's dress at the waist, gentlemen."

When Florence raised one snobbish, arrogant eyebrow, Haven moved to where she stood with her hand on Oscar's shoulder, lifted her hand just a little, and added, "Or from soiling a gentleman's fine white shirt with the moisture and oils that tend to linger on our hands, ladies."

Florence scowled, her face turning as red as a radish. And although Haven was never pleased at having to correct, scold, or embarrass anyone at all, she knew no other way to get the point across to Florence than to offer her a spoonful of her own bitter tonic.

Johnny grinned with gratitude when Haven's gaze caught his for a moment, and she winked at him.

"Now to 'The Blue Danube' . . . more slowly than I will play it later," Haven commenced, "One, two, three and . . . da da da da daaa . . . da da . . . da da."

At once, Haven's fatigue lightened, as did her heart. The joy she felt at watching the children waltz so near perfectly was fodder to her soul. They waltzed so well that she was prompted to comment, "Beautiful. Just beautiful! Have you all been practicin' outside of class this week? Each and every one of you is waltzin' just marvelously! Oh, I adore it!"

Even the boys couldn't keep from grinning at such a gushing compliment offered by their young dance instructor. And as her students continued to waltz near flawlessly, Haven hurried to the piano at one end of the room.

"Oh, we must have music!" she chimed. "Even if I am not the greatest of pianists."

As Haven sat down and began to play "The

Blue Danube" on the newly tuned piano, she was almost giddy over thinking of how wonderful it would be to have Arabella teach the etiquette, decorum, and social dance classes with her, for Arabella was a far, far, far superior pianist. It was as if she had been born with some sort of soulful kinship to the instrument, and Haven knew the children would delight in her playing. And without having to play herself, Haven would be able to focus solely on the children's steps and dancing rhythms. Of course, she hoped Arabella would be willing to teach some subjects as well; Arabella was ever so soft-spoken, graceful, and intriguing, and Haven knew the children of Fletcher would benefit in associating with and knowing such a kind and elegant young woman as Arabella Barnes.

As she played then and watched the children waltz about the room with surprising dexterity, Haven noticed sweet Edith Crabtree encouraging shy Johnny with a smile. In thinking of the Crabtree family, Haven mused that perhaps, just perhaps, she and Arabella could begin to hope a little in Fletcher. Maybe they were not destined to live their lives out alone as spinsters the way the Sandersan sisters did.

Years before, during one of their late-night conversations, Arabella and Haven had together concluded that because of their individual secrets of lineage, neither should ever hope to find love, nor to marry. After all, what men would have them, when their blood was so "tainted," as the world oft proclaimed? She and Arabella had decided that very night years ago that they would bury their desires for marriage and family, for to them, it all seemed so entirely unobtainable. Haven's heart had been further reconciled to this fate when she arrived in Fletcher and spent time in the company of Wynifred and Merigold Sandersan. They seemed quite content with their individual spinsterhoods—happy older ladies with much to keep their minds and still-nimble fingers busy.

And yet what woman did not long for a man's adoration, did not dream of having children and a handsome husband with whom to raise them? It simply seemed a dream beyond her reach.

But then Haven had met the younger Crabtree family—Walter Crabtree, his wife, May, and their children, Edith and Walter Jr. Haven was told that Mrs. May Crabtree had been married once before and widowed just after Edith was born. The moment Haven observed the contrast in Edith and her half-brother, Walter, Haven did not merely suspect; she knew. Edith Crabtree and her mother, May, both shared a secret like Arabella's. There flowed through their veins the blood of another continent—from which people had been taken from their own far-away home and sold to other humans as slaves.

Edith and her mother were uniquely attractive, just as Arabella was. They owned the same dark, dark hair Arabella did. And though May and Edith owned brown eyes instead of the bright blue of Arabella's, their olive skin spoke to betray their secret. Most wonderful to Haven, however, was that, even for their obvious partial ancestry, no one in Fletcher seemed to notice at all. Or if they did, they were not concerned about it. And *that* was what gave Haven hope. Perhaps Mipsie and Joe were right. Perhaps folks out west *were* far less concerned about whether a body's blood was pure of one race or the other. Perhaps both she and Arabella could—perhaps would—find love one day.

Yes, hope had begun to well in Haven's heart: hope that she might capture the attention of a handsome man the likes of Sheriff Sterling, that a man might not consider her ancestral secret some sort of repulsive flaw, that a man might truly fall in love with her.

Haven had the children waltz thrice more to "The Blue Danube" before ending her playing and applauding with sincere admiration of their performance.

"Oh, my darlin's!" she exclaimed with delight. "You all are doin' so wonderfully! It truly enchants me so to see you dancin' with such apparent ease!" Placing her hands over her heart, Haven sighed, shaking her head with admiration.

"You all should feel very satisfied with the way you're dancin'," Haven continued. "It isn't a trivial thing, the waltz. It takes concentration to learn and perform and—as y'all are aware—practice to perfect."

Edith Crabtree raised her hand.

"Yes, Edith," Haven said, nodding in giving permission to the girl to speak.

"Miss Abernathy," Edith began, "I don't even have to think about countin' my steps out anymore. It just comes naturally to me now."

Haven smiled and again nodded, this time with affirmation. "Yes, it does. Once you've learned the steps and repeated them over and over and over again, it becomes a routine that your mind knows without having to remind you. And," she continued, nodding to Johnny, "you, Johnny, may take a great amount of recognition for bein' such a capable partner. When a man knows how to lead the waltz . . . that is when his partner is free to simply enjoy the dance. Bravo, Johnny! Bravo!"

Haven led the class in applauding Johnny, whose ears turned red as summer geraniums from the attention. Haven had quickly discovered that the entire McGhee family was as bashful as bunnies. And yet as hard as it was for Haven to force Johnny into accepting praise from others, she knew that it was paramount he learn to accept compliments, join in social conversation, and endure the attention of his fellow townsfolk if he were to weather adulthood well and with refinement. And so even though her tender heart and compassion for Johnny ached each time she saw his ears blush red with embarrassment, Haven pressed Johnny, and he had indeed begun to bear her compliments with much less visible agony.

"And now that you have all nearly mastered the waltz," Haven said as she moved through the group of children, pairing them with alternate partners, "let us enjoy the Virginia reel, shall we?"

Florence's eyes narrowed a little as she scowled at Haven when Haven directed her to stand before Andrew instead of Grover.

"And everyone remember this," she began, allowing one eyebrow to arch as she looked at Florence. "No matter how uncomfortable you may be in any given social situation, do not let your expression betray you. Smile, everyone!"

As each student smiled—some with sincerity and some with little to no genuineness—Haven called, "Take your places please . . . for the Virginia reel!"

Gesturing that the boys and girls should take their positions across from one another—boys lined on one side, girls on the other—Haven began, "Let's tap it out first. I think we should make sure we haven't all forgotten anything. Then, again, I'll accompany a bit later."

"Yes, Miss Abernathy," came the scattered responses.

"All right, everyone ready?" Haven asked.

When each student nodded, Haven began to clap her hands in rhythm. "Ready and forward, two and three and bow, then right elbows, swing!"

Haven was so delighted by how well the children were doing with the first few steps that her voice immediately dropped into the more familiar call for the dance. After all, counting out the dance wasn't nearly as fun as calling it.

"Left hand turn . . . two hands turn," she called as she continued to clap out the rhythm. "And do-si-do! Left shoulder . . . top couple gallop down! Gallop on back! Now stretch the willows!" Giggling with delight, Haven chimed, "Wonderful! Just wonderful! Keep going now."

Hitching up her skirt just a bit, she hurried back to the piano at the far end of the room. Taking her seat, she began to play "Turkey in the Straw."

"Annnnd top couple gallop back to the top . . . and pass it off! Everyone forward and back," she continued to call as she played. Oh, she could not wait until Arabella arrived! Haven enjoyed calling out the dance, instructing the children, and playing the piano, but doing all together tended to make her feel as if everything were not as smooth as she would like.

"Right hand . . . now the left! That's it!" she continued to call as she played. "Both hands, turn . . . do-si-do . . . left shoulder . . . top couple gallop down . . . stretch the willows! And remember, my darlin's, you may clap out the rhythm as you dance. It's all part of the fun!"

Haven's smile broadened as she craned her neck to watch the children as she played. "That's it! Wonderful! Oh, you are all doin' so well!"

She giggled as she saw Margie Shaffer's pretty young face blush pink as a raspberry when Andrew Henry linked his arm with hers during the reeling between different partners. Haven well knew the glee every girl knew in dancing with the boy who made her heart leap with delight—and by the sparkle in Margie's eyes and the raspberry glow on her cheeks, she knew that in that moment Margie Shaffer was happier than a dog with two tails. That in turn made Haven happy, as well. And as she continued to play "Turkey in the Straw" and call out the Virginia reel, Haven thought then that she was very glad the townsfolk had asked her to teach a few social graces to their children. After all, however tiring it could be at times, it was always entertaining!

After three turns at the Virginia reel, the children were quite worn out.

"Everyone take a seat please," Haven instructed

as she rose from the piano bench and hurried to where she'd hidden the sack of lemon drops on a chair near the large window that looked out onto Fletcher. "There's a pitcher of water and some glasses on a tray in the millinery shop, Grover," Haven began. "Will you please pour everyone a glass of refreshment? And remember to serve the ladies first, right?"

"Yes, Miss Abernathy," Grover rather grumbled.

"And with willin'ness, Grover . . . however feigned it may be," Haven added with a giggle.

Haven turned and watched as Grover carried in the tray laden with nine small glasses he'd filled with water.

Going to Florence first, he offered, "Miss Ray?"

"Thank you, Mr. Lewis," Florence blushed as she chose the closest glass to her.

"You're welcome," Grover said, smiling at Florence.

Haven held her breath, knowing that Grover had been overjoyed to serve Florence but wondering whether he would remember his manners and appear just as delighted to serve the other young ladies.

"Miss Crabtree?" Grover asked once he'd moved to stand before Edith.

Smiling with pleasure, Edith nodded and said, "Thank you, Mr. Lewis."

Haven exhaled the breath she'd been holding as

Grover repeated the phrasing and accompanying smile as he served Nancy and Margie as well. Indeed, he even managed to serve the other young men with the polish of a British butler.

And then, looking up and hurrying toward Haven, Grover offered, "Miss Abernathy?" The expression of concern on Grover's face indicated to Haven that he realized he should have served her when he'd served the other girls, before he'd served the boys and most likely first out of everyone. Haven let it pass.

She winked at him, nodded her approval, and said, "Thank you, Mr. Lewis. And well done indeed."

Grover exhaled a sigh of relief before taking the final glass from the tray, tucking the tray under his arm, and gulping the water with the gusto of a pelican ingurgitating a large fish.

Haven inhaled slowly, knowing there was still a lot to be taught—even if the boy *did* waltz like a little prince. Haven sipped a bit of water out of her glass, depositing it on the windowsill behind her as she readied the sack of lemon drops for dispersal.

"Now, in a very orderly fashion, ladies first, as always," Haven began, "everyone come to the front of the room. Bein' that I suspected you all would dance so very well today—and with very little complainin' I might add"—Haven looked to Florence, offering a final albeit silent reprimand

on the girl's treatment of Johnny McGhee—
"I stopped in and purchased some lemon drops
from Mr. Crabtree this mornin'."

Instantly the children were on their feet,
moving toward the front of the room with sweet
anticipation at receiving a lemon drop.

"Properly, now, ladies and gentlemen . . .
properly," Haven softly instructed as the excited
children lined up to receive their lemon drops.

As she handed each child in turn a piece of
candy, she said, "We still have some class time
left today, and I do want to review our table
manners."

Oscar Dalton raised his hand.

"Yes, Mr. Dalton?" Haven prodded.

"When it comes to things like hard candy and
such," Oscar began, "I mean, we're supposed to
chew our food with our mouth closed . . . but do
we suck with our mouth closed too?"

Oscar's sister Nancy rolled her eyes with
embarrassment at her brother's seemingly silly
question. "Oh, for Pete's sake, Oscar," she
mumbled.

"Well now, let's just think about this for a
minute, shall we?" Haven mused. "Oscar, I
would say that in the case of, for instance, a large
lollipop, one would need to be careful about not
lickin' or suckin' with too much vigor . . . even
though one must continually open one's mouth
in endeavorin' to consume it. That bein' said,

however . . . yes, one should always suck on a piece of hard candy with one's mouth closed, at least while in the company of others."

Oscar nodded to indicate Haven's response made sense.

"Also, you all be careful with these lemon drops, all right?" Haven advised. "I wouldn't want someone chokin' on one."

Margie Shafer raised her hand, and Haven said, "Yes, Margie?"

"Miss Abernathy, why don't you have us come into the instruction room through the front door in here? Instead of havin' us all tramp through your shop?"

"Well, it seems the lock is broken on this door, Margie," Haven answered. "The Misses Sandersan said it stopped workin' years ago, and I just haven't taken the time to have it fixed."

As Haven turned to look at the sealed door herself, she popped a lemon drop into her own mouth. After all, she had worked hard playing the piano and instructing the children; therefore, she thought she might enjoy a little treat herself.

Yet just as she turned around—and just as Andrew Henry asked, "Who's that man, Miss Abernathy?" without raising his hand—Haven gasped as she looked out the large window before her to see an astonishingly handsome, incredibly formidable-looking man on the boardwalk just outside. He paused in his stride, turning and glaring through the window directly at Haven.

Haven's body tried to gasp again, for the intensity of the man's jade-colored eyes seemed to burn through her with a fierceness she had never even fathomed could exist. Yet she could not draw a breath, for when she had gasped at first seeing the man, the lemon drop in her mouth had been sucked to the back of her throat. She was choking! After having just warned the children of the dangers of hard candy, she, their teacher, was choking!

Frantically Haven's hands went to her throat as she tried to cough up the lemon drop. But being unable to draw a breath, she was therefore unable to push a breath to a cough.

"Miss Abernathy? Are you all right?" she heard Johnny McGhee ask from behind her.

Haven could feel her mind beginning to dizzy, felt her face was red from the strain of her body not being able to breathe. Her panicked gaze still held the fierce one of the stranger through the instruction room window, and she saw his dark brows pucker in a frown.

"She's chokin'!" Oscar hollered. "Miss Abernathy is chokin' on a lemon drop!"

"Is this one of our manners lessons, Miss Abernathy?" Nancy inquired.

Again, Haven's body attempted to gasp as, all at once, the door leading from the outside boardwalk to the instruction room burst open, splintering throughout the room—the stranger with the fierce and fiery stare stepping across the threshold.

"She's chokin' on a lemon drop, mister!" Margie cried.

The stranger said nothing—simply strode to Haven, reached out, and slapped her hard on the back. But the lemon drop did not dislodge from her throat.

"She's gonna choke to death right here with us watchin'!" Florence shrieked.

Again the man pounded on Haven's back. Nothing. She still couldn't breathe!

"Well, then . . ." she heard the man's low, imposing voice rumble.

Haven felt the man's arms suddenly go around her waist—felt more dizzying effects as he flipped her upside down and began shaking her.

"Cough it up, lady," the man growled, "else you're gonna commence yer dirt nap right here in front of these kids."

Holding Haven upside down with now just one arm around her waist, the man pounded on her back once more. At last, the lemon drop dislodged from Haven's mouth and, seeming to have a will of its own, leapt out of her mouth and went bouncing across the wooden planks of the instruction room floor.

Windmilling her around and back onto her feet, the man held her shoulders, steadying her as the fierceness of his jade eyes bore into the bright green of her own. He didn't say a word to her— simply nodded in affirming that she was all right and breathing again.

"Thanks, mister," Johnny McGhee offered.

"Mm hmm," was the man's only response.

As he turned and made his way toward the scattered remnants of the broken-down door, he looked up to Haven, remarking, "My apologies for your door, ma'am. I'll come back and fix this for you later on."

"Th-thank you," Haven managed to stammer in a weak and breathless voice.

The man nodded, touched the brim of his worn brown hat in a polite gesture of taking his leave, stepped over the threshold, and strode away down the boardwalk.

"Good Lord, Miss Abernathy!" Grover exclaimed. "That man plum saved your life!"

Swallowing hard and wondering if she'd ever want to eat a lemon drop again, Haven nodded. "Yes, he did," she affirmed. "But we mustn't use the Lord's name as an exclamation, Mr. Lewis. Yes?"

"Yes, ma'am," Grover mumbled.

"Are you all right, Miss Abernathy?" Edith asked, approaching with the timidity of a butterfly.

"Yes . . . yes, I'm fine, Edith," Haven assured the girl. Forcing a smile, she retrieved her glass from the windowsill and slowly drank the refreshing water remaining inside it. Her throat hurt from the abrasive sugar coating of the wicked lemon drop.

"Who was that man, Miss Abernathy?" Andrew Henry asked.

Haven shrugged, answering, "I don't know. I've never seen him before."

"His name is Mr. Briscoe," Edith offered. "I was in Grandpa's store when Sheriff Sterlin' came in, and I heard the sheriff say there was a new man in town named Briscoe. I'm sure that's him. There ain't no other new men in town."

"*Aren't* any other new men in town," Haven kindly corrected.

"That's what Edith just said, Miss Abernathy," Grover pointed out, one eyebrow quirked in confusion.

"Well, he sure is handsome!" Nancy noted aloud.

"You're disgustin', Nancy Dalton!" Nancy's brother Oscar scolded. "Why, that man's prob'ly old enough to be your daddy!"

"I think he's handsome too," Florence chimed in.

Grover scowled at Florence, growling, "Is that so?"

"Very well, we have had a bit of excitement, but let's not let it overly distract us from continuing our lessons today," Haven announced, motioning

69

that the children should take their seats once more.

As four sets of youthful male shoulders slumped with disappointment, Nancy leaned closer to Haven, asking, "But don't *you* think he was handsome, Miss Abernathy?"

"Why . . . I hardly had moment to notice, Nancy," Haven answered—although quite untruthfully.

"I'm not surprised, Miss Abernathy," Grover interjected. "I mean, you was heels over hind-end with your petticoats and bloomers swishin' every which way. It's no wonder you didn't get a good look at him."

As Haven felt her face blush crimson with humiliation, it was Andrew Henry who came to her rescue.

"Don't worry none about what Grover says, Miss Abernathy," Andrew assured her. Offering a comforting smile, he added, "It was all just a mess of cotton and ruffles to us. I couldn't have made sense of it if I tried."

Touched by Andrew's well-meaning, albeit distressing, attempt at encouragement, Haven smiled. "Thank you, Andrew. I do feel better in that. Please take your seats again, everyone," Haven said, walking with the children toward the other end of the room.

"Here you go, Miss Abernathy," Johnny said, offering Haven the villainous lemon drop that had leapt from her throat. "I figure if you rinse it off, it'll taste good as new."

The boy was a sweetheart! "Thank you, Johnny," Haven said as the boy dropped the sticky piece of candy into the palm of her outstretched hand. "I'm sure you're right. I'll just plop it in my pocket and rinse it off a bit later."

"Yes, ma'am," Johnny said, smiling with pride at his thoughtful deed.

Exhaling a heavy sigh, Haven determined she would wait until she was in the privacy of her little house before she allowed her humiliation to drive her to sobbing. There were still minutes of class time remaining and children to be taught. She'd think about the fact that she'd nearly died of choking on a lemon drop later—the fact that the most beautiful man she'd ever before seen had seen her at her absolute worst, bloomers and petticoats and all, while he saved her life!

"Now, speaking of table manners," Haven began as the children settled into their seats, "who can tell me the proper manner in which to eat soup?"

Haven was pleased when most of the children raised their hands in willingness to answer. Yet even as she called on Margie—even as she listened to Margie's correct description of the proper manner of soup bowl and soupspoon usage—all she could think about was the handsome man who burst through the instruction

71

room door to save her from choking to death.

In that moment, every part of Haven Abernathy knew that the image of the man's face and form—of his strength and power—was emblazoned on her mind forever. The man was far from the cliché tall, dark, and handsome; he was tall, dark-haired, and light-green-eyed and preposterously good-looking! Handsome did not come close to describing him. And it seemed his name was Mr. Briscoe—the Mr. Briscoe who had purchased the Vickers' farm—the Mr. Briscoe who was now her neighbor.

"Are you feelin' all right, Miss Abernathy?" Oscar inquired. "You look a bit too pink in the cheeks."

Haven nodded, smiled comfortingly, and answered, "Oh yes. I'm fine, Oscar. Still a bit rattled, I suppose."

And rattled she was! In fact, Haven realized she was trembling, her heart was fluttering an unfamiliar sort of quiver in her bosom, and she felt quite flustered indeed. Each thought of Mr. Briscoe caused the palms of her hands to begin perspiring a little. And yet Haven determinedly convinced herself that almost dying because of a lemon drop had left her so unsettled—and not Mr. Briscoe.

CHAPTER THREE

Valentine Briscoe scowled. As he strode along the boardwalk toward the livery where he'd left his wagon and team, he grumbled with irritation.

"Now I gotta waste the rest of the damn day replacin' that woman's damn door," he growled to himself. "Not two full days in this town and already some woman is draggin' me outta my way."

He exhaled a heavy sigh of frustration and paused for a moment. Removing his hat, he raked a hand back through his dark hair. "Dammit all to hell," he exclaimed under his breath—but not quietly enough it would seem. The two little towheaded boys using a couple of sticks to dig through a pile of fresh horse manure in the road nearby glanced up at him, broke into snickering, and hurried off.

But Val didn't worry about it too much. Fletcher was made up of farmers, horsemen, and cattle ranchers. He was certain the two boys had heard more cussing from their own fathers airing their lungs than they just had from him. Anyhow, he wasn't a bit concerned about what the boys thought of him. In fact, it would go better for him and them if they stayed clear of his path.

Valentine Briscoe had no great love for people. Other than his own family, he figured life would be much less demanding, much more peaceable, without them. It had been one reason he had taken pause in listening to his folks' advice about moving to Fletcher—people. Denver was just too darn close for Val's liking. The silver barons and their silver strikes had filled the big city near to busting its seams, and he knew that eventually more people would tire of the city and head out toward Fletcher and its separation.

Still, although his folks had the idea that they had managed to talk Val into moving to Fletcher to afford himself the chance of healing—to remove himself from his home in Limon east of Fletcher in an effort to find some peace of mind with the past—Val's true intentions were much more akin to exactly what his folks wanted him to escape. Fact was, the only reason Val had appeared to take heed of his parents' advice and leave Limon was because of what one of the deputies in Limon had confided in him—that a renegade band of Comanches was hiding out somewhere near to Fletcher.

Val clenched his jaw at the thought of the band. He wished them nothing but misery and death. And if he ever did manage to find them, well, that's exactly what he would be certain they got—brutal misery and torturous deaths. He didn't try to explain it to anyone, but his gut assured him that the band of Comanche Indians that was holed up somewhere in the vicinity of Fletcher was the same band Val and his father had been searching for near to a year. Val had learned long ago to trust his gut. Therefore, if his gut was telling him that moving to Fletcher might bring him closer to meeting up with the devils that had ruined his family's lives, then he'd do exactly what his gut said to do.

Shaking his head and exhaling another sigh in an effort to settle the rage that was flaming inside him again, Val crossed the street to the livery. Mr. Griggs was standing just outside the livery straightening out the tracings on Val's team. He still wore his smithy apron, and by the way his graying brown hair hung moist with perspiration, Val figured the man had just finished shoeing Clover.

Val arched one eyebrow, somewhat impressed, for it was obvious Mr. Griggs had taken the time to brush Clover and Peaches after replacing one of Clover's shoes. To Val's way of thinking, a livery owner and farrier who took to such detail was a good horseman indeed.

"This is quite a team you got here, Mr. Briscoe," Mr. Griggs announced with admiration as Val approached. "A finer team than I've ever seen round Fletcher before, that's for certain."

"Thank you," Val said, trying not to let pride well in him. "They're a good pair. My daddy and me raised 'em from birth, and they've been good to me."

Val reached into the front pocket of his trousers, removing a handful of carrots. He divided them evenly into his hands and fed them to Clover and Peaches.

"There you go, girls," he chuckled. "Did you have fun bein' primped up by Mr. Griggs, hmmm?"

Peaches whinnied and nodded her head. Val smiled. He might hate people, but he sure loved his horses.

He glanced up and into the livery for a moment. "Looks like you've got some nice stock yourself, Griggs," he commented aloud as he studied the four Thoroughbreds stabled in the livery.

"Oh, they ain't mine," Mr. Griggs said, "though I wish they were. They're beautiful animals and every one of them a pedigreed Thoroughbred . . . Tennessee born, I believe."

Val arched his brows in admiration. "Tennessee Thoroughbreds out here in Fletcher?" he asked. "Are they meant for racin' in Denver or somethin'? Seems odd that an owner would keep racehorses out this far from the city."

"That's 'cause they ain't racehorses," Mr. Griggs informed him. "They come up from Georgia with Miss Abernathy. Seems she has a relative or somethin' she's tryin' to coax to movin' out here with her, so she brung the horses out to tempt him."

Val frowned a moment and then quirked one eyebrow with disbelief and curiosity. "Miss Abernathy?"

Mr. Griggs's smile broadened. "Yes, sirree!" he exclaimed with obvious admiration of the Miss Abernathy who owned the Thoroughbreds. "She owns the hat shop in town," he explained. "And she teaches et'kit, decorum, and social dancin' to the children a few afternoons a week."

"Oh," Val mumbled as his brows fell into a glower. "The damsel in distress I just met."

"Damsel in distress?" Mr. Griggs asked, puzzled.

"Young woman with black hair, green eyes, and a room full of young'uns dancin' the Virginia reel?" Val offered.

Mr. Griggs's smile broadened to the breadth of the Mississippi. "That'd be her! Prettiest thing I ever did see . . . just as *fine* as cream gravy!"

Val's eyes narrowed as he studied Miss Abernathy's horses from a distance a bit longer. "She don't seem like someone who would settle so far out west," he commented. "And neither do her horses."

Mr. Griggs shrugged. "I know. But she did. Seems her folks died off in India or England or some such faraway place. But the Misses Sandersan sisters coaxed her out here to sell her hats is the way I hear it. I guess those silver barons out in Denver have themselves some wives that fancy frilly hats, and Miss Abernathy's hats are the ones they fancy most."

"Hmm," Val mumbled. He didn't want to talk about the woman who had loused up his day by needing her life saved, and a new door to boot.

"How much do I owe you, Mr. Griggs?" Val asked, reaching into his front pocket.

"A dollar oughta cover it," Mr. Griggs answered.

Handing Griggs a silver dollar, Val patted Clover and Peaches on the noses, saying, "Well, girls, we best head home. I gotta fix a door somehow before evenin'. Thank you, Griggs. We'll be seein' you."

"Thank you, Mr. Briscoe," Mr. Griggs said with a nod.

Val climbed up onto the wagon's seat, released the brake, and snapped the lines at the backs of Clover and Peaches.

The team lurched forward, and although it wasn't a long ways to the farm he'd purchased, Val was glad to get out of town. There were too many people in town and no one but him when he was at his farm. That's the way he liked it.

Still, as the wagon rattled along, Val found himself thinking of the hat lady, Miss Abernathy. When he'd first passed her shop on his way to the general store to have Crabtree order in some feed for him, he'd glanced in through the big window near the hat shop and seen children waltzing—heard a piano playing "The Blue Danube." Still, he hadn't thought much of it. But on his way back to the livery, he'd paused when he'd glanced through the same window to see a young woman standing just on the other side of the same window.

When she'd turned and looked at him, her eyes had widened to the size of saucers, and at first he'd thought she was just aghast to see a stranger in town. Yet it had only taken Val a moment to realize the young woman was choking—on what, he hadn't known. But he could see that she was in danger. So he'd been impulsive, knocked down the door, and turned the girl head over bloomers, shaking her until he saw a lemon drop fall out of her mouth and go rolling across the floor.

In truth, the incident had nearly caused his heart to stop. He'd known a little girl in Limon who had choked to death years before, and the memory had flashed into his mind when he realized what was happening to Fletcher's social dance teacher.

Val felt a breath of a chuckle escape his throat then—allowed one corner of his mouth to curve up with amusement. Now that the woman was no longer in danger, he was struck by the humor of the fact that Fletcher's refined southern belle—its instructor of etiquette, decorum, and social dance—had found herself pinwheeled upside down and being bounced about with her petticoats flying hither and yon by a man she didn't even know.

His smile broadened to include both corners of his mouth, and he nodded, speaking aloud to Clover and Peaches, "She didn't melt into a bawlin' mess of embarrassment though, now did she, girls? Just thanked me and went on about her business."

Drawing a deep breath of fresh Colorado air, Val shrugged broad shoulders. "I expect hangin' a new door for her won't be too awful inconvenient. After all, the woman nearly died. She oughta at least have a door, hmm?" Val grinned again. "As fine as cream gravy, is she? That's a good way of sayin' she's pretty, I suppose."

As Val rode on—as the thought of smooth, delicious cream gravy caused his mouth to water a bit—he mumbled, "Yep. That's a real good way of sayin' it."

＊ ＊ ＊ ＊ ＊

Haven buried her face in one hand, groaning. "Oh, I've never been so humiliated in all my life!" she exclaimed. Looking over to Wynifred and Merigold Sandersan, she shook her head as new tears filled her eyes. "Whatever am I to do?"

"Well, it seems to me," Miss Wynifred began, "that you can either worry yourself sick over it or laugh about it."

Haven stared at Miss Wynifred with astonishment. "Laugh about it? Laugh about it? Have you lost your ever-lovin' mind, Miss Wynifred?"

But as both Miss Wynifred and Miss Merigold smiled with understanding, Miss Merigold offered, "I think Wynnie is right, Haven. Fortunately you're alive . . . thanks to Mr. Briscoe. Now if you were dead, it wouldn't be amusin' at all. But since you're here with us still, I think all we can do is just find amusement in the whole situation."

As Haven stood utterly dumbfounded, Miss Wynifred continued. "Look at it this way, Haven honey. That new man in town . . . well, he isn't gonna forget you any time soon. And you said he was handsome, didn't you?"

Haven smoothed her hair up in the back—tucked a stray strand behind her right ear. "As handsome as a June day is long," she admitted, "which only makes it that much worse."

Both the Misses Sandersan were still smiling with amusement—although compassionate amusement.

"Which only makes it that much better!" Merigold proclaimed. "What woman in this town wouldn't give her hind teeth to have a handsome man pick her up and save her life?"

"He saved me from chokin' on a lemon drop," Haven reminded the sisters. "It wasn't like heathens were draggin' me off to make me into

81

soup and eat me. I was chokin' on a lemon drop! Like a little girl in short skirts!"

Again Wynifred and Merigold giggled.

"Oh, quit stewin' over it so much, Haven," Wynifred instructed. "Let's just hear again how handsome this new Mr. Briscoe is. Merigold and I are true admirers of handsomeness, through and through we are."

Haven exhaled a sigh of defeat as she gazed at the two older ladies sitting perched on the edge of their sofa as if waiting to hear some intricate tale of murder and mystery. She shook her head, smiling. There was no defeating the two ladies in their determination to make everything exciting and wonderful.

"Very well," Haven said, rather plopping into the soft chair opposite the sofa in the Sandersan sisters' parlor. "I give up. If you two refuse to give me any sympathy for the fact that I was nearly humiliated to ruination today, then I guess I'll give in and tell you about our handsome Mr. Briscoe."

Turning to face her sister, Miss Wynifred inquired, "That's what we want, isn't it, Merigold?"

"Yes indeed," Miss Merigold affirmed. "We want to hear about Mr. Briscoe."

Looking back to the Misses Sandersan, Haven smiled. She had fallen in love with these two ladies faster than a hat flew off in a hurricane.

They were so supportive, so encouraging and kind, so loving, and so quick to amuse and be amused. How could anyone linger in gloom and glum when the Sandersan sisters were at hand?

And so she surrendered. "Very well, you two silly Susans," Haven conceded. "In all my twenty years of livin' on this green earth, I have never seen a man so handsome in face and in form. Standin' on the other side of the glass, his dark brows furrowed into a frown, stood the most exquisite, the most fascinatin', the most beautiful man I have ever set eyes upon!"

Haven was delighted when Miss Merigold sighed with enchantment.

"He was tall . . . ever so tall," Haven continued, "with hair as the color of midnight and eyes like two jade gemstones. His jaw was square, his chin defined but not too pronounced, with a few days' whisker growth."

"Oh, I just love that on a man!" Miss Wynifred exclaimed. "Just a few days of whiskers—not more'n a week, of course. Just enough to make him look rugged and capable."

"Capable of what?" Haven asked, curious.

Miss Merigold arched one brow slyly. "Why, of anything, Haven dear," she explained. "Of anything."

"Do go on, honey," Miss Wynifred prodded.

Haven noted the way her heart fluttered all at once as she thought of Mr. Briscoe's strength—

the strength so obviously revealed in the way he picked her up and windmilled her about as if she were no more than a rag doll.

"He has quite defined musculature, of that I am sure, for I could feel it as he held me," Haven continued. "And his shoulders? Why, they are as broad as a barn door, at least!"

Miss Merigold began to laugh, and then Miss Wynifred laughed. In the next moment, even Haven was laughing. It was, after all, the most ridiculous of circumstances—the etiquette and decorum teacher in Fletcher so clumsily choking on a lemon drop, the mysterious and very handsome stranger in town happening upon her at just that moment, wheeling her around like a pinwheel, and shaking the lemon drop from her mouth.

Through her laughter, Miss Merigold offered, "And think of poor Mr. Briscoe in all this!" She gasped for breath a moment before adding, "Not knowing anyone in town from Adam, and the first woman he meets is the local milliner. And . . . and he has to pick her up and shake a lemon drop from her!"

Miss Merigold barely managed to finish her sentence before such a wave of laughter so overtook all three women that Haven, for her part, could not draw breath.

"And those poor children!" Miss Wynifred whooped, wiping tears of mirth from her cheeks.

"What a sight indeed! They won't soon forget that Virginia reel, now will they?"

Again all three women were overtaken with breathless, reeling amusement. Miss Merigold stamped her feet in attempting to settle herself. But this only caused her to be further drowned in convulsions of hilarity.

Miss Wynifred leaned back against the sofa, gasping, "Oh, my back! Oh, my back! This hurts me so!" Yet even as she complained, her laughter increased, tears of merriment streaming from her eyes.

"Have I avoided chokin' to death, only to suffocate from hysterics with you ladies?" Haven sighed, finally able to draw breath.

"Oh!" Miss Wynifred breathed at last. "No, dear, I would hope not."

Miss Merigold offered one final giggle before sighing with relieved breath. "Oh my! I haven't laughed like that since . . . well, since I don't know when." She looked to Haven, dabbing the tears from the corners of her eyes with the handkerchief she kept tucked in one sleeve. "Oh, what joy you do bring us, Haven dear," she breathed. "I don't know how we ever got along before you came to us."

"You're far too kind, Miss Merigold," Haven said. "But I am glad that, in the least, I can festoon your heads with my hats and cheer your hearts with my misadventures."

"And you do both with such apparent ease, my dear!" Miss Wynifred added. "And now, I've one more question for you concernin' this Mr. Briscoe of yours."

Haven was acutely aware of her heart all of a sudden—as if it had begun to beat more quickly at the mention of Mr. Briscoe's name.

"And what might that be?" she prodded Miss Wynifred.

Miss Wynifred and Miss Merigold both leaned forward, and in a rather conspiratorial tone, Miss Wynifred asked, "Do you mean to tell us that this Mr. Briscoe is more attractive even than our own Sheriff Sterling? Hmmm?"

Haven smiled. It had not taken long for her to determine that both Sandersan sisters shared her own admiration for a dazzlingly comely man. And though Sheriff Sterling was near sublimely handsome, Haven offered her answer to Miss Wynifred's query.

"As I said," Haven began in her own clandestine tone, "I have never seen, nor can I imagine that there even exists anywhere, a more physically beautiful, a more pulchritudinous man than Fletcher's newly acquired Mr. Briscoe."

"How delicious!" Merigold exclaimed with delight.

"Delicious indeed!" Wynifred agreed.

"But will you stay for supper, dear?" Merigold asked without prompting.

"Oh yes, darlin'! You must stay for supper," Wynifred added. "We must hear more concerning your letter from Madame Lefebre, as well as any creative millinery ideas you're cookin' up."

Haven shook her head, however. "Oh no. No, I couldn't impose . . . not again," she assured the Sandersans. "Not after you had me twice last week for supper. Why, you'll think I'm a vagrant beggin' for—"

"Oh, nonsense!" Miss Wynifred interrupted. "We've got a whole chicken in the oven, and you know we love your company, dear."

"We'll not take no for an answer, you realize, Haven," Miss Merigold added.

Haven exhaled a sigh of forfeit. "You two will make me reconsider stoppin' in after my classes with the children if you don't stop spoilin' me like this."

"Oh, fiddle-faddle, Haven," Miss Wynifred said, tossing a wave in the air as if Haven's suggestion were a trifle. "You know we love havin' you! We'd have you livin' here with us if we could convince you of it. And it's well you know it."

Haven studied the two older ladies for a moment, her heart warming at their presence, their friendship, their affection for her.

"I cannot wait for Arabella to meet you both," Haven sighed. "You will adore her! And she will fall in love with you as quickly as I have, that I can promise."

"Well, we're impatient to meet Arabella, as well you know," Miss Merigold reminded. "What fun we four will have, hmmm?"

"What fun indeed!" Miss Wynifred agreed. "Now, let's off to the kitchen and enjoy a yummy supper together. What hats have you been workin' on this week, sweet pea? Anything that might tempt me in particular?"

"Perhaps," Haven said as she rose and followed Miss Wynifred and Miss Merigold from the parlor to the kitchen.

"Well, I want somethin' the likes of what Baby Doe Tabor bought from Madame Lefebre's shop in Denver," Merigold remarked. "I'm thinkin' for Christmastime. Somethin' really lavish. Do you know what I mean, Haven?"

Haven giggled. "I most certainly do," she said.

Miss Merigold—though the less talkative of the two Sandersan sisters—did indeed enjoy flamboyant hats. When the Sandersan sisters had first begun to order hats from Haven, Miss Merigold had explained that she preferred her hats to be "as flashy as a rat with a gold tooth." Haven had quickly discerned that the more flamboyant the hat, the more Miss Merigold liked it. Furthermore, since quitting Covington, Georgia, for Fletcher, Haven had realized (though she was not sure that Miss Merigold herself was exactly conscious of it) that just about the only way Merigold Sandersan could draw attention away from her talkative sister when they were at social gatherings or strolling about town was by donning a somewhat ostentatious hat. And while Miss Merigold's practice of wearing hats to draw attention to herself was a bit exhibitionistic, Haven and everyone else in Fletcher seemed to admire her courage. Thus, Haven worked particularly hard when designing and making hats for Miss Merigold Sandersan—for she loved the woman's individualist attitude.

Haven smiled as she assisted the Sandersan sisters in setting the table and preparing the food. She felt at home in their home and in their company. And she could not wait for Arabella to arrive, to know that Arabella would savor the same comforts with the Sandersan sisters as Haven did. Warmth, friendship, laughter— the scent of bread fresh from the oven and slathered with butter, of roasted apples covered in cinnamon and sugar—and the feeling of being accepted, of being loved, no matter what. All the things that were wonderful about the Sandersan sisters for Haven would bless Arabella's life as well. Haven knew they would. She and Arabella would find an unspoken liberation together in Fletcher—and she wished Arabella could be there already, instead of two weeks hence.

✳ ✳ ✳ ✳ ✳

"Did ya see it, Miss Abernathy?" Ronald Henry asked, reaching out to take Haven's hand in his own.

Haven smiled as she gazed down at Ronald. He fell into step beside her.

"Did I see what, Ronald?" she asked him.

"Did you see the new door that feller hung up for ya?" Robert Henry asked, racing up from behind and taking Haven's free hand in his.

"New door?" Haven asked. She remembered then—what Mr. Briscoe had muttered upon taking his leave after saving her life earlier in the day. He'd quite unnecessarily apologized for breaking down the door to the instruction room—mentioned that he'd fix it later on in the day. Haven hadn't thought he'd been serious, however. After all, it wasn't his fault that he'd had to break it down in order to save her from choking to death.

"Yep. We seen him do it," Ronald offered. "We seen him drive his wagon back into town, tie up right in front of your shop, and pull a door out of his wagon bed."

Haven had quickly learned the way between the Henry twins; everything with them was done in turns—back and forth, back and forth—even their conversations with others. Thus, she knew it was Robert's turn to talk.

90

"He truly hung a new door for me?" Haven asked Robert.

"Yes, ma'am, Miss Abernathy," Robert assured her. "He give me and Ronald a penny each just for holdin' his hammer and such. A shiny penny each, just for standin' there and watchin' him really."

"Well, why don't you two boys escort me to my shop so I can inspect this new door, hmm?" Haven giggled, squeezing each boy's hand with affection. Oh, certainly the Henry twins' hands were dusty—a bit dry from a hard day of play in the dirt and grass. But Haven didn't mind. Little boys' hands weren't meant to be perpetually clean and soft. Haven had always thought a good definition of a boy was "noise . . . with dirt on it." And Ronald and Robert Henry were about as rough and tumble as little boys came. Naturally they tested her patience whenever she was wrangling them during afternoon etiquette class. But she loved them for their rambunctious, gleeful natures.

"See there, Miss Abernathy?" Ronald said, pointing to the new door that now hung where the old one had been.

"See?" Robert unnecessarily added.

"I *do* see," Haven mumbled—for she was quite astonished that Mr. Briscoe had indeed hung a new door for her.

"And it works too," Robert said, releasing

Haven's hand and racing up onto the boardwalk. "Look!"

And indeed the door did open.

"I . . . I suppose you children can start comin' into the instruction room through this door now," she said.

"Yep!" Ronald agreed. "And Mr. Briscoe said he left the key right there in the 'struction room for ya."

"I'll get it, Miss Abernathy!" Robert exclaimed, letting go of Haven's hand and sprinting toward his brother.

"Aw, Robert," Ronald whined. "She can get her own dang key."

"Well, this way, she don't have to," Robert argued. He disappeared into the instruction room for a moment, reappeared with a key, closed the door, and very adeptly locked it.

Jumping down from the boardwalk, Robert offered the key to Haven.

"There ya go, Miss Abernathy," he said, smiling up at her.

Haven couldn't keep from smiling at him in return. Robert and Ronald, though not as calm and well mannered as their elder brother, Andrew, were both as cute as buttons. Tawny hair, dark lashes, and the smattering of freckles across their noses and cheeks—why, a body couldn't help but smile at their mischievous, albeit well-meaning, characters.

It was why Haven always thought of Ronald and Robert as the Henry Buttons. As a child, she'd known a family in Covington that comprised a mother, a father, one sister, and also four handsome little boys born only a year apart each. The family's last name was Taylor, and everyone in town referred to the Taylor boys as the Taylor Buttons—for they were indeed as cute as little buttons. The Taylor Buttons were as mischievous as the day was long. No other brothers in the fine state of Georgia caught more polliwogs, wrestled in more mud puddles, or set more things on fire than the Taylor Buttons. And since Robert and Ronald Henry were ever and always in mischief, ever and always proving boys were noise with dirt on it, Haven had dubbed them the Henry Buttons. Just as the Taylor Buttons had grown from boys into fine, hard-working, God-fearing men, Haven knew the Henry Buttons would, as well.

"Why, thank you, Robert," Haven said. "Thank you for fetchin' the key for me and for lockin' up the instruction room." She bent, placing an affectionate kiss on the top of Robert's head—a cute little towhead that smelled like dirt and strawberries.

"I helped too, Miss Abernathy!" Ronald said, leaping off the boardwalk and hurrying toward her. "I'm the one who told ya about the new door in the first place."

"Yes, you did, Ronald," Haven said. She bent and placed another kiss on another dirt-and-strawberry–scented head. "And I am so grateful."

"You'll have to be sure and thank that feller that fixed yer door," Ronald reminded his teacher. "It'd be the polite thing to do . . . wouldn't it?"

"Indeed it would be," Haven agreed—a measure of pride in knowing that something she'd said had managed to sneak into Ronald Henry's mind. "And I will be sure and thank him, as soon as I can."

"Yes, ma'am," Ronald said, smiling at her.

"Robert! Ronald?"

Haven smiled at the sound of Mrs. Henry's voice calling out for her two youngest children.

"Supper's on, boys!" Mrs. Henry called. "You best get home . . . and I mean *now!*"

As both Ronald and Robert's shoulders went slack with disappointment, Haven encouraged, "All good days end with a good evenin', boys. Now you run along home to your supper, all right?"

As Ronald and Robert nodded, turned, and began dragging their feet in the dirt of the street to make their short walk home as long as they possibly could, Haven called, "And thank you again, boys. You are turnin' into such gentlemen!"

Val watched from his place at a table inside the diner across the street—watched as the two little towheaded boys that had near talked his ears off while he was hanging the new door for the hatmaking lady headed for home. He'd figured it had been *their* mama who'd started hollering about supper. He suspected that woman had her hands full with twin boys the likes of those two little dickens. He knew how full his own mother's hands had been with him and his sisters—and there weren't any twins in the mix.

Val's eyes narrowed as he watched the milliner stroll on up to inspect the new door he'd hung. Using the key he'd left for her, she unlocked the door, opened it, and seemed to study it a moment.

The young woman shook her head and smiled, and Val mumbled to himself, "Well, there you go, Mama. My good deed for the day."

Val's mother had taught her children that, no matter what life heaped on a body, performing a good deed once a day helped protect against giving up on faith and hope—helped a body to survive. And though at times Val wanted nothing more than to give up on both, he didn't. He may have given up on things like happiness, on ever feeling anything other than fury and hatred. But he'd never given up hope. He figured it was his mother who kept him soldiering on—not just what she'd taught Val and her other children but her faith, her unceasing hope, even for everything taken from her.

And so a good deed he had done for the day.

And as he watched the Miss Abernathy lock her new door again, deposit the key in the pocket of her skirt, and start for home, Val exhaled a sigh of discouragement mingled with fatigue. Yep, he'd done his good deed and even had himself a nice supper of ham, butter biscuits, and cream gravy.

Gazing out the diner window once more, Val watched her continue to sashay down the boardwalk.

"As fine as cream gravy," he mumbled to himself. But even for the truth of what Mr. Griggs had said—even for the fact that the Abernathy woman was indeed a fine and pretty little thing— Val felt nothing but anger, hatred, prejudice, and frustration.

For near to a year, Valentine Briscoe had known nothing, felt nothing, but fury and loathing—nothing but the desire for revenge. Certainly his mother's confidence kept the tiny spark of hope Valentine had left flickering, but it was nearly out—Val could feel it. With each passing day, Valentine Briscoe could sense his soul darkening—could sense his heart had grown stone cold.

CHAPTER FOUR

As the train slowly chugged to a stop, Haven struggled to contain her excitement. In a matter of mere minutes, she and Arabella would, at last, be together again!

"For pity's sake, Haven honey," Miss Wynifred chuckled, "calm yourself, before you have a fit of apoplexy!"

"You're wound tighter than a three-day clock, sweetie," Miss Merigold noted. "I've never seen you in such a state!"

Haven knew her cheeks were flushed with eager enthusiasm—thought her heart might beat itself right out of her bosom with impatience.

"I can't remember a time before this one when I *was* in such state, Miss Merigold!" Haven admitted. "I'm just so overjoyed that Arabella is finally here, that we're back together, that she had the courage to leave Georgia and everything there, to trust me enough to come out to Fletcher. Why, I'm as giddy as a songbird in the spring! I just can't seem to settle myself."

"Well, you're as pretty as a songbird in the spring, that's for certain," Miss Wynifred said. She linked her arm with Haven's in an effort to abate Haven's dizzying agitation. "I suppose you might as well be as giddy as one."

The black iron horse crawled to a stop, releasing a long, tired sigh of steam. In that instant, Haven thought the train did indeed appear weary. Its extensive expiration of hot mist seemed to mirror her own emotions just then— for the sigh she exhaled in knowing Arabella was with her in Fletcher at last brought a sudden awareness of the emotional fatigue she had borne while separated from her family for the previous months.

A porter hopped down from the steps at the front of the passenger car coupled just behind the wood car. Haven held her breath and felt her eyes widening as she watched the porter turn around to face the passenger train exit. The porter held out his hand, and in the next moment, Arabella began to gracefully descend the passenger car steps.

"Is that her?" Miss Merigold asked in a whisper, linking her arm with Haven's free one.

"Of course that's her, Merigold," Wynifred answered before Haven could even begin to respond. "Look how beautiful she is! She looks exactly the way Haven described her to us."

Arabella, dressed in her finest blue dress and donning the hat Haven had made for her to complement it, stepped off the train and onto the platform. Although Haven was determined to maintain all appearances of self-control and poise, the moment Arabella turned and looked at her, any ounce of decorum Haven had planned to adhere to was forgotten, as she and Arabella both broke into delighted shrieks of joy, racing to one another with arms swung wide in beckoning a mutual embrace.

"Oh, Bellie!" Haven cried as she and Arabella met, hugging one another as tightly as physically possible. "Oh, how I've missed you! I'm so glad you're here!"

Haven's eyes filled with tears, and Arabella wept as their cheeks pressed together firmly.

"Havey! We've all been so miserable without you!" Arabella confessed. "I thought I might die from missin' you so!"

No matter how she tried, Haven could not keep her tears from replenishing themselves in her eyes and trickling down over her cheeks. Oh, how she'd missed Arabella! And now that Arabella was there—bringing with her the scents of green things, flowers, and even Mipsie's cooking—Haven's heart began to ache for want of the closeness of the rest of her family.

Sniffling, the two young women finally separated. "You're here, Bellie! You're really here!" Haven whispered in comfortable awe.

"Yes, I am," Arabella agreed, smiling. Yet it was a weak smile, and Haven knew Arabella was frightened—as frightened and as terrified as Haven had been the day she'd arrived in Fletcher herself.

But just as they had Haven, Wynifred and Merigold Sandersan were there to meet Arabella. Thus, taking Arabella's hand in her own in a gesture of support in taking courage, Haven turned Arabella's attention toward Miss Wynifred and Miss Merigold.

More tears filled Haven's eyes as she saw that the two older ladies stood, arms linked, with tears welling in their eyes as well.

"Arabella Barnes, please meet Miss Wynifred and Miss Merigold Sandersan," she offered.

Arabella dipped a quick curtsy, saying, "It's a pleasure to meet you, Miss Wynifred . . . Miss Merigold."

No sooner had Arabella nodded to each woman in turn than both Wynifred and Merigold burst into excited, gleeful greetings as they rushed forward, each hugging Arabella in turn.

"Oh, Arabella darlin', you are even more beautiful than Haven described you to be!" Miss Wynifred exclaimed. Taking Arabella's shoulders, the woman held her at arm's length, studying her for a moment.

"Isn't she just beautiful, Merigold?" Wynifred asked.

"Oh, indeed!" Miss Merigold exclaimed. Miss Merigold quickly walked a circle around Arabella, studying her from head to toe. "You look like somethin' that stepped right off a per-formin' stage! Aren't you somethin' to behold?"

Although she could see that Arabella was uncomfortable under such scrutiny, not to mention bashful at such gushing compliments, Haven giggled.

"They're very complimentary," she said to Arabella. "But you'll get used to it, I promise."

"I-I-I . . . why . . . why, thank you both," Arabella managed.

Like Haven, Arabella did not enjoy receiving compliments or gifts. Receiving made her uncomfortable, just as it did Haven. Haven would always and ever rather give a gift or a compliment a million times more than she would like to receive either. Still, during her months in Fletcher, Haven had learned that there was no stopping the tide of admiration, encouragement, and pure adoration that traveled with Wynifred and Merigold Sandersan. Hence, she knew Arabella would learn to accept their adulation just as she had.

"Oh, you must come for supper tonight, Arabella," Merigold insisted. "Won't you both come for supper, Haven? I know we tend to dominate your time, dear, but we would so love to have you both. But wait!" Interrupting her own resolve to have supper guests, Merigold changed her venue. "Why, I'm sure you two have so much catchin' up to do! What am I thinkin', tryin' to impose on your first night together after so long? You two enjoy your privacy and catchin' up tonight, and we'll have supper another time."

"Very wise, Merigold," Wynifred concurred. "Very wise. Still, would you allow us to walk with the both of you into town? At least 'til we get close to the turn toward our own home?"

Haven exchanged glances with Arabella—smiling glances of understanding—and Arabella said, "Of course, ladies. I feel honored to have so much happy company, especially as I enter town for the first time. No doubt strangers are rare here, and I am not in particular fond of bein' noticed. So havin' three others with me will indeed comfort me."

Haven giggled as both Wynifred and Merigold smiled with pleasure and pride.

"Well, then we might as well square our shoulders and get to it, hmmm?" Wynifred suggested, linking her arm with one of Arabella's, as Merigold linked hers with one of Haven's.

"Here we are, all four of us," Miss Merigold began, "as brave as the first man to ever eat an oyster, I'd say."

"Indeed, Merigold! Indeed!" Wynifred agreed.

Arabella looked to Haven, smiling. Haven could see a measure of her friend's fear waning, and it soothed her own heart.

"You are goin' to love the folks in Fletcher," Haven assured Arabella. "I promise."

"Yes, you are gonna love them," Merigold added as they began walking. "We've even got a new, delicious-lookin' man just arrived in town. Haven herself says she's never seen a more beautiful man in all her life."

"Is that so?" Arabella asked, arching one eyebrow with piqued curiosity as she studied Haven a moment.

"He *is* beautiful to look at," Haven brazenly admitted. "But so is the devil, some folks say."

"Well, the devil didn't hang a new door on the shop, now did he?" Merigold teasingly reminded.

"A new door on the shop?" Arabella inquired. "Your shop, Havey?"

Haven nodded, but it was Wynifred Sandersan who answered Arabella.

"Yes, on your and Haven's shop," she began. "And it was a true act of kindness on his part, even though it was Mr. Briscoe who busted the door down. He only did so to save Haven's life, after all. So you see, Arabella, my angel, it wasn't even his responsibility to replace the door. But he did anyway, and at no cost to Haven."

Stopping in her tracks, Arabella exclaimed, "Save your life? How did he save your life? And how on earth was your life in danger?"

But Haven shook her head, assuring her friend, "Oh, it wasn't as serious as that, Bellie."

"Of course it was!" Wynifred and Merigold asserted in unison, however.

"Mr. Briscoe was just happenin' by the millinery shop and glanced through the window

103

just in time to see Haven begin chokin' on a lemon drop," came Wynifred's dramatic response.

"And we obviously have a new hero in our midst, for without pause, Mr. Briscoe broke down the door, picked Haven up, and shook that lemon drop right out of her throat," Merigold finished with equal theatrics.

Arabella's eyes were as wide as the moon as she studied Haven a moment.

"You choked on a lemon drop and were rescued by the most beautiful man you've ever seen?" she asked. "And you neglected to tell me about it?"

Haven shrugged. "It only happened two weeks ago . . . just after I posted my last letter to you. I didn't have time to get another letter to you before you left Covin'ton to travel to Fletcher," she explained.

"Well, I-I suppose all is well that ends well," Arabella said, exhaling a sigh of residual concern.

"And that's exactly right," Wynifred said, tugging Arabella along as she began walking once more. "And although he doesn't linger in town, that Mr. Briscoe is as pretty as a diamond flush! So Merigold and me figure Haven was just about the luckiest woman in the county, havin' him be the one who broke down her door, swooped her up in his arms, and rattled that lemon drop outta her. As far as we know, Haven's still the only woman the man has spoken to since he arrived in Fletcher."

The uncomfortable feeling of deep guilt—a feeling Haven was all too familiar with and had been for most of her life—washed over her as Arabella looked at her with encouraged inquisitiveness. Although Haven's heart leapt at seeing the hope in Arabella's blue eyes, Haven had to find a way to communicate to her friend that, though many things they'd both longed for had happened in Fletcher, romance had not.

Oh, certainly, things *were* different in Fletcher. Old prejudices and opinions weren't as paramount here as they were in the South—at least not toward those with African or slave ancestry. There didn't abide in Fletcher the constant concern over the purity or impurity (as some viewed it) of one's blood heritage. May and Edith Crabtree living happily as influential members of the community was proof of that.

But it certainly didn't mean that Haven had flounced into town and lured any man into an infatuation with her, let alone the mysterious Mr. Briscoe. And though Haven knew the Misses Sandersan's discussing Mr. Briscoe's good looks and heroics on her behalf had given Arabella cause to begin thinking that Haven had found romance, there could be nothing further from the truth. Yes, Mr. Briscoe had saved her life. Yes, he had kindly replaced the door to her instruction room even when the burden had not been his at all to bear. But beyond that, Haven had hardly glimpsed the man in the two weeks following the incident. And even on the few occasions when she had seen him in town, he'd not said a word to her or even glanced her way. As optimistic as Haven was that Arabella would find a measure of carefree happiness in Fletcher as Haven had, the like she had never known before, she knew it would still be imperfect—and that the secrets she and her cherished friend both carried in their hearts would need to ever remain secrets.

"Oh, it wasn't so dramatic as it sounds, Bellie," Haven began, shrugging in feigning the lemon drop incident had been trivial. "Why, I haven't exchanged one word with the man since, and from what I hear, he avoids any conversation at all if he can manage it."

"Oh, I see," Arabella said. Her countenance visibly changed from hopeful to worrisome.

"You're goin' to love Fletcher, Bellie!" Haven exclaimed, moving her arm from its linking with Merigold's to an encouraging link with Arabella's. "The weather is simply divine! I've heard the winters are like nothin' we've ever known before. Oh, but the summer was beautiful! And I'm sure autumn will be extraordinary in its beauty. And the people here are so kind, so friendly and helpful."

"We are good folks here in Fletcher, sweet Arabella," Wynifred assured the newcomer. "So many wonderful folks have chosen to live here . . .

and now we've got one more to add to the pot."

Haven exhaled a quiet sigh of relief as Arabella's expression brightened once more.

"I'm just so scattered about it all," Arabella admitted. "Leavin' my mama and daddy was . . . well, it was more than I thought I could bear."

Merigold reached out and caressed Arabella's cheek with the back of her wrinkled hand. "Well, don't you worry on it, honey. We'll coax your folks out here one way or the other, now won't we, Wynnie?"

"Of course we will," Wynifred agreed. "But for now, let's get you on into town so that you can rest after your travel and catch up on all your news with Haven."

"Yes, ma'am," Arabella said, smiling.

Merigold laughed with amused admiration. "Oh, I do love the good manners they engender in the South. I do hope you've included the importance of addressin' one's elders properly in your etiquette classes with the children, Haven."

"Yes, ma'am," Haven confirmed with a nod.

"Good," Merigold approved. "Now let's get you girls home. Arabella must be plum wrung out, hmmm?"

Again Haven felt herself exhale. The Sandersan sisters were God-sent to her and Arabella, and she silently thanked heaven for them. Without them she certainly would never have found the courage to leave Covington for Fletcher—for she had Wynifred and Merigold to go to. And now, she could see that Arabella needed them more than perhaps even Haven had upon her arrival.

Yes, God-sent they were. And as the four women chattered on their way back to town, Haven thanked Him for providing her with such a blessing as were the Sandersan sisters.

❋ ❋ ❋ ❋ ❋

"And this is the general store," Haven pointed out to Arabella as they approached Mr. Crabtree's place of business. "Mr. and Mrs. Crabtree are the proprietors and very kind people."

"Mr. Crabtree handles the post as well, doesn't he?" Arabella inquired.

"Indeed," Haven confirmed. "Oh, and their son, Walter, owns a vast and very lovely apple orchard out west of town."

"Oh, I do love apples!" Arabella sighed.

"And I've already asked Walter Crabtree if we can pick some of his apples ourselves when he's ready to harvest," Haven added. "That way we can bake apple pies and apple crisps and simmer apple butter until the bouquet of apples has permeated our entire bein's."

"You are so dramatic, Havey," Arabella giggled. Shaking her head as she gazed at her friend a moment, she added, "Oh, how I've missed you."

"And I you, Bellie," Haven whispered, emotion rising in her throat. "But you're here now, and that's what's important. And anyway, I'm sincerely serious about the apples. And once they're harvested and gone for the year—and our cellar shelves lined from top to bottom with applesauce and apple butter—then we'll beg some of the farmers in Fletcher to let us immerse ourselves up to our elbows in pumpkins! Why, we'll bake our bustles off with pumpkin pies, pumpkin breads, pumpkin butter. Oh, what an autumn it will be!"

At that very moment, May and Edith Crabtree stepped out of the general store, onto the boardwalk, and toward Haven and Arabella.

"Oh! Hello, Miss May . . . Edith," Haven greeted with a smile.

"Hello, Haven," May responded, also smiling.

"Good afternoon, Miss Abernathy," Edith offered, cheerful as ever.

"How is your day so far, Haven?" May inquired.

Haven did not miss the manner in which both May and Edith studied Arabella. She wondered if they saw something familiar in her—something shared.

"My day is wonderful!" Haven exclaimed with excitement. "And all for the fact that . . . well, I would like to introduce both of you to my dearest, sisterly friend, Arabella Barnes. She has finally arrived from Georgia, just this very day."

"Why, it is such a pleasure to meet you, Miss Barnes," May said, offering a hand.

Arabella paused a moment—for in truth, she was not accustomed to strangers offering their hands to her, nor to accepting the offer.

Standing close, Haven lightly pinched the back of Arabella's arm through the sleeve of her dress.

"As it is to meet you, Mrs. Crabtree," Arabella managed as she accepted May's hand with her own graceful, kid-gloved one.

"Oh, do call me May, please," May insisted. "Or Miss May, as Haven does. She explained to us long ago the South's tradition of offering a 'Miss' before a woman's given name . . . and I find it so pleasant!"

"Thank you, Miss May. And Arabella for me, if you don't mind," Arabella kindly countered.

"I'm Edith," Edith chirped, taking Arabella's hand the moment her mother released it. "And I am so delighted to finally meet you, Miss Barnes! Miss Abernathy has talked and talked of you for so long, I was beginnin' to wonder if you were real."

Arabella giggled with delight, smiling at Edith as she said, "Well, here I am. I hope I'm not a disappointment, especially after all this waitin' on me you've had to do."

But Edith shook her head, her eyes sparkling like summer stars. "No, ma'am! Truth is, I think you're just about the most beautiful woman I've seen!" Seeming to drop into worry a bit, Edith looked to Haven, adding, "I mean, you were the most beautiful woman I had ever seen before when you arrived, Miss Abernathy—other than Mama, that is. And now, now with Miss Barnes standin' right here . . . the two of you are just divine!"

Haven giggled, not at all offended by Edith's compliment to Arabella. After all, Haven agreed with Edith: Arabella was the most beautiful woman Haven had ever seen as well.

"Well, thank you, Edith," Haven said, placing a warm palm to the girl's face. "Aren't you just the kindest thing."

Edith's cheeks pinked up with being thoroughly enchanted by the lovely Arabella Barnes.

For her part, Haven exhaled a sigh of pleased contentment. The last five months had been wonderful, yet they had likewise been expressly challenging. Haven had departed her family and home in Georgia—the only family and home she'd ever known. She'd traveled west to a place she'd never been. She'd set up the millinery shop, begun teaching etiquette, decorum, and social dance, and made acquaintance with an entire town of new people—not to mention nearly dying when she almost choked herself into the grave on a lemon drop. And all this she had done without her dearest friend and sister at her side.

For a moment, Haven stood astonished by her own strength and endurance. She'd arrived in spring to mountains blanketed in white and downy snowfalls that lingered for days. Having never known snow or seen mountains the likes of the great Rockies, Haven had borne a hefty insecurity indeed for a time. Still, with the encouragement and care of the Sandersan sisters, she had acclimated to Fletcher's spring, its summer, and its townsfolk. Now, autumn was already beginning to make itself known. The morning air was just a bit cooler than it had been even one week before. And several trees in the aspen grove just east of town were already boasting clusters of gold-gilded leaves mid their loftiest perimeters.

Yet it was the instant Arabella stepped off the train car step that Haven had realized just how much she had acclimated, as well as how much she had changed, and she knew her dearest friend would as well—wonderful, liberating acclimation and change!

"Oh, Miss Abernathy," Edith began in a near whisper, jostling Haven from her musings.

"Yes, Edith?" Haven inquired in her own whisper.

"We just seen that Mr. Briscoe inside the general store," Edith continued quietly.

"Oh . . . well, how nice," Haven said, smiling and trying to ignore the manner in which her heart leapt with a wallop she thought might knock her off her feet.

"Me and the other girls in the older etiquette class . . ." Edith continued, "well, we still think he's the handsomest man any of us has ever seen, Miss Abernathy! And since I just had a closer-up look at him inside just now . . ." Edith shook her head, emphasizing that what she was about to say was pure, perfect, undeniable truth. "Why, I just envy you for havin' your life saved in his arms!"

"For heaven's sake, Edith!" May gently scolded, blushing for her daughter's forthrightness. "Miss Abernathy nearly *died* from that lemon drop that day! I'm sure the last thing that was on her mind was whether Mr. Briscoe was handsome."

Haven was overcome by the desire to hurry past the general store as quickly as possible so that she did not risk coming face to face with Mr. Briscoe when her heart was pounding so madly and her composure entirely frazzled.

"Oh, it's fine, Miss May," Haven quickly assured Edith's mother. Then, winking and smiling at Edith, she whispered, "And I do understand your admiration of the man's attractiveness, Edith."

Quickly linking her arm with Arabella's, Haven said, "Well, we must be off. There is just so much I need to catch up on with Arabella, and I'm sure you two ladies have things tuggin' at your time, as well. It was so nice to visit with you all. Have a wonderful evenin'!"

"Uh, yes, goodbye!" Arabella politely communicated as Haven began to tug on her arm in an effort to hurry her along.

"What is wrong with you, Haven?" Arabella asked in a whisper. "All of a sudden you're as jumpy as a turkey in November! I would think you *would* want to see your Mr. Briscoe again."

"I-I . . . I can't face him, Bellie . . . not today," Haven stammered in attempting to explain her actions and near rudeness to the Crabtrees. "But . . . but truth be told, I haven't yet found the fortitude to thank him for fixin' up the instruction room with a new door! I just cannot speak to him today, not when I haven't thanked him in two whole weeks. He entirely unravels me, Bellie . . . entirely!"

"You haven't thanked him for savin' your life yet?" Arabella gasped, digging the heels of her shoes into the boardwalk to pull them to a halt. "Why, Haven Abernathy! You are the etiquette teacher here!"

Turning to face Arabella and taking her hands in her own, Haven whispered, "I thanked him for savin' my life. That I did do, the very moment after he did so! But I . . . I just haven't been able to find a . . . a way or a . . . a time to thank him for the door. And I just don't feel up to it right now and . . ."

As Haven released one of Arabella's hands in order to press her own firmly to her bosom in a futile effort to calm her raging heart, she inhaled a deep breath in an attempt to soothe herself. She also took a step back—and, in doing so, felt the ball of her foot step firm on the boardwalk beneath her. But the same was not true of the heel of her shoe.

Squealing as she began to fall backward, Haven held tight to Arabella's hand, pulling her toward her.

"Haven!" Arabella yelped as she followed Haven in tumbling off the boardwalk.

"Oof!" Her collision with the ground when her backside hit it hard forced the air from her lungs a mere instant before Arabella came tumbling down beside her—facefirst into the dirt.

Unable to draw a breath, Haven could only lay there in the street in front of the Crabtrees' general store, gulping like a landed catfish.

She looked to Arabella, now perched on all fours as she too tried to breathe.

But Haven couldn't speak to apologize—couldn't ask her friend if she had been injured in their fall. For audible words required oxygenation in one's lungs, and Haven had none.

"You ladies all right there?" Haven heard Mr. Crabtree inquire.

Haven looked up to see Mr. Crabtree, his daughter-in-law May, and his granddaughter

Edith looking down at her with worried expressions. And then, to her utter mortification, she also saw the looming, intimidating, ethereal comeliness of Mr. Briscoe scowling down at her.

When Haven was still unable to respond—a sense of panic washing over her as she had yet to draw a breath—Mr. Briscoe rather growled, "Hmm," and then jumped down off the boardwalk, took hold of her hand, and none too gently yanked her to her feet.

The lurch of his yank on her arm, and consequent uprightness it afforded her, caused Haven's body to gasp, and she was able to fill her lungs with air at last.

"Ma'am?" Mr. Briscoe mumbled to Arabella.

When no response came from a stunned Arabella (still on all fours facing the ground), Haven watched as Mr. Briscoe bent down, taking Arabella's small waist between his two powerful hands and lifting her to her feet as well.

Turning Arabella to face him—his hands still steadying her at her waist—Mr. Briscoe inquired, "You all right, ma'am?"

As Arabella's eyes widened to the size of china serving platters, Haven knew that she and Edith Crabtree were not the only women in town that day to recognize Mr. Briscoe as the handsomest man either had heretofore seen.

"You must be Mr. Briscoe!" Arabella breathily exclaimed.

Mr. Briscoe's scowl deepened to a suspicious frown as he nodded. "Yep."

He turned and looked to Haven as he dropped his hands from Arabella's waist.

Haven gulped down the lump in her throat and managed, "Th-thank you, Mr. Briscoe . . . again." As his eyes narrowed, the dam within her broke, and Haven began to babble. "And thank you so much for hangin' that new door for me . . . the one you hung the day you saved my life two weeks ago. I've meant to thank you—every day I've meant to—but I have a sense that you enjoy your privacy, and I was . . . well, to be quite sincere, I was apprehensive about approachin' you when I did see you were in town. But I just want to take this second opportunity I've had of your assistance to thank you for this, as well as the new door, and to inquire as to what sum is owed to you by me . . . f-for fixin' the door . . . and of course the door itself." Haven laughed nervously, continuing, "I mean, doors aren't free! I'm quite aware of that fact. I mean, they were never free in Georgia, so I'm certain they're never free here, where they must be much more difficult to come by. And I do want to make whatever restitution, to offer whatever remuneration, I can. You see—"

Arabella's soft squeeze at her elbow finally stopped the flood of burble flowing from her mouth. Haven immediately blushed red as a bitter blister but somehow succeeded in regaining

117

her poise and quite composedly offering, "I would hope you would allow me to repay your kindnesses, sir."

Mr. Briscoe's eyes were still narrowed as he studied Haven a moment longer. Mr. Crabtree, May, Edith, and Arabella all stood in silence, as if waiting to hear something that perhaps no one in Fletcher had ever heard before: a sentence from Mr. Briscoe.

"Nope," Mr. Briscoe began. "Just doin' my part as a member of the town."

The deep, resonating tone of his voice caused Haven's knees to weaken a bit. Yet she still was able to speak.

"I really would like to thank you, Mr. Briscoe," she reiterated.

Mr. Briscoe inhaled a deep breath, as if he were struggling to keep his temper.

"No, thank you, ma'am," he said. "You do your part here with teachin' and your business and such. And I intend to do mine . . . whatever it may be. That includes hangin' doors for folks."

"As well as diggin' graves without chargin' nobody."

Haven and Arabella both turned to see Sheriff Sterling had arrived behind them at some point during the incident.

He smiled, asking, "You ladies all right? That was quite a tumble you both took."

"Yes," Haven sighed, humiliated.

"I don't believe I've had the pleasure," Sheriff Sterling said, removing his hat and offering a rugged, callused hand to Arabella. "Dan Sterling."

Haven looked to Arabella to see the color completely drained from her face one moment and pinked up like a spring tulip the next.

This time—in full opposition to the moment May Crabtree had offered Arabella *her* hand— Arabella accepted the sheriff's gesture at once, placing her small, kid-gloved hand in his.

"Arabella Barnes," Arabella replied, her voice as sweet and enthralling as ambrosia. "It's a pleasure to meet you, Mr. Sterling."

For his part, Sheriff Sterling's eyes were bright, near to sparkling with admiration.

"The pleasure is mine, Miss Barnes," Sheriff Sterling said. "And please call me Dan."

Sheriff Sterling's smile broadened, further adding to his own handsome features, and Haven bit the inside of her lip a little to keep from giggling with merriment and gladness as she noted the way in which Arabella expertly restrained the urge to sigh with felicity.

"Are you sure you're all right, Miss Abernathy?" Edith inquired from the boardwalk.

Turning to respond to her, Haven quickly inhaled when she saw how very close to her Mr. Briscoe was still standing.

A slight frown puckered his gorgeous brow as

119

he seemed to study her from head to toe with lingering concern—or curiosity—or perhaps disbelief that, once again, he'd had to come to Haven's aid.

Fairly having to wrench her attention away from him and to Edith—for he was ever so bewitching to gaze upon—Haven smiled and answered, "Oh yes! I'm fine, Edith. Just a little rumpled, I suppose."

Edith nodded, and Haven returned her attention to Mr. Briscoe as the sheriff said, "Well, I saw it all from across the street, and I'm sure glad to see both you ladies seem no worse for the wear. Glad you were here too, Val."

"Val?"

Haven was horrified when she realized she had whispered his name out loud.

Yet Mr. Briscoe seemed unaffected. He nodded toward the sheriff. Then, nodding to Arabella, he offered his hand, "Valentine Briscoe, Miss Barnes. Folks call me Val."

"It's a pleasure to meet you, Val," Arabella said, placing her hand in his. "And thank you so much, for your heroic service to Haven and me."

Haven watched as Valentine Briscoe arched one eyebrow with curiosity. "Just glad you both didn't get banged up any worse."

Haven quickly studied Arabella's appearance. Save a little dust on the skirt of her dress where her knees had been on the ground, there was nothing whatsoever out of place about her. Arabella's hat was as snug and upright on her beautifully piled hair as ever it had been.

Realizing that if Arabella hadn't been "banged up," then she must be, Haven put a hand to her head. Indeed, her hat had slipped to one side during her fall—or else her rescue—and now hovered askew above her right ear. Likewise, a long, long, long strand of her coal-colored hair had escaped its pin and hung from her left temple to her waist.

"Well, thank you, everyone . . . Mr. Briscoe in particular," Haven began, forcing a smile. "And everyone else, of course, for your kind concern. But I best be gettin' Arabella on home now. We've got so much catchin' up to do, and dear Mr. Latham has promised to bring Arabella's travelin' trunk and things home from the station this evenin'. We wouldn't want to miss him."

"Mr. Latham?" Sheriff Sterling asked.

"Why yes," Haven assured him. "I spoke with him last evenin' about bringin' Arabella's things out to the house."

The sheriff cleared his throat and seemed uncharacteristically uncomfortable. "Well, um, Miss Abernathy . . . Mr. Latham passed on in the night. His wife fetched Doctor Perkins first thing this mornin'." The sheriff nodded toward Valentine Briscoe. "Val here has agreed to dig Mr. Latham's grave, and his wife plans on holding his wake the day after tomorrow."

"But . . . but I haven't paid him yet!" Haven exclaimed. "I owe him for his services today. I promised him that when he brought Arabella's things over from the train station, I'd settle with him at once. He can't possibly have died without havin' collected what I owe him."

Haven's eyes widened as Valentine Briscoe reached out and took her chin in one strong hand. He turned her head one way and then the other, appearing to inspect her thoroughly.

"You sure you didn't bang your head harder when you fell just now?" he asked.

As she stared into the infinite handsomeness of his face, Haven realized how ridiculous the worry she'd expressed was.

"I guess I won't have the chance to settle with him after all," she breathed.

"I'll see to gettin' your trunk and things from the train station for you, Miss Barnes," Sheriff Sterling offered.

"Why, thank you kindly, Sheriff Sterling," Arabella said, her voice sounding like the chimes of heaven, once again.

"My pleasure, ma'am," the sheriff said, still smiling at Arabella.

"And maybe one of us outta see the ladies home," Mr. Crabtree suggested from his place on the boardwalk. "I'm not sure Miss Abernathy is quite herself yet."

"Oh, fiddle-dee-dee," Haven chirped, even though a place at the back of her head had begun to throb mercilessly. "We'll be just fine. You all are so sweet to be concerned, however. Thank you."

Yet as she turned to start toward home, Haven was overwhelmed with a dizzying sensation. She stumbled forward two steps, and then backward three, and next found herself being swooped up into the powerful cradle of Valentine Briscoe's arms. Instinctively, Haven's arms encircled his neck in an attempt to steady herself.

"I'm so very sorry, Mr. Briscoe," Haven managed as the throbbing at the back of her head commenced to spread thoroughly throughout it.

"Havey! Are you all right?" Haven heard Arabella's worried voice echoing through the pounding inside her head.

"Yes, of course, Bellie," Haven breathed.

"There's nothin' all right about her," she heard Valentine Briscoe growl. And it was the last thing she heard before feeling her body go completely limp as the lamp flame of her consciousness flickered out.

CHAPTER FIVE

Here she comes," she heard a man's voice saying. "She's comin' around just fine now."

Haven opened her eyes to see Arabella and Doctor Perkins leaning over her. Doctor Perkins offered an encouraging grin even as worry puckered Arabella's lovely brows.

"You're right as rain, Miss Abernathy," Doctor Perkins said.

Haven noted how well Doctor Perkins's faded blue eyes complemented the silver of his hair. And he had such a kind, reassuring smile.

But in the next instant, Haven remembered what had happened.

"Oh my!" she exclaimed. "Did I faint? How Southernly cliché of me!"

Haven blushed as she glanced beyond Arabella to see Valentine Briscoe and Sheriff Sterling standing at the foot of the bed upon which she lay. Both men were scowling at her—scowling with concern and not irritation, or so she hoped.

She assumed, from her unfamiliar surroundings, she was lying in Doctor Perkins's office.

"Is she truly well, Doctor Perkins?" Haven heard Edith Crabtree inquire.

Indeed, Edith and her mother stood behind Arabella. Had the entire town been witness to

Haven's weakness? Her blush of humiliation deepened as she quickly sat upright. Instantaneous pounding commenced in her head, however, and the heavy dizziness returned.

"Oh, fiddle-faddle," she grumbled. "My head feels like it's caught between a hammer and an anvil."

"I believe you hit your head harder than you realized when you fell, Miss Abernathy," Doctor Perkins explained. "You've got a pretty big lump on the back of it. It'll be sore for a time, I'm afraid. Still, it's swellin' out instead of in . . ."

Doctor Perkins paused as he lifted one of Haven's eyelids to study her eye and then repeated the process on her other.

"But your pupils look fine," he concluded. "I think gettin' the wind knocked out of you had as much to do with your fallin' unconscious as hittin' your head did. But you're fine, Miss Abernathy. Just fine."

Even for Doctor Perkins's reassurance, Haven did not feel fine. Nevertheless, what was a woman to do but pretend otherwise?

"So she's good enough to go home, Doc?" Sheriff Sterling inquired.

"Oh yes," Doctor Perkins assured. "Of course, you're welcome to stay here in my office and rest, Miss Abernathy."

"Goodness no!" Haven declared. "As you said,

sir, I'm right as rain and anxious to get home and settle Arabella in."

May Crabtree stepped closer to the bed on which Haven sat.

"Well, now that we know you're well, Haven, Edith and I will be headin' on home," May said, smiling with kindness. "You rest up now." May offered her hand to Arabella, adding, "And it is so nice to meet you, Miss Barnes. So very nice, indeed."

"Likewise, Mrs. Crabtree, I assure you," Arabella said.

Even with the headache that was making her miserable, Haven could see the hope rising in Arabella. Knowing that May and Edith Crabtree lived happily in Fletcher had given Arabella a glimpse of a different sort of life than she'd known in Georgia, and it made Haven's heart swell with joy in knowing her friend anticipated more happiness than she had known before.

Valentine Briscoe opened the door for May and Edith as they made their way out of the doctor's office.

"Thank you kindly, Mr. Briscoe," May said, acknowledging the man's manners.

"Ma'am," he returned with a nod.

Haven felt her mouth go dry as the handsome, brooding man turned his attention to her then. His eyes narrowed as he studied her a moment—

seemed to be summing up for himself whether she were well.

Turning his attention to Sheriff Sterling, Valentine Briscoe said, "Well, I got a grave to dig." He looked to Arabella and touched the brim of his hat, adding, "Welcome to Fletcher, Miss Barnes."

"Thank you, Mr. Briscoe," came Arabella's melodic reply.

"Thank you for patchin' her up, Doc," Valentine thanked Doctor Perkins.

"I'm happy to help," Doctor Perkins responded. "I'm glad you had the prudence to bring her to me the way you did."

It was then that Mr. Briscoe looked at Haven again—nearly glaring at her. "You take more care, Miss Abernathy. Way things are goin' for you of late, I might be diggin' another grave here pretty quick if you don't."

Haven was humiliated, and her temper flared, as well. How dare the man chasten her as if she were no more than a child! Her bruised ego wanted to lash out at him—to remind him that she had only had two incidents of being in danger or hurt since moving to Fletcher. And both incidents occurred when he was somewhere nearby. In fact, she fought the urge to flat out accuse him of being her bad luck.

But instead, Haven simply gritted her teeth and offered Valentine Briscoe a smile. After all, she was the etiquette and decorum teacher in

Fletcher. What kind of example would she be setting if she proceeded to chew into Valentine Briscoe for getting her dander up?

"Thank you for your sound advice, Mr. Briscoe," Haven said in a voice that mimicked that of an angel. "And for your assistance . . . again. I'm beholden. Truly beholden."

Valentine Briscoe's eyes narrowed with wariness—as if he could see right through her polished yet somewhat insincere gratitude.

Then Haven remembered something else. "Oh! And Mr. Briscoe," she began, "about that new door you hung for me . . ."

"Forget about the damn door, Miss Abernathy," he growled. "Just take better care. I ain't got the temperament for damsels in distress."

Haven's pride was then far too pinched, and she angrily retorted, "I am *not* a damsel in distress, Valentine Briscoe!"

Valentine glared at Haven once more and then groused, "I got a grave to dig. Good day," and stormed out of Doctor Perkins's office.

Haven looked to Sheriff Sterling when she heard an amused chuckle resonate in his throat.

"Seems to me like Mr. Briscoe there could use a bit of your proper manners instructin', Miss Abernathy," he proposed, winking with sympathy at Haven. Haven exhaled a tired sigh as he continued, "Even so, in my experience, a man that young and already so cantankerous . . .

well, a man like that's most likely got a past, and a hard one at that."

Haven waved a hand, as if dismissing Valentine Briscoe's gruffness. "Oh, I'm grateful for his help—on both occasions that he's proved to be my rescuer. I'll just try to stay out of his way from here on out, I suppose."

She looked to Doctor Perkins, desperate to change the course of the conversation. "So I'm all right to be on my way home, sir?"

"Yes, indeed, Miss Abernathy," Doctor Perkins assured her. He smiled a rather fatherly smile, adding, "Just settle yourself in a comfortable chair for a bit if you're able. You do need some rest. I'll give you a little dose of tonic for your headache. But other than that particular discomfort, you're just fine."

"Thank you, Doctor Perkins," Haven said. She looked to Sheriff Sterling, adding, "And thank you, as well, Sheriff. You're so kind and thoughtful to all of us who live in Fletcher."

"It's my pleasure, ma'am," Sheriff Sterling contended.

Haven watched as the handsome sheriff's gaze lingered in locking with Arabella's beautiful one. Why, she could've sworn two tiny stars had fallen from the heavens and straight into Sheriff Sterling's eyes! Oh, Arabella *would* be happy in Fletcher. Haven's heart and soul just knew she would!

● ● ●

Valentine growled under his breath. He had things to do! Digging a grave was no easy task, and he still had chores waiting. He hadn't had the time to waste in carrying the fainting southern belle to Doc Perkins's. And he certainly hadn't had the time to stay and make sure the woman came around and was well.

Val felt his scowl soften, however—even felt a hint of amusement tugging at the corners of his mouth as he thought over the incident. Now that he knew that Fletcher's little hatmaking etiquette teacher hadn't suffered any permanent damage, the vision of Miss Abernathy and her friend tumbling off the boardwalk and into the street plum tickled him. Oh, he knew how mortified both ladies must've been—still probably would be for some time—in knowing their fine southern manners did nothing to help them appear any more proper than anyone else in the world when they went tumbling down in a flurry of blue and green dresses, petticoats, and bloomers. And he certainly did not find amusement in the possible injuries either one or both might have sustained from the fall. But the expression on Haven Abernathy's face when he'd yanked her to her feet had been priceless! Shock, bewilderment—he couldn't put a name to the expression exactly, but the memory of it tickled him all the same.

The woman seemed to find herself rolling in the mud of disaster more often than a pig on a hot summer Sunday. The fact that Miss Haven Abernathy had been in need of serious assistance, in one way or the other, both times Val had crossed her path led him to worrying a bit over her, and his frown returned. What was a woman like her doing out west all alone anyhow? Then again, it would seem that she wasn't all alone anymore. Miss Barnes had arrived that very day, and Val exhaled a sigh of dismissing himself of the unexpected feeling of responsibility over Miss Abernathy's well-being that had begun to rise in him. It made sense to assume that Miss Barnes was the second half of the Abernathy and Barnes Millinery shop in town, as well. Thus, Val concluded that hopefully Miss Barnes could keep her friend out of trouble from then on out. Still, what in tarnation were two young southern beauties doing all alone and so far out west?

Val frowned again as his apprehension returned. He didn't have time for worry over anyone—not the townsfolk of Fletcher and certainly not two young women who had somehow failed in reeling in a couple of husbands to protect, provide, and care for them.

And yet both women hailed from Georgia. Things were different in the South. He thought of May and Edith Crabtree—the slight coffee in their creamy complexions that no one in Fletcher seemed to even notice. It was the one thing he liked about living out west, instead of east or south. Folks didn't seem to put as much care and gossip into the color of a person's skin, or lack thereof, for that matter.

Val tried to gulp down the familiar burden of prejudice that crept into his mind, but as always it proved difficult. Why couldn't he be a saint like his mother and not judge a whole race of folks to be evil simply because there were a few bad apples among them? There were bad apples in every race, every nationality, every corner of the world. One race did not own the patent on evil above another. Evil was Satan's doing, and the devil did not take note of differing races, religions, or genders. He pulled everyone he could into hell with him.

Nevertheless, it was a daily fight for Val to try to view anyone as honest, good, and worthy of admiration, let alone the heathens who had caused such pain and tragedy to him and his family. Too much had happened at the hand of evil—too much tragedy, loss, and pain—and Val's anger because of it had been building inside of him for far too long. It had taken root, firm root.

Even so, he again remembered his mother's counsel: that every day a man ought to do at least one good deed. It was what kept the devil from laying claim to his soul. Hence, he would dig a grave for some poor old man he'd only met once—and hopefully keep the devil at bay for one more day.

Val mused, grumbled, and fought a silent, inward battle with himself all the way to the small cemetery where he'd left his shovel earlier. Stripping off his shirt, he pulled his suspenders over his shoulders with a smart snap and started in to digging a resting place for Mr. Latham.

"Poor old cuss," Valentine mumbled as he drove the shovel into the dry dirt, stomping on its shoulder with his boot to drive it deeper.

He shoveled only a couple shovelfuls of dirt aside before the memory of Miss Abernathy's startled expression when he'd pulled her to her feet leapt foremost to his mind once more. Again, Val allowed the corners of his mouth to curl into a grin. If nothing else, Miss Abernathy and her misadventures were entertaining—and it had been a long, long time since anything had cheered Valentine Briscoe enough to make him smile.

❉ ❉ ❉ ❉ ❉

"Oh my heavens!" Arabella exclaimed in a whisper as she stared through the parlor window to the small cemetery nearby. "I just cannot fathom that he's out there with hardly a stitch of clothin' on at all!"

134

"Why not?" Haven exclaimed, fairly leaping out of the chair she'd been sitting in. The quick movement caused her headache to make itself known again, but she paid it no mind as she hurried to the window.

Arabella had been peeping out the parlor window since the moment she'd watched the attractive lawman, Sheriff Sterling, ride away in his wagon after delivering her trunk and other baggage. Once the sheriff was out of sight, however, Arabella had noticed that Mr. Briscoe was indeed just across the way digging a grave for Mr. Latham. Arabella had been astonished at how brazen Valentine Briscoe was to be working out in broad, public daylight without his shirt on—and also his strength and musculature so prominently displayed as he worked at digging Mr. Latham's grave.

Certainly, Haven was as curious about Valentine Briscoe's improper state of undress, but after this, the fourth time Arabella had mentioned it to her, Haven found her curiosity could not be settled.

"Oh my, indeed!" Haven breathed as she stood next to her friend, gazing out the window to where Valentine Briscoe was working. Haven's brows puckered into a frown of concern. "It's awful hot out today," she mused aloud, trying to ignore the way she wanted to simply stare at him forever. "He must be terribly parched."

"I don't see that he's brought any water with him at all," Arabella noted.

Haven endeavored to squelch the worry that instantly surged through her—but to no avail.

"Miss Wynifred told me that they found an old prospector just east of here," Haven began. "In truth, they found the bones of an old prospector *and* his mule, just east of here—found him about five years back but figured he'd been dead for decades. Folks determined he'd run out of water and died of thirst."

Arabella giggled. "Oh, for pity's sake, Haven, Mr. Briscoe isn't gonna die out there from thirst. Why, town is just a short walk away! And anyway, we're right here . . . and you've got that rain barrel and that pump out back."

Haven nodded. "Oh, I know. But my experience with Mr. Briscoe has led me to believe he's as stubborn as that old prospector's mule, at least! He'd probably rather drop dead diggin' that grave than knock on my door and ask for a drink."

Arabella sighed and nodded herself. "Well, I've only just met the man today, but I do tend to share your opinion of him in that regard."

Looking to Arabella, Haven pleaded, "Oh, do please take him a pitcher of water, Bellie! We just cannot have the man droppin' dead out there in the graveyard. Not after he's saved my life twice!"

Arabella's smile faded, however. "*You* take the

water to him," she countered. "I don't even know the man! I can't just waltz out there without a chaperone and offer him a drink."

But Haven shook her head. "But I can't possibly face him again. Not twice in one day," she explained. "And anyway, things are different out here. Folks don't care so much about men and women socializin' with one another without proper chaperonin'. You'll be just fine."

But Arabella shook her head. "I just couldn't, Havey," she insisted. "You know how nervous I get around new folks."

Haven put a hand to her forehead. Her headache was better but still present. Yet she knew Arabella was right. Valentine Briscoe had saved Haven from choking to death on a lemon drop. Valentine Briscoe had carried her to Doctor Perkins's after she'd made a fool of herself falling off the boardwalk in town. She knew she should be the one to take a pitcher of water out to him.

"You're right, Bellie," Haven conceded. "And I'm sorry for pressin' you. It's just that . . . well, the man makes me as jittery as a June bug on a pole line. I can't figure why, exactly, but he does. No one else in town intimidates me anymore—no one but that man out there."

"I'm sure it's just because he's as handsome as the day is long," Arabella offered.

Haven shrugged as she made her way to the

kitchen sink and began working the pump. "The sheriff is handsome, and I don't get all June-buggy when he's around," she pointed out.

As the water began to spill from the pump, Arabella hurried into the kitchen as well. Finding a pitcher and a glass in one cupboard, she handed them both to Haven.

"Maybe it's because you feel indebted to him for all his heroics where your well-bein' is concerned," Arabella suggested.

"Maybe," Haven sighed as she filled the pitcher with cool water from the pump. Taking the pitcher in one hand and the glass Arabella offered to her in the other, Haven quietly confessed, "Bellie, the truth is . . . I've dreamt about Valentine Briscoe every night since I first saw him. Every single night for two weeks! And that cannot be healthy for a woman."

Arabella grinned with understanding compassion. "Then when you get back from waterin' him, I think you and I need to do some talkin' about that half-naked man out there nearly dyin' of thirst, don't you?"

Haven nodded. "I'm fearful that somethin's wrong with me, Bellie," she whispered. "I've just been pushin' my dreams and such to the back of my mind, for it makes no sense whatsoever. But I suppose talkin' it out with you will help me to sort it out." Haven smiled at her beautiful, beloved friend. She smiled, so grateful to have the company of her sister-friend there with her at last. "Talkin' with you *always* helps me to sort things out. Oh, Bellie . . . I'm so thankful you're here!"

Arabella's eyes misted with tears. "Me too, Havey."

"Truly?" Haven asked.

"Truly," Arabella assured her.

Inhaling a deep breath of courage and resolve, Haven nodded with determination to make certain Valentine Briscoe didn't drop dead of thirst. As Arabella opened the kitchen door leading to the back porch for her, Haven straightened her posture and left the house. Mr. Briscoe wouldn't die of thirst digging Mr. Latham's grave that day. Not while Haven Abernathy was nearby.

"G-good afternoon, Mr. Briscoe."

Val looked up to see none other than the prissy little milliner standing at one side of the hole he was standing in. A long-absent susceptibility to feeling relief washed over him as he noted the young woman seemed no worse for the wear after her fall earlier in the day.

"Afternoon," he managed to respond. He'd be polite to the girl, even if her unwelcomed appearance had stopped the momentum of his labor.

"I-I've glanced out the window a time or two while you've been workin', and I haven't noticed that you've had even one sip of water since you started," she began. She was nervous; Val could tell by the way she was stammering and twisting her hips this way and that, making her skirt swish back and forth.

"Can't say that I have," Val admitted. He was dry—too dry. But he hadn't noticed it until the woman had said something.

"Well, I thought maybe you could use some cool water, so I've brought you a pitcher and glass. I-I hope you're not angry with me for intrudin'," she managed.

"Nope," Val assured her. Driving his shovel deep into the dirt, Val put his hands on the side of the grave that was near to five feet deep already, hoisting himself out of the hole to stand next to the pretty milliner.

"Thank you kindly, ma'am," he mumbled as she offered the glass to him.

Haven gulped down the large lump that had formed in her throat between the back porch of the house and Mr. Latham's grave. Still, another lump instantly took its place as she looked up, up, and up into the mesmerizing face of Valentine Briscoe.

Valentine accepted the glass, holding it as Haven's trembling hand filled it with cool water from the pitcher.

"It would appear that you're nearly finished

here, Mr. Briscoe," Haven forced herself to comment.

"Yep," the man answered.

Haven watched as he drank the entire glass of water lickety-split, holding it out to her so that she could fill it from the pitcher once more.

"Well, it was kind of you to offer to do this for poor Mr. and Mrs. Latham," Haven said, "just as it was kind of you to help me today . . . again."

She watched as Valentine inhaled a deep breath, exhaling it slowly as if struggling to restrain his temper.

"I don't take well to bein' thanked," he said, " 'specially when I'm just doin' what anyone oughta do in a situation."

"So I've gathered," Haven admitted. "B-but if you would allow me to say that . . . that . . ."

"That what?" the man prodded.

Haven glanced away from him, for his ethereally disturbing attractiveness was somehow greatly intensified by the fact that he stood not a breath from her—his broad, sun-bronzed shoulders and chest staring her in the face. She'd never experienced anything the like of standing so near a half-unclothed man, let alone a man the caliber of Valentine Briscoe.

Nonetheless, calling upon every ounce of bravery she could muster, Haven explained, "Well, I know it's often uncomfortable to be thanked. But it is proper to allow someone to

141

offer their thanks . . . especially when they are indebted to you as deeply as I am."

"I ain't much for propriety," the man remarked, holding his empty glass out to her again.

"I-I know, but . . . but it's not the propriety that's important," Haven said, filling his glass once more. "It's givin' the receiver of your service the opportunity to feel he or she has acknowledged you and what you've done, thereby alleviatin' he or she from bearing the heavy burden of indebtedness."

The handsome man's green, green eyes narrowed. "So I'm supposed to let you thank me so that *you* feel better? Is that it?"

"Oh, exactly!" Haven exclaimed with relief and delight. "I have felt just terrible these past couple of weeks—at not thankin' you properly for savin' my life and hangin' a new door and all! I know you told me to forget about it, but I just can't, and I do want to offer my thanks for that incident and the one today."

Valentine's narrowed eyes relaxed. He shrugged his broad, broad shoulders and said, "Well, then, thank me proper, if it'll make you feel better."

"It will," Haven assured him. Swallowing another lump that had taken up residency in her throat (albeit a much smaller lump than the first two), she said, "Thank you so much for all you've done to help me, Mr. Briscoe. I am truly grateful."

The man inhaled deeply, causing his massive chest that was glistening with perspiration to rise up and out until Haven need only lean forward a bit to find her nose smack between the defined muscles just below his collar bone.

"You're welcome," he managed to accept—though she could see he was uncomfortable in doing so.

"Thank you, Mr. Briscoe," Haven sighed, smiling up at him. "I do feel much better in havin' properly thanked you."

The man nodded and glanced away for a moment. Inhaling deeply again, he rather muttered, "While we're at all this proper pomp and circumstance," he began, "I hope you'll forgive me for cussin' at you earlier today . . . at the doc's place. I ain't a soft man—in any regard, I suppose. But that's no excuse for cussin' at a woman or grouchin' at her either, for that matter."

Haven blushed and breathed a nervous giggle. The fact was, she hadn't minded that he'd sworn—or that he'd grouched for that matter either. She didn't know why she hadn't minded, but she hadn't.

Still, she was the etiquette teacher in town. Furthermore, she'd just given Mr. Briscoe a lesson on propriety too. It would not do for her to tell him that she hadn't minded his grouching.

"Thank you, Mr. Briscoe," she therefore responded.

Valentine nodded. He held the empty glass toward her.

"Thank you for the water, Miss Abernathy," he said.

"You're very welcome," Haven assured with a nod. Accepting the glass from him and realizing he'd drunk the pitcher dry, she added, "And please, if you are thirsty, our house is just a dash away. There's a pump right out back if you don't want to knock for us, and I've got a rain barrel just off the back porch you can use for refreshin' your . . . your . . . yourself if you like."

Haven tried not to stare at the man's bareness, but she couldn't keep from it! His arms were so bulging with muscles they were like immense tree limbs. And his shoulders, chest, and stomach reminded her of photographs she'd once seen in a book—photographs of sculptures of Greek gods.

In fact, Haven was suddenly so completely unnerved by Valentine Briscoe's half-naked nearness that she took a step back from him—not realizing that she stood with her back to Mr. Latham's freshly dug grave.

"Whoop! Careful now," Valentine exclaimed, taking her waist in his powerful hands and pulling her forward and against the granite of his firm body. "I doubt gettin' another bump on your head today would do you any kind of good."

Breathless for the feel of being so close to

144

him—for being right up against him, in truth—Haven nearly dropped the glass she was holding in one hand and the pitcher she was holding in the other.

"Oh, I'm quite certain it would not," Haven breathed. "Thank you, Mr. Briscoe."

"You can call me Val," Valentine told her.

The green eyes of Valentine Briscoe stared at Haven then. He seemed to very intently study her face—her eyes, her nose, her cheeks, her lips.

Suddenly, the voice inside Haven's head silently warned, *Get away! He'll know!* startling her from the warm, blissful distraction of it all.

Therefore, even though Haven had never felt a euphoria like she was experiencing at being held by Valentine Briscoe—being held against him as he studied her—Haven quickly ducked around him and away from the open grave.

"Very well, Mr. Briscoe," she called over her shoulder as she hurried toward the house. "And remember, do please keep yourself cool and well-watered while you're workin'. And do let myself or Arabella know if you need anything."

Hastening back to the house, Haven burst through the back kitchen door, slammed it behind her with one foot, set the pitcher and glass down on the nearby counter, and collapsed into a chair at the table.

"What on earth, Haven?" Arabella exclaimed, rushing into the room from the parlor. "You took off faster than a buttered bullet! What did he say? Did he say somethin' to unsettle you?"

"*He* unsettles me, Arabella!" Haven blustered. "The man's very existence unsettles me. And then, just now . . . well, you saw what happened! I nearly fell into Mr. Latham's grave! I was so nervous at talkin' with the man, I almost went head over tail into that grave. And he saved me . . . *again!*" Haven put a hand to her bosom in attempting to slow the mad pounding of her heart. "And then . . . he just held me there! Just held me there, right up against his bare skin! And he was studyin' my face. I'm sure he guessed, Arabella! I'm just sure he did!"

"Well, I'm sure he did not," Arabella soothed. She took a seat in a chair across the table from Haven. Reaching out, she took Haven's free hand in her own, clasping it with warm reassurance. "You just imagined that he did, that's all."

"Somethin's wrong with me, Bellie," Haven whispered, tears filling her eyes. Shaking her head, she explained, "This isn't like me at all! To be so clumsy, so . . . so entirely intimidated! Why, I'm probably just as ruffled-lookin' when I'm near Valentine Briscoe as all the Fletcher schoolgirls are when Andrew Henry swaggers into the schoolhouse. What is wrong with me, Arabella? I was fine, just fine, up until that man arrived in town." Haven moved the hand at her bosom to press her palm against her forehead.

"Maybe I've taken ill with somethin'. Maybe I've got some ghastly disease or . . . or . . ."

Arabella's amused laughter—the laughter that sounded like a thousand fairies were mirthful—drew Haven's attention away from her dramatic feelings.

"Oh, Havey!" Arabella laughed. "Really? You're not really this naïve. I know you're not! You're just not wantin' to admit it to anybody . . . includin' yourself."

Haven frowned, and even though she knew exactly what Arabella meant, she didn't feel ready to say it herself. She'd let Arabella say it for her. "Admit what?"

Arabella arched one lovely brow. "Oh, you know what. And I know you, Haven Abernathy! You've always considered that if you don't admit somethin' is so, then it can't be so. But we both know you always learn this lesson the hard way."

"What lesson?" Haven asked, feigning ignorance—for Arabella was right. Haven did tend to imagine that if she didn't acknowledge something to be real, then it wouldn't be.

"The same lesson you learned when Daddy gave us Orville," Arabella began. "I knew Orville was meant to be our Thanksgivin' dinner all along. And so did you. And even though I was as heartbroken as you were when the day came that Daddy wanted to butcher him, you pretended all those months that if you didn't admit to yourself that Orville was meant for supper, then all would be well."

"But all was well where Orville was concerned," Haven playfully reminded. "He ended up not bein' our Thanksgivin' dinner that year."

"Only because your daddy and mine couldn't bear to break both our hearts. And you know it," Arabella giggled. She sighed with compassion, smiled at Haven, and said, "So tell me about this Mr. Valentine Briscoe you've been tryin' to convince yourself you're *not* attracted to."

Haven inhaled a deep breath of forfeit. Sighing she said, "I don't know why, Arabella, for he's about as soft as a bed made out of thorny brier stem. But whenever I even set eyes on the man, I can hardly keep from faintin' away at how fast my heart starts poundin'! And I've dreamt of nothin' but that grouchy neighbor-man of mine since the day I met him."

Arabella laughed. Shaking her head with merriment, she needlessly noted, "Well, you've done a dandy job of makin' sure you have had his attention here and there."

"Not on purpose!" Haven wailed as tears filled her eyes. "You know I'm not like that silly Sophia Stuckerman back home. Why, she was always feignin' at faintin' or gettin' somethin' caught in her eye. You know I don't do that. I've just turned into a clumsy imbecile somehow."

Still smiling, Arabella suggested, "How about

we bake a batch of cookies, strip off our bustles and stockin's, plop down in the parlor, and just talk all through the night like we used to, hmm? You can tell me all about this new ghastly disease called Valentine Briscoe you've contracted. What do you say?"

Haven smiled and felt calm returning.

"Very well," she agreed. "And after we've discussed my new ghastly disease, we can discuss the way lookin' at you made Sheriff Sterlin's eyes light up like candles on a Christmas tree!"

Arabella blushed, shook her head, and scolded, "Don't tease me so, Havey. You know right well I think your sheriff is as handsome as a harvest moon."

"Yes, I do," Haven admitted. At last she smiled at her friend. "So bake cookies first . . . then strip off our bustles?"

Arabella giggled and nodded, "Yes!"

Haven studied her friend a moment—the fascinating blue of her eyes, her perfectly straight and narrow nose, her full lips, and her perfectly coifed hair. Everything about Arabella Barnes comforted Haven—somehow gave her strength to do and face things she might otherwise not find the strength to do or face. Oh, how she'd missed her beloved sister.

CHAPTER SIX

Haven covered her mouth with one hand to hide a yawn. She and Arabella had stayed up until almost sunrise. There was just too much that needed verbal catching up—how Mipsie and Old Joe were faring back home, how Arabella had enjoyed her train travel, how handsome Arabella thought Sheriff Sterling was. Not to mention the fact that Arabella needed reassurance that she'd done the right thing in leaving Covington for Fletcher—as well as Haven needing reassurance that just because she had finally, consciously admitted to being perniciously attracted to Valentine Briscoe, it didn't mean she was on the brink of insanity.

Yes, Haven and Arabella had talked, giggled, cried, expressed worries, and offered reassuring comfort to one another all through the night. And now a blurry-eyed Haven was wondering how she would ever make it through the morning, let alone teaching etiquette classes that afternoon.

Still, as Haven looked up from the hat she was working on and gazed out the window to see Arabella adeptly painting gold, crimson, and orange leaves on the shop's front windows, she exhaled a heavy sigh of happy contentment. Arabella had made it to Fletcher! And Haven was more certain than ever that her beloved Mipsie and Old Joe would find their way out west too— someday.

Placing her millinery project on her worktable, Haven stood, stepping out of the shop and onto the boardwalk so that she could better see Arabella's embellishing art.

"Oh, Bellie!" Haven gasped as the beauty of Arabella's painting came full into view. "How beautiful! Oh, everyone will love it. Look how perfectly it brightens up the town!"

Arabella smiled. "I'm glad you like it, Havey. I'm figurin' we can change the subject matter several times a year, perhaps seasonally. Leaves for autumn, snowflakes for winter . . . things like that. I heard of a man who embellishes store windows in Savannah just like this. And I want our shop to be as pretty on the outside as your hats are when they're sittin' on Baby Doe Tabor's head!"

"Well, I doubt any hat I ever did create was as pretty as these leaves, Bellie," Haven sighed with admiration. "I just love the way you've got that big old tree trunk and tree limb to the side and above there, leaves rainin' down so soft and pretty."

"It is comin' out nicely, I think," Arabella agreed.

"Oh! Could you do pumpkins in October?" Haven asked with delighted anticipation.

"Of course," Arabella assured her friend. "And maybe holly and mistletoe for Christmas!"

"Yes, please!" Haven exclaimed. "And we can hang some mistletoe just inside the shop entrance." Lowering her voice and winking as Arabella glanced over to her, Haven added, "And then we can lure your handsome sheriff into the shop, and you can catch him under the mistletoe and get yourself a Christmas kiss from him!"

Arabella blushed with delectation. "Now, hush, Haven. I swear, you can be so silly sometimes."

"But I'm not bein' silly. I'm bein' serious!" Haven countered. "Why, I thought Sheriff Sterlin's blue eyes were gonna bug right out of his head when he first saw you! I swear, he looked as happy as a dog with two tails. I thought his jaw was goin' to drop clean off!"

Still blushing, Arabella shook her head, however. "Havey, I've been here all of one day . . . and not even a whole day, at that! I'm sure the sheriff hardly noticed me at all."

"You think so?" Haven teased.

Arabella had gone back to painting. Therefore, she hadn't seen Sheriff Sterling approaching from across the street the way Haven had.

"Well, let's see about that," Haven said. Waving a welcoming hand at the sheriff, Haven called, "Good mornin', Sheriff! How are you today?"

Arabella straightened her posture so quickly a body would have thought someone had shoved a broom handle up the back of her dress.

"Good mornin', Miss Abernathy," the sheriff said as he stepped up onto the boardwalk.

"Oh, for pity's sake, Sheriff," Haven began. "I've been tellin' you for months now, please call me Haven."

Sheriff Sterling's blue eyes twinkled as he chuckled a bit. "Well, I don't know what folks in town might think if I start callin' the etiquette teacher by her first name."

Although Haven continued to smile at the sheriff, the familiar sensation of disappointment she'd begun to feel at being branded "the etiquette teacher" in Fletcher rose in her chest. She had enjoyed the etiquette classes with the children; she still did. But she had begun to feel a heavy, albeit invisible, burden weighing on her. Haven perceived she must always be the perfect example of a proper, finished lady—that she must never make the mistake of stepping out of line where acceptable decorum or manners were concerned. It was another secret she bore in silence, and it was beginning to taint her cheerfulness now and again.

Nevertheless, she was profoundly grateful that the good folks of Fletcher had been and were so unquestioningly accepting of her. And she knew better than to discount that blessing in favor of wishing for another.

"And good mornin' to you too, Miss Barnes,"

Sheriff Sterling offered to Arabella then. "Goodness sakes! You're an artist as well as a milliner? My, my, my! You two ladies certainly have brought more than just your rare beauty to the town of Fletcher."

Arabella turned to face the sheriff, her face as pinked up as a baby pig's curly-tailed fanny.

"Oh, it's just a little embellishment to pretty up the shop," Arabella explained.

Haven smiled, all too aware of Arabella's discomfort, even though the southern beauty masked it perfectly.

The sheriff studied the falling autumn leaves scene Arabella was painting. Shaking his head in admiration, he complimented, "If you ask me, it's prettyin' up the whole town. What in the world did I do to deserve havin' such a talented young woman as an acquaintance?"

Gazing back at her own work, Arabella exhaled a sigh of nervous delight. "I'm so glad you approve of the window dressin's, Sheriff," Arabella managed. "I do hope it brings a little gladness to the community."

Sheriff Sterling's smile faded. "Well, the Lord knows the community certainly could use a bit more gladness of late."

Haven's brow puckered with concern.

"Is somethin' wrong, Sheriff?" she inquired.

Sheriff Sterling removed his hat and raked his fingers back through his hair.

"I'm afraid so," the man sighed. "It seems Mrs. Latham has followed her husband in passin' away."

"What?" Haven and Arabella exclaimed in unison.

"Yep," the sheriff confirmed. "Doc Perkins stopped in first thing this mornin' to see how she was holdin' up. When Mrs. Latham didn't answer her door, Doc let himself in." He paused, his frown deepening. "Doc found her curled up in her bed, a soggy handkerchief clutched in her hand. He figures she died of a broken heart." He shrugged. "Least ways that's how he put it. Doc says her heart stopped—said he's seen it before, 'specially in cases of older folks who lose a spouse. So looks like we'll be havin' a wake tomorrow for both Mr. *and* Mrs. Latham."

"How sad," Haven said, her own heart aching to its center.

"Yes," the sheriff agreed.

"But . . . well, at least they're together again, instead of one bein' left behind to mourn alone for who knows how many years," Arabella offered.

Sheriff Sterling nodded, and Haven brightened a little. "That's true." She paused, feeling her own familiar heart ache. "Just like Daddy and Mama," she mumbled, tears brimming in her eyes.

"Mornin', Dan."

Haven was startled by the sound of Valentine

Briscoe's voice behind her. All at once, the only image in her mind was that of Valentine Briscoe's shirtless, sun-bronzed body rippling with muscles as he'd steadied her to keep from tumbling headlong into Mr. Latham's grave the day before.

"Mornin', Val," Sheriff Sterling said. He turned, offering a hand to Valentine Briscoe.

Haven felt her brows arch with surprise as Valentine actually accepted the sheriff's handshake.

"Mornin', ladies," Val said, nodding first to Haven and then to Arabella.

"Good mornin'," Haven returned.

"Mr. Briscoe," Arabella greeted with a smile.

Haven watched as Valentine studied the shop windows a moment.

"Nice leaves," he mumbled.

Arabella smiled. "Thank you, Mr. Briscoe."

Inhaling a deep breath, as if acknowledging three at once had sorely tried his patience, Valentine turned his attention back to the sheriff.

"Doc Perkins tells me you're in need of another grave to be dug?" he asked.

The sheriff nodded and returned his hat to his head. "Yep. Mrs. Latham passed on in the middle of the night, and Doc Perkins says that . . . well, Mr. Latham will be a bit . . . um . . ." Sheriff Sterling glanced at Arabella. "If you'll excuse me, ma'am, for my crudeness." Looking back to

Valentine, he continued, "Doc says Mr. Latham will be far too, um, ripe . . . if we wait another day. So he thinks it'd be best if we just plant both tomorrow. I know it's a lot to ask, Val, but might you have it in you to dig another grave today? If you've got the time, of course."

"I can do it," Valentine answered without pause. "Glad you told me early on. I got a load of work waitin' at my place, so I best get to diggin' as soon as I can."

"The town will be more'n happy to pay you for diggin' them graves, Val," the sheriff offered.

But Valentine Briscoe shook his head. "Nope. I'm fine without pay."

"Yoo hoo! Sheriff! Mr. Briscoe!"

Haven bit her lip with amusement as the group of four turned to see none other than Miss Wynifred and Miss Merigold Sandersan hurrying toward them from up the street. She almost laughed out loud when she heard a low, breathy groan escape Valentine's throat.

"We've brought cinnamon rolls! Fresh from the oven!" Miss Merigold called.

"Enough for everyone!" Miss Wynifred added.

Indeed, each Sandersan sister carried a large baking pan fairly stuffed with large, frosted cinnamon rolls. The very next instant, the sweet scent of yeast, flour, cinnamon, and sugar reached Haven's senses, and she was astonished at how suddenly soothed she felt.

158

"Good mornin', ladies," Sheriff Sterling kindly greeted.

Haven exchanged understanding glances with Arabella. The Misses Sandersan were amusing, and it was clear that Sheriff Sterling appreciated their kind eccentricities. Haven knew that Arabella would find the sheriff all the more attractive because of it. The shining approval in Arabella's beautiful blues as she stared at the back of the sheriff's head as he faced the Sandersans was proof of it.

Valentine reached up, rubbing at the two- to three-days' whisker growth on his chin. His eyes darted quickly in all directions, and Haven knew he was looking for a means of escape. The Sandersan sisters were as social as social butterflies came. Valentine Briscoe was not.

"And don't you gentlemen worry one whit, 'cause Merigold and I thought ahead and brought some old muslin napkins along with us," Wynifred explained as she and her sister climbed the steps leading up to the boardwalk and the shop's entrance. "As ever, we used the confectioner's sugar we have Mr. Crabtree order in for us and thick, rich cream fresh from Esmeralda's udder yesterday mornin' for this icin'. It's as smooth and fine as any icin' we ever did make before. I declare to you I was salivatin' whilst I was drizzlin' it over the cinnamon rolls. Mmmm!"

159

"We made enough so that you girls can give one to each of your students today too, Haven, honey," Merigold chirped. "Wynnie and I were certain you'd be wantin' to celebrate the arrival of your sweet Arabella with them today, and Wynnie thought it might be a better idea to feed the children cinnamon rolls instead of lemon drops this time," the old gal said with a wink.

Haven felt her cheeks burst into a flaming blush of humiliation. But Miss Merigold was hardly finished unintentionally embarrassing her.

"Still," Merigold continued, nudging Valentine's arm with one elbow, "let's hope you'll be passin' by this afternoon, just in case Haven's bad luck with lemon drops carries over to cinnamon rolls, hmmm?"

Valentine mumbled, "Maybe, ma'am."

Valentine glanced to Haven then, and she thought she saw one corner of his mouth twitch for a moment, as if he were almost going to smile. She wasn't offended that he appeared to be somewhat amused by Haven's discomfort. It fact, she liked that he was. After all, though the memory of nearly choking to death was horrifying in one regard, the fact that the handsome Valentine Briscoe had saved her was deeply romantic in another. Especially being that Haven lived through it.

"Now, here you go, Sheriff," Wynifred began to instruct. "Just take a piece of muslin out of my apron pocket here . . . oh, go on and get four, would you mind? One for each of you. Then choose a cinnamon roll. I promise your mouth will think it's sippin' ambrosia."

"Why, thank you, Miss Wynifred . . . Miss Merigold," Sheriff Sterling said. The sheriff reached into Wynifred's apron pocket and removed several pieces of muslin. Counting out four, he shoved the remaining pieces back into her pocket.

Arabella looked at Haven, her eyes as wide as twin harvest moons. But Haven smiled at her friend with reassurance. She knew Arabella was astonished at the familiarity between Sheriff and Miss Wynifred. Southern etiquette had probably felt a blow to its heart over such goings-on. But life out west was different. It wasn't such a shocking thing to see a man reach into a woman's pocket and remove a piece of cloth if she asked him to.

"Mmm, mmm!" he sighed, looking over the pan of cinnamon rolls Miss Merigold offered to him. "These do look delicious, ladies. I will not deny that they sent my mouth to waterin' already. No, I will not!"

Haven watched Arabella as Arabella watched the sheriff choose his cinnamon roll. She half expected wings to sprout from Arabella's besotted heart and take flight. The pretty pink blush on her cheeks and the sparkle in her eyes gave Haven's heart wings, as well. She knew Arabella would be happier in Fletcher than she ever had been in all her life!

"Is it all right if I just put this other pan for the children in your instruction room, Haven, honey?" Miss Wynifred asked.

"Oh, of course, Miss Wynifred," Haven assured her. "And you are so kind to think of them that way . . . and Arabella and me. Thank you so very much."

"We'd love a little visit with you girls once you're finished with your gentlemen callers," Merigold said. With a wink at Haven and a quiet "tee hee" of a giggle, Miss Merigold disappeared through the new door leading into the instruction room, as well.

"Those two are just the most charmin' lavender-scented old gals I've ever known," Sheriff Sterling chuckled. "Seems they're always doin' somethin' for somebody."

"Yes. They are," Haven agreed. She was thinking, of course, of all the Sandersan sisters had done for her. She would not be where she was without them. They had made her happiness possible, and she would be forever grateful.

"That there's a mighty good cinnamon roll," Valentine commented. He arched one handsome brow in being impressed and then took another bite.

Haven was surprised by the inflection of

gratification in his voice. She realized then that she'd never heard an ounce of joy, happiness, or contentment in his voice before. The obvious expression and the way it changed the intonation of Valentine's voice—from deep and brooding to deep and rich like cream icing drizzled over a cinnamon roll—caused butterflies to begin flittering about in her stomach.

"You got that right," the sheriff agreed. "I think I coulda put a whole pan of these away."

Haven glanced back to Valentine to see him staring at her. She immediately felt uncomfortable—nervous that he might recognize something in her that she did not want him to recognize.

Nervously, she ran the tips of the fingers of her free hand over her forehead. "Why, Mr. Briscoe," she began, feigning a lighthearted nature, "by the way you're lookin' at me, I feel quite like you're expectin' me to truly choke on this cinnamon roll."

"No, ma'am. Not at all," Valentine responded—though he continued to stare at her as he took another bite of the roll in his hand.

As fine as cream gravy. It was the thought that traveled through Val's mind every time he studied the pretty little milliner. Yet as the smooth, soft, sweetened spice of the bite of cinnamon roll caused his entire body to feel warm and somewhat less surly, he derived that more than cream gravy, Miss Abernathy was akin to the icing with which the Sandersan sisters had topped their cinnamon rolls. She was too sweet to be cream gravy slathered on a warm, buttered biscuit. Nope, Fletcher's little milliner was sweet and spicy—a confectionary pleasure to Val's senses.

Nonetheless, suddenly aware that his thinking was roosting on sugars and spice and everything nice about the town milliner, Val recognized a not-so-mild uneasiness in himself and knew he could linger no longer.

"If you'll excuse me," he began, touching the brim of his hat in a proper farewell to Haven and then her friend. "Seems I got another grave to dig. And it won't wait." He turned and offered a hand to the sheriff. "I'll take care of it, Dan. Mrs. Latham can be put to rest right next to her husband come tomorrow."

Sheriff Sterling nodded, grasping hands firmly with Valentine. "Thank you, Val. Truly."

"Mmm hmmm," Val mumbled.

As he stepped down off the boardwalk, he shoved the last bite of the cinnamon roll into his mouth and the scrap of muslin into the back pocket of his britches. It truly was the best thing he'd tasted in years. Or so it seemed. As he strode toward the livery where he'd left his wagon and team, he realized that he couldn't remember ever having eaten anything that made him experience a lift in his mood the way that cinnamon roll had. At least not for the past year—not since . . .

"I guess I better head home and snatch up a shovel," Val grumbled to himself. He exhaled a heavy sigh, for his arms and back were still sore from digging Mr. Latham's grave the day before. Yet he knew hard work brought sound sleep— and sound sleep was another thing he hadn't had much of for near to a year.

* * * * *

"Tell us everythin', Haven honey," Miss Wynifred demanded. "We heard straight from May Crabtree herself that you and Arabella took a tumble off the boardwalk in front of the general store yesterday."

"And that you plopped down right in front of that handsome Mr. Briscoe," Merigold added as she sat, eyes wide as serving platters in anticipation.

Before Haven could respond, however, Miss Wynifred turned her attention to Arabella. "May also tells us that Fletcher's handsome young sheriff turned as drooly as a hound puppy lookin' at a lame rabbit when he set eyes on you, Arabella Barnes. Now, do tell," Wynifred prodded.

In truth, Haven was relieved Miss Wynifred had turned her attention so quickly from Haven's despicable display of impropriety and clumsiness the day before to Arabella's instantaneous acquisition of Sheriff Sterling's enthrallment. After all, Arabella's situation was much more pleasant to ponder. Though the memory of being swooped up into Valentine Briscoe's strong arms did cause Haven's heart to flutter. Good gracious! How he affected her!

"Well, I don't really know about that," Arabella humbly began.

The four women were seated in the instruction room, each enjoying a cinnamon roll. Both Haven and Arabella had been quite astonished when Wynifred and Merigold Sandersan suggested the two younger ladies enjoy a second cinnamon roll. But once Miss Merigold explained that no one was nearby to witness such gluttony and thereby no one was nearby to judge it as gluttony, Haven and Arabella both agreed to relishing a second warm, sweet, near decadently buttered and iced cinnamon roll.

"Now don't you?" Merigold teased. "Why, to hear May tell it, the sheriff was near to pantin' with cupidity at the sight of you!"

Arabella blushed, and Haven giggled, amused by her friend's bashfulness, as well as Miss Merigold's verbiage.

"At least admit to us that you think Sheriff Sterling is as handsome as the day is long," Wynifred coaxed. "Come on now. We'll take the secret to our graves, I promise."

Arabella's smile broadened so as to give the Mississippi River itself something to admire.

"He is very handsome," she admitted. "I swear, he quite put my stomach to floppin' around like a fish out of water yesterday. And today, if you must know."

As Wynifred and Merigold burst into peels of delight, Haven's brows arched in surprise. It was quite unlike Arabella to admit to something so personal to anyone but Haven—especially two women she'd only just officially met the very day before. Still, it was proof to Haven—proof that Fletcher would be good for her friend.

"And then there's you," Merigold said, wagging an index finger at Haven. "Faintin' dead away and right into the arms of that tall drink of water, Valentine Briscoe!"

It was Haven's cheeks that pinked up with a blush this time. "I hardly fainted into his arms, Miss Merigold," Haven bashfully corrected. "I . . . I just hit my head when I fell and knocked the wind out of me too, and then . . . and then . . . the world just started spinnin' and . . . and . . ."

"And Valentine Briscoe swooped you up into his strong arms and carried you all the way to Doc Perkins's place," Miss Wynifred finished. She sighed with blissful admiration—as if she'd been the one carried in Valentine Briscoe's arms instead of Haven.

"And I hear he stayed at your bedside until

you were conscious once more," Miss Merigold contributed.

"He most certainly did not," Haven corrected, even as her heart beat more quickly, remembering Valentine there in the same room when she'd come to in Doctor Perkins's office. "It was Arabella at my side," Haven said, smiling at her friend, "though Mr. Briscoe was there, in the back of the room. So I guess he did stay until I was better." Haven felt a slight frown pucker her brow as she added, "Of course, he swore at me as he was leavin'."

"Oh, how divine!" Miss Merigold exclaimed. "He must've been really concerned over you . . . to let his proper guard down enough to swear in front of folks."

"Oh my, yes!" Wynifred agreed with a nod. She glanced over her shoulder, as if making certain the four of them were indeed alone. "Truth be told, I think a man oughta be able to swear when he's worried. If he's been hurt too . . . or if the need arises in some other form." She winked at Haven. "I love a man who can swear a bit—not too much and not too often. Just a bit, when it's called for . . . and with good form and technique."

"Oh, me too!" Merigold agreed.

"You do?" Haven asked, surprised. The truth was, Haven had felt the same way—all her life she had. She was reminded of the time her father caught a man in town calling out obscenities to

Mipsie one day. Haven's father had stridden right up to the man and sworn at him good before laying the man out with one punch. She'd never thought about the fact that some folks would've thought her father ill-mannered and crass for the use of profanity, especially in public. In truth, it wasn't until Haven had relayed the story to her mother later in the day—her mother then gently scolding her father for having sworn at the villain first—that Haven had even thought of the impropriety of it. Yet even in that very moment, Haven did not fault her father—only thought of him as a hero who had defended Mipsie's honor. Thus, it gave her comfort to know that she was not the only woman on earth who did not disparage a man for swearing a bit here and there.

"Oh my, yes!" Merigold assured her. "Though I do agree with Wynifred. It has to be done properly, and with strength. But any woman who faults a man for a little cussin' here and there . . . well, she might as well devitalize her man in every other regard as well."

"Valentine Briscoe puts me in mind of our own daddy," Wynifred interjected. "Don't you think so, Merigold?"

"Oh yes!" Merigold exclaimed. "Handsome, tall, and as masculine as any man ever born. That was our daddy, girls!"

Haven and Arabella exchanged understanding

glances, their smiles each broadening with amusement.

"Why, our daddy was six feet and four inches," Merigold offered with obvious admiration.

"Yes! Daddy was so very tall," Wynifred added. "Folks could see Daddy coming a mile away—knew it was him, just because he was so tall. Now, I don't think Mr. Briscoe is as tall as Daddy, do you, Merigold?"

Merigold's brows puckered together thoughtfully a moment. "No, no, indeed not," she answered at last. "But he's tall, all right. Tall enough he could hunt geese with a rake, I'd say."

"But we're runnin' off on a tangent now," Wynifred said, shaking her head. "I want to hear about yesterday. And about the sheriff haulin' your things out to you, Arabella." She frowned then. "Poor Mr. Latham," she said, shaking her head.

"Poor Mrs. Latham too. I think Paulina just couldn't go on without ol' Wilson," Merigold said to her sister. "Those two had been attached at the hip since they were children, or so Paulina once told me."

"Mm hmmm. Mm hmmm," Wynifred agreed, nodding. "I suppose when two people have loved each other for near to sixty years—if you're gonna go, it's best to go close together, so one isn't left behind alone for too long."

"Oh, Wynnie!" Merigold suddenly exclaimed.

"That funeral is tomorrow, and you've got that seam splittin' out in your black crepe!"

"Oh dear! That's right!" Wynifred gasped. "I've got to get that mended before tomorrow!"

As both women quickly stood up, readying to take their leave, Wynifred said, "I'm so sorry, ladies! We've got to run on home. I'm afraid we'll have to visit another time."

"Oh, that's just fine," Haven said as she and Arabella rose from their chairs as well. She'd finished her second cinnamon roll and offered the square of muslin she'd been using to Miss Wynifred.

"No, no, dear, you just keep that for later," Miss Wynifred said. With a friendly wink, she added, "In case you and Arabella get a cravin' for another cinnamon roll before the children start arrivin' this afternoon, hmmm?"

Haven giggled. Miss Wynifred and Miss Merigold were true kindred spirits if ever she and Arabella had ever had any.

"And thank you so much for thinkin' of the children," Haven said, looking from Wynifred to Merigold and back. "You two just do so awful much for me! I'll never be able to thank you for everything!"

"Your friendship is all we care about, Haven honey," Merigold offered, smiling. "We love doin' for you, and now we have Arabella to dote on as well. Why, you two girls have brought us so much happiness that . . . well, we'll never be able to thank *you* for everything."

"So true," Wynifred concurred. "So very true."

Wynifred leaned over, placing a loving kiss on Haven's face as Merigold kissed Arabella's cheek. Then Merigold pressed a kiss to Haven's cheek as Wynifred kissed Arabella's.

"And now we're off to mend our mournin' attire," Merigold said. "Just drop the bakin' pans off on your way home . . . or tomorrow or whenever you have time."

"We will," Haven assured her. "And thank you again, ladies . . . so very, very much!"

"Of course, sweetheart," Miss Wynifred called as she and her sister quickly exited the instruction room by way of Mr. Briscoe's new door.

Once the door had closed behind them, both Haven and Arabella collapsed back into their chairs.

"Whew!" Arabella breathed. "Are they always that fizzy?" She laughed a little, amused by the energy of the Sandersan sisters.

Haven shook her head. "No, not always," she answered. "But when they have somethin' to fizz about . . . yes! I love them so much, but there are times when they just tire me out." Haven giggled, thinking of how adorable, kind, and helpful Wynifred and Merigold were.

Looking to the clock hanging on the instruction room wall, Haven began, "How would you feel about runnin' on home for a bit, just for a little catnap before the children start to arrive for lessons?"

Arabella smiled. "I would feel wonderful about it!" she chirped. "I swear all that sweetness I just ate is implorin' me to lie down and close my eyes for a spell. And I do want to be fresh and spritely when meetin' the children."

"As do I," Haven agreed. "Then let's close the shop and pussyfoot home for an hour or two. We'll be glad of it."

The Sandersans' warm, sweet cinnamon rolls had lulled Haven's mind and body into a state of deliciously blithe drowsiness. And as she locked the millinery shop's front door, she wondered how on earth Valentine Briscoe was ever going to manage to dig a grave for Mrs. Latham—for she had no doubt that the delectable, confection-drizzled delights had had the same effect on him.

CHAPTER SEVEN

Val paused in his digging. He surely did want Mr. and Mrs. Latham to rest in peace next to one another—wanted their services the next day to go smoothly. Doc Perkins said Mr. Latham was already pretty ripe, so Val knew the elderly couple needed to be buried as quickly as possible. And yet his back was aching something terrible. Offering to dig two graves in two consecutive days—what in tarnation had he been thinking?

Still, Val knew that moaning and groaning to himself wouldn't get the job done. Furthermore, the hard work was good for him, as well as the benefaction the grave would provide for poor Mrs. Latham. Nevertheless, he hoped the good deed he stumbled upon needing doing the next day was a little less physically laborious in nature. He was already wondering if he'd be too darn sore come morning to even attend the services for Mr. and Mrs. Latham, let alone be capable of doing some other good deed.

Val wiped at the perspiration on his forehead with one forearm. It was hotter than hell outside, and he wondered when autumn might make itself known in Fletcher. Seemed to him, it being early September and all, it was about time for things to cool off. Walter Crabtree had been in the general store just that morning telling his father to let folks know his apples were ripe for the picking if anyone cared to pick their own and save a penny or two. Yet to Val, standing there in a hole up to his knees with still another four feet to go, it felt like mid-July out under the blazing afternoon sun.

And why hadn't he thought to bring his own water? Val was irritated with himself for not thinking of water when he'd raced home to grab his shovel. He was about as parched as a sun-blanched bone!

Thirsty to the core, he glanced over toward the milliners' little house nearby. The day before, when Haven Abernathy brought him the glass and pitcher of water, she'd made sure he understood that he was welcome to the water at her pump out back of her house, as well as her rain barrel. Still, Val paused in putting his shovel down and going to either place for a drink. He didn't want to run the risk of bumping into Miss Abernathy and her hatmaking friend. He didn't have the time or tolerance for any more socializing. Look what talking to folks in town had gotten him into just that very day already—digging a grave and eating a cinnamon roll that was so good it got him to thinking there might still be something in life worth experiencing. But his thirst wasn't going to quench itself. And anyway, he figured that the milliner and her friend would be at their shop, working their dainty little fingers away making hats for some rich man's wife somewhere. Either that or they'd be busy with one of the etiquette classes she held for the children in town.

Therefore, still angry with himself for not bringing water with him, Val drove his shovel into the dirt, stepped up out of Mrs. Latham's would-be grave, and headed for the pump behind the house.

As he strode past the front of the house, Val noted that the pansies and petunias planted around the front porch steps were the same colors and size of the ones planted on every grave in Fletcher's little boneyard. He'd never noticed it before, but now that he had, he figured it made sense that the Abernathy woman would have been the one to plant the flowers at all the graves. Likewise it stood to reason that her house was the only one close enough to easily carry water from to nurture the flowers in the little cemetery. Val thought for a moment that it was a kind thing to do—to plant flowers at the graves of folks a body didn't even know and care for them as Miss Abernathy had obviously done. Still, the girl could've had a more selfish reason to do it. After all, what woman in her right mind would want her parlor window looking over a boneyard? Maybe she planted the flowers just to improve her own view.

Regardless, Val knew it had been the Abernathy

woman who had beautified the boneyard, and whatever her reasoning, he couldn't fault her for wanting to add some color to the world.

Val stopped in his tracks when he reached the rain barrel at the back of the house, however. For there, right next to the rain barrel, stood a small table, and on the table sat a pitcher of water with a cloth covering it to keep bugs and dirt out, a glass turned upside down for the same purpose, and two small, neatly folded towels with a note beside them and held still by a small rock.

Frowning, Val read the note, mumbling, *"Please use these towels for whatever purpose, Mr. Briscoe—whether bathing your face or dabbing perspiration away. And thank you for your service to Mr. and Mrs. Latham. With Sincerity, Haven Abernathy."*

Glancing about to make sure no one was watching him, Val did indeed remove the cloth from the pitcher to see several sprigs of mint leaves and quite a few lemon wedges floating in the water. Shrugging in thinking he might as well enjoy the water the woman had so thoughtfully prepared and left for him, Val picked up the glass and poured it full of the water from the pitcher.

The moment the cool mint- and lemon-flavored water touched his lips—his tongue—he was refreshed. And far more so than he would've been had the water been merely plain from the pump. In truth, Val was astounded at how cool the minted water felt in his throat, how instantly it seemed to slow his perspiring.

Once he'd drunk the pitcher empty, he shrugged again, picking up one of the soft, white towels and plunging it into the rain barrel. Wringing the excess water out, he wiped his face and placed the cool, wet towel on the back of his neck. Reaching into the empty pitcher, he retrieved one of the sprigs of mint therein, tore off a few leaves, popped them in his mouth, and began chewing them. He knew chewing the mint would refresh him even further.

For a moment, Val was almost glad that the hatmaking etiquette teacher lived so near to the cemetery—for she certainly knew how to refresh a man.

The sudden, unexpected shrieking startled Val so completely that he about jumped out of his skin! Hurriedly looking about for the source of the women's screams, Val's eyes widened with amazed curiosity as he watched Miss Abernathy and her friend backing out of the outhouse some distance away, continuing to shriek and squeal as if the devil himself were chasing them out.

Val watched, awed into silence, as the women squealed, hopped around, and continued to scramble backward away from the outhouse. He drew in a quick breath as he watched the heels of their shoes get caught in the long fabric covering the bustles of their dresses, tripping them up and landing them both on their bottoms.

At once he was worried that they were hurt—especially Miss Abernathy. He figured she was probably still not right in her head, considering what she'd been through the day before. So without another thought, Val ran to assist them.

"Ow!" Haven exclaimed, simultaneously bursting into laughter.

"I think that knocked a few of my teeth right out!" Arabella giggled as both she and Haven collapsed on their backs into the grass.

"I told you, Bellie! I told you!" Haven gasped through her chortling. "You *have* to drop fire down in that hole before you do anything else! And even then, you have to be so quick about your business. Oh, I just hate spiders! I just hate them to my very core!"

"And I've never seen a black widda! Not in real life, Havey," Arabella said, shivering with the residual nervous shakes the fear of seeing the poisonous spider had caused in her. "I mean, I've read about them, but how in all the world am I supposed to do my private business in the company of somethin' so awful?"

"I take to the tree line behind the house sometimes myself," Haven admitted. She slapped her forearm, having thought she felt something crawling there. "I swear I'd rather squat down behind a tree than face that malicious husband-eater every time I need to go. But with the weather beginnin' to cool off—"

"Are you ladies all right?"

Instantly Haven was frozen—petrified as the horror of who was nearby settled over her. Quickly pulling herself to a sitting position, Haven turned where she sat to see none other than Valentine Briscoe hurrying toward them. Once again, he wasn't wearing his shirt. His muscles distended with the visible strength of a steam engine as he approached.

"Oh, Bellie," she breathed in embarrassment.

"Oh, Havey," Arabella breathed in understanding.

"What happened?" Valentine asked, dropping to one knee next to Haven. "Are you hurt?" he asked. He reached out and took her chin in one strong hand, turning her head from side to side as he inspected her.

"No, sir," Haven managed. "Just terrified and startled near to death by a . . . by a . . ."

"By a what?" Valentine asked, releasing her and studying Arabella a moment.

"By a spider, sir," Arabella answered. "A big ol' shiny black widda!"

"A black widder? You mean . . . a spider?" Valentine asked, frowning.

"Yes!" Haven affirmed strongly. Her skin began to crawl as she thought of the spider again. "I've been burnin' her web down every time I go in there! And still she just spins another one—a bigger one than before! She and I are havin' a battle of wills, and I'm afraid I'm losin', Mr. Briscoe."

Valentine's frown softened. He offered a short nod and then stood, saying, "I'll take care of it for you."

And that was when Haven thought she might drop dead of embarrassment. Scrambling to her feet, she called, "Oh no! Please, Mr. Briscoe, don't go in there! We can take care of that old hag ourselves! I really don't think you need to—"

But it was too late. Valentine Briscoe opened the door to the outhouse and stepped inside.

Exchanging understanding glances of mortified humiliation with Arabella, Haven leapt to her feet. Valentine Briscoe could not truly be in their outhouse! Why, what would he think of her? Certainly everyone in Fletcher owned outhouses—used them. But to think that Valentine would now know for certain that Haven used one, as well. And what she used them for— it was beyond disgracing!

"He's in there, Havey!" Arabella gasped in horror. "He's in your privy!"

"I know it!" Haven exclaimed, tears brimming in her eyes. "And it's our privy, Bellie, not just mine."

Hurrying to the outhouse, Haven reached out and opened the door. There, just inside, stood

Valentine Briscoe. But he wasn't looking down the outhouse hole at the she-devil spider. No, instead he was studying the walls—the walls Haven had painted a lovely, soft purple—lilac—to mirror the flowers that would bloom forth on the lilac trees that surrounded the outhouse come spring. Instead of looking at the thick, shiny, sticky web the female spider had built, Valentine studied the pretty basket, filled with twelve copies of the most recent issue of the *Farmers' Almanac*, the bottling jar filled with water and fresh flowers that Haven had attached to one wall using wire and a nail, and the lovely etching of a mermaid Haven had cut from one of the Chatterbox books she owned and carefully tacked to the one wall.

"Mr. Briscoe," Haven ventured, "I'm truly sorry we disturbed you . . . worried you. It's only that . . ."

Valentine Briscoe then looked into the hole in the seat of the outhouse. Haven felt her face grow red with embarrassment. To know that the man she could not quit thinking about was staring down into . . . into . . . it was more than she thought she could bear.

"Yep. She's a nasty ol' biddy. I can see that from the size of her web," Valentine remarked. "You say you've been burnin' her web?"

Gulping down her pride, Haven answered, "Yes. I started with strikin' matches and droppin' them in. At first, that scared her away long enough for me to . . . to . . ."

"Tend to business," Valentine finished.

"Yes," Haven admitted, her fiery blush of humiliation returning. "But the last couple of days, it takes two or three times of droppin' a burnin' piece of paper or somethin' to get her to scramble. We just decided to come in here today and do battle until we were the only ones left alive. But when I dropped a piece of fiery paper in just now, why, the thing just came runnin' up out of the hole and chased us out!"

Haven—though still mortified with embarrass-ment—watched as Valentine rubbed at the whisker growth on his jaw and chin. "I see," he mumbled.

Haven relaxed a bit, for it appeared that Valentine understood the dilemma.

"Well, why don't we just lift up the lid and smash her?" he suggested. "Then she'll be gone for good. And the next time one shows, just smash her before she entices you to battle. Hmm?"

Haven looked at Arabella. Arabella looked at Haven.

Go on, Arabella mouthed to Haven.

Summoning every ounce of courage she could, Haven asked, "What do you mean, lift the lid?"

Valentine turned, staring at Haven. As one brow arched, he asked, "You did see the hinges back here, didn't you?" he inquired, pointing to the back of the seat. "I mean, you painted them purple . . . so I figured you knew that this seat lifts up."

There was never a red geranium put on the green earth by heaven itself that was a brighter shade of crimson than were Haven's cheeks at that moment. She did not know that the seat lifted!

However, she was loath to admit her lack of observation. Therefore, she tried to appear less dimwitted than an earthworm and offered, "But she'll just run at us all the same, won't she?"

Valentine shrugged. "I don't know. Let's find out."

But as Valentine Briscoe reached out and began to lift the lid of the outhouse seat, Haven and Arabella simultaneously shrieked, turned, and fled the minuscule building.

Moments later, Haven heard the outhouse seat drop shut once more. And as Haven and Arabella clung to one another, Valentine stepped out and said, "She's dead. And I knocked down her web for good."

"Are you sure she's dead?" Arabella asked.

Holding up his right boot so that both Arabella and Haven could see the sole of it, Valentine answered, "There she is."

Haven grimaced as Valentine scraped the dead spider off his boot by sliding his foot along the grass beneath him.

Swallowing the thick lump of disgust, fear, and humiliation that had gathered in her throat, Haven humbly offered, "Thank you, Mr. Briscoe. I know you must think we are just the silliest ninnies, but—"

"I don't like spiders either," Valentine assured her. One corner of his mouth curved up in a half grin for a moment. "And I'm glad to help. So if you ever get another she-devil you don't wanna mess with, you just holler, all right?"

In that moment, Haven's heart swelled to near bursting with admiration of Valentine Briscoe. He was so handsome! So helpful! So heroic! He'd dug two graves in two days and still managed to find the time to help two ninnies like herself and Arabella with killing a nefarious spider.

"Thank you, Mr. Briscoe. Truly!" Haven gushed. "Please let me do somethin' to thank you this time."

But Valentine shook his inordinately handsome head. "No, ma'am. I'm just glad I could help you with somethin'."

"Oh, please!" Haven pleaded, however. Then a thought struck her. Quickly she dashed into the newly exterminated outhouse, snatched a copy of the *Farmers' Almanac* from the basket within, and hurried back out to where Valentine stood.

"Please," she begged, offering the almanac to Valentine, "please take this as a thank you this time."

Valentine slowly moved to accept the booklet. "But I already have a copy, Miss Abernathy."

And before she could think better of it, Haven began prattling. "I'm sure you do—one copy, for the use for which it was printed. But Mr. Crabtree explained to me that most of you all out here use corncobs and straw and things for . . . for . . . when you're . . . you're takin' advantage of the outhouse. And I just couldn't bring myself to try corncobs, for pity's sake! Not on my . . . not when I was used to . . . to somethin' else. So please . . . please take this one for your own use in . . . in times of need. And remember that I'm so grateful to you for everything. Every time you use it, please remember me and my gratitude."

A mischievous bewitchery enveloped Val then. As he studied the almanac the milliner was offering to him—as he studied her dark hair, the strands that had escaped her coiffure and were scattered this way and that, as he gazed into the deep emerald of her eyes—something burbled up inside him that he'd nearly forgotten existed. As he thought of the predicament he'd found her and her friend in—as he thought of the lavender walls inside the outhouse, the basketful of the *Farmers' Almanac*, the fresh flowers—his hatred, anger, and determination to stay cold and distance floundered.

He almost didn't recognize the sound of his

own laughter as it escaped his throat. He almost didn't recognize the emotions he was feeling: amusement, delight, diversion, happiness.

There was something else he'd nearly forgotten, as well: desire. And it also escaped. Escaped before Val even knew it meant to.

"You want me to think of you every time I use a page of the almanac?" he chuckled. "Damn, woman! You *do* entertain me."

And before his normally rational self had a chance to stop him, Val tucked the *Farmers' Almanac* into his back pocket, took the hatmaker's soft, beautiful face between his hands, and kissed her directly on her pretty, berry-colored mouth.

He knew at once that he'd made a mistake, for the frenzied heat that traveled through him head to toe was more affecting than the Sandersan sisters' cinnamon roll had been early in the day. In fact, that sweet, confection-drizzled cinnamon roll was nothing compared with what the feel of Haven's lips against his did to him.

Still, Val did not want to reveal, in any tiniest of measures, the consequences kissing Haven Abernathy had had on him.

So mustering another chuckle, he simply released her, saying, "You're a funny little thing, I'll give you that."

Forcing an amused-looking smile to linger on

his face, Val quickly turned, striding back toward the front of the house and the graveyard beyond.

Tossing a short wave in the air, he called, "And thank you kindly for the water, Miss Abernathy. It was truly refreshin'."

Val then called upon the darkness that had taken up residence in him a year before—willed it to return. Commanding the abhorrence, rage, and vengeful conviction that the hatmaker had managed to squelch for a moment to rise up within him again, Val stormed toward the small cemetery. He did not have time for women with purple-painted outhouses to distract him! He had retribution to dispense; he had men to find. He had men to kill.

Arabella stared at Haven, her mouth gaping open in wonderment.

"Arabella?" Haven whispered. "Did that man just . . . did he just . . ."

"He kissed you!" Arabella breathed. "He kissed you straight on the mouth! Right here in full daylight! Right here with me lookin' on!"

Haven's heart was beating so quickly, hammering with such force, that she could hear it rattling in her own ears! Placing a hand to her bosom in an effort to calm its mad racing, she looked to Arabella, smiling.

"I swear, I'm near to swoonin', Bellie!" she confessed. "Every inch of me is covered with goose bumps, and I feel as giddy as a goat hoppin' about a peach tree!"

"I can imagine you are," Arabella giggled. "My goodness! Kissed on the lips by the man you've been dreamin' over every night for weeks? Why, I'm surprised you didn't drop in a faint on the spot."

Straightening her posture and attempting to smooth some loose strands of her hair back up to its place, Haven inhaled a deep breath. "Well, I can't allow myself to remain so disheveled over it all. The younger children will be gatherin' in the instruction room in less than an hour. We best tidy ourselves a bit, I suppose."

Haven's resolution to recapture the appearance of grace and poise was short-lived, however. In the very next instant, she reached out, taking Arabella's hands in hers, and with pure felicity beaming in her countenance gushed, "Did you see his smile, Bellie? Why, he's already too handsome when he's frownin' and broodin' the way he does. But that smile! I thought my heart might truly come leaping up through my throat and right out of my mouth, I was so affected!"

"Dazzlin' is the word that comes to my mind," Arabella chirped. "Valentine Briscoe's smile is truly dazzlin'!"

Haven released Arabella's hands, placing her palms to her cheeks. "Why, my cheeks are on fire. I've got to cool this blush before we start class with the younger children."

"Well, let's go in and settle ourselves down a bit," Arabella suggested, "put a comb through our hair and have a cool glass of water. We've got a little time."

Haven nodded. "Yes, I surely do need to gather myself. It would not do for the children to see me so undone."

Arabella smiled again. "He kissed you, Havey! He really did kiss you!"

"Oh, I know!" Haven sighed, breathless at the memory of Valentine Briscoe's lips so firmly pressed to hers—so warmly pressed to hers.

❋ ❋ ❋ ❋ ❋

"And the night of the Harvest Festival would be just so perfectly fittin' for the children's recital. Don't you agree, Miss Abernathy?" Mrs. Henry said, wrenching Haven's attention back to the matter at hand and away from the lingering memory of Valentine Briscoe's kiss.

"I-I beg your pardon, Miss Claudine?" Haven stammered.

Claudine Henry exchanged amused glances with Elenora Dalton, May Crabtree, Sara Shaffer, and the other mothers of Haven's students.

"Why, our young'uns must've completely wrung you out today, Miss Abernathy!" Clotilda Lewis giggled. "Didn't you hear what Claudine suggested just now? That we have the children's recital as part of the Harvest Festival on the night of the harvest moon?"

"Oh my!" Haven exclaimed, offering a broad smile and an air of innocence. "I think it must be those cinnamon rolls the Misses Sandersan brought by. I swear their warm sweetness has got me primed and ready for a late afternoon catnap."

The women in the room smiled, laughing lightheartedly.

"My, yes!" Bridget Ray agreed. "Florence saved part of hers for me, and I've never eaten somethin' so decadent in my life."

"I had one of Miss Wynifred and Miss Merigold's cinnamon rolls last spring," Elenora mentioned. "Mmm mmm, what a treat!"

"Yes indeed," Catherine Bernard agreed with a pronounced nod of affirmation.

Haven exchanged glances of relief with Arabella, glad she'd managed to turn the subject from her own inattention.

"But back to the recital," Claudine Henry said. "What do you think, Miss Abernathy? Shall we couple the children's recital with the town's Harvest Festival? I for one think it would make for a wonderful evenin' altogether. Don't you?"

Haven nodded, agreeing, "Yes, I do. I can just imagine how lovely it all will be. And I think the children would enjoy showin' what they've learned to everyone in town instead of just their families."

"Oh, absolutely," May Crabtree said.

"The *Farmers' Almanac* says September 24 will be the harvest moon this year, and since we always hold the Harvest Festival under the harvest moon, then our date is set in stone," Clotilda Lewis informed. "Why don't all of us involved in plannin' out the festival have a meetin' tomorrow mornin' at my house and see what needs to be done to involve the recital?"

Haven gasped and leapt to her feet, exclaiming, "The *Farmers' Almanac*?" With horrific and sudden understanding, Haven looked to Arabella. "I told him to think of me every time he used it, Bellie!" she choked.

Arching one eyebrow and smiling with amusement, Arabella softly confirmed, "Yes, you did. You're just now realizin' that, Havey?"

"Pardon me, dear?" Sara Shaffer asked. "Is somethin' wrong?"

As her cheeks nearly burst into flames with a blush so profuse it seeped all the way to her bones, Haven smiled, smoothed her hair, and answered, "Oh, not at all, Miss Sara. I just . . . I just remembered somethin' that I need to attend to as soon as I can is all."

Gracefully sitting back down in her chair, Haven attempted to look serene and unruffled. "I think havin' the children show what they've learned as far as dancin' at the Harvest Festival and also bein' able to implement their newly polished etiquette and decorum mannerisms would be a benefit to them as well. It will give them all the opportunity to truly see, for themselves, how much they've grown."

Haven gulped down the putrid lump of chagrin that was gathering in her throat. Even as the mothers of her students began to talk with one another, excited by the prospect of involving the children in the Harvest Festival, Haven's stomach churned with the bitter nausea that accompanied disquietude.

In her haste and desperation to thank Valentine Briscoe for helping her rid their outhouse of the she-devil spider, Haven had with good intentions offered him a fresh, clean copy of the *Farmers' Almanac* to use as he needed in his own outhouse. But when the realization had finally been remembered to her consciousness— for she'd been too caught up in blissful day-dreaming of having been kissed by Valentine to reflect on it earlier—she was suddenly aware of both how improper it had been for her to offer the almanac to Valentine and the fact she had actually asked him to think of *her* every time he used it! And now, every time Valentine Briscoe used the *Farmers' Almanac* to . . . to . . . to attend to his outhouse needs, he *would* think of her! How could he avoid thinking of her whenever he tore a page from the almanac to use in place of a rough old corncob when . . .

"If you both have the time, that is, of course," Claudine Henry was saying as Haven felt the woman's hand alight on her shoulder.

"Oh, we are honored that you would include us, Miss Claudine," Arabella chirped. Winking at Haven, Arabella conveyed that, although Haven had not been paying attention to the ongoing conversation among the kind mothers of the Fletcher children, Arabella had.

"Wonderful!" Claudine chimed. "And would you be so kind as to ask the sisters Sandersan to attend as well? We would never present a Harvest Festival worth a penny if Wynifred and Merigold didn't help us."

"Of course," Arabella said. Offering a hand to Claudine Henry, she added, "And it is so very nice to meet you." Arabella looked to each woman in turn. "To meet each of you. I won't deny that I was nervous leavin' home and comin' west. I wasn't at all certain I would enjoy it. But all of you, and of course your darlin' children . . . well, I know I made the right decision in comin' to Fletcher."

Amid the gracious "thank yous" and "we are so pleased to have you in Fletchers" the other women offered at once, May Crabtree stepped forward, clasping Arabella's hand with her own. "I know you did too," she said. Haven smiled, her nausea lessening a little as she saw the true under-standing in May's eyes as she winked at Arabella. "And we're beside ourselves with delight at havin' you join our wonderful township."

"Thank you, Miss May," Arabella humbly offered.

"All right, ladies," Clotilda Lewis called as the group of women began to disperse. "Remember, my house, tomorrow mornin' at nine a.m. See you all there!"

Managing to keep a friendly smile on her face until the last of the women had exited the instruction room by way of Valentine Briscoe's door, Haven allowed her shoulders to sag, burying her face in her hands the moment the door closed behind them.

"Bellie! Oh, my gracious, Bellie! What have I done?" Haven wailed as tears brimmed in her eyes.

She looked up when she heard Arabella's soft laughter.

"You think it's funny?" Haven squeaked.

"Of course I do, sweetie!" Arabella admitted. "Why, you're forgettin' the best part of it all!"

"And what best part could there possibly be?" Haven asked, a tear trickling down her face. "I told the man to think of me every time he . . . every time he . . ."

"Every time he uses a page of the *Farmers' Almanac* to—"

"Don't say it out loud!" Haven interrupted. "Oh, for pity's sake, don't speak it!"

Arabella laughed again. "But you're forgettin' what he said to you! He said you entertain him . . . and then he kissed you, Havey! I think he was diverted from whatever keeps that perpetual frown on his face, that he had a few moments of pure amusement. And it made him so happy, he kissed you, Havey! He might not have kissed you if you hadn't made him smile and chuckle the way you did."

"Oh, so his kissin' me was just the same as when I kissed Ronald Henry today for makin' me laugh when he asked me why his grandma has a mustache like his grandpa does?" Haven asked, weeping.

Arabella giggled. "No, silly goose! And you didn't kiss Ronald Henry on the mouth either, now did you?" Putting a loving, comforting arm across Haven's shoulders, Arabella explained. "I don't think anything has made your Mr. Briscoe smile in a very long time. I recognize the kind of pain and anger in his eyes. I remember seein' it when I was a little girl. I remember a woman in town lookin' at me as I walked with Mama, holdin' her hand. That woman looked at me as if I were the devil's own child. She hated me; she wanted to hurt me. A body doesn't forget that expression. And . . . and I've seen that kind of hate and anger burnin' in Mr. Briscoe's eyes. Not

197

directed at me, of course, but he's angry and hurt about somethin'. I think you know that, don't you?"

Haven brushed the tears from her cheeks, nodding. "I do," she admitted. "But to be honest, most of the time I'm just so swept away to near swoonin'—at how handsome he is and how fast my heart beats when he's near to me—that I try to push that look in his eyes to the back of my mind." She looked to Arabella, frowning. "I don't want to see the kind of hate and anger in him that that woman you spoke of carried."

Arabella nodded, her smile fading. "Because you're afraid that if he ever found out the truth about you . . . that hate might be for you?"

"Yes," Haven admitted.

But Arabella shook her head. "No. I don't think that bigotry is what puts that flame of fury in Valentine Briscoe's eyes. I think it's somethin' else."

Nodding, Haven whispered, "I do too. But what if that somethin' else has the same outcome where I'm concerned in his thinkin'? What if—"

"He kissed you, Haven!" Arabella interrupted. Her beautiful smile returned, and she added, "Remember that he kissed you! A man like that doesn't kiss a woman that way if there's any chance of him bein' hard and malevolent enough to hate her in any way. So you just enjoy knowin' that Valentine Briscoe kissed you! *And* that you made him happy enough to laugh for a moment or two."

Haven gazed into the beautiful blue of her cherished friend's sapphire eyes. Oh, how she wanted happiness for Arabella! How she wanted to see her sister settled into a warm and cozy house, with a handsome, loving husband and children.

It was then that Haven realized she'd spent much too much time weeping and carrying on over her own matters. Arabella had only been in Fletcher a few days, and although the children of the etiquette classes and their parents had received her with welcoming smiles, words, and handshakes, there was one person Haven knew would love to welcome her more thoroughly and with open arms—Sheriff Dan Sterling!

"You're right, Bellie," Haven said, taking Arabella's hand in her own. "I *did* make him laugh. And after all, isn't laughter the best medicine for anyone, ever?"

"It is," Arabella agreed.

"Come on then," Haven said, rising from her chair. "I know someone else who could use a little more beauty and laughter in his life."

"Who?" Arabella asked, rising from her seat as well.

"Our sheriff!" Haven exclaimed with excitement.

"Oh, Havey, no. No, no, no, no!" Arabella argued, her face draining of color.

"Now come on, Bellie," Haven encouraged as she hurried into the millinery shop to lock the front door. "Poor Sheriff Sterlin' has been sitting over there in his office in the jail-house for hours, waitin' for ol' Mr. Bixler to dry out from his weekly compotation of spirits with Mr. Garvey just outside of town. Now how monotonous is that? And we have several of Wynifred and Merigold's cinnamon rolls left. So why don't we pay a quick visit to our handsome sheriff and share our good fortune of remaining confectionary delights with him, hmmm?"

"Oh, Havey, I just don't think I could . . ." Arabella stammered.

"Didn't Sheriff Sterlin' go after your trunks and other things over at the train station yesterday? Didn't he haul it all back to the house for us?" Haven teasingly reminded. "And now I hear that with the Reverend Hillyard gone up to Denver to visit his sister, poor Sheriff Sterlin' has to preside over Mr. and Mrs. Latham's burials tomorrow. Don't you think he deserves a couple of those sweet cinnamon rolls?"

Arabella smiled, revealing once again her attraction to the sheriff. "He is the handsomest lawman I ever did set eyes on," she sighed.

"And just think," Haven giggled, "maybe

you'll say somethin' embarrassin' and ridiculous and end up with a kiss of your own."

Arabella laughed, the pretty pink returning to her cheeks. "Haven Abernathy! You do so much to cheer and encourage my soul."

"Come on then," Haven chirped. "Let's go visit your handsome lawman, shall we?"

Arabella nodded, excited enthusiasm sparkling in her eyes.

Haven knew Arabella would be happy in Fletcher, just as Haven was. Yet her heart skipped a beat in thinking that Mipsie and Old Joe were still so far away. Nevertheless, a few minutes later, as she and Arabella crossed Fletcher's main thoroughfare, arms linked and heading toward the jailhouse, a voice inside her head and heart assured her that she would find a way to bring her whole remaining family together again—and in Fletcher.

* * * * *

Valentine collapsed into the big chair in the front room of his house. He was worn to the bone! His back, shoulders, and arms were already aching so bad from grave digging two days consecutively, he worried he'd be too stiff come morning to attend the services for the poor old couple that had passed.

Still, he liked being tired out from hard labor. And he liked the feel of a cool bath before bed.

He'd sleep well that night, of that he was certain.

Val's attention fell to the *Farmers' Almanac* lying on the small table to one side of the chair. Instantly a chuckle bubbled up in his throat. He'd never forget the expression of desperate sincerity on Haven Abernathy's face as she stood before him, disheveled from her attempts of battling the spider in her outhouse, pleading with him to think of her every time he used the almanac.

He wondered if she'd ever realize what she'd actually asked him to do, and it made him chuckle again. Picking up the almanac and rising from his chair, Val strode to the back door and pulled his boots on over his bare feet.

"No time like the present, I suppose," he sighed as he swung the back door open.

Val thought for a moment that his mother would not approve of him waltzing on out to the outhouse wearing nothing but his boots. But being that Val knew no one was about, and that it was as dark outside as a sack of black cats, he pushed his mother's disapproval to the back of his mind. And with the most recent edition of the *Farmers' Almanac* in hand, he sauntered toward the outhouse.

He smiled as he walked, remembering how soft and sweet Haven Abernathy's lips had been next to his. Val had regretted kissing the little hatmaker at first, for he had a mission he'd promised himself he'd complete and would not be deterred by anything—even a pretty little southern belle like Haven Abernathy.

Yet as he'd thought it over while he'd finished digging Mrs. Latham's grave that afternoon, he decided that Haven Abernathy had experienced far too much humiliation of late—and seemingly always in his presence—and that she deserved a kiss simply for that fact, and for being so amusing. After all, she had made him smile for the first time in a year.

CHAPTER EIGHT

Haven and Arabella had enjoyed the gathering of ladies to discuss plans for Fletcher's Harvest Festival that morning. Clotilda Lewis was a kind and generous hostess. Still, knowing how difficult her sons Grover and Cleveland could be during etiquette, decorum, and social dance lessons, Haven had been somewhat relieved to find that Mr. Lewis had taken the two boys out to Valentine Briscoe's farm to help harvest pears.

Haven's heart leapt at the mention of Valentine's name at the Lewis home that morning. And it was leaping at that very moment, as well—even as she stood dressed in her mourning clothes and listening as Sheriff Sterling read Bible verses as he stood at the head of Mr. and Mrs. Latham's open graves. She thought herself morbid, of course, being so affected by the fact that Valentine stood just behind her, listening to the funeral services. How demented must a person be to be delighted for any reason at a funeral service? Especially services for two sweet people who had so recently passed?

Still, demented or not, Haven's heart hammered within her chest, nearly as hard as it had hammered the day before when Valentine had kissed her. She could literally feel him standing behind her—as if his body gave off a heat or vigor that lured her to him!

Forcing her attention back to the matter at hand, Haven tried to concentrate on what Sheriff Sterling was saying.

"And so we commit the souls of Wilson and Paulina Latham into your hands, Lord. May their earthly remains rest in peace until such time as bodies and spirits are reunited on that great and glorious day of resurrection. Amen."

"Amen," Haven spoke in unison with the rest of Fletcher's townsfolk who had gathered to pay respects to Mr. and Mrs. Latham.

"Val?" Sheriff Sterling inquired, taking one shovel in one hand and a second in another and looking to Valentine. "If you don't mind."

"You bet," Val said, stepping from behind and around Haven as he strode toward Sheriff Sterling.

Haven watched as Sheriff Sterling stomped on his shovel's shoulder, driving it into the mount of dirt next to Mr. Latham's grave. It was not an unexpected process to Haven. She had attended funerals before and had been present when the first several bladesful of dirt were shoveled into the grave—onto the coffin.

But as Valentine dug his shovel into the dirt he'd mounded next to Mrs. Latham's grave while digging it the day before, Haven startled at the sound and was instantly overwhelmed with emotion, with grief. But not grief for Mr. and Mrs. Latham—grief for her own parents!

As Sheriff Sterling and Valentine continued to shovel more dirt into the open graves, Haven's heart, still racing, began to ache. In truth, the pain that had suddenly gripped the life-giving muscle in her bosom commenced in beating with such agony, Haven feared she was at death's door.

"What's the matter, Havey?" Arabella whispered as Haven's hands clutched her own chest.

"Mama and Daddy," Haven wept quietly. "They'll be so cold come winter. They're probably already so cold, if England is as cold and dreary as Aunt Alice described in her letters." As tears began streaming over Haven's cheeks, she whispered, "I'll never see them again, Bellie. I'll . . . I'll never be able to visit their graves . . . to plant pretty flowers for Mama. They're so far away, Bellie!"

"I know, Havey," Arabella comforted softly. She put an arm across Haven's shoulders and suggested, "Let's get home and settled where we can talk a bit."

"They're gone, Bellie!" Haven choked. "And I was such an insensitive daughter. I never understood how Mama could just leave us all behind . . . Daddy too. I never understood how she could just let my grandma wither away out there in Oklahoma. But that doesn't mean I didn't love her, love them both. I did love them, Bellie, but I was not the daughter I should have been."

"Come on, let's just get home, all right?" Arabella urged, turning Haven in the direction of the house.

"Are you all right, honey?" Miss Merigold asked as Arabella and Haven moved past them.

Haven could only nod and force a smile of reassurance through her tears as she glanced to Merigold and then Wynifred.

"A reminder of your own recent loss, sweetie," Miss Wynifred offered with understanding. "It takes time, dear—more time than any of us realizes at first. You just go on home and rest. It'll be all right. I promise."

Again Haven nodded, even as more tears spilled from her eyes onto her cheeks.

"What's wrong with me, Bellie?" Haven asked as she and Arabella hurried toward the privacy of the house. "I cried for a week straight after Aunt Alice's letter arrived. And then here and there, especially at night, for these past months. I-I . . . I feel like my heart is breakin'! The ache inside me is awful, all of a sudden."

"It's all right, Havey," Arabella softly soothed. "We'll get changed out of these mournin' dresses, have a cool glass of water, and just rest. You just need to rest."

• • •

Val felt his brows furrow into a deep frown of concern as he watched Haven Abernathy and her friend hurry back toward their house. He hadn't realized the Abernathy woman had been so fond of Mr. and Mrs. Latham. She seemed downright distraught.

Still, he figured any young woman who had the patience to make hats, let alone the patience of Job it would take to teach young'uns proper manners, would have to be a sensitive soul. He remembered how upset she'd been the day her friend had arrived—how she'd been worried because Mr. Latham had passed on before she'd had a chance to pay him wages for something he never was able to do. Where Val had nearly forgotten what any emotion felt like other than hate and rage, Haven Abernathy appeared to have a very tender heart indeed.

He remembered the way she'd looked, the sincerity of her countenance, when she'd begged him to accept the *Farmers' Almanac* the day before; she'd truly meant to do him a kindness. And she had, for not only had Haven Abernathy managed to make him smile—caused him to laugh and forget about the horror of his lot for a moment—she'd also introduced him to a much more comfortable means of cleaning up matters when he'd finished his outhouse business.

Val gritted his teeth to keep from smiling at

the memory. After all, it wouldn't do to have the townsfolk thinking he found amusement in filling up the grave of a dead woman— not when he was hoping the folks of Fletcher would harvest the bushels and bushels of ripe and ripening pears he had waiting in the pear orchard.

Still, the expression on Haven Abernathy's face as she'd begged him to accept a copy of the *Farmers' Almanac* lingered at the forefront of his mind. Even so, Val found himself concerned for the little social dance teacher. She had seemed a mite more undone by the funeral goings-on than he had expected, and he couldn't keep himself from wondering why.

✳ ✳ ✳ ✳ ✳

"I remember how upset you were when you found these," Arabella remarked as she picked up one of the photographic cabinet cards lying on the table.

Haven shook her tired head as she studied the card she held. "I just don't understand why Mama kept these from me."

"I'm sure she meant to give them to you someday, Havey," Arabella offered. "And then . . . well, I suppose that's why Mama says we shouldn't wait to do good things—because the opportunity might pass us by."

Haven nodded as Arabella breathed a sigh of

knowing disappointment of her own—of missing Mipsie and Old Joe.

Returning her attention to the photograph she held, Haven studied every tiny detail about the woman in it—her mother's mother, her own grandmother. Looking back at her from the image on the cabinet card, an elderly woman wearing a simple gingham dress and seated in a very plain chair smiled. The photograph of her maternal grandmother was rare and unusual and for many reasons. First of all, Haven had only seen one other photograph in all her life wherein the subject was smiling, as her grandmother was in the one she held—and that was of famed James Butler "Wild Bill" Hickok. Why, it was positively scandalous for a body to smile when being photographed! And yet there her grandmother sat—straight-postured in a plain chair, sitting near a tree trunk, with eyes so bright and alive Haven felt she might suddenly find some magical way to step right out of the photograph. Her grandmother's hair was smoothed back into a tight coil at the back of her neck, and her dark, no doubt sun-bronzed, and frail-looking hands lay clasped in her lap.

Although Haven knew the information her own mother had written on the back of the card, she turned the card over and read the writing once more.

"Amadahy 'Forest Water' Adair," Haven read

aloud. *"Taken on this 19th day of August, 1883, for my daughter Tayanita 'Young Beaver' Merial Adair Abernathy and my granddaughter, Haven Hialeah Awinita 'Beautiful Meadow Fawn' Abernathy."* Turning the card over again, Haven read the printed information beneath her grandmother's photo. *"Delaware District, Indian Territory, Oklahoma."*

As Haven's eyes again filled with tears, she asked, "This photograph card was taken only two years ago, Bellie. Why wouldn't Mama have at least shown it to me? And there are three copies here . . . and these other photographs I found after Mama died." Haven shook her head as she lovingly touched the other photographs laid out on the kitchen table before her. "She could still be alive, Bellie. My grandmother could still be alive . . . and Mama never told me? All I ever had of her before I found these were my mother's iris . . . the ones my grandmother had left in Georgia when she went west. Why didn't mother tell me there were photographs? And obviously correspondence?"

Arabella shook her head, brushing a tear from her own cheek. "I don't think anyone livin' can answer that, Havey. Maybe my mama or daddy, but I . . . I just don't know."

Haven nodded at Arabella, offering a smile to convey that Arabella should not worry so about it. Then, gazing again at her grandmother's photograph, she said, "My grandmother, Amadahy Adair, could still be alive and living in Oklahoma . . . in the Indian Territories there."

"Yes," Arabella answered. "She very well could be there still. After all, she appears quite healthy and robust in the photograph of two years ago. I think it's entirely possible that she is there, still living."

"I should write to the postmaster there, if there is one," Haven mused aloud. "I'm sure my grandmother would want to know about . . . about Mama and Daddy passin'."

"And about how well you are doin' for yourself too," Arabella encouraged.

Haven laid the photograph down on the table's top to join the others. Her heart was aching again. Thoughts of her grandmother's plight— of her history—were mingling with her revived grief over her parents' deaths. She knew that if she did not busy herself with something at once, she would be reduced to tears and sobbing again.

Gathering the photographs on the table into a pile, Haven pushed her chair back and stood, saying, "I need to get those iris in the ground soon. What good would it have done to have you bring some of Mama's iris on the train with you if I don't take proper care of them?"

"Oh, I'm sure they'll last another day or two out of the soil," Arabella remarked as Haven placed the photographs of her grandmother in the drawer of the small desk in the hallway. "Daddy put a good bunch of moist Georgia soil in that box with them. They'll keep awhile longer."

"And I'm so grateful for the lemons Mipsie sent up with you too, Bellie!" Haven exclaimed sincerely. "Oh, how I've missed the lemon and mint water she always served us in summer."

"Mama was certain you would enjoy the lemons. I'm sorry I couldn't bring more with me." Arabella paused a moment and then began, "Remember how she used to have to hide them from us when we were little?" She giggled, "Poor Mama."

Haven felt a light laughter escape her throat at the memory. "Oh, I do! And remember how we squeezed all those lemons that one day to make our own lemonade . . ."

"And stirred in an entire half a pound of sugar?" Arabella added.

"That was the best lemonade I ever did have," Haven laughed.

"Oh, me too. Me too! And that evenin' afterward—that was the worst tummy ache I ever had!"

It felt good to laugh. Haven's mood since the Lathams' service had been dark and gloomy indeed. But as ever, Arabella was there to cheer her up.

A knock on the door startled them, and they both giggled at how easily they had been alarmed.

214

"Who could that be?" Arabella asked. "It's nearly dusk."

As Haven strode through the parlor toward the front door, she called, "Oh, it's probably Robert and Ronald Henry up to somethin'. You know they knocked on my door a month or so back and asked if I knew where they could find somethin' dead to poke a stick at."

"Did you?" Arabella chirped.

Haven shrugged and giggled again. "Would you believe that I did? I had seen a dead squirrel out behind the millinery shop earlier that mornin'."

As Arabella expelled a delighted laugh, Haven opened the front door of the house to find none other than Sheriff Sterling himself standing on the porch.

"Well, good evenin', Sheriff," she greeted.

"Evenin', Miss Abernathy," Sheriff Sterling returned.

Haven grinned with silent amusement, for it was obvious by the way Sheriff Sterling was spinning his hat between his hands—as well as the fact his hair was combed back as if he'd just run a comb through it seconds before—that Sheriff Dan Sterling had come to see Arabella.

"Oh my! Good evenin', Sheriff," Arabella chimed, walking into the room so gracefully one would think she was floating on air. "And may I commend you on offerin' such fine services for Mr. and Mrs. Latham today?"

"Thank you, Miss Barnes," Sheriff Sterling said, accepting her compliment.

"How may we help you?" Haven asked. Oh, she was being a dickens, feigning ignorance the way she was. But she couldn't help it! The man was just too darling in his nervousness not to fiddle with a little bit.

"Well . . . uh . . . well . . ." Sheriff Sterling stammered.

"A well? It's a big hole in the ground, Sheriff," Haven said. "At least, that's what Mipsie Mama always says."

"Who?" the sheriff asked.

Realizing she did not want to explain at that very moment who Mipsie Mama was, Haven stepped aside, saying, "Why don't you come on in for a minute? I need to run outside and take care of some waterin' of the flowers over at the cemetery, so I hope you don't mind if Arabella keeps you company."

"Oh, not at all, ma'am," Sheriff Sterling sighed with relief. Lowering his voice, he looked past Haven to Arabella. "Truth be told, I was hopin' to have a word with Miss Barnes anyway."

"I figured as much, Sheriff," Haven said, offering the man an understanding wink. "So, if you'll excuse my rudeness, I'm off to carry some water over to my dry little flowers."

Without even pausing to snatch up a warming shawl in case the night air turned cool before the sheriff and Arabella were finished with their "word," Haven simply lit out the front door, closing it behind her and hurrying down the porch steps and around to the back of the house, where an old bucket stood next to the rain barrel.

The night air was cool—cooler than she'd expected it to be at only dusk. Still, Haven found the temperature invigorating. She could hear frogs croaking in the tall grass and lilac trees out near the outhouse, and she knew the crickets would begin to play their soothing evening melodies once the sun had set.

As Haven took hold of the bucket's handle, dunking it into the rain barrel to fill it, she inhaled deeply the refreshing scents of summer giving way to autumn. The essence of still-green grass was there, mingled with the comforting bouquet of cedar burning in a hearth to warm a home that evening. The delicious spice of an apple pie baking in someone's oven lingered in the air as well, filling Haven's heart with delight. She wished she had thought to bake an apple pie that day.

A meadowlark nearby but unseen was trilling, its beautiful call softly echoing on the breeze in a manner it ever could have in Georgia. Haven thought then that she did not miss the plethora of birdcalls in Covington—so many birds calling all at once that the sound could seem deafening at times. Yes, she much preferred to hear fewer birds calling, especially in the early morning when she would be awakened by two mourning doves exchanging loving warbles to one another amid the peacefulness of sunrise.

The water sloshed in the bucket as Haven carried it toward the cemetery. Yes, dusk was a wondrous, almost magical time to Haven, and most evenings a trip to water the flowers she'd planted at the base of each tombstone gave her a feeling of happiness—as if perhaps the ghosts of those long past were there, smiling at her as she watered and removed spent blooms from the plants.

But this night it was different, for Haven knew Mr. and Mrs. Latham; she had known them, at least. And as she pushed open the small gate that was the entrance to the cemetery, the sense of loss and sadness that had overwhelmed her earlier began to settle over her once more. She tried not to look at the freshly filled graves of Mr. and Mrs. Latham. But the fact that they were, indeed, only recently filled made it difficult not to glance at the two rounded mounds at the far end of the place. Haven knew that the rain, the snow, and the sun would all combine to see that the graves of the more recently deceased would one day be as flattened and unremarkable as all the others.

Setting the pail down near a small headstone she had grown to favor, Haven knelt and began to pinch the spent petunia blooms from the flowers there. She thought again of her parents—of her father and mother—their bodies buried in the cold, dark earth so very far from their warm and beloved Covington, Georgia. She thought again of the flowers she would never be able to plant for her mother at her resting place and hoped that there was a spring in heaven, that her mother might bathe in the perfume of lilacs and wisteria forever.

Haven thought of her father—of his kindness early on toward Old Joe, Mipsie, and Arabella when so many were cruel to those who had been slaves. She remembered her father saying that Joe Barnes was a better man than any other he had ever known, white, black, or otherwise. Haven loved her father all the more for his holding Joe in the high regard he deserved.

Upon thinking of the vile, repulsive, and immoral practice of enslaving other human beings, Haven was soothed somewhat in remembering that her mother had long ago told her that her Grandmother Adair had not owned slaves, as many others who had been driven out of Georgia did. The fact comforted her in that moment, just as it had years before when her mother had assured her of it.

But no line of thinking could keep Haven's tears of grief and loss, of missing her father and mother, from streaming over her cheeks in profusion. Oh, she knew her parents were safely in the arms of Heaven, that their souls were freed from earthly pains and worries, that even it may be they had already begun the work of being guardian angels—that they could well be watching over her in that very moment. Yet even for knowing their souls were free and happy, safe and warm, the pain in her chest, the wrenching of her heart, still ached.

Haven was glad Sheriff Sterling had come calling on Arabella. Being out in the cool of the early evening, tending to the flowers, breathing in the calming aroma of cedar, the baking apples somewhere in town—it was what she needed in those moments. It was what would help soothe her aching heart.

※ ※ ※ ※ ※

Val stepped out of the diner and paused a moment before heading home. The sun was beginning its evening descent, and already the sky and the clouds drifting in it were painted soft with pastels of blue and pink and purple. Val did enjoy sunsets. They always gave him a sense of respite and relaxation. Even in winter, when darkness came earlier than other seasons, he enjoyed the setting of the sun—the way the sun seemed to bid goodnight and the moon rose to take its place amid a tapestry of midnight velvet and jeweled stars.

As he stepped off the boardwalk and into the street, he let out a heavy whoof when the soreness in his shoulders made itself known again. Digging graves for two days consecutively and then filling one up again had plum worn him out, and he couldn't wait to get home, strip down to his birthday suit, and fall into bed. He needed a good night's sleep if he was going to be up and ready before the townsfolk began arriving to harvest pears from his pear trees.

When he'd purchased the farm from Joseph Vickers, Val had been so focused on simply finding a place he could stay while he searched that he hadn't really noticed how quickly harvest would be upon him. And though he did not have the time nor the inclination to harvest, haul, and sell his crop of pears in Denver that year, he knew that he would need to do so the following year. Therefore, the trees needed to be picked and tended to. Most of all, however, Valentine could not tolerate the idea of a whole crop of pears going to waste. He figured it was better to give them away than to pick them himself, be too busy to do anything with them, and end up with a mess of rotting pears to deal with. Yep, loath as he was toward socializing, he needed the citizens of Fletcher to accept their fill of his pears.

Rubbing at his left shoulder to try and ease the soreness there, he started toward home. As he neared the cemetery that had contributed so greatly to his aching muscles and fatigue, however, Val frowned when he saw someone kneeling before one of the smaller tombstones.

"What in tarnation is someone doin' sittin' out in the boneyard at this time of day?" he muttered under his breath.

Yet as he drew closer, he recognized at once that the person in the cemetery was a woman—and not just any woman but Haven Abernathy. He noted the way she brushed at her cheeks, as if wiping tears away—noted how her normally straight, though slight, shoulders were slumped, and he heard her sniffle.

At first Val thought he'd just make a turn, head out around back of Miss Abernathy's house, and avoid intruding on whatever had found the woman kneeling in the cemetery, sniffling at sunset.

Nevertheless, as he thought of the moments of pure amusement—of downright mirth—Haven Abernathy had gifted him the day before, Val realized he hadn't yet done a good deed for his mother's sake that day. Sure, he'd filled in Mrs. Latham's grave, but that wasn't really a good deed in itself. It was more like tying up the good deed he'd begun the day before when he'd dug her grave.

Nope, he'd have to check in on Miss Abernathy, else he'd never get to sleep that night. And he knew he needed his sleep that night if he was going to face a town full of pear pickers the next morning.

"Evenin', Miss Abernathy."

Quickly brushing the tears from her cheeks and hoping that the hazy dusk of sunset would hide her no doubt red and puffy eyes, Haven forced a smile, looked up, and said, "Good evenin', Mr. Briscoe. What has you out and about in town so late in the day?"

"Oh, I've been too busy to cook for myself these past weeks," he began. "Been too lazy too, in truth. So I've been havin' my supper over at the diner most nights. I'm just on my way home."

Still forcing her smile, Haven looked down at the petunias she'd been tending. "Well, I'm glad you had your supper. I just love the biscuits and cream gravy over at the diner. Mine never seems to be as satisfyin' to me."

"Hmm," Valentine mumbled. "Fact is, I've had the biscuits and cream gravy most nights when I'm there. It is good food."

"Well, I'm glad you had a nice supper, Mr. Briscoe," Haven offered. "And I'm quite certain you must be very tired after all that diggin' you've been doin' the past couple of days. I know I wouldn't be able to lift a hand to do anythin' else at all. But at least your head won't hit the pillow hungry, hmm?"

"I was glad to do the diggin'," Valentine said. He paused a moment, and Haven looked up at him, still managing to smile. "Might I say, ma'am, that this does seem an odd time for you to be out pickin' dead flowers. Everythin' all right?"

Haven shrugged, even as fresh tears brimmed in her eyes. "Yes, yes . . . everythin' is fine," she answered.

"You sure, Miss Abernathy?" Valentine asked. "Where's your friend? Seems to me the two of you are joined at the hip most of the time."

"Arabella? Why, she's back at the house with . . . with . . ."

"With?" Valentine prodded.

"Well, she's back at the house speakin' with Sheriff Sterling," Haven admitted. After all, Valentine Briscoe hardly spoke to anyone except Sheriff Sterling. So what harm could there be in telling him the truth? "I mean, I can see the house fine from my place here . . . so it's not as though it's entirely inappropriate for them to be conversin' all alone."

Haven looked up to Valentine when she heard a short, quiet chuckle rumble in his throat.

He was smiling, and again Haven was mesmerized by how much more handsome he was with his dazzling smile.

"I expect you've figured by now," he began as he actually sat down beside her, "that I don't bother much in other folks' business. And although there's no doubt that you are a fine, polished, respectable woman, *I* don't give too much thought to what people think of me. So Dan and your friend can stay up all night alone in that house, and nobody would hear it from me."

Haven's smile was sincere then. She'd known he could be trusted; how she'd known she wasn't sure, but she had known it.

He looked down at the flowers at the base of the little tombstone. "Is that the only reason you're keepin' the dead company out here this evenin', ma'am?" he asked. " 'Cause it seems to me you're not quite yourself."

Haven shook her head, trying to make her giggle sound as if what he'd said was a ridiculous notion. "Oh, fiddle-faddle!" she chirped. "Of course I'm myself. Why would you think otherwise?"

"I s'ppose cause you ain't chokin' to death, fallin' off somethin', or shriekin' over a spider."

She looked over to him, her heart leaping inside her when he winked at her.

"I seem to have made quite an impression on your memory, Mr. Briscoe," she breathed. "And truth be told, I am a titch melancholy this evenin'. You see, my father and mother died this past spring. And Mr. and Mrs. Latham's funeral today . . . it brought to mind the depth of the loss, the fact that I will never see them again, in this life anyway, and the reality that I cannot even plant flowers to bloom over my mother's grave . . . bein' that my parents are buried in England."

Valentine was silent for a moment. And Haven was astonished at what he said next.

"Well, it might not seem like much comfort to you, Miss Abernathy . . . but you're fortunate in knowin' they *are* dead."

"I beg your pardon?" Haven asked, still awe-struck with his seemingly unfeeling statement.

"What I mean is, someone told you that your folks died, right?" Valentine asked.

"Yes, but—"

"But nothin'," he interrupted. "Since you say they're buried in England, I imagine they were traveling abroad when they passed?"

"Yes, but—"

"And how do you know they died?"

Haven, though still flabbergasted by Valentine's remark, explained, "A letter . . . a letter from my Aunt Alice, who was attending them when they died."

"Well, there you go then," Valentine said, nodding with firm assurance. "What if your aunt hadn't been there with them? What if you simply had never heard from your parents again? What if they'd simply never come home? You never received a letter of any kind anything or anyone tellin' you what had happened?"

Haven exhaled the breath she'd been holding

as understanding washed over her. "I suppose I would spend the rest of my life wonderin' what had become of them, wonderin' if they'd just abandoned me for some extravagant life abroad—whether they'd been murdered, whether one had died and not the other. It would haunt me forever."

Valentine nodded again. "It would eat you up inside," he grumbled. "So although I know your heart feels like it's gonna bust clean to pieces in knowin' you'll never see your folks again . . ." He paused, grinned at her, and continued, "Well, in this life. You do at least know what happened to them. You at least know for certain that they've passed on and where they're laid to rest."

As the heaviness in Haven's heart lifted a little, her eyebrows arching in admiration of Valentine's wisdom, she said, "Why, that was nothin' less than profound, Mr. Briscoe. You are a very wise man. And you're right." Haven shook her head, continuing, "Not knowin' what had become of Daddy and Mama . . . why, that would've been unbearable. I am blessed in knowin' about them. And so I suppose I'm wrong to grieve so hard for them."

But Valentine shook his head. Frowning, he said, "It's never wrong to grieve hard." His voice was deeper for a moment, it seemed, and filled with sincere emotion. "You grieve as hard and as long as you need to, Miss Abernathy. And don't let nobody tell you to get over it quick. The grief that comes with a loss like yours . . . it don't happen on anybody's time but your own. And it ain't nobody's business but your own neither."

He offered a nod of affirmation, and Haven smiled at him sincerely.

"Thank you, Mr. Briscoe," Haven sighed as her mood rallied. "I feel better. I really do. Thank you."

"Well, bein' that you're the etiquette teacher and all, and that I'm sure and certain you're teachin' your students to accept a body's thanks graciously," he began. He smiled, adding, "And bein' that I already got one lesson from you on graciously acceptin' thanks . . . I s'ppose I'll just say you're welcome and leave it at that."

Haven giggled, even though she blushed with humiliation at remembering how she'd scolded him.

"Oh, I can be a dickens sometimes," she admitted. "I don't know what gets into me." She breathed a soft laugh, adding, "Probably my mama's determination that I be a proper lady and that no one ever find out that . . ."

Haven barely managed to keep from confessing her deepest secret to a man she hardly knew! There was such an ambiance of trustworthiness about Valentine Briscoe—an aspect of unusual heroism—and she did wonder for a moment what he would think of her if he knew about

228

her maternal grandmother's origin—about her mother's—about her own.

And then Valentine asked, "And that no one ever find out what?"

Haven knew she must never risk telling any man about herself—her secret—especially not Valentine Briscoe, the only man who had ever made her heart race so fiercely, the only man who had ever made her heart race at all.

And so she answered, "That no one ever find out how truly clumsy, graceless, and downright silly-hearted I am at times." She winked at him, adding, "No one other than Arabella and you, of course. Goodness knows you've been witness to my antics more times than I care to remember."

Valentine chuckled. "Oh, everybody's got their own antics, as you call them," he assured her. "Three things nobody in all the world is safe from fallin' into—humiliation, pain, and a grave."

"I would argue there are four things nobody in all the world is safe from fallin' into," Haven playfully argued.

"Four, huh?" Valentine asked, obviously curious.

"Yes," Haven assured him.

"And what's that fourth thing nobody's safe from fallin' into, Miss Abernathy?" he prodded.

Exhaling a heavy sigh, Haven turned her attention toward the house just beyond the cemetery and offered, "Nobody in the world is safe from fallin' in love."

Again she heard Valentine breathe a quiet laugh. "You may be right about that," he agreed. "I've seen the way Dan Sterlin' gets all daffy-eyed whenever your friend Miss Barnes is in his sights. Is she as sweet on him as he is on her?"

Haven nodded. "Oh my, yes!" she declared. "Sweeter than a baby with a sugar flower in its mouth."

"A sugar flower?" Valentine asked. "What's a sugar flower?"

Haven looked back to him. "You've never heard of a sugar flower?" When Valentine shook his head, Haven exclaimed, "Why, Valentine Briscoe! Were you raised in a cave?"

"It would seem so," he answered, smiling.

As warm bliss rinsed over Haven at the sight of Valentine's smile, she still felt bound to explain a sugar flower to him. "When a baby is fussin' and nothin' can soothe, a mama takes little square of cloth, moistens a teaspoon of sugar or honey, wraps the cloth around the sugar, twistin' it tight, and gives it to the baby to suck or chew on. It's called a sugar flower because when the baby is suckin' on the sugar, the part of the cloth hangin' out of the baby's mouth looks like the petals of a flower. You see? A sugar flower."

Valentine burst into laughter. He laughed so hard his sore shoulders hurt!

"It really isn't that funny, Mr. Briscoe . . .

although I am glad you're amused," the pretty little hatmaker said.

Val figured his laughter must've been contagious because as he continued to laugh—wholeheartedly laugh as he hadn't laughed in perhaps years—Haven Abernathy began to laugh too.

Through her laughter, she finally asked, "What on earth has you so tickled, sir?"

Gasping for breath and wiping at the mirthful tears gathered in the corners of his eyes, Val answered, "You! Only you—Miss Etiquette, Decorum, and Social Dance—only you could come up with somethin' proper and pretty to call a sugar teat!"

"A what?" Haven Abernathy laughcd.

"A sugar teat," Val managed to repeat. "That's what my mama always called them. A sugar teat."

"A sugar teat?" Haven repeated. "You mean like a . . . like a teat . . . on a cow's udder?"

Val would never be able to explain if anyone asked him why Haven's inquiry made him break into another round of near painful laughter, but it did. Something about the way she said the word *teat*—as if she were being daring enough to cuss—coupled with the manner in which her sweet southern voice almost sang "cow's udder," did indeed tickle him! It tickled him all the way to his center.

"Yes, ma'am!" he laughed. "That is exactly what I mean."

Her laughter began to subside, and she said, "Hmmm. I guess that does make sense. I mean, baby calves suckle on teats. And I suppose one could call it somethin' far more inappropriate than a sugar teat." She sighed, smiling at him and saying, "But I prefer sugar flower all the same. That's what Mama and Mipsie always called them."

Val noted the way Haven's smile lessened— and the way she seemed to leap into drawing his attention back to Dan and her friend conversing in the house beyond.

"But yes, I do think Arabella is as sweet on Sheriff Sterling as I hope he is on her," she concluded.

Val, however, was still feeling mighty entertained and a bit too mischievous. And so he tossed, "Do you think they're in there sparkin' a little?"

Haven's eyes widened with wonder, as if she'd never considered the matter before.

"Oh! Oh, surely not," she whispered. "I mean, they've hardly known one another long enough to . . . to merit any kind of intimacy the likes of kissin' each other."

Val reached up and rubbed at the whiskers on his jaw. He knew he should just stand up and walk on home—knew it would be best for her, for the both of them. But the laughter they'd shared had a sort of intoxicating consequence on him, and he wasn't sober yet.

"Well, I kissed you yesterday, Miss Abernathy, didn't I?" he teased. "And we haven't really known one another much longer than them two."

She blushed, and he smiled. She liked his flirtation; he could see it in the sudden twinkle in her eyes, as well as by the warmth that had risen to her cheeks.

"Well . . . well, that was different," Haven stammered. "You . . . you simply felt sorry for me for bein' so ridiculous in handin' you that *Farmers' Almanac* like a ninny."

"I didn't feel sorry for you," Val assured her. "And anyway, I'm appreciatin' that almanac. It sure is softer on my fanny than the old corncobs I've been usin'."

"Your *fanny?*" Haven exclaimed, as if he'd committed some sort of blasphemy.

"Yep," he assured her, feeling an amused chuckle tickling his throat. "And bein' that you're so insistent on people allowin' others to thank them, I'd like to thank you for that fine, soft *Farmers' Almanac* you gave. Would that be all right?"

She blushed again, and he could see her fighting the urge to smile—to laugh.

"Well, I suppose it wouldn't do for me not to practice what I preach," she said. "So yes, Mr.

233

Briscoe, you may thank me for that silly *Farmers' Almanac*."

"Yes, ma'am," Val mumbled as he reached out, taking Haven's face in his hands and pressing a kiss to her soft, sweet mouth.

Haven's heart leapt with such vigor inside her bosom that, had her lips not been otherwise occupied in being kissed by Valentine, she would have worried that it would leapt right out of her mouth.

The butterflies flapping inside her stomach were rendering her breathless, and when Valentine kissed her a second time, Haven was glad she was already sitting down—for every one of her limbs went limp with staggering rapture!

"Wh-what are you doin', Mr. Briscoe?" Haven breathed as Valentine ended their kiss and stared at her a moment, his eyes narrowed and simmering with an emerald glow.

"Why, I'm thankin' you, Miss Abernathy," he mumbled as he again drew her mouth to his.

Haven forgot every ounce of etiquette, decorum, and even social dance as Valentine kissed her again and again—as his lips claimed hers, began to govern her will in coaxing hers to part. And as she felt the warmth of his mouth mingle with her own, Miss Haven Abernathy of Covington, Georgia—Miss Haven Abernathy, graduate of Mrs. Josephine St. Bernard's Finishing School—

did not give a whit for how improper anyone in the world would've thought she was being in sliding her arms over Valentine's shoulders as he stood them both up, gathering her into the power of his arms and against the firm strength of his body.

Haven had never known anything the like of what she was feeling! Never known a man could cause a woman to feel so absolutely euphoric that she would throw propriety to the wind in favor of continuing to kiss him!

Certainly, she knew he had no serious intentions toward her—for she instinctively knew he was not the sort to pay formal courting traditions. In truth, she wasn't even sure he was overly fond of her. For all she knew, the fact that she unintentionally amused him was the only thing about her he did like. Yet in those moments—with Valentine Briscoe's strong arms banded around her, the flavorsome warmth of his mouth shepherding hers to enjoy his kiss as thoroughly as she was able—in those bliss-filled, dreamborne moments, Haven didn't care.

After some time—Haven did not know how long, though she did know it was not long enough—Valentine broke the seal of their lips.

Taking her face between his warm, callused, strong yet gentle hands, he gazed at her through narrowed eyes and mumbled, "I oughta walk you home now. The sun is almost set, and it'll be dark here in a bit."

"Yes . . . yes, it will," Haven managed to respond.

She wondered for a moment if her weakened knees could even carry her home. Furthermore, how would she bid goodnight to him once he had walked her home? Their moments of exchanged affections in the cemetery would make a simple, "Goodnight, Mr. Briscoe," seem ridiculous.

Therefore, Haven suggested, "I'm fine to walk home on my own, Mr. Briscoe. I mean, the house is right there . . . hardly a stone's throw away."

But any hint of amusement or cheerfulness disappeared from Valentine's expression then as he said, "A woman ought not to be walkin' alone in the dark, Miss Abernathy. No matter how close your house is . . . I'm seein' you on home."

The tone in his voice was firm and determined—almost threatening in a manner. Therefore, Haven forced a smile, nodded, and said, "Well, I do hate to delay you any longer, but if you insist . . ."

"I do," Valentine grumbled.

And there it was—the anger, the impatience that was in him most all of the time she had been in his company. Knowing it would do no good to press him about anything, let alone what had just transpired between them, Haven nodded. After all, who was she to request that Valentine explain why he had kissed her and whether he truly had any liking for her? Didn't she have

236

her own secrets that she wanted kept? Whatever caused Valentine Briscoe to laugh one moment, bathe Haven in delectable bliss the next, and yet subsequently turn cold as stone toward her—it was his secret to keep.

Thus, as she offered a smile and a pleasant goodnight to Valentine as he touched the brim of his hat once they'd reached the back door of the house, she let him go without another word—without begging for an explanation of his actions—without even a questioning expression of any kind.

And as she quietly stole into the house—intent on not disturbing Arabella and the sheriff, whose voices she could hear still coupled in conversation—as she crept through the kitchen and back to the bedroom she and Arabella shared, Haven made up her mind to do exactly what Mipsie had always advised when faced with something wonderful yet fleeting.

"Don't you be cryin' 'cause sometin 'tis ova, Miss Haven," Mipsie had counseled so often. "You just be smilin' dat it ever did happ'n in da first place, you hear?"

And it *had* happened! Under a purple-curtained sky, freckled with glimmering, glittering stars, Valentine Briscoe had kissed her—really kissed her—kissed her into an ethereal sort of intoxication she wished never, ever to forget.

"I'm just smilin' and happy that it happened in

the first place, Mipsie," Haven whispered to the silence.

Going to the small desk against one wall in the room, Haven removed several sheets of paper, an ink pen, and ink. She would write to the postmaster in the Delaware District of the Oklahoma Indian Territory. She would try to contact her grandmother Adair—or at least attempt to discover whether she were still living.

As she sat in the chair at the desk, Haven sighed, shaking her head as she thought about her grandmother and the fact that she knew nothing of her condition.

"He's right," she said to herself. "It is better to know that someone has died, rather than spend a lifetime wonderin' what became of them."

CHAPTER NINE

The pounding in his head woke Val up. Frowning, he struggled through the fog of having fallen into a deep, deep sleep but not until the early hours of morning. Without opening his eyes, he rolled over, groaning as the soreness in his shoulders told him he must not have moved an inch once he had finally gotten to sleep.

The truth was, he'd been awake until well after the clock struck three in the morning. His mind had been heavily taxed with scolding himself where Haven Abernathy was concerned. The night before, when he'd come upon her in the cemetery and decided to do a good deed and offer solace to her unsettled state, he had faltered in the end. Val had let his attraction to the little hatmaker of Fletcher weaken his steadfastness of purpose for a time, and he'd been up most of the night thereafter, scolding himself for having veered from his chosen path and also rebuilding his hardhearted conviction to succeed at what he'd set out to do, no matter what. It had taken hours and hours, but he had at last managed to right his direction of thinking and, in doing so, fallen asleep at last.

More pounding—and Val realized the sound

wasn't in his head but rather at the front door of his house.

"What the hell?" he grumbled as he rather teeteringly rose from his bed and stood. Grabbing the quilt from the bed, he wrapped it around his waist and stomped out of his bedroom toward the front of the house.

Taking hold of the latch of the door, Val growled, "What do you want?" as he pulled the door open.

He was not at all prepared for what, or rather who, he found standing on his front porch, staring at him. Rubbing the sleep from his eyes, Val frowned as he glared at none other than Haven Abernathy, both elderly Sandersan ladies, Dan Sterling, and Dan's paramour, Arabella Barnes.

"Uh . . . mornin', Val," Sheriff Sterling greeted.

For her part, Haven gulped at the magnificent sight of Valentine Briscoe standing just inside his door, hair tousled as if he were a schoolboy, and not a stitch of clothing about him save a quilt he'd haphazardly wrapped around his waist.

"Pardon us for wakin' you, Val," the sheriff continued as Val continued to hold the quilt at his waist, yet reaching up and resting his free hand on the top of the open door. "But folks have been arrivin' for near to half an hour, and everyone's wonderin' where you'd like them to start at pickin' pears."

"My goodness!" Haven heard Wynifred exclaim in a whisper to her sister. "I think he's full unshucked under that quilt!"

"Yes, I believe he is," Merigold agreed. "And isn't it a wondrous sight indeed?"

Haven thought that perhaps she'd slipped into the devil's hands for a moment, for she entirely agreed with Merigold's assessment of Valentine in such a state: it was truly a wondrous sight! In the first place, his sleepy-eyed expression was not only handsome but also quite adorably endearing. His dark hair, still tousled even for the fact he'd raked his fingers back through it before resting his hand on the top of the door, only added to his physical allure. And of course there was the fact he was not at all bashful about the world having full view of his broad, muscular shoulders, strong arms, expansive chest, and firm stomach. Furthermore, the manner in which he held the quilt at his waist—loosely, as if he weren't at all worried that it might slip away and flabbergast the lot of them with a wildly inappropriate visual lesson in human anatomy—Haven admired his obvious lack of concern for what other folks might think of him.

In truth, Haven loved him all the more for his apparent inattention to propriety in that instant.

She frowned at once, however—disturbed that a form of the word *love* had been what her mind chose to associate with Valentine Briscoe just then.

"Pears?" Valentine asked. A body would've thought the man had completely forgotten he'd asked anyone wanting pears free for the picking to meet at his home that morning to help harvest his orchard.

"Yep," Sheriff Sterling affirmed. "You wanted everybody in town who was willin' to meet out here at your place this mornin' for pickin' pears." The sheriff chuckled. "You have a rough night there, Val?"

Nodding, Val admitted, "And then some." He rubbed at his tired eyes again with his hand that wasn't holding the quilt at his waist. "Pears . . . yeah . . . the pears." Again he nodded. "Just have folks who have brought their own baskets and boxes start to pickin' wherever they choose, if you wouldn't mind, Dan. I'll throw on my britches and boots and start haulin' out some extra bushel baskets for folks who don't have enough or any at all."

"I sure will, Val. No problem," the sheriff responded.

Looking straight at Haven then, Val said, "Sorry for oversleepin' this mornin', ladies. It ain't like me. I just had a herd of thoughts stampedin' through my mind all night and didn't get to sleep 'til nigh on sunrise."

"Oh, that's just fine, Mr. Briscoe," Wynifred

answered, her smile as broad as was the Mississippi wide. "We understand completely."

"My, yes!" Merigold added, studying Valentine from head to toe. "We don't mind one whit."

Arabella leaned over, giggling as she whispered into Haven's ear, "And you better roll your tongue up and pop it back into your mouth, Haven Abernathy. Why, you look just like a starvin' dog watchin' a butcher cleavin' up a cow!"

Haven closed her gaping mouth just as Sheriff Sterling said, "We'll be on our way then, Val. We'll see you out there in the orchard in a bit."

"That'll be fine," Val said, still staring at Haven. "And forgive me for not offerin' a proper good mornin' to you ladies."

"Oh, don't you worry your head one bit about it, Mr. Briscoe," Wynifred chirped. "We're just sorry we interrupted your hard-earned sleep."

"Well, good mornin' then," Val said, raking his free hand back through his hair. "I'll be right behind you."

Val closed the door and tossed the quilt he'd been holding tight at his waist into a nearby parlor chair. How in the world could he have overslept? Especially on the one day he had asked people to gather on his property?

By unintentionally luring him into falling prey to her feminine wiles the night before, Haven Abernathy had surely messed up his thinking.

And yet, even as Val grumbled while he dressed and readied for a day of enduring the company of townsfolk, he found himself worrying over the pretty little etiquette teacher. She had lost her parents. Furthermore, by what he had gathered, she had no other family to cling to. Otherwise, why would she move plum clear across the country—alone? The thought traveled through Val's mind that even if he lost his parents—which he knew was an eventual inevitability—he'd had siblings to grow up with, a few aunts and uncles and cousins nearby. Although he had no desire to be with any extended family at the time, he knew that if he ever did want or need the company of blood relations, he had them. It seemed that Haven Abernathy had none. Of course she had her friend, Miss Barnes, and the two Sandersan ladies certainly mothered her like she was their own—and Val was glad. But he imagined it was still different than having a flock of uncles, aunts, and cousins to sympathize with the loss of a body's parents, to offer support— especially to someone as young and vibrant as Haven Abernathy.

As Val pulled on his undertrousers, tying the drawstring at his waist—as he stepped into his britches—he thought about Haven Abernathy's raven black hair, her emerald green eyes, her small and perfectly straight nose, and her slight but curvaceous figure. She was a pretty thing, and that was dangerous—dangerous to any man who had set his mind to following through with something. A woman like Haven could be a mighty detrimental distraction to a man with a purpose like Val's. Oh, certainly Val knew his mother would encourage him toward Haven—tell him he ought to get to know her, want to go courting her. But his mother also thought Val had picked up, bought a farm and orchards, and moved to Fletcher intending to start a new life—to attempt to move beyond what had happened to his family the previous year.

Pulling on his socks and his boots, Val felt the familiar grip of guilt clutch his heart. His mother would indeed be disappointed to know his true reason for quitting Limon for Fletcher. In truth, she'd be heartbroken. But it was what Val had to do, and he wouldn't rest—or find happiness or go courting a pretty little southern belle—until he'd done what he'd set out to do. Even if it took him the entirety of his miserable life to do it.

Shoving his arms through the sleeves of a clean black shirt, Val left his house and headed for the barn.

"Hey there, Val!" Griggs called as Val approached.

"Mornin', Griggs," Val answered.

"Sheriff says you've got some bushel baskets and such in your barn that need haulin' out to your orchards, so I pulled my wagon and team around," Griggs explained, hopping down from his wagon seat. "Figured I could get them there faster since my team is already harnessed and such."

"Good thinkin'," Val said with a nod. "Thank you, Griggs."

"Anything I can do to help," Griggs said, smiling. "And might I say, it's right generous of you to give your whole crop of pears away."

Val shrugged. "I'm just helpin' those who are willin' to help me. Ain't nothin' generous about it."

Griggs chuckled. "Whatever you say."

"Let's get them bushel baskets and boxes loaded," Val sighed as he strode into the barn. He had to get busy—had to get to some hard work—had to get Haven Abernathy off his mind so he could concentrate on what truly needed concentrating on.

He glanced at the woodpile next to the barn. He'd need to start putting in some wood in preparation for the cold months ahead. As almost a reflex, he wondered whether Haven and Arabella had thought of having someone haul wood for them—worried a little that they wouldn't have enough wood ready when winter hit.

Exhaling a sigh of frustration, he lifted his hat, raked his fingers back through his hair, and growled a little.

Misunderstanding Val's reaction, Griggs slapped Val on the back as he looked at the pile of bushel baskets and wood boxes stacked up in the barn.

"Don't worry about it, Val," Griggs said, smiling. "We'll have these loaded and out to the orchard in no time."

Val nodded and headed into the barn to start loading up the wagon.

He hoped his parents had hired enough hands to harvest the farm back home in Limon. He hoped his daddy was able to bring in enough wood to last through the winter. He wondered who would help his daddy with that chore now that Val was in Fletcher. And even though he tried not to think of Haven Abernathy, he figured he'd better check in with her to make sure she had hired someone to haul wood for her.

"Worryin' over her is gonna be the death of me," Val grumbled as he picked up a stack of bushel baskets and headed for Griggs's wagon.

"What's that, Val?" Griggs asked.

"Nothin'," Val lied. "Nothin'."

* * * * *

Haven just could not help herself! No matter how she tried to keep from glancing around the orchard in looking for Valentine Briscoe's whereabouts, Haven could not keep from looking for him. Of course, her perch atop the ladder and in the upper branches of the pear tree hid her curiosity from anyone—anyone save Arabella, who stood atop another ladder next to her.

"He's behind us, helpin' Mrs. Bernard pick the tree she's been workin' on," Arabella said quietly.

"Oh, fiddle-faddle, Bellie," Haven chimed, feigning a carefree attitude. "You don't have to tell me where he is every livin' moment of the day."

But Arabella smiled. "Well, bein' that you want to know where he is every livin' minute of the day . . . I thought I'd just help you out a bit."

Haven smiled at her friend as she placed another pear in the basket on her arm.

"Well, it seems to me that you're just as concerned about where our handsome sheriff is every livin' minute of the day," she playfully countered.

Arabella blushed, and the sight sent happiness racing through Haven.

The truth was that when Sheriff Sterling had bid Arabella goodnight the night before, Haven had not said one word about her romantic interlude with Valentine Briscoe in the cemetery. The expression of pure bliss on Arabella's face as she enthusiastically related everything that had transpired between her and the sheriff during his visit had been so wonderful, Haven knew that it was Arabella's time to be euphoric. Haven had enjoyed her euphoria in the cemetery and written a letter to the postmaster in the Oklahoma Indian

Territory and it was then her turn to listen to her friend's expression of joy and hope. Furthermore, Sheriff Sterling had been perfectly proper during his visit. He'd taken Arabella's hand in his, raised it to his lips, and kissed the back of it in bidding her goodnight. Therefore, Haven was not at all certain Arabella would approve of the fact that Haven had found herself blissful in Valentine's arms while they'd shared impassioned exchanges of affections. No, the night before had belonged to Arabella and *her* happiness. After all, it was obvious Sheriff Sterling had serious intentions toward Haven's sister-friend. Whereas Valentine Briscoe's intentions toward Haven—she wasn't quite sure he had any intentions toward her at all. Most likely he'd simply felt sorry for her, being that he'd happened upon her while she was tired and emotionally weak.

"I do not deny it," Arabella admitted, smiling. "He's over helpin' the Crabtrees load their bushel baskets into their wagon." Arabella sighed, even as a slight frown puckered her beautiful brow. "Havey, do you think . . . do you think that I should discourage the sheriff's attentions? I mean, my secret . . . the fact that . . . if he finds out . . ." Arabella shook her head, her frown deepening. "But if I don't tell him, then it would be akin to a lie . . . wouldn't it? Still, I'm certain if he knew my secret, he'd run from me as fast as he could."

Haven shook her head, however. "No. No, he would not, Bellie," Haven reassured her friend. "Out here . . . well, you've seen the Crabtree family. No one spurns May or Edith, no one at all. I think it's a different sort of town than most." Yet Haven exhaled a sigh of discouragement. "For you, anyway."

"Why for me and not for you?" Arabella asked. "If folks eventually figure out particular things about me and . . . and I'm not hated and cast out, then why would it be any different for you?" Arabella shook her head and returned her attention to the group of pears hanging in the tree just within her reach. "It won't do for you to tell me to hope for the things that I dream of to come true if you don't hope for yourself."

"Nevertheless, Bellie, it *is* different for me here," Haven whispered. "May and Edith, you— it's slave ancestry runnin' in your veins. The blood of Africa, stolen away and sold into horror. But mine . . ."

"There's Indian blood runnin' through your veins," Arabella interrupted. "Your secret should be less offensive when discovered than mine."

"Not out west," Haven corrected. "Out here many tribes were brutal . . . did terrible, tortuous things to farmers and their families. It seems every family I've met since comin' west has some awful, ghastly, grisly, horrid story of relatives murdered in some abominably gruesome manner.

250

And those grudges are fresher in their minds . . . more personal."

Lowering her voice, Haven leaned toward Arabella, whispering, "Clotilda Lewis had a great-aunt and great-uncle who were skinned alive and then slowly roasted until they died." She shook her head again. "And I know you're goin' to say that it's all nonsense, Bellie, but it's not." Haven picked another pear and placed it in the basket on her arm. "My grandmother's people were not the violent sort of tribe, but other tribes were, and folks here are far more hateful of Indians than they are of black folks. Especially wildly beautiful quadroons with a lovely cream-in-your-coffee complexion likes yours, Arabella, and you know it."

Arabella sighed. "Well, we intruded on the Indians—mistreated and murdered them." She shrugged. "So it seems to me like your secret people have a right to be angry and vengeful."

Haven smiled, realizing the futility of it all. Near everyone in America had mixed background of some sort—white and Indian, Irish and African, Chinese and British. In truth, she figured that someday the time would come when a body wouldn't be able to discern the ancestry of another person just by looking at the color of their hair or skin, the shape of their nose, or the cleft in their chin. Still, that time was in the long-distant future. And in Haven's time, many folks out west hated Indians, many folks up east hated Irishman, and many folks down south hated black people. Odd and quite equally unfair, people often considered those of mixed blood as being more hateworthy than they did those who possessed a pure lineage of a different race. Haven knew that by leaving home she and Arabella would have a chance for a freedom of self they'd never have in Georgia. And they had—would continue to. It even appeared as though Arabella might find love—true, unconditional love. Nonetheless, Haven had begun to think that while Arabella's quarter of black blood lifted her from the burden of having been born into slavery, Haven's quarter of Indian blood might be to her detriment. *If* anyone ever discovered it, that was.

"Oh, let's just toss it aside for now," Haven suggested. Smiling at Arabella, determined to return to enjoying her new life out west, Haven said, "Tell me again what Sheriff Sterling said to you as he was leavin' last night, just before he kissed your hand."

Arabella's cheeks pinked with a blush of remembered delight.

"He took my hand in his, gazed into my eyes, and said, 'Why, Miss Barnes, you are the loveliest, kindest, and downright smartest woman I have ever had the pleasure of knowin'.' Then he kissed my hand. And it wasn't a quick kiss either!

But long and lingerin' . . . like he never wanted to stop kissin' it."

Haven exhaled a sigh of pure proxied pleasure. "How entirely romantic, Bellie," she said.

And as if the Fates themselves had been waiting to hear the joy in Arabella's voice when she told the story again, Haven heard Sheriff Sterling's voice just below them.

"Miss Barnes?" he began.

Arabella looked down from her graceful perch on the pear-picking ladder and said, "Yes, Sheriff?"

Haven could see that it was time for her to empty her nearly full basket of pears. She wanted the sheriff and Arabella to have their privacy, after all, and unless Haven climbed down her ladder and distracted the Sandersan sisters standing below them, there would be no privacy to be had.

"Might I have word with you for a moment, ma'am?" Sheriff Sterling asked, his eyes twinkling with admiration as he stared up at Arabella.

"Of course," Arabella assured him.

Haven hurried down her ladder, saying, "Well, this basket is gettin' far too heavy. Miss Wynifred, Miss Merigold, would you two mind helpin' me lug our baskets over to a fresh bushel box?"

"Not at all," Wynifred chirped, winking at

Merigold as Haven stepped off the ladder and Arabella began to descend hers.

However, Haven was somewhat exasperated when both Miss Wynifred and Miss Merigold paused in turning toward the empty bushel boxes setting under a lately picked pear tree. Certainly they turned their back to the sheriff and Arabella, thereby offering a whiff of privacy, but they did not move farther—even when Haven arched her brows as she looked to them, nodding in the direction of the bushel box stack.

"What might I do for your, Sheriff?" Haven heard Arabella ask as she stepped off the ladder.

"Well, the truth is," Sheriff Sterling began, removing his hat and nervously spinning it between his hands, "I was wonderin' if you might like to take supper with me over at the diner this evenin', Miss Barnes."

Haven saw Miss Wynifred and Miss Merigold exchange delighted glances, and Haven widened her eyes at Wynifred to scold her for eavesdropping as the woman nudged Haven with one elbow to make certain Haven had heard the sheriff's invitation to Arabella.

I heard him, Haven silently mouthed to Miss Wynifred.

"Why, that would be divine, Sheriff," Arabella chirped with enthusiasm. "Oh . . . of course, if Haven doesn't mind takin' supper alone tonight, that is."

"Oh, of course," Sheriff Sterling said with a firm nod.

Instantly, Miss Wynifred spun around, Miss Merigold following suit.

"Why, we were just gettin' ready to ask you girls if you wouldn't mind joinin' us for supper this evenin'," Wynifred exclaimed. Placing a hand to her cheek and feigning innocence, Wynifred offered, "Oh, forgive me, Sheriff, but I couldn't help but overhear your invitation to our dear Arabella, and it struck me just this moment that, since Merigold and I had planned on havin' Haven and Arabella to supper tonight, it's just as easy for Haven to have supper at our house and Arabella to join you at the diner. Isn't that right, Haven honey?"

Haven felt chagrin at Wynifred Sandersan's embarrassing lack of manners, for the woman had not only eavesdropped and interfered but also seemed to have no remorse for doing either!

"Why, that would be just wonderful, Miss Wynifred," Haven chimed. "Just wonderful!"

"Lovely!" Merigold interjected. "Then we'll see you for supper at five, Haven." She looked to the sheriff and Arabella then. "And you two enjoy your supper together at the diner. I swear that cook Hugh Ray hired on at his diner last spring makes the most delicious biscuits and cream gravy I ever have had in all my life."

"Well, now that that's all settled," Wynifred said, linking an arm with one of Haven's, "let's the three of us run on over and help the Henrys load their bushel baskets, shall we? I see their wagon just over yonder a ways."

Merigold linked her arm with Haven's free one. "Why yes, let's. Come along, Haven. You and I can help wrangle those twin boys of Claudine's while Andrew helps his daddy load up."

"I'll be back as quick as a cat, Bellie," Haven called over her shoulder as the Sandersan sisters fairly dragged her along with them.

Once Haven was certain the sheriff and Arabella were enough distance behind them, Haven giggled as she scolded, "You two are far too impish for your own good! Why, I've never seen such terrible manners in two ladies who should know better."

But Wynifred and Merigold Sandersan simply laughed.

"Oh, come now, Haven," Wynifred began. "You were too stunned at hearin' Arabella prove what a lady she is by not wantin' to leave you home alone while she went to supper with that handsome sheriff of hers to think of anything better. Now weren't you? Admit it."

"And besides," Merigold added before Haven could confirm that Wynifred was indeed correct in her assumption, "it's far better for two old ladies to forget their manners than for the etiquette and decorum teacher of Fletcher to forget them."

Haven giggled, shaking her head, too amused by the Sandersan sisters' brazen matchmaking to remain exasperated with them for any length of time.

"You two," she laughed. "Oh, how you cheer my heart! Why, I'm so excited for Arabella's sake, I can hardly keep from squealin' with joy!"

Wynifred and Merigold laughed as well.

"Oh my!" Wynifred sighed, still smiling with amusement. "I haven't had that much fun in tossin' propriety aside in ages."

"Oh, but I have," Merigold countered.

"You have?" Haven asked with surprise. Of the two Sandersan sisters, Haven had learned long ago that Wynifred was the stronger personality. Haven figured Wynifred spoke ten times as often as Merigold did. And it was why she was surprised the less assertive sister had claimed to trump what her sister had just done.

"Indeed," Merigold assured her.

"Whenever have you tossed propriety aside of late, Merigold Sandersan?" Wynifred playfully challenged.

"I'll have you know, there is a benefit to bein' the less talkative of us two, Wynnie," Merigold stated.

"And what might that benefit be?"

"Well, while we were all standin' at Mr.

Briscoe's door this mornin'," Merigold began, "while the sheriff was talkin' and you, Haven here, and even Arabella were avertin' your eyes from Mr. Briscoe's state of undress—bein' that that was the proper thing to do in the situation—why, I just had my fill of lookin' that man up and down and admirin' the firm sculpture of his body that heaven blessed him with!"

Haven gasped and blushed at the memory of Valentine's appearance at his own front door wearing nothing but a quilt around his waist. Oh, it truly had been a magnificent sight to behold! And yet Merigold was right; Haven had glanced about nearly anywhere to keep from staring at Valentine then.

Wynifred burst into laughter, and Haven couldn't keep from joining her in it.

"Why, Merigold Sandersan," Wynifred chortled, "you are nothin' if not incorrigible!"

As Merigold giggled, she added, "But I do admit to thinkin' that the man was fortunate he snatched up a quilt to cover himself, rather than a length of dotted swiss! Even I'm not that incorrigible."

Haven gasped and covered her gaping mouth as the full meaning sunk into her thinking. Dotted swiss was a sheer, gossamer fabric embellished with tiny white dots. Susan Thompson, Haven's friend back in Covington, had sewn her wedding veil from dotted swiss. Had Valentine somehow managed to snatch up a length of the nearly transparent fabric instead of the quilt . . .

"Hush, Merigold," Wynifred laughed. "You'll give our sweet Haven here a fit of apoplexy talkin' about such things."

But Haven was still blushing—for the corruption to her imagination had already been done.

Val rubbed at the two-days' whisker growth on his chin. Something about the way the two old Sandersan ladies were laughing—like Mark Twain had just told them to go to heaven for the climate and hell for the company. His curiosity was further piqued when Haven Abernathy broke into waves of laughter as well.

As the three women stood near the Henrys' wagon trying to regain their poise, Val noticed that he had been grinning as he watched them. For one thing, he couldn't get Haven's expression, when he'd met her and the others at his front door that morning wearing nothing but a quilt and a frown, out of his mind. He figured that she hadn't even realized she'd gone from astonishment with eyes as wide as Thanksgiving turkey platters to grinning like a possum eating a sweet potato as she'd tried over and over not to look at him.

Fact was, Val liked the fact his appearance had made the prim and proper etiquette teacher blush and smile. He'd liked the way she'd blushed and smiled the night before too—in the cemetery when he'd lost his ever-loving mind and kissed her.

Still, as he watched Haven and the Sandersan sisters trying to corral the two Henry twins, his smile faded. What in tarnation had possessed him to accept the old Sandersans' invitation to supper that night?

Of course, they'd said they wanted to thank him—for letting the town harvest and have his pear crop without paying. And since Haven's little lecture to him on allowing folks to thank him, Val had discovered he'd been working on it. Furthermore, they'd asked him while he wasn't really paying too much attention—while he and Griggs had been loading baskets and boxes into the wagon from Val's barn.

Nonetheless, Val figured it wouldn't be too taxing to share a nice meal with two lonely old ladies. If their cinnamon rolls were anything that the rest of their cooking could be measured by, he knew he'd be having a very tasty meal that night indeed. Maybe the old gals would even whip up a fresh batch of cinnamon rolls for dessert.

Rubbing at his whiskers again, Val swallowed the excess moisture that had gathered in his mouth at the thought of the Sandersan sisters' cinnamon rolls—or at the thought of kissing Haven Abernathy the night before. Realizing he couldn't be sure which thought had caused him to salivate, he turned and strode to where Jarvis McGhee and his two children were struggling to load the boxes of pears they'd picked into Jarvis's wagon.

"It's the cinnamon rolls doin' it, that's for damn sure," Val grumbled as he rather stormed toward the McGhees. Only thing was, his mouth didn't water when he thought of the cinnamon rolls again.

CHAPTER TEN

And Arabella says that right before the Harvest Festival she'll remove some of the leaves she's painted on the tree on the store window and add a few more on the ground beneath the tree, and some pumpkins too," Haven explained as she drizzled icing over the freshly baked pan of cinnamon rolls sitting on the small table in one corner of Wynifred and Merigold's kitchen.

"Oh, that will be just lovely!" Merigold exclaimed.

"And does she have other plans for the shop window for October?" Wynifred inquired as she stirred the thick beef stew simmering on the stovetop. "Perhaps some jack-o'-lantern faces and things?"

"Oh my, yes!" Haven exclaimed with excitement. "I'm certain our shop's window will just become more and more beautiful now that Arabella views it as a blank canvas for her to work on. Oh, I do love to see the end results of her work process. Can you just imagine the beauty that must linger in her mind every livin' minute of the day?"

"Not at all!" Merigold admitted. "Why, I can't imagine bein' able to draw and paint the way Arabella does. For that matter, however, I can't imagine how *you* dream up a different hat creation every day either, Haven." Merigold shook her head with admiration. "I just stand in awe of such creativity."

"Oh, me too," Wynifred agreed. "Of course, we all have our gifts and talents, don't we? Why, look at these cinnamon rolls you and I have been bakin' all these years, sister. Anyone who has ever tasted one swears ours are unparalleled anywhere! Mr. Crabtree told me himself—old Mr. Crabtree, that is—that when he was out to New York as a younger man, he had himself a cinnamon roll every mornin' on his way to his office. He swore he'd never tasted anything so delicious and perfectly satisfying in all his life as those cinnamon rolls from that New York bakery—that is, until he had a taste of ours. Isn't that right, Merigold?"

"Indeed he did," Merigold agreed.

"So there, you see? Everyone has their own gifts and talents. It's just that some are more visible than others."

"Oh my, yes! Everyone has talents," Merigold concurred. "Of course, I think we all agreed that Mr. Valentine Briscoe holds a rare talent himself."

"That being?" Wynifred prodded, winking at Haven.

Haven smiled, even blushed a little. For she

264

knew Merigold Sandersan well enough to know exactly what the woman was about to say.

"That being his Adonis-like physique, his muscles! Why, they look as if they were sculpted from pure granite. And that dark hair, those jade-green eyes . . . that face of his! Bein' that beautiful? Now, *that* is a talent!"

Haven giggled, even for the fact she whole-heartedly held to Merigold's opinion of Valentine.

Laughing, Wynifred corrected, "*That* is a gift, Merigold! Mr. Briscoe's *talent* is evident in the way he presents that gift. Answerin' his door this mornin' wrapped in nothin' but a quilt at his waist and hangin' onto the top of his door with one hand so we had a perfect view of his long, strong arm? Givin' us women a mass of butterflies in our stomachs the way he did? Now *that's* his talent!"

"And then some!" Merigold exclaimed, joining her sister in laughter.

For her part, Haven could only shake her head with delighted disbelief at how unguarded the Sandersan sisters were, especially in the privacy of their own home. She thought how wonderful it was to linger with them and know she was safe to laugh as loudly as she felt inspired to, eat as much as she wanted, discuss any subject on the face of the earth without the worry of offending, and share any secret without fear of being betrayed. Well, she felt she could share some secrets at least—not all, but some.

It's how she'd felt whenever her parents had been away. The truth was, Haven had never felt quite so free and able to be herself when her parents had been home. Only when they had gone did she feel comfortable enough in her own skin to be true to herself, keeping nothing about herself hidden. Mipsie, Old Joe, and Arabella had made home feel like home to Haven, not her parents. Haven's greatest secret always seemed like it was something to be ashamed of with her parents, even for her mother's part in it. But not with Mipsie and Joe, and certainly not with Arabella. And the Sandersan sisters and their cozy, comfortable sanctuary of a home felt the same way to Haven—snug, intimate, and secure.

"Oh, come on, Haven honey," Wynifred teased with a giggle. "Admit it to us. Admit it out loud that you think Mr. Valentine Briscoe is the Adonis of Fletcher, Colorado!"

Haven laughed, shook her head, and confessed, "You know I think he is. I swear, that man makes my mouth water . . . just the same way these cinnamon rolls do!"

As Wynifred and Merigold burst into squeals of delight, Haven thought of Valentine as he had appeared that morning. The truth was, she wasn't a fan of viewing folks immodestly dressed. She'd seen shirtless men before, frequently in fact. But the sight had never struck her as anything to think twice about—that is, until she'd first seen Valentine digging Mr. Latham's grave. But goodness sakes did she think twice about Valentine's being half dressed—about how incredibly attractive he'd appeared that way. And then, when he'd answered the door that morning when Sheriff Sterling had suggested the group of them knock on Mr. Briscoe's front door to see if all was well? Well, the truth be told, Haven had been nothing short of mesmerized at the sight of him. And anyway, she was in her safe, secure place—the home of the Sandersan sisters—where she needn't pretend she was anything other than spellbound by the man.

Still giggling with delighted amusement, Wynifred and Merigold each placed an arm around Haven's waist, hugging her warmly.

"Oh honey, we just love you so much!" Wynifred exclaimed. "You know that, don't you?"

"You're like a daughter to me, Haven," Merigold added. She studied Haven a moment and reached back behind Haven, taking Haven's long black braid and pulling it to rest over her right shoulder. "And you're such a jewel. I don't understand why on earth you don't wear your hair down like this. It's such a crownin' beauty, after all. It's like silk."

"You know it's not at all proper for a woman to display her hair so audaciously, Miss Merigold,"

Haven reminded. "Whatever would people think of me?"

"That you're a rare enchantress indeed!" Wynifred answered. "It makes me wish you woulda been stung by a bee long ago, if that's what it took for us to see your silken, raven tresses."

Haven tossed her head back a little, laughing. "My silken, raven tresses?" she chirped. "Oh, come now, Miss Wynifred. And anyway, I don't ever want to be stung like that again . . . on my head!" Reaching up to press on the sore place at the right side of her head, Haven added, "This sting hurts like the dickens! I thought Arabella would never find that stinger and pick it out. I don't know why that nasty ol' bee chose me to sting while we were pickin' pears today."

"I would think it chose you because you were sweeter than anything else out there. And of course we don't like to think of you in pain, dear," Wynifred agreed. "But do promise that someday you'll let us brush this sable mane of yours, hmmm? I used to love to brush our little sister's hair."

"Me too," Merigold said—although quietly and with reverence.

"You have a sister?" Haven asked.

"We had a little sister, yes," Wynifred answered. "She died very long ago."

Haven noted the pain of loss that settled in

Wynifred's and Merigold's eyes then. And when Merigold pasted on a smile and said, "Now let's get to finishin' up supper," Haven knew not to press the sisters for any further information concerning their sister.

"Why don't you set the table, Haven honey?" Wynifred suggested.

"Of course." Haven adored helping the Sandersans put supper on the table. It was another reason she felt so comfortable in their home; they treated her like she belonged there, not as a guest.

Going to the cupboard, Wynifred removed four plates, handing them to Haven.

Puzzled, Haven asked, "We only need three, don't we?"

Yet Merigold shook her head. "We need four."

"But Arabella won't be joinin' us, remember?" Haven reminded.

"Oh, we know," Wynifred assured her.

There was a knock on the front door of the house then.

"That's our fourth, I would imagine," Merigold chirped. "Would you mind gettin' the door, Haven? I've got to see to this stew."

Seeing that Wynifred was busily gathering utensils and napkins for the table, Haven agreed, "Yes, ma'am," even though she was somewhat put out for a moment that her solitary time with Wynifred and Merigold was being interrupted—

that her time of safety and freedom with them and in private serenity was being intruded upon. But she smiled and set the plates on the kitchen table, wiping her hands on her apron as she hurried to the door.

Opening the Sandersans' front door, Haven saw none other than Valentine Briscoe standing on their porch.

"Oh! Well, good evenin', Mr. Briscoe," she managed, even as her heart leapt up into her throat. He was so handsome! Haven wondered how it could be that she was never prepared for the awe that always washed over her when she faced him.

Valentine's brows furrowed a little, but only briefly.

"Evenin', Miss Abernathy," his low voice rumbled in return. "Have I arrived too soon? I . . . uh . . . Miss Sandersan and Miss Sandersan invited me for supper, but I—"

"You're not a moment too soon, Mr. Briscoe," Wynifred chimed as she appeared just behind Haven. "And I do so admire a guest who is prompt. Won't you please come in? We're puttin' supper on the table just now, in fact."

Valentine's eyes narrowed as he gazed at Haven a moment.

"I . . . I . . ." Haven whispered to him, shrugging to indicate her innocence in the matter.

She could see that he thought she was a party

to the Sandersans' scheming, and she wanted to make certain he understood she was not.

"We invited Haven to join us this evenin', as well," Wynifred explained as she simultaneously reached out, took Valentine's hat from his head with one hand, and grasped his forearm and pulled him in over the threshold and into the house with her other.

"Yes," Merigold confirmed as she rather sashayed into the parlor as well. "When we found out that our gallant Sheriff Sterling had invited Miss Barnes to supper at the diner, we remembered that we see you there far too often, Mr. Briscoe. And always dinin' alone. So Wynnie and I decided it was high time we had you to our house for supper. And havin' Haven join us means you're not trapped with just Wynnie and me all evenin' long."

"Um . . . thank you, ma'am," Valentine said. "I do appreciate you thinkin' of me."

Haven smiled as she studied Valentine, however. As calm and collected as he appeared on the outside, Haven knew Valentine well enough to know his insides were squirming like a worm on a hot brick.

"Oh, we always think of you, Mr. Briscoe," Wynifred gushed. "Out there, all alone on your farm, with no one to cook for you? We figure you need to come by at least once a week and have a nice sit-down supper with us."

"Oh . . . oh, Miss Sandersan, I couldn't impose like that. No, ma'am," Valentine stammered.

Valentine's attention returned to Haven then, and he grinned as he studied her from head to toe.

"Did you get the bee sting all taken care of, Miss Abernathy?" he inquired.

For a moment, Haven was flattered at the way Valentine's gaze seemed to travel over her hair—exactly as if he were admiring her *silken, raven tresses*. Yet as he continued to study her, his attention lingering on her hair, Haven remembered exactly why she never wore her hair down, or braided for that matter. And it wasn't for propriety's sake.

When she was just about twelve, her mother forbade her to ever wear her hair braided again.

"Indian women weave their hair into plaits, Haven," her mother had informed her. "And you're gettin' old enough now that you look just like your grandmother Adair when you wear braids. It'll send people to wonderin' if you're pure through and through. Do you understand?"

Haven had understood, and she'd lived in fear of someone discovering her one-quarter blood ever since. Were she ever to be entirely honest with anyone concerning her heritage, Haven would admit to often braiding her hair into plaits and studying herself in the mirror at times. She would stand before the mirror, wondering if she really did look like her Cherokee grandmother—wondering whether anyone else would ever see the Cherokee in her.

"Uh . . . why yes, thank you, I did," Haven answered Valentine. "I . . . I had to wash my hair after Arabella plucked the stinger out of me, and . . . well, it takes it so long to dry, and I didn't realize you . . . I do apologize for my very casual appearance, Mr. Briscoe."

Valentine's grin broadened. "Well, I think you look mighty fine, Miss Abernathy," he said. "Seems like I should be the one apologizing . . . for *my* very casual appearance this mornin' when I answered my door."

Haven felt her cheeks blush crimson as the vision of Valentine's very casual appearance that morning leapt to the forefront of her mind.

"Oh, nonsense, Mr. Briscoe!" Merigold laughed. "Why, Wynnie and I haven't had such a treat as catchin' you unshucked and oversleepin' in a long, long time."

A bit of color rose to Valentine's cheeks as he rubbed at the whisker growth on his jaw and chuckled, "Well, I don't know quite what to say about that, ma'am. Thank you, I guess?"

Wynifred linked her arm through Valentine's then. "You just come on in and sit down to supper, Mr. Briscoe. We've got beef stew and a fresh-baked batch of cinnamon rolls to enjoy together."

As Wynifred escorted Valentine into the kitchen, Haven caught Merigold's arm to stay her a moment.

"What on earth were you two thinkin'?" she scolded in a whisper. "Why, I look exactly like somethin' the cat drug in! Flour all over me, hair down and ridiculous—"

"You look lovely, Haven," Merigold interrupted, patting Haven's cheek. "And we just thought we oughta thank Mr. Briscoe somehow—you know, for givin' away his entire crop of pears." Merigold shrugged. "And then when the sheriff invited Arabella to supper at the diner . . . well, three's a crowd, and you make four. Four is always better than three for supper."

"But, Miss Merigold—" Haven began.

"Now, you hush, honey," Merigold whispered. "Just enjoy his company! I bet you've never had a better lookin' dinner companion than Valentine Briscoe, now have you?"

"No, but—"

"Just enjoy it, sweetie," Merigold said with a wink. "I certainly plan to."

Merigold was off then, heading for the kitchen, where Wynifred was already pointing out a chair at the table next to Valentine.

Exhaling a heavy sigh and trying not to panic, Haven tossed her long braid to hang down her back. She figured she would look less like her grandmother Adair then. And after all, Miss

Merigold was right: Haven couldn't think of anything more appetizing to look at during supper than Valentine Briscoe.

✳ ✳ ✳ ✳ ✳

"I could not believe Merigold had suggested such a thing!" Wynifred Sandersan said. "Ridin' a horse astride? Why, it just wasn't done back then!"

Merigold Sandersan giggled. "Oh indeed! And when I suggested we ride astride whenever we were ridin' alone, I swear Wynifred looked at me like I had just suggested skinnin' a baby with a spoon!"

"Well, it just wasn't done then," Wynifred repeated.

Val looked across the table to where Haven Abernathy sat listening to the Sandersan sisters relate the tale of their youthful rebellion. Damn, the girl was pretty! Especially with her hair freer than it usually was. He noted that she looked nearly a foot shorter with her hair down and no hat propped up high on her head. Val found himself stealing glances at her far more than was safe.

"And so we've been tellin' Haven she ought to let Merigold and me exercise her horses once in a while," Miss Merigold said, pulling Val's attention back to the conversation at hand.

"Oh, that's right," Val contributed, suddenly

remembering what Griggs had told him. Looking to Haven, he continued, "Griggs keeps—what is it?—four horses in the livery for you, Miss Abernathy?"

"Yes, sir," Haven confirmed.

"I've seen them," Val began. "They're magnificent animals. I'm right surprised you didn't just sell them before you moved out west. Seems that woulda been easier than payin' to have them stabled and findin' folks to make sure they get ridden."

Val saw a pallor of guilt wash over Haven's pretty face.

"Well, I . . . I . . ." she stammered.

"Oh, go on, honey," Wynifred Sandersan encouraged the young woman. "I'm sure Mr. Briscoe will understand."

Val's interest was piqued. He'd always wondered why the hatmaking etiquette teacher owned four Thoroughbred horses and why she kept them locked away in a livery. So Wynifred's remark tickled his curiosity all the more.

"I'm sure I will," he said, directly to Haven.

He didn't feel comfortable admitting it—even silently to himself—but such a mingling of powerful emotions toward Haven rose in him, not to mention the physical attraction he was feeling toward her, that he wondered whether he could resist dragging the woman out to the cemetery and making love to her again the way he had the night before. She looked so vulnerable— so worried that he would think badly of her for whatever she felt guilty about—and it stimulated every ounce of his protective nature.

"Well, you see," Haven began, "as you know, Mr. Briscoe, my own parents have passed on. However, two of the people who cared for my family's properties—who are family in my own heart—they're still in Georgia. And I just know they would be happier out here with Arabella and me. I just know it! When I left Covin'ton, I knew Arabella would join." Haven shrugged. "It took some convincin', I'll not deny that, but I knew Arabella would move to Fletcher. And, well, you see, I hoped Old Joe and Mipsie would come out when Arabella did. But I had my doubts that they would be willin' to leave Georgia. It's familiar to them, after all."

Haven paused, her eyes searching Val's as if asking a silent question—as if hoping for understanding. She sighed with what seemed to be disappointment and then continued, "And, well, to be honest, J-Joe loves those horses. They were my daddy's horses, but it was Joe who cared for them, rode them, loved them. And I was hopin' that if I brought the horses with me out here . . . that it might be somethin' else to lure Joe and Mipsie here, as well."

"Somethin' more than just you and Miss Barnes," Val offered—for he did understand.

Leaving home took courage, no matter what. Even for Val it had been difficult to leave Limon, and Fletcher was only seventy-five miles away. He couldn't even imagine how hard it would be to leave home for Fletcher when home was so far away. He understood more, as well.

"Yes," Haven admitted, as if she'd committed some horrible sin by casting a lure to this Joe. "I just thought Joe would be happier here if he had the horses to care for . . . to own."

"You're gonna give him those Thoroughbreds?" Val asked. He wasn't surprised, not in the least. He'd seen with his own eyes how kind, softhearted, and giving Haven was. But to give away such magnificent and valuable animals? Well, it seemed like the little hatmaker would never cease to amaze him.

"Of course," Haven answered, as if she'd been puzzled by his question. "After all, Joe loves them more than anyone else does, even me. And they love him. I can tell they're anxious, wonderin' where Joe is, wonderin' if he's comin' to see them. So yes, I'm hopin' the horses will help Joe and Mipsie have the courage to come out west with Arabella and me."

Haven's gaze locked with Val's. The unspoken questioning had returned to her beautiful green eyes, and Val narrowed his as he gazed at her. He knew what she was worried about—knew that the appearance of this Joe and Mipsie might throw speculation onto Miss Barnes. After all, he figured they were Arabella's parents, or at least one of them was her parent. Arabella Barnes was far too attractive a woman to be made up of just plain old white blood. Valentine had always thought Arabella most likely shared a lineage along the same lines as did May and Edith Crabtree—a part African lineage. Val also postulated that Joe and Mipsie were once slaves, that perhaps Haven's father had owned them at some point, kept them on as workers after the war and the emancipation proclamation. And although anger rose in him at thinking of Haven's father having possibly owned human beings, Val knew he was not guiltless in holding resentment against those of another race. Certainly, he never looked at another human being of any gender, color, or ethnicity and thought of them as anything but his brothers and sisters as God's children. But he did hold malice toward evil men, in particular those who had brought such pain, tragedy, and loss to him and his family— men from a race that he knew often butchered and murdered other human beings. And no matter what wrong had been done to these savages to indeed make them savage, it did not warrant what they had done to their fellow human beings. Just as slavery did not warrant black men killing white men—even for the fact that their white masters had killed their kin before—Indians stealing, torturing, and murdering white men was not warranted because of what had been done to them. It was all an abomination—slavery, Indian removal. Yet Val's hatred nested in him like a black crow, picking at his heart and mind—always.

Nevertheless, Val softened his gaze. "Well, I for one hope you're successful in persuadin' them into comin' out," Val stated. "Fletcher needs a good horseman like your Joe. And I'm sure he and his would find Fletcher to be a right welcomin' and friendly town."

The pink of hope that rose to Haven's pretty cheeks made Val realize he'd done his good deed for the day. He'd managed to convey to Haven that he suspected Joe and Mipsie were former slaves and that the townsfolk of Fletcher would most likely be more welcoming to them than anywhere down south. It made him feel good to know he'd given hope to the little etiquette teacher he'd done some sparking with out in the cemetery the night before.

"Here you go, Mr. Briscoe," Merigold Sandersan said as she set a plate boasting a large cinnamon roll on the table before him. "Let me get you a glass of milk to go with that."

"Thank you kindly, ma'am," Val said as his mouth began to water. The problem was, he was still looking at Haven, so again he wasn't certain if it was the anticipation of the cinnamon roll that had set him to salivating—or the reverie of having kissed Haven Abernathy the night before.

"Oh, I wish you could've coaxed Joe and Mipsie out in time to be here for the Harvest Festival," Merigold sighed. "It's always such a wonderful occasion, especially this year with the children showin' off what they've learned from Miss Haven Abernathy, Fletcher's own etiquette, decorum, and social dance teacher!"

Haven blushed with embarrassment as Valentine grinned with mild amusement, arching one eyebrow as he nodded to her and said, "Indeed. It oughta be right entertainin' to see the children usin' what they've learned."

"Oh, I do hope the weather cooperates," Wynifred whined. "Why, two years back, it started snowin' just before the festival. And although folks tried to linger and enjoy themselves, after an hour we were seein' the beginnin's of a blizzard, and everyone had to hightail it home. Of course, everyone was tucked in nice and cozy for the evenin', but it was a great disappointment."

"Oh, I don't think you need to worry none at all, Miss Sandersan," Valentine offered. Nodding to Haven, he added, "Why, thanks to Miss Abernathy here, I happened across a page in the *Farmers' Almanac* just this afternoon. And the almanac promises perfect weather for that week of the Harvest Festival."

"Well, that's awful nice, Haven honey," Wynifred cooed. "How thoughtful of you to see that our newest farmer had a fresh copy of the almanac!"

"You have no idea how thoughtful it truly was, Miss Sandersan," Valentine said, smiling. "Why, to be honest, I've found it more useful and appreciated than any gift I've ever received in all my life."

Merigold smiled and took Haven's face between her soft, wrinkled hands. "Oh, Haven! You are just the sweetest thing, always lookin' out for others. Isn't she just the sweetest thing, Mr. Briscoe?"

"Yes, ma'am," Valentine chuckled.

Haven had never known such a burning blush! Had she had a hand mirror handy, she knew she would find that her reflection would show her cheeks the deepest shade of crimson a body had ever seen.

Still, in an effort to display as much dignity as possible under the circumstances, Haven said, "Well, I am glad to know you're findin' it helpful, Mr. Briscoe."

The broad smile that spread across Valentine's face and the deep chuckle rumbling in his throat made Haven feel a little less humiliated and more mirthful herself. It was obvious that her *gift* had benefited Valentine with more than just a softer trip to the outhouse; it had also provided him with ongoing amusement. And that was a thing Haven sensed he needed more of. Therefore, Haven decided to try and not be so mortified every time Valentine made reference to the *Farmers' Almanac*. No, she determined she would make the effort to see it from his point of view—see the humor in it and be good-naturedly amused herself if the subject ever arose again. After all, as far as Haven knew, she was the only person in Fletcher who had managed—albeit unintentionally—to give Valentine Briscoe a reason to laugh. And as Mipsie had always taught her, "Laughin' is da best tonic God dun give us. It heals mo' wounds dan anytin' else in da worl'." And once again, Haven was reminded of how wise Mipsie was—and how much she missed her.

✳ ✳ ✳ ✳ ✳

It was near to dusk, and Val still had chores to finish up once he got home. It was past time for him to take his leave of the Misses Sandersan and Haven. Yet for the first time in a year, he found himself wishing to linger. But the cows needed milking, and he was worn out from being around people all day long. The pear pickers had all been kind and hard working, but Val was peopled out for one day.

Yet as he stood and strode to the door to take his leave of the Misses Sandersan's home, he felt an unhappy sort of melancholy rinse over him. Not only had they fed him a delicious meal, but they'd also been very pleasant to converse with. Even when Val wasn't involved in actually talking during a given conversation with Wynifred and Merigold Sandersan, he found their lively laughter and chatter quite charming.

Most of all, however, it was the company of Haven Abernathy he found most pleasant and downright fascinating. The young woman was so beautiful—not just her face and figure but also her mind, her compassion, her patience, her kindness, and her sense of humor. Once Val had determined to just relax and enjoy the company of the three ladies, he'd begun to see deeper into Haven's heart and soul—even more than he had the night before when he'd savored the sweet flavor of her kiss out in the boneyard.

Of course, he still knew his purpose, his calling, especially with what needed to be done. And as he stood at the threshold of the Sandersan sisters' door ready to say his thanks before taking his leave, the small glimmer of happy distraction and miniscule softening of his heart departed, leaving him cold and angry inside once more.

"Thank you, ladies," Val managed. Even though he wanted to escape in those moments and retreat to his home, where he was more comfortable with his anger and loathing, he pasted on a smile. "I can't recall when I had such a delicious meal . . . not to mention such lovely supper companions."

The Sandersans blushed with delight, and Merigold cooed, "Oh, go on with you now, Mr. Briscoe." She wagged an index finger at him, playfully scolding, "And you just remember this: flattery will get you anything you want around here!"

"Miss Merigold!" Haven exclaimed, even as she giggled.

It was one of the things Val liked most about Haven Abernathy—the way she always acted astonished, near to taking offense, when someone spoke or acted improperly. Yep, Val really, really liked that. It revealed not only Haven's rare sense of humor but also that she wasn't a self-righteous, judgmental old prude. And now, knowing what he knew about her affection for and desire to do right by Miss Barnes's parents—well, it was only further proof of her lack of bigotry and prejudice. Something Val wished he possessed more of.

Haven's eyes twinkled as she looked at him, still giggling over Miss Merigold's impropriety.

"Well, that's good to know, Miss Merigold," Val responded. "Good to know!"

"And I mean it too," Merigold affirmed with a wink.

Val smiled, offered another, "Thank you, ladies. Truly," and then opened the door to let himself out.

"Thank you for comin', Mr. Briscoe," Wynifred said. "I hope you'll come to supper again soon."

"Yes, ma'am," Val said, touching the brim of his hat in offering his farewell.

"And do sleep well tonight, Mr. Briscoe," Haven added then.

She was smiling at him, her beautiful green eyes appearing as emerald embers.

"Thank you, Miss Abernathy," Val said with a nod. And then, before he could think to say otherwise, he said, "Would you mind if I spoke with you for a moment, Miss Abernathy? In private?"

Haven felt the color drain from her cheeks—tried to ignore the breathless anxiety that was rising in her. Valentine seemed so suddenly stoic. He'd been smiling and laughing just moments before, but now his smile was gone and his eyes narrowed as he looked at her.

"Of . . . of course," Haven stammered.

"Well, we best see to those supper dishes, Merigold," Wynifred said, tugging at her sister's arm.

"Oh yes, indeed," Merigold agreed, following her sister out of the parlor.

Haven watched as Valentine rubbed at the whisker growth on his chin and jaw.

"What is it, Mr. Briscoe?" she ventured. "Have I . . . have I done somethin' to upset you in any way? If so, I'm so sorry! I just—"

"No. No, not at all," Val muttered. He looked

straight at her then, his eyes flaring with a jade wildfire. "I . . . uh . . . I just wanted to offer my apologies for . . . for my behavior last evenin' . . . in the cemetery."

Instantly Haven's heart sank to the very pit of her stomach. All day long she'd fought off daydreaming—bathing in reveries of Valentine Briscoe kissing her the night before. And that was after having hardly slept a wink just after it happened. The most wonderful, delicious, marvelous moments of her life had transpired in the cemetery, being held in Valentine's powerful arms as his mouth claimed hers. Pure, thrilling, thoroughgoing bliss had intoxicated her, and all for the fact that it was Valentine Briscoe administering such ambrosial affection to her. And now—now he stood before her apologizing? There was a pain pinching her heart all of a sudden.

"Your behavior?" Haven asked in a whisper, trying to rally the courage to offer her own apology. After all, Valentine Briscoe was obvious in his opinion that their romantic interlude was a mistake. "I'm the one who was the fool, allowin' the Lathams' funeral to . . . to waken my emotions and . . . oh, what you must think of me!"

"No, no, no," he interrupted, reaching out and taking her shoulders.

Haven looked up at him, willing the tears brimming in her eyes to stay where they were— to not spill over onto her cheeks—for the moment was humiliating enough without her bursting into weeping like a scolded child.

"I just want to make certain you know that I'm no kind of rascally villain just out to lure ladies into . . . uh . . . meanin'less mischief," he assured her. "You're a mighty beautiful woman, Miss Abernathy, and I admire you—your goodness, all you do for folks. And I . . . I know I shouldn'ta nudged you so hard into sparkin' the way I did." He grinned and winked at her, adding, "Not that I'd take it back if I had the chance. I just want you to know that I'm no philanderer. Mighta been a bit of a flirter in my youth . . ." He lowered his voice, whispering, "But I don't kiss a woman just for the entertainment of it. I just come along last night and saw you there so hurt over your folks, and well . . . fact is, I couldn't resist sparkin' with you. And I hope you won't think badly of me for it."

Haven smiled at him, and her heart leapt back up into her chest. He hadn't said he'd regretted kissing her the way she feared he might. He just didn't want her to think he was running all over town kissing every unmarried woman in it. And he'd said he wouldn't take it back if he had the chance! That meant everything to Haven.

"Never," Haven assured him. "I only hope you don't think I'm some scarlet-petticoated saloon girl. What you were thinkin' of me, why, I can't even imagine, and I—"

"I was thinkin' that you're a pretty young lady with a kind heart and the patience of Job," he chuckled.

It wasn't what Haven dreamt of hearing Valentine say to her; it wasn't, *I've fallen in love with you, and will you marry me, Haven Abernathy?* But it was wonderful all the same.

"Well, thank you, Mr. Briscoe," Haven began. "But what you said before is probably more correct."

Val frowned. "What did I say before?"

"In Doc Perkins's office," she reminded him. "You referred to me as a damsel in distress. And I might need admit to myself one day that maybe that has more truth to it than I care to concede. It seems I'm always and ever in distress whenever you're just innocently walkin' by."

Val glanced away for a moment. "I did say that, didn't I?"

"Yes, you did. And obviously you are correct," Haven offered.

"Obviously I'm a horse's . . . a jackass," he said.

Haven bit her lip to keep from giggling, finding it quite endearing that Val would not only change what he had begun to call himself but also that he would think there was a great deal of difference between the two.

"I'm sorry, Miss Abernathy," he sighed with a heavy exhale.

"No need to apologize for speakin' the truth, Mr. Briscoe," she assured him.

Valentine shook his head, rubbing at his temples. "I didn't get a wink of sleep last night, and I suppose my bein' so tired is what has me ramblin' on like a magpie." He looked at her again then, and Haven could see the fatigue in his countenance. "Thank you again for supper." He paused, his handsome brows wrinkling as he added, "It'll be dark here pretty quick. Do you want me to walk you home?"

Remembering how determined he had been to walk her home after the tryst the night before, the butterflies in Haven's stomach woke up and took flight.

Shaking her head, however, she answered, "No, I'll be leavin' in a minute here. But thank you so much for offerin'."

Valentine's tired eyes narrowed. "I'm more'n happy to wait on you. You're sure you'll be home before dark?" he reiterated.

"Of course," Haven assured him. "And even if I'm not, it's not far, and I'm perfectly safe in Fletcher."

"Just say you'll be home before dark. For my own peace of mind, all right?" he pressed.

"All right," Haven agreed. "I'll be home before dark. And I think you best be on your way. A man does need a good night's rest."

Valentine still seemed a bit distrustful, and

Haven wondered why he would be so concerned about her being home before dark. It wasn't as if they lived in the heart of one of the crime-ridden alleys in Atlanta.

"All right. Goodnight, Miss Abernathy," Valentine said.

"Goodnight, Mr. Briscoe," Haven replied.

Valentine left the Sandersans' house then, closing the door behind him.

It was no more than a matter of a few seconds before Wynifred and Merigold descended upon Haven, shooting out questions faster than buttered bullets.

"What on earth was that about?" Wynifred asked.

"Did he kiss you goodnight?" Merigold inquired.

Haven rolled her eyes and giggled. "Oh, for pity's sake, no, Miss Merigold," she said—though goose bumps broke over her arms and legs at the thought of his having done so. "He just wanted to make certain I was home before dark . . . wanted to wait to walk me home if I wasn't plannin' on it."

"And you didn't go with him?" Wynifred exclaimed. "What on earth were you thinkin', girl?"

Haven smiled. Oh, how she loved the two older ladies! They nearly mother-henned her to death sometimes—and she adored it!

"Well, I'm certainly not gonna leave the two of you with supper dishes to do and—" Haven began.

"Oh, poppycock!" Merigold fussed. "That man likes you, Haven! Why, you march right out that door, take hold of that handsome piece of muscle's arm, and let him walk you home!"

Haven felt a strange need—a feeling akin to desperation.

"It doesn't matter if he likes me, Miss Merigold," she quietly countered.

"What? Why not?" Wynifred asked, frowning.

"Because . . . because I have a secret," Haven confessed—surprising herself with what she then meant to do. "And . . . and if Mr. Briscoe ever discovered what my secret is, I promise you, he would not just stop likin' me. He'd hate and loathe me. Everyone would."

"Oh, nonsense!" Merigold argued. "Everybody's got secrets, Haven honey. I guarantee Mr. Valentine Briscoe himself has secrets."

But Haven shook her head. "Not like mine," she breathed, tears welling in her eyes.

"Oh, now come on, honey," Wynifred said, putting a consoling arm around Haven's shoulders. "No secret is so bad that it would make a man run from a woman like you."

"This one would."

Haven watched as Wynifred and Merigold exchanged glances of deep concern.

"Well, what is it then, sweet pea?" Merigold asked. "What kind of secret could a pretty, young thing like you possibly have that would keep a man away?"

Summoning every ounce and breath of courage in her being, Haven said, "I'm an Indian. I'm one-quarter Cherokee Indian."

Wynifred and Merigold exchanged glances once more—this time glances of astonishment. If the two women who treated her like their own daughter found surprise and disgust in her revelation, then what would anyone else think of her now—especially Valentine Briscoe?

CHAPTER ELEVEN

"My mother's mother, my grandmother Adair, was born in Georgia in 1818," Haven began as she sat on the sofa in the Sandersans' parlor. She brushed tears from her cheeks, for she was frightened that, in spite of their encouragement, Wynifred and Merigold would no longer love and adore her as nearly their own kin once they'd heard the whole of what she meant to confide in them. And yet something deep within Haven felt driven to reveal her secret. Perhaps it was the fact that her parents were gone; with her mother not having to bear the scandal such a revelation would've brought to her, perhaps Haven felt liberated somehow. Or perhaps it was just the desire to be entirely forthcoming with the two older ladies who had encouraged, helped, and cared for her. Whatever the reason, Haven knew that if she didn't tell Wynifred and Merigold everything, she would regret it in some manner.

Thus, she continued. "Her name was . . . her name *is* Amadahy. It means Forest Water. I . . . I found photographs of her made as recent as two years ago—photographs my mother had never shown me. I have always thought she was dead— long ago dead—for my mother spoke of her as if she only ever existed in the past."

Haven paused, gripped by a mingling of emotions—regret, fear, sadness, loneliness, even anger at her mother's having never told her that Amadahy Adair was still alive.

"Go on, sweetheart," Wynifred urged gently. "You just tell us everythin'. We're not goin' anywhere."

Haven nodded and brushed more tears from her cheeks. "Amadahy's family, bein' members of the Overhill Cherokee, knew further change was inevitable and thus wished to make peace with the frontiersmen, the farmers, even the merchants who began migrating inland after the Revolutionary War—unlike the lower and river town peoples who fought against change and integration. Amadahy's family—her parents, at least—were even wealthy in a fashion. Though I am chagrinned to admit it, they even owned African slaves . . . treatin' their slaves no better than any other people that owned human bein's."

Haven hesitated as her throat constricted with more emotion. Before that moment, only her father and mother, Mipsie, Joe, and Arabella knew Haven's secret. And even for her adoration of and trust in Wynifred and Merigold, fear of reprisal continued to grip her.

"Go on, honey," Merigold tenderly prodded. "There's not a thing in all the world that can surprise us or make us feel differently toward you, I promise." Merigold exchanged

296

understanding glances with Wynifred, and when Wynifred nodded, indicating permission to her sister, Merigold added, "We have ancestors who owned people, as well. And it is not somethin' we talk about or share with others either. It wasn't us, it's in the past, and we are not sullied with that loathsome sin. Neither are you. Remember that."

Nodding and swallowing the lump of anxiety in her throat, Haven progressed.

"Well, it would seem that my grandmother was a very beautiful woman," Haven introduced.

"Oh, I'm certain of that!" Wynifred quietly exclaimed. "Aren't you, Merigold?"

"Oh, absolutely," Merigold softly agreed with a strong nod of affirmation. "If she looked anything at all like you, Haven, I'm sure your grandmother was stunnin'."

Haven grinned a little, comforted, as well as somewhat amused, at the efforts the sisters were making to settle her. And she noted that she was not as afraid as she was even a minute before. She had told them she was Indian, and yet there they sat, smiling, encouraging, comforting her, just as they always had. It gave hope a venue to begin rising within her.

"But go on, sweetie," Wynifred said. "I'm sorry for interruptin'."

Inhaling a new breath of determination, Haven indeed soldiered on.

"My grandmother was said to be very beautiful, and by the time she was nineteen, she had married my grandfather—John Adair, a Scotsman whose family had left their homeland when he was just a boy. Just over a year after their marriage, my grandmother gave birth to my mother, naming her Tayanita, or Young Beaver. My grandfather, however, wanted my mother to avoid bein' characterized 'a half-breed' and therefore added Merial as her first given name. Tragically, my grandfather Adair died of consumption just after my mother was born. And so my grandmother took my mother and returned to her family."

"Did your grandmother, havin' married a Scotsman . . . was she exempt from relocatin' when the Cherokee people were driven out of Georgia then?"

Haven shook her head, sniffling. "No. Although she had been married to my grandfather Adair, she was livin' with her own parents when President Jackson chose to enforce the Indian Removal Act, upon which President Van Buren gave the final order of removal. Knowing my mother would have a greater chance of survival, as well as a better life, with my grandfather's people than with her own, my grandmother went to John Adair's brother and his wife, beggin' them to take my mother, to raise her as their own—for she felt obliged to accompany her family durin' the relocation to the Indian

Territory west of the Mississippi." Again Haven paused, sniffling in trying to stay her tears. "My grandfather's brother agreed to raise my mother, thus savin' her from almost certain death, as well as ensurin' that she was raised in white society. It was always a heartbreakin' tale for me to think on, for only my grandmother survived the death march to the Indian Territory. Every single member of her family—her parents, her brothers, her sisters, all of them . . . even the slaves they brought with them—all of them perished along the trail, leavin' my grandmother as the lone survivor of her kin to be settled there."

Daring to glance up to Wynifred and Merigold, Haven was astonished to see both women brushing tears from their own cheeks.

"The Trail of Tears, they call it," Merigold whispered. "And all because men are greedy when it comes to gold . . . value it more than human life itself!"

"The Georgia Gold Rush, the Trail of Tears . . ." Wynifred sighed with heartache. "I remember Daddy and Mama talkin' about it when we were girls, don't you, Merigold? Talkin' about what an abhorrent abomination it all was."

Merigold nodded. "I do. Oh, I most certainly do."

"And to think, after all she sacrificed . . . givin' up her own child!" Wynifred exclaimed. "After everythin', she lost her family . . . her entire family."

Haven gulped down the pain she was feeling—empathy for her grandmother's plight. "She was not yet twenty-one when she crossed the Trail of Tears," Haven offered. "I . . . I never knew any more about her. I never knew Mama did—not until I found the photographs of her after Mama and Daddy died."

"Well, do you know where the photograph was taken?" Merigold piped up. "Or . . . or can't you write so someone down there in the territory where they settled the Cherokee can inquire about her?"

Haven inhaled a breath of slight reprieve as Wynifred added, "Why, yes! Can't we just send a telegram or somethin' down there? Surely someone knows somethin' about your grand-mother and whether she's still livin'. No doubt she would love to know she has a granddaughter who cares for her!"

Smiling with further relief as she realized that the Sandersans did not seem prepared to disown her over her ancestry, Haven confessed, "I posted a letter to the postmaster there, in the northern territory, where the photograph was taken. And I will admit that I am so hopeful in hearin' good news in return."

Merigold gleefully clapped her hands together, exclaiming, "Oh yes! That was so clever of

300

you, Haven. Surely someone will have heard of a beautiful old woman there. Oh, I do hope they have a postmaster who's willin' to help!" Merigold frowned a moment, put one index finger to her chin, tipped her head to one side, and said, "Hmmm. I hope they have a postmaster at all. I hear it's quite spacious out there."

"Just think, Haven honey," Wynifred declared, "you might still have a chance of findin' her, maybe meetin' up with her one day. Oh, how wonderful that would be!"

Haven felt as if a sudden heaviness had been lifted from her shoulders. Why, the Sandersan sisters didn't seem at all disturbed by what she had revealed about herself. In truth, they seemed quite pleased and excitable about it.

"So . . . you're not disgusted with me or . . . or regrettin' havin' made my acquaintance . . . or that you encouraged me to move out here near you? You don't hate Indians?" Haven ventured. It all seemed so unexpected, Wynifred's and Merigold's lack of astonishment.

"Oh, for pity's sake, Haven! Of course not!" Wynifred exclaimed as if she were a bit offended by Haven's inquiry. "Why on earth would we feel any differently about you? And we don't hate Indians! Why would we hate Indians?" Wynifred paused as if Haven had asked her the most horrifying question she ever could have. "I do admit to loathin' evil, and there's evil in every peoples. Indians aren't an evil people. Freedmen aren't an evil people. You know that. Why, evil don't nest accordin' to color, race, or language. It just chooses to settle in those who allow it to. And besides, for my part, I find you all the more interestin' for your heritage, young lady. Don't you, Merigold?"

As Wynifred looked to her sister, Merigold did not hesitate in the least in saying, "Yes indeed, my oh my! A beautiful Cherokee princess . . . right here in our parlor!"

Haven arched one doubtful eyebrow, even giggled a little, and said, "Oh, fiddle-faddle, Miss Merigold! Now you're just bein' plain preposterous."

"No, I am not," Merigold defended herself, however. "And how do you know you're *not* a Cherokee princess, hmmm? Your mama didn't tell you a whole lot about her mother's family . . . so it's just as possible that you are as it is that you are not."

"No wonder that Valentine Briscoe couldn't take his eyes off you durin' supper," Wynifred offered. "Might be he has some royal lineage of his own and his soul recognized you as royal blood as well."

"I wonder what Mr. Briscoe would think if he knew he had a princess right under his nose?" Merigold offered.

"Oh no! He can never know! Never!" Haven

gasped, leaping up from her seat on the sofa. Her throat felt as if it were constricting, and her heart began to pound furiously at the thought of Valentine Briscoe's ever discovering her secret. "Oh, he'd hate me! I know he would. Everyone in town would if they ever found out!"

"Haven honey, settle down, dear," Wynifred soothed. "It wouldn't be the end of the world if—"

Dropping to her knees before the two older ladies, Haven begged, "Please! Please promise me you'll never tell another livin' soul about me . . . about my secret! Promise me! Please!"

Tears were once more streaming down over her cheeks, and Haven found she was trembling. Fear had again gripped her. What if Valentine Briscoe ever *did* find out about her? Oh, she couldn't bear the thought of him looking at her with disgust instead of pleased amusement. She couldn't bear it!

"Oh, sweetie!" Merigold chirped, a deep frown furrowing her already wrinkled brow. "We would never tell anyone someone else's secret . . . never! Your secret is so safe in our hearts. So very, very safe."

"We will take it to our graves, Haven," Wynifred confirmed. "You know that, don't you?"

"Y-yes," Haven stammered.

"And anyway," Merigold sighed, "it's not as if

you're the only one in town with a secret as big as that."

Feeling somewhat soothed once more, Haven nodded. "Oh, I know, I know," she admitted. "I knew the minute I saw May and Edith Crabtree that they shared a secret like Ara . . . like mine. I know that."

But when neither Sandersan sister said anything further to confirm or deny the obvious truth of May and Edith Crabtree's lineage, Haven stared at them for a moment.

"That's not what I meant," Merigold whispered. "I meant that there are many secrets held here in Fletcher. Everyone has a secret, Haven—May and Edith Crabtree, you . . . and me and Wynnie."

Haven frowned. Merigold's eyes were moist with new tears, as were Wynifred's.

"What do you mean?" Haven asked. "Do you mean . . . do you two hold a secret lineage the way May and I do?"

But Merigold shook her head. "No," she answered. Then she shrugged and added, "Well, maybe, somewhere way back. I'm not sure. But it's not the secret we cache most desperately. No, it is not."

"I don't understand," Haven sighed. She was tired, thoroughly fatigued from revealing what she'd kept to herself for so very, very long—for nearly her entire life.

Wynifred looked to Merigold, smiled rather sadly, and said, "Run get a hairbrush, Merigold, will you?"

"Of course, Wynnie," Merigold answered. Without hesitation, Merigold stood and walked toward the back of the house.

"A hairbrush?" Haven asked, entirely confused.

Wynifred nodded. "Yes. Because if Merigold and I are gonna talk about our secret—about our boys—then I want the pleasure of brushin' your hair while we do it. It'll help you to settle down. And it'll help me too."

"But I—" Haven began.

Wynifred held up one trembling hand to stay Haven's question, however. "Let's wait until Merigold is back with us. After all, it's her secret too."

❋ ❋ ❋ ❋ ❋

"Well, where should I begin?" Wynifred inquired of Merigold.

Haven sat in one of the kitchen chairs, quiet as a mouse, as Wynifred began brushing her hair. And, oh, it did serve to soothe her! Even for the slight soreness in the place where the bee had stung her, Haven felt that with each stroke of the hairbrush through her long hair, Wynifred Sandersan brushed a little more of her cares and anxiety away.

"Start with that fact that you and I are not

the spinster Sandersan sisters the way we lead everyone to believe," Merigold answered.

"What?" Haven asked.

She watched as Merigold plunged a fork into the large cinnamon roll sitting on the plate on the table in front of her. Using the fork, Merigold tore a portion of the cinnamon roll away, discarded the utensil then, and simply picked the sweet bread up with her fingers.

Taking a big bite, Merigold uncharacteristically did not finish chewing before she said, "Wynnie and I are not spinsters. The Sandersan brothers were our husbands—Herbert and Hubert Sandersan. They were twins. And what their mama was thinkin' namin' them Herbert and Hubert, I will never know! That's why Wynnie and I called them Bert and Rusty. Bert is Wynnie's husband, and Rusty is mine."

"You . . . you were both married?" Haven inquired—for in truth, she was quite astonished. Everyone in town assumed Wynifred and Merigold Sandersan had never married. Thus, to know they had married—and married twin brothers at that—it was quite astonishing.

"The way we see it, we still are married," Wynifred answered, her brushing of Haven's hair never breaking rhythm.

"Wynnie was eighteen when she married Bert," Merigold offered. "We had a double weddin', even though I was only sixteen at the time.

Daddy liked Rusty, knew he was a good man, so he granted us permission to marry when Bert and Wynnie did."

"Oh my goodness!" Haven breathed. "I-I had no idea!"

"That's because no one here knows. That's how we want it," Wynifred explained. "We had our wills drawn up before we moved to Fletcher, and they're with our solicitor in Denver. My will states that when I pass on, my tombstone is to read, *Mrs. Herbert Sandersan. Wynifred to her friends*. And no one will know until I'm dead."

"And mine will read, *Mrs. Hubert 'Rusty' Sandersan. Merigold to her friends*. And no one will know until I'm dead," Merigold stated.

"But . . . why?" Haven couldn't keep from asking. "Why is it such a secret? Are your husbands outlaws or somethin'?"

Both Wynifred and Merigold chuckled and exchanged amused glances.

"No, sweet pea," Wynifred began. "Bert and Rusty were the greatest of men . . . heroes. Devoted husbands and wonderful fathers."

"You have children?" Haven exclaimed. "How could it be you have children but still manage to live as if you were never—"

"We have children," Merigold whispered, "but none still livin', honey."

Instantly, Haven's eyes filled with tears as realization began to strike her. By her estimation,

Wynifred and Merigold were maybe ten to fifteen years older than her own mother had been—exactly the right age to have had grown children at the time the war broke out. Haven's mother had not given birth to Haven until she was nearly thirty. Born to a young bride like Wynifred or Merigold, Haven could easily have been in her forties by now—in her early twenties at the time of the war.

"Did the war take them?" Haven ventured as tears spilled from her eyes.

Merigold sniffled, stuffed another large bite of cinnamon roll into her mouth, and nodded. "My little Lulabelle died when she was just five years old. She had a terrible fever one day, and then . . ." Merigold paused and tore another piece of cinnamon roll. "But my sons grew up into men—fine young men indeed." She smiled, even though more tears trickled over her cheeks. "Then Carthel was killed at Chickamauga, and my Loren died in Andersonville prison in '64."

Merigold was silent then, and Haven brushed tears from her cheeks—wondered at how much heartache and loss people could endure before they would die of a broken heart the way Mrs. Latham had done.

"I lost both of my boys at Chickamauga—September 19, 1863—the day before Carthel was killed," Wynifred said. "Both of my boys and both of my nephews." She was quiet for a moment. Her voice cracked with emotion when she added, "We lost Bert and Rusty at Gettysburg, on the same day—July 2, 1863."

Merigold smiled up at her sister through her tears. "Wynnie and I have always been thankful that Bert and Rusty went together. It seemed fittin' for twins."

Haven started to pull her hair out of Wynifred's hands.

"Oh, let me brush it awhile longer, sweet pea," Wynifred's weak voice pleaded. "It helps me . . . calms me as much as it will you."

"But I can't just sit here, lettin' you brush my hair, knowin' the pain and loss you all have suffered!" Haven wept. "Oh my goodness! And to think, there I was just minutes ago, thinkin' I had a burden to bear. How foolish I've been all this time. Everyone *does* have secrets—painful, nearly unendurable secrets. I've been so selfish, so self-centered, and—"

"Hush, now, honey," Merigold cooed. "You're no fool, Haven. You're sharp as tack, beautiful as a princess—"

"Talented, kind, lovin', thoughtful," Wynifred continued. "And I know your worries are valid where your secret is concerned. I know there are people, even round about here, that have suffered greatly at the hands of Indians—who forget how the Indians have suffered so greatly at the hands of settlers. I know. Just like in Georgia, where some folks no doubt blame free black people for bein' free. It's hate, it's prejudice—all around it is. But maybe someday things won't be that way."

"But your husbands! Your children!" Haven sobbed.

Merigold reached across the table, placing a somewhat sticky hand over one of Haven's in a kind, comforting manner.

"And that's why we keep it to ourselves," she said, forcing a smile. "It *is* painful. There were times when neither Wynnie nor I thought we could go on livin'. And that's when we decided to do what we've done."

Haven wiped at the tears on her cheeks. "To move somewhere where no one knew you or your pain and loss," she offered. "Somewhere where you could just be the rather eccentric spinsterly Sandersan sisters."

"See?" Merigold chirped. "I told you she was smart, Wynnie!"

Haven smiled a little as Merigold patted her hand again before returning to tearing apart the remains of the cinnamon roll before her.

"It's less painful when you don't have to bear the constant sympathy of others . . . or answer questions about your past when thinkin' on your past hurts so much," Wynifred explained.

"Though we can think of Rusty, Bert, the boys, and my Lulabelle now . . . and remember the happy times without feelin' like we would rather die," Merigold added. "It took years. It took leavin' our homes and movin' west where we did not know a soul. But we healed. We've got deep scars and plenty of them, but I think you can see that we're truly happy. Maybe not as happy as we could've been if the war had never come along. But we do know happiness."

Wynifred stopped brushing Haven's hair then and leaned over her shoulder, pressing one wrinkled cheek to Haven's smooth one and saying, "And you, my angel love, are one of our greatest happinesses. Truly the most wonderful, joyful thing we've had in our lives in twenty years."

"And that's why we want you and that handsome Valentine Briscoe to quit fightin' the sizzlin' attraction the two of you feel for one another," Merigold said, smiling once more at last.

Haven laughed—wholeheartedly laughed. "Miss Merigold, have you lost your mind? Valentine Briscoe? Why, that man is too much man for me . . . no matter how I pine away for him in secret."

"I knew it! I knew it!" Merigold squealed. "I just knew you were taken with that man. And he's taken with you. It's as plain as the nose on his handsome face!"

"No, no, no," Haven countered, shaking her head. Even as the memory of the night before—

being in Valentine's arms, the reverie of the sensation of his lips claiming hers—washed over her, causing goose bumps to prickle her arms, Haven shook her head. "No, no. It could never happen," she said firmly.

"Well, why ever not?" Wynifred inquired. "Merigold's right! He couldn't quit starin' at you all through dinner!"

"More than likely he was just waitin' for me to do somethin' ridiculous," Haven suggested. "And besides, if he ever found out that I'm . . . that I'm . . ."

"That you're an Indian princess?" Merigold offered with a wink.

"Miss Merigold," Haven whined, "please don't tease me. Valentine is from here . . . from very near here. I doubt he's any lover of Indians, princess or otherwise."

"How will you know unless you give him the opportunity to tell you one day?" Merigold asked.

"Never!" Haven said, fairly leaping up from her chair. "And anyway, I promised him I would be home before dark, and I've already broken that promise," she added, realizing that the sun had indeed already set.

Wynifred took Haven by the shoulders, looking at her intensely. "Now, you listen to me, Haven. I love you like my own daughter." Wynifred nodded toward Merigold. "And so does Merigold. We want happiness for you. We do. More than anything we want that. But we do understand the weight of secrets, and we do understand that some secrets must be kept, no matter what."

"We will never tell a soul your secret, Haven," Merigold firmly assured. "Never. Even if we do want you to find your way into Valentine Briscoe's bed one day . . ."

"Merigold! For pity's sake!" Wynifred scolded, although giggling as she did so.

"I meant his weddin' bed, of course," Merigold said with a wink. "Get your mind out of the mud, Wynifred Sandersan." Merigold smiled. "We won't ever tell him . . . or anyone, Haven. We've trusted you with our secret, haven't we? And you need to trust us as much as we've trusted you."

Haven did feel a calming peace come over her then. She knew the Sandersan sisters would never share her secret. And she would never share theirs—never.

"I'm sorry," she breathed. "I suppose I'm just tired. I didn't sleep a wink last night, and then all that pear pickin' today . . . and supper . . ." She leaned forward, placing a tender kiss to Wynifred's cheek—turned then and kissed Merigold's. "I cannot imagine what my life would be without the two of you. I love you both so much. So very much!"

"Oh, we love you too, honey!" Wynifred and Merigold chimed in unison.

With the sensation of having had a burden lifted

once more—even for the new, empathic pain she now held for her cherished friends—her heart felt freer, as if it had been moved into a larger space where it could beat without being quite as fearful.

Val remained in the shadows of the north side of the Sandersan sisters' house. He'd been too worried about Haven getting home safely to leave. Dusk had turned into sunset and sunset into moonrise before the front door of the cozy little house finally opened.

Stepping further back into the shadows, Val watched and listened as the two old spinsters exchanged pleasantries and goodnights with Haven. Then, once Haven had begun her walk home, Val followed her, silently keeping to the shadows. He was only mildly miffed that she hadn't kept her promise to be home before dark. After all, he was not unfamiliar with the ways of women when they got to cackling like hens in the coop. It was a joy that men did not understand. Yet a good man respected the fact that it was a woman's joy, whether or not he understood it. At least, that's what Val's daddy had always taught him.

As he followed Haven, Val realized how truly in peril she could be had it not been for his following her—had it instead been men bent on . . .

The sudden glint of moonlight on Haven's long raven hair distracted Val from his anxious thoughts. It was only then, in silver light of the moonrise, that Val realized Haven's hair was no longer braided but hung long and straight down her back to below her waist, like soft, sable silk—though even darker than sable—black. The sight was mesmerizing in its beauty and allure.

Val felt his eyebrows arch in astonishment as the idea leapt to his mind that her hair would feel like velvet next to his skin. A sudden desire to take Haven in his arms, throw her to the ground, and kiss her—no. He wanted to take Haven in his arms, throw himself to lay on his back on the ground so that as he kissed her, the soft raven of her hair would descend upon him like a silken veil.

And then, in the next moment, Haven reached up, running her hands over her head as she combed her hair. Val stopped. Dead in his tracks he stopped. As Haven walked on, Val watched the way her hair swayed back and forth in rhythm with her steps—and the familiarity of the sight began to prick at his mind.

Slowly he recommenced in following her, for he was concerned for her safety. Perhaps there were no evil men in Fletcher. He certainly hoped not. But there was a saloon. And some men who were otherwise good men had been known to turn to evil once enough liquor had been poured into them. Still, as he followed Haven—as he watched her hair swing back and forth, imagined how such black velvet would feel on his skin—his thoughts continued to be pricked by something, something so familiar and yet still elusive to explanation.

Val watched and followed, determined to serve as Haven's invisible protector—at least for that night.

As they neared the cemetery so close to her house, Haven reached over her shoulders, parting her hair at the nape of her neck and pulling it forward before running her hands over her head, combing it again with her fingers.

Again Val stopped. But this time, he knew what was familiar about Haven's hair and her mannerisms with it. He'd seen hair like hers before. Not nearly as beautiful but just as long and just as black.

Swallowing the lump in his throat as heinous and painful memories began to flame inside him, Val breathed, "Indian."

CHAPTER TWELVE

H e took the train to Limon to visit his folks for a bit," Robert Henry explained.

"Oh, well, that's nice," Haven commented.

She smiled, glancing to her right as Robert held her hand and then to her left as Ronald held her other hand. The boys were walking along at a rather leisurely pace, and Haven guessed it was because they were trying to stretch out the errand their mother had sent them on with Haven. Haven understood perfectly. When she and Arabella were little girls, many were the times they had stretched an errand to last as long as possible in order to avoid whatever chores or other responsibilities awaited them when they returned. Haven knew Robert and Ronald would much rather be escorting her out to Mr. Briscoe's farm—so Haven could offer Valentine the opportunity to judge the apple butter contest at the Harvest Festival—than they would be back home doing chores.

"Yep," Ronald concurred. "And he paid us each a whole silver dollar for feeding his animals and such while he was gone!"

"My goodness! That is quite a lot of money indeed!" Haven said dramatically.

"Yep," Robert agreed. "And he said we done a

right good job of takin' care of things . . . said he'd hire us again the next time he went over to Limon to visit his folks."

Ronald tugged at Haven's hand, saying, "We might not be the best in the etiquette class, Miss Abernathy, but we're mighty hard workers."

Haven smiled down at Ronald and let go of his hand just long enough to tousle his sunshine-colored hair.

"Why, you and Robert are fine young men, Ronald," Haven assured him. "And your manners and social dancin' skills are outstandin'! Don't you ever let me hear you talkin' them down like that, all right? You're wonderful, both of you, and I'm so glad I've had the chance to meet you and teach you and be your friend. I can certainly see why Mr. Briscoe chose the two of you to tend to his farm while he was away. Why, you're just the most trustworthy, dependable boys I know. Mr. Briscoe reveals himself to be a very wise man in trustin' you boys."

Haven's smile broadened as both Ronald's and Robert's chests puffed with pride.

"Thank you, Miss Abernathy," the boys said in unison.

"We do try," Robert added.

"Oh, I know you do, both of you," Haven confirmed.

"I love the Harvest Festival," Ronald sighed. "All that apple pie and such. I hope the Sandersan sisters bring some of their cinnamon rolls again this year. They're my favorite!"

"The Sandersan sisters bring their cinnamon rolls every year, Ronald," Robert rather grouched. "Why wouldn't they bring them this year?"

Ronald shrugged. "I don't know. I've just been worried that they won't."

"Well, I'll make sure and put a bug in their ears for you, Ronald," Haven promised, "just to make sure they don't forget, all right? But why didn't you just ask them yourself?" Haven inquired. "I know they would be just heartbroken to know you've been worryin' over it."

Again Ronald shrugged. "I don't know. I suppose because older people kind of make me nervous," the boy admitted. "I'm always afraid that they don't want me talkin' to them or somethin'."

"Older people love children," Haven assured the boy. "At least most do. And I happen to know that the Misses Sandersan would be tickled pink if you took to visitin' with them once in a while. Why, I bet if you planned a day ahead—let them know you were comin' by one afternoon—well, I'm certain they'd have somethin' baked and yummy waitin' for you when you arrived."

"Do you really think so, Miss Abernathy?" Ronald asked with excitement.

Haven laughed. "Oh, I know so, sweetie! I know so. I myself have never been to visit with

Miss Wynifred and Miss Merigold without havin' some sort of delicious treat waitin' for me."

"I'm gonna do it, Miss Abernathy!" Ronald stated with exuberance. "I'll wait until a few days after the festival though. I don't want them bakin' themselves to death."

Haven giggled quietly. "I think that is very thoughtful and well mannered of you, Ronald. You truly are a gentleman."

"Look at the leaves today, Miss Abernathy," Robert sighed with admiration. "I just love when the quakies are yellow!"

"It is beautiful country here," Haven affirmed as she glanced around the Colorado vista of pine and gold.

The air was indeed much cooler, even than it had been the day before. Autumn came early to Fletcher, and with it brought the beauty of the year's serene repose. Indeed, the pines on the foothills and mountains, tall and straight and maintaining their deep virility, were occasionally interlaced with the bright xanthous of Aspens. The combination—such stark evergreen and vivid yellow—was awe-inspiring in its perfect contrast. Here and there were also groves of only aspens assembled, standing like tall kindred— timbers of treasure with royal manes of gold.

In truth, though the colors of the leaves of the aspens were not so diverse as the crimson of the maples nor the oranges of the dogwoods of

Georgia, there was something about the cool of the air in Fletcher, the dry quality, that made it lighter than the heavy humidity of the South. And the lovely gold of the aspens offered Haven a tranquility she had never known before.

As beautiful and in complement to the trees, the sky was a perfect canvas of blue, dappled with large, fluffy clouds hither and yon and an occasional arrow of geese flying south overhead. The grasses were yet green, but not so green as they had been in summer, as if they were preparing to settle in for the long nap winter would bless them with. It was a beautiful place to be.

"Are you glad you came to live in Fletcher, Miss Abernathy?" Robert inquired, exactly as if he'd read her thoughts.

"Oh yes, Robert!" Haven exclaimed with honesty. "And for so many reasons." She winked at Robert, adding, "One of the best of which is meeting you."

Robert blushed, smiled, and hung his head a moment.

"You think Mr. Briscoe will agree to judge the apple butter, Miss Abernathy?" Ronald asked.

Inhaling a deep breath as her heart began to beat more quickly at being reminded she was on her way to see Valentine, she answered, "I certainly hope so, Ronald. I can't imagine why he would refuse. Although one never can be sure what a person might do in these kinds of situations."

"I think he'll do it," Robert said. "Mr. Briscoe ain't the kind to have a yeller stripe down his back. He ain't afraid of nothin'.""

Haven smiled at Robert's assault on proper grammar. But she wasn't holding an instruction class, so who was she to correct him? Furthermore, Haven had a fondness toward the manner of speech of those who had grown up out west. She found it quite delightful and often felt as if something important might be lost if the children of Fletcher were to lose their colloquial way of conversing.

"He sure ain't," Ronald agreed. "And Daddy says he ain't never seen a man work so hard in cuttin' and haulin' timber before."

"Do you mean to say Mr. Briscoe has been preparin' his firewood for winter? And that's why I haven't seen hardly hide nor hair of him in almost two weeks?" Haven asked.

The truth was, Haven had been awash with worry and anxiety nearly all day, every day, since she had enjoyed supper with Valentine and the Sandersan sisters the evening following the pear picking at Valentine's orchard. She'd begun to wonder if perhaps she had offended him in some way—or even worse, if he'd somehow managed to guess her secret and found himself loathing her. In fact, ever since she'd sent the letter to her grandmother Adair—since the moment Mr.

Crabtree had mumbled, "Indian Territory, huh?" under his breath as he'd marked an X over the stamp with his pencil—she'd worried that someone would become suspicious. After all, what reason did anyone have to post a letter to Indian Territory unless a body was acquainted with Indians—or related to them?

"Yep," Ronald responded. "He's been bringin' in so much wood that Mama says everybody in town will be toasty warm all winter long."

Exhaling a sigh of relief—relief that had been elusive to Haven for near to two weeks—Haven said, "Well, that makes sense then. Between visitin' his family and haulin' wood . . . well, that *would* keep a man mighty busy."

"Yes, ma'am," Ronald agreed.

"Mama says that's why Mr. Briscoe fills his shirt out so nice," Robert mentioned. "She says that after fellin' the timber, cuttin' it, and splittin' it, Mr. Briscoe must have muscles like a Greek god . . . whatever that is."

Haven bit her lip to keep from giggling. It seemed other women in town had noticed how muscular Valentine was.

"And Daddy told Mama that if he had nothin' better to do all day than swing an ax, he could fill out his shirt like a Greek god too," Ronald added.

"Then Mama told Daddy that he already filled out his shirt plenty perfect," Robert continued.

"And then Daddy and Mama took to smoochin'! Right there in front of all us children!"

Haven couldn't keep from laughing then. And when the boys both looked up to her with inquisitively wrinkled eyebrows, she said, "But, boys, daddies and mamas are supposed to smooch in front of their children. That way the children gain reassurance that their parents love one another."

Robert frowned, grumbling, "I don't need to see no insurance that my parents love each other. I know they do."

Ronald, however, smiled as big as an opossum eating a sweet potato. "I can't wait 'til I'm old enough to go sparkin'," he stated. "And I know just who I'm gonna go sparkin' with."

"And who might that be?" Haven couldn't resist asking.

"Why, Fanny Dunklin, of course," Robert answered for his brother. "Ronnie is as sweet on Fanny as a baby suckin' on a sugar teat!"

"Yes, I am," Ronald confirmed. "And I ain't ashamed to say it!"

"Well, good for you, Ronald," Haven encouraged. "You should never be ashamed of carin' for somebody."

"Uh . . . but don't go tellin' Fanny, all right, Miss Abernathy?" Ronald added. "I ain't quite ready for her to know. I figure in another five or ten years I'll tell her."

"I understand," Haven promised. Oh, how she adored the Henry boys—even more now that they had informed her that Valentine had been gone gathering timber for winter and visiting his family. Maybe he hadn't been avoiding her after all.

* * * * *

Val growled, rolled over, and opened his eyes when he heard the knock on his front door.

Raking a hand back through his hair, he grumbled, "Who's got reason to be beatin' on my damn door now? The pears have all been picked. I've been scoutin' and haulin' wood. You'd think folks would know not to go wakin' snakes."

As Val rather stumbled out of bed, he pulled his quilt up, wrapping it around his waist. Still groggy as he stomped toward the front door, he did note that the sun was bright. He'd overslept again.

"I gotta start gettin' more sleep," he yawned.

Taking hold of the door latch, he pulled the door open to see none other than Haven Abernathy and the two Henry twins standing at his threshold.

"Mornin', Mr. Briscoe," one of the towheaded boys greeted with a friendly smile. Val didn't know which Henry boy it was, as he still had trouble determining which one was Ronald and which one was Robert. And that was when he was full-wide awake.

"Mornin', boys," Val managed. "Mornin', Miss Abernathy," he added with a wink.

Val couldn't keep from grinning as he watched Haven unconsciously look him over from head to toe. She looked so astonished that he wouldn't have been surprised if her eyes had bugged right out of her head.

"What can I do you for this mornin'?" Val asked.

Just for his own amusement, he purposely pushed down the quilt bunched in his hand at his waist to rest below his navel, nearly bursting into laughter as Haven's eyes grew even wider. She even took a step back, as if seeing a man standing before her in such a casual state of undress had shoved her a little.

"Well, me and Ronald and Miss Abernathy here have been dispatched to give you an invitation, sir," the boy said.

"An invitation?" Val asked, looking from the boy who must be Robert to his brother and back. Danged if he still couldn't figure a way to tell them apart.

"Yes, sir," Ronald confirmed. "The town committee in charge of the Harvest Festival tomorrow would like for you to serve as the judge for the apple butter contest."

"Is that right?" Val inquired, staring at Haven.

He'd almost forgotten how beautiful she was, the silken quality of her hair. He was disappointed to see that she was, once again, the vision of propriety, wearing her hair piled on her head, with a perky green hat adorned with feathers and ribbons as her crowning glory.

"Yes, sir," one of the boys answered. Val hadn't been looking at the Henry boys, so he wasn't sure which one of them had responded.

"Will you do it, Mr. Briscoe?" the one standing on Haven's right pressed.

Val gazed at Haven a moment. His eyes narrowed as he studied her face—her perfectly angled, high-set cheekbones; straight, dainty nose; and most of all, her mesmerizing emerald almond-shaped eyes, so alluringly flattered by thick, long, dark lashes.

"Damn," he mumbled with admiration.

"What's that, Mr. Briscoe?" one of the Henry boys asked.

"Uh . . . I meant to say, sure thing, boys," Val stammered. "I think I can manage to taste a few apple butters made by the lovely ladies of Fletcher."

Haven smiled, exhaling a breath as if she'd expected him to refuse.

"Well, that's just fine, Mr. Briscoe!" the other Henry boy exclaimed. "That sure is a good answer for us to take back to our ma . . . to the committee, sir."

Val reached out, tousling one boy's straw-colored hair and then the other's. "What time should I be there?"

The Henry twins leaned a little forward and looked around Haven to each other while shrugging.

"I believe the festivities are set to begin at six o'clock, Mr. Briscoe," Haven answered for them.

Val nodded. "Then I'll be there at six o'clock sharp," he assured her.

"Thank you," she said. She paused in taking her leave, however. "We haven't seen much of you around town of late, Mr. Briscoe. I hope you're doin' well."

"Yes, ma'am," Val said with a nod.

"Miss Abernathy, we already told you that he was out visitin' his family, haulin' wood, and such," one of the Henry boys whispered so loudly Val figured everyone in town heard what he said.

"Oh . . . oh, I know," Haven responded, blushing so red Val was afraid she might burst. "But I . . . I . . ."

"I think your etiquette teacher here is tryin' to say that a body ought always to inquire after someone's well-bein' when visitin'," Val tossed out in an effort to save Haven from any further discomfort.

Both Henry boys nodded, and one of them said,

"Oh, I see. That makes sense to me. Does that make sense to you, Ronald?"

"It surely does," the one who must be Ronald agreed. "I would think that is especially true when one goes callin' on a neighbor and they come to the door almost plum necked." Looking up to Haven, the boy added, "Would that be right, Miss Abernathy? When someone comes to the door necked, a body ought to surely inquire about their well-bein'?"

Blushing even more crimson than she had before, Haven stammered, "I . . . I suppose so, boys. But why don't we take our leave and let Mr. Briscoe get back to . . . to whatever he was doin' before we interrupted him?"

"Looks to me like he was waitin' for his underwear to dry," said one of the Henry boys, smiling at Val as if he now held the greatest secret he'd ever held in his short, little life.

"Well, that may well be," Haven said, taking each boy by the hand, smiling up at Val, and adding, "Thank you for your time, Mr. Briscoe. We look forward to seein' you tomorrow at the festival."

"Yes, ma'am," Val said. And then, simply because something about Haven Abernathy awakened the imp in him, Val chuckled, "Have a nice day, Miss Abernathy," letting go of his hold on the quilt as he simultaneously closed the door in front of him.

"Good Lord, Miss Abernathy!" Ronald exclaimed. "Why, if Mr. Briscoe hadn'ta shut that door in time, we mighta all seen his—"

"Well, he did close it in time, so let's just focus on not using the Lord's name as an exclamation for now, shall we?" Haven babbled as she hurriedly turned the boys around, nearly dragging them down Valentine's porch steps.

"Did you see them muscles in his arms, Ronald?" Robert asked as Haven towed them along with her. "When I grow up, I want to have muscles just like Mr. Briscoe's."

"Me too!" Ronald agreed. "And you know what else, Robert?"

"What else?"

"Well, I can tell you that if Mama thinks Mr. Briscoe fills out his shirt like a Greek god because of his muscles, then she's broad-faced lyin' to Daddy about him fillin' his shirt out the same way."

"I was thinkin' the very same thing, Ronnie," Robert admitted. "I suppose she's just lyin' to Daddy to keep from hurtin' his feelin's though."

"Yep," Ronald agreed. "But at least we done our duty and got Mr. Briscoe to judge the apple butter contest at the festival tomorrow." Looking up to Haven, Ronald added, "Ain't that right, Miss Haven?"

"Yes, Ronald, that's right," Haven managed.

Yet she didn't slow her pace—not one whit. Haven wanted to get as far away from Valentine Briscoe's farm as she could. Why, the man was near next to a heathen! Who in the world answered their door half naked—not once, but twice?

"Can we run on ahead, Miss Abernathy?" Robert asked. "We're near enough to town, don't you think?"

Haven smiled at Robert and then Ronald. She tousled their hair and nodded. "Oh, I suppose," she relented. "Just stay close enough that I can see you until we get back to the millinery shop, all right?"

"Yes, ma'am," Ronald promised.

Haven shook her head, amused by her own protectiveness of the boys. After all, everyone in town knew the Henry twins were always off by themselves getting into some kind of mischief. Still, she did feel responsible for them, being that their mother had asked her to walk with them to Valentine's place to "dispatch" the judging invitation, as Claudine Henry had termed it.

Yet as the Henry Buttons raced ahead of her, Haven slowed her walk a little. Yes, Valentine had rattled her nerves something fierce! But now that he was no longer standing right in front of her wearing nothing but a handsome smile and a quilt wrapped at his waist, she found she had relaxed. She was even able to find amusement in the incident. Oh, he was indeed a bit of a scoundrel—dropping the quilt just as he shut the door. Haven knew darn well the man had meant to unsettle her. But she found that, instead of being chagrinned as she should have been, she was rather charmed by the sense of humor he allowed himself to show here and there.

She thought of his talking about the *Farmers' Almanac* when they'd shared supper with the Sandersan sisters. He'd intentionally teased her about it—and without either Wynifred or Merigold being any the wiser.

Haven giggled to herself, thinking of how just downright adorable the man was when he'd been woken from a deep sleep—hair tousled, eyes squinting. She sighed, wondering whose apple butter Valentine would choose the next night as the best in town. Of course, she and Arabella were entering their own apple butters. But no one but Mrs. Henry would know whose was whose, being that Mrs. Henry had assigned a number to each jar of apple butter entered in the contest and kept the list solely to herself.

It was a silly thing to daydream over, but Haven did it anyway—imagined that something about her had somehow been infused into her apple butter and that Valentine Briscoe would taste it and declare that Haven Abernathy's apple butter was pure ambrosia compared with all the others.

"Oh, fiddle-dee-dee, Haven," Haven giggled,

scolding herself. "You're a young woman, not a schoolgirl! No doubt one of the Sandersan sisters will win the apple butter contest, so put your mind to hatmakin' for today and worry about the festival tomorrow."

Still, it was a difficult task to manage, considering that when she arrived back at the millinery shop, it was to find Arabella adding large, round pumpkins to the painted mural on the shop window.

"Oh, Bellie!" Haven exclaimed. "It's beautiful—just beautiful!"

Arabella stepped back from the window, studying it herself for a moment. "Oh, I'm glad you like it. I do think it turned out quite lovely. I hope Dan approves."

Haven's smile broadened as she watched the light of true love glistening in Arabella's eyes.

"Dan is it now, hmm?" she teased in a whisper.

"Oh! I mean . . . I meant Sheriff Sterlin'," Arabella corrected herself, turning rather pale all at once. "I hope Sheriff Sterlin' approves of it—bein' that it's his job to make certain everything is presentable and things."

"Bellie," Haven whispered, "don't worry about referrin' to your beau by his first name. He's your beau! It's fine to enjoy that familiar first-name intimacy. Goodness knows that as much sparkin' as the two of you do, you undoubtedly should be usin' one another's given names."

The color in Arabella's cheeks returned tenfold. And as the scarlet blush pinked her cheeks, she whispered, "Havey! Hush, now! What if someone hears you? I don't know if Dan . . . if Sheriff Sterlin' is wantin' the whole town to know that we're courtin'."

Haven burst into laughter—such strong laughter that it took her several moments, as well as Arabella grabbing her by the arm, dragging her into the shop, and closing the door behind them, before it settled down a bit.

"And what on earth is so funny?" Arabella scolded. "You know I'm worried about Dan and me—the Sheriff and me—about what people will think if . . . what Dan will think if he finds out about . . . about me."

Haven took Arabella's hands in her own, gazing with love and sincerity into the beautiful blue of her friend's eyes. "Bellie, he won't care. He'll love you all the more, I know he will," she said, attempting to calm Arabella's anxieties. "You know in your heart that he knows already . . . don't you?"

Arabella shrugged. "I . . . I don't know for certain," she whispered.

"Then tell him, Bellie. If you love him, tell him . . . and soon. Your mama and Joe, they're truly set on movin' out here with us. And when they do . . . are you gonna lie to Dan? Not acknowledge your mama as your mother and break her heart?"

Arabella gulped, her eyes misting with tears.

"I . . . I received a letter from Mama just today, Havey," she said. "And she . . . she told me that she and Joe won't come to Fletcher if I don't promise to keep the fact that she's my mother and Joe my father a secret from everyone here."

Haven frowned—felt her heart begin to ache with pain.

"No . . . no. Absolutely not," she breathed. "The whole point of us comin' out here, of leavin' home, was to escape the problems in Georgia. We didn't come out here to continue to hide who we really are."

Arabella reached out, taking Haven by the shoulders. "Then tell me this, Havey. Do you ever plan to tell anyone who you really are? Anyone other than Miss Wynifred and Miss Merigold? Because I don't see you runnin' up to Valentine Briscoe and—"

"Valentine isn't in love with me the way Sheriff Sterlin' is in love with you," Haven interrupted. "Dan Sterlin' will be askin' for your hand in marriage any time now. And all I have with Valentine is a secret tryst—and in a cemetery at that—and a knowledge of how perfect his physique is."

"But you're in love with him, Havey," Arabella stated. "And—"

"And he just thinks of me as the clumsy, silly woman who makes hats," Haven interjected.

"You know it's different, Bellie. And you know it's time for you to tell Dan everything about yourself. You don't want to live the secret, only to have it revealed at a time not of your choosin'."

"I know," Arabella admitted, exhaling a heavy sigh. "But what about Mama? She doesn't want me to tell anyone that she's my mother."

Haven straightened her posture. Digging down to find the courage and determination she needed at that moment, she said, "Well, talk to Dan about that. I'm confident he will want you to let others know that she is your mother when she arrives. So talk to Dan about it . . . and then we'll discuss it further."

Arabella nodded with forfeit. "You're right. I need to tell him. And I won't wait. I'll tell him tomorrow night . . . after the Harvest Festival when he's walkin' me home. I will," she promised.

Fear leapt so furiously into Haven's heart that it nearly knocked her off her feet. But she did not let it show in her expression. Dan Sterling was a good man—a good man who loved Arabella. He would not cast her away simply because she was of mixed blood. Haven knew he wouldn't; at least, she silently prayed that he wouldn't.

"But I have a condition," Arabella unexpectedly added.

"A condition?" Haven asked, curious.

Arabella nodded. "Yes. I will tell Dan tomorrow

night; I swear it. But you have to do somethin'
for me . . . to help me be brave in goin' through
with it, all right?"

"Anything!" Haven promised. "You know
I'd do anything if it will help you find your
happiness, Bellie."

Arabella smiled. "Good. Then tomorrow night,
I want you to wear your green formal dress to the
Harvest Festival and—"

"I can do that!" Haven assured Arabella. "I
mean, it might be considered a little too formal
for an event such as the Harvest Festival by most
people's standards. But as long as you don't
think anyone will find it too . . . too revealing,
bein' that it is off my shoulders a bit, I can find
the courage to wear it."

"And . . ." Arabella continued.

"And?"

"And . . . I want you to make an effort to flirt
with Valentine Briscoe," Arabella finished.

"What?" Haven exclaimed. It was her turn for
the color to drain from her face. "Bellie, no! I
couldn't possibly—"

"Do it," Arabella demanded, however. "Do it
for me . . . and do it for yourself, Havey. Why,
it took Dan nearly a week of sparkin' before he
kissed me the way you said Mr. Briscoe kissed
you out there in the cemetery. Of course, I didn't
know you'd been sparkin' with the man until that
night you came home after tellin' the Sandersans

about your grandmother." Arabella arched an accusing eyebrow.

"I'm sorry I didn't tell you right away, Bellie," Haven apologized again. "I . . . I just didn't know what you'd think, and I wanted you to bathe in the bliss of gettin' to know your Dan, and—"

"Just promise me that you'll make an effort to let Valentine know you like him," Arabella urged. "I'm not askin' you to confess your love . . . not yet. But do it for me and for my mama and daddy, all right? And do it for yourself."

Haven exhaled a heavy sigh. She did love Valentine Briscoe, although she really couldn't have explained to anyone other than Arabella how she'd fallen in love with a man she hardly knew. And she did want Arabella to be happy—to know that Dan Sterling would love her no matter what, to have the freedom of claiming Mipsie as her mother to anyone and everyone.

"All right," Haven agreed. "I'll wear my green frock and flirt with Valentine Briscoe. There. Does that make you happy?"

Arabella smiled, throwing her arms around Haven and hugging her tightly. "It does! Oh, it does!"

Haven returned Arabella's hug. All would be well—it had to be!

"Now, how did your dispatchin' of the invitation with the Henry boys go, hmmm?" Arabella asked, releasing Haven and reaching for a cloth hanging nearby. "I swear! *Dispatchin'* an invitation? You would think Claudine Henry was a West Point graduate."

"Oh, it went well," Haven said. "Of course, Valentine answered the door in the nude again."

"What?" Arabella exclaimed, pausing in wiping the paint from her hands with the cloth she held.

"Well, he wasn't completely nude," Haven offered. "Still, it was a good thing he closed the door so quickly. Otherwise, when he dropped the quilt, the Henry boys and I might have seen more than would've been revealed if he'd been wearin' that dotted swiss Miss Merigold mentioned last time."

"What?" Arabella squealed with laughter as the bell to the shop jingled. "Oh, Havey! You just have to tell me all about it. You just have to!"

"Tell you all about what?" Sheriff Sterling asked as he stepped into the store.

Haven and Arabella exchanged conspiratorial glances.

"Oh, I think it can wait, Sheriff," Haven said. "At least until after you've approved Arabella's additions to our shop window."

"Well, how about you show me your additions then, Miss Barnes?" the sheriff said, his eyes glistening with adoration as he gazed at Arabella.

"I would love to, Sheriff!" Arabella chirped.

Haven watched as Sheriff Sterling opened the door, gesturing for Arabella to precede him in exiting the shop. Once they'd stepped out onto the boardwalk, closing the door behind them, Haven allowed the quiet, selfish part of her to think for a moment. She'd moved west to find happiness, the same happiness she'd dreamt of for Arabella. And yet the tiniest part of Haven was saddened by the fact that Arabella's happiness had come so all at once—almost instantly the moment she had arrived in Fletcher. Whereas Haven's? Well, Haven had known for weeks that her happiness might never be complete—not when Valentine Briscoe held her heart in his hands without even knowing—without even wanting it.

CHAPTER THIRTEEN

M iss Abernathy! Miss Abernathy!"
Haven turned to see the little Henry
Buttons running toward her. Robert and Ronald
each held a large cinnamon roll in one hand.
Haven giggled, delighted as the two towheaded
boys waved with exuberance. She felt a thrill
of wonderment travel the length of her as a soft
autumn breeze swept a few fallen aspen leaves
from the ground, swirling them up into the air. It
looked as if pretty pixies were flittering about the
Henry Buttons as they hurried toward her. The
evening was heavenly, and it seemed everything
was more beautiful for it. So many wonderful
scents were on the breeze—fresh-baked goods,
mulled apple cider. And someone had even
managed to come by a few pumpkins that were
ripe enough to carve into early jack-o'-lanterns;
thus, the aroma of candle-flame-heated pumpkin
mingled with the other beloved Indian summer
essences to lend an ambrosial bouquet to the
night air.

"You were right, Miss Abernathy!" Ronald
announced as he and Robert reached the place
where Haven stood.

"About what, sweetie?" Haven asked—though

341

she already had an idea of what she had been right about.

"Them Misses Sandersan," Robert began, "they give us a whole cinnamon roll each just now . . . *and* they said we can come to their house for a visit in a couple of days after et'kit instruction, and they'll make sure they have pie or cinnamon rolls or cookies or somethin' the like waitin' for us!"

Haven smiled, adoring the boys with all her heart. "You see? Miss Wynifred and Miss Merigold are just the kindest ladies I've ever known."

"Yes, ma'am!" Ronald exclaimed. "And look at the size of these cinnamon rolls they give us! Why, a man could eat a week on one of these, if he had the need to."

"That's true," Robert agreed. Then taking a large bite out of the cinnamon roll he held, Robert said, "But since we don't have the need to, I'm gonna eat the whole of mine right now!"

Haven laughed, amused as well as gratified by the boys' delight and glad for their intentions of visiting the Sandersans. For all Wynifred and Merigold's denial of it, Haven knew that they longed for company—for conversation, socializing, and people to love and dote on. And who better to dote on and share their own kind of mischief with than the playful and often quite impish Henry Buttons?

"We'll see you later, Miss Abernathy!" Robert and Ronald called in unison as they bolted off toward who-knew-what next.

"Those two little rascals sure do like you."

Goose bumps raced over Haven's arms as she turned to see Valentine standing behind her.

"Well, the feelin' is mutual," she said, smiling as the warmth that always washed over her when standing in Valentine's presence manifested itself. "They may be a little rambunctious and naughty at times . . . but that's what boys are supposed to be, right?"

Valentine smiled, nodding with agreement.

"And congratulations to you, Mr. Briscoe, on survivin' the judgin' of the apple butter contest without reducin' any of the ladies to tears," Haven offered.

The Harvest Festival had been in full swing for near to two hours, and although she had spoken with him on multiple occasions, Haven still had not found the courage to "flirt a bit" with Valentine as Arabella had made her promise to do. He was so handsome—so intimidating standing there rather towering over her— perfectly gallant in his white shirt, burgundy vest, black four-in-hand tie, and black frock coat.

"I'll not deny that I was a bit rattled about it . . . to say the least," Valentine admitted in a lowered voice. "All those ladies lookin' on, starin' at me while I was tastin' the butters—like each one of them was tryin' to bedevil me into choosin' her own." Valentine shook his head, adding, "I'm glad it's over with."

Haven giggled, amused by his obvious lingering disquiet.

"Well, I for one know that you gave the first-place ribbon to exactly the woman who deserved it," Haven offered reassuringly. "I myself have enjoyed many servin's of Miss Merigold Sandersan's apple butter, and I have never tasted any other more delicious than hers in all my life. Not even Miss Wynifred's." She smiled at Valentine as she reached out, smoothing the lapel of his frock coat. It wasn't much of a flirt, but it was all she could muster just then. "You were the perfect judge for the job."

Valentine grinned down at her. "So you're not huffy with me for not choosin' your apple butter as the winner? Or even second or third place?"

"Oh, fiddle-dee-dee," Haven said, waving a hand to indicate she thought it would be silly to be huffy over not winning the apple butter contest—no matter what her ridiculous daydreams of it had been the day before. "Of course not, Mr. Briscoe." She beamed at him, brazenly winking as she said, "However, had it been a peach butter contest—well, I was raised a Georgia peach, and peach butter is one of my specialties. Consequently, had we had a peach butter contest and mine had not won . . . then I might have been inclined to pout just a little."

For a moment, Val wondered if someone had poured something other than apple cider into the mug he'd watched Haven drink from earlier in the evening. The girl was grinning like a fresh-carved jack-o'-lantern. Furthermore, she'd touched him—well, touched the lapel of his coat anyway. If he hadn't known better, Val would've thought that Fletcher's etiquette-teaching hat-maker was flirting with him.

"It's a lovely evenin', isn't it?" Haven inquired of him.

"It is indeed," he agreed.

Val grinned as he studied Haven from head to toe. Something about the flicker of the flames from the lamps set atop nearby poles and the burnished gold the bonfire added to the night combined to enhance an amber adornment to Haven's already radiant beauty. Val was pleased she had chosen to wear her hair differently— not all twisted tight and piled on her head but a softer set to it, with long, raven ringlets draping pendulous down her back. Her green gown was the same emerald reflected in her already-sparkling eyes. And Val would not deny to himself, nor to anyone who might ask, that the neckline of her dress profoundly appealed to him—for it was cut low, revealing the crest of her shoulders, the alluring hollow of her throat, and a dainty-looking clavicle. It was true Haven was always stunning to look at, but there in the glow of the firelight, she was nigh unto irresistible.

"Of course, as you well know," Val began, needing to distract himself from the ravishing Georgia peach who had transplanted herself out west, "the *Farmers' Almanac* predicted the weather would be just as nice as it indeed has turned out to be this evenin'."

Haven blushed and giggled a little. "You are never goin' to let me forget that, are you?" she asked him.

"Of course not," he admitted, mesmerized by her smile.

As he gazed into her brilliant green eyes, Val thought about the conversations he'd had with his parents earlier in the week and how they had encouraged him to move on from the horror of the year before—to endeavor to live a full life, to fall in love, to wed and start a family of his own. Of course, he'd explained to his father and mother his attraction to Haven Abernathy—even confessed to them the hunch he owned concerning part of her lineage. The truth was, he had been surprised when neither his father nor his mother had held instant ill will toward the Georgia peach they didn't know. In fact—though his mother had wept bitterly when he'd told of Haven's rare silky raven hair and unique appearance otherwise—both his parents had counseled him to somehow soften his hard heart enough to pay court to her. Yet even as he stood there admiring her—considering how thoroughly he liked her, even wanted to go courting her—he felt the stone cold in his chest stand firm, and he wondered whether he would ever find a way to warm it up even a little. Would he ever be able to accept and let go of what had happened the year before—give up his mission of revenge? In truth, he was afraid he would not. The atrocities inflicted upon Val's family were unforgivable, the wounds unhealable.

"And now, ladies and gentlemen," Dan Sterling called out, startling Val from his thoughts. Stepping onto the wood-planked dance floor the men in town had constructed, Dan continued, "Gather round! Gather round. We're about to start the dancin'. But before we do, Miss Abernathy's etiquette, decorum, and social dance students are gonna show us what they've learned!"

Val watched Haven as everyone applauded. Her posture straightened to an even more perfect stance than the one she'd held the moment before, and he could see empathy overtake her countenance as she watched the children gather. No doubt every child preparing to dance was bundled tight with nerves. The thought traveled through Val's mind that he was glad he wasn't one of the boys having to show what he'd learned in front of the whole town. He remembered when his oldest sister, Alberta, had taken it upon herself to teach him social dance the year he'd turned twelve. It had been a nightmare for him! And yet, in the end, Val had been grateful to Alberta for pushing him so hard to learn. After all, it was his waltzing skills that had won him a kiss from Dalia Sue Lynstrum at the Christmas social that same year.

Still, he felt sorry for each and every one of the boys as they gathered on the dance floor behind the sheriff. Noticing the way the color had drained from her cheeks, he figured Haven was just as nervous as the children were.

"Oh, I know they're just terrified," she whispered aloud. Val wasn't sure whether she was talking to herself or to him.

But he decided to offer a bit of comfort to her anyhow. "They'll be fine once they get started."

Haven nodded and nervously sighed, "I do hope so."

Val watched as Jarvis McGhee, clutching his fiddle, moved to stand near the makeshift dance floor. And as none other than the quiet, ever-frowning, oldest Mr. Crabtree stepped up to stand near Jarvis, Val asked, "Old Man Crabtree? Does he fiddle too?"

Inhaling a deep breath, as if she were about to jump from a cliff, Haven answered, "Believe it or not, he's goin' to call the Virginia reel once the waltz is over."

"Hmm," Val mumbled. "I woulda never taken him for a dancin' man . . . or a dance-callin' man, for that matter."

Haven smiled at him, her eyes flashing with excitement. "Me neither," she admitted.

Jarvis tuned up his fiddle a little as the children all took their places, each and every one of them looking to Haven for reassurance.

You're fine! she mouthed, nodding and flashing a beautiful smile of encouragement. *Go on now.*

" 'The Blue Danube.' A waltz," Old Crabtree announced.

Then, as Jarvis began to play, the children of Fletcher did indeed perform the waltz, and with more perfection than Val had ever seen in children so young. Fact was, he'd never seen a group of adults waltz so well.

It was obvious that the citizens of Fletcher were pleased with what they were watching, for they did not even wait for the dance to end but rather began applauding at once.

"Oh, good!" Haven said, smiling up to him. "That will give the children confidence!"

"I would guess so," Val chuckled as he joined the applause.

Val couldn't keep from smiling as he vacillated between watching Haven's expressions of joy for the children's sakes and watching how wonderfully the children were waltzing. One thing was for certain: Haven Abernathy had proved herself a fine social dance teacher indeed.

Haven's heart was beating with such delight for the children's sakes. They were waltzing marvelously—flawlessly! All of them, each couple, waltzed with such fluidity, the younger children waltzing as well as the older children. She couldn't keep from giggling with joy as she noted the way Robert and Ronald had near instantly gone from two little mischievous, cinnamon-roll-munching Button boys to two quite dashing gentlemen. She did wonder for a moment if the boys had managed to wash the Sandersans' cinnamon roll icing from their hands before taking their partners, Fanny Dunklin and Addie Bernard, in waltz position. Still, both girls were smiling—beaming with pride—so Haven guessed Robert and Ronald weren't too sticky.

"My, my, my, Miss Abernathy," Valentine said aside to her. "You are a downright miracle worker, if you ask me. Those children are somethin' else! I've never seen such perfect waltzin' . . . especially in ones so young."

Feeling a blush of satisfaction rise to her cheeks, Haven offered, "Thank you so much, Mr. Briscoe. But it really is the hard work put in by the children that has them so polished, you know."

As the waltz ended, Haven was confident that such applause and cheering of praise had never been heard in Fletcher before. Pride filled her bosom as the children all managed to remain quite poised as they moved about the dance floor, meeting new partners and repositioning themselves to perform the Virginia reel.

As the crowd quieted down, Mr. Crabtree announced, "The Virginia reel."

Jarvis McGhee tucked his fiddle beneath his chin again and began playing an introduction to "Turkey in the Straw."

"And . . . forward and back!" Mr. Crabtree began to call. "Right hand turn . . . left hand turn."

All onlookers began applauding with joy and admiration, and the applause quickly turned to everyone clapping in rhythm as the children reeled.

Unable to control her excitement and glee any longer, Haven squealed with happy enjoyment. Reaching out and placing her hand on Valentine's strong forearm, she looked up to him, saying, "Oh, aren't they just adorable? Aren't they just the cutest things you've ever seen in all your life? Why, look at them! Just dancin' like they've been doin' it their whole lives. And I know they're havin' fun too!"

Pausing, she felt a wave of humility and gratitude wash over her—even felt the moisture of emotion rise in her eyes. "Thank you, Mr.

Briscoe," she said with full sincerity. "Thank you so much . . . so very, very much!"

Valentine arched one handsome brow. "Why are you thankin' me?" he chuckled. "I didn't have anything at all to do with it. You did all this."

But Haven shook her head, brushing a tear from the corner of her eye. "No," she stated. "I may have taught the children—been teachin' them anyway. But had you not come along in time to save my life, to save me from chokin' on that lemon drop that day . . ." Again Haven shook her head, overwhelmed with gratitude. "Well, I wouldn't have been able to help the children polish their steps in time to perform here tonight, in time for them to feel confident and proud of what they've accomplished."

Valentine frowned. "You mean, you're sayin' that this is somehow partly my doin'? Because I shook a lemon drop outta your throat the day we met?"

Haven smiled. "Yes. Exactly."

Valentine's frown disappeared as he burst into laughter—wholehearted, profoundly amused laughter.

Haven gasped as Valentine reached out, taking her face between his warm, strong hands.

"Haven Abernathy," he chuckled, "you are the most entertainin' woman—the most entertainin' person, for that matter—that I have ever met in all my life!"

"Is . . . is that a compliment, Mr. Briscoe?" Haven stammered—for she was entirely mesmerized by his smoldering gaze but not truly certain whether being the most entertaining person a body had ever met was a good thing.

Again Valentine laughed. Then, shaking his head with lingering amusement, he said, "Yes, that is a compliment. And my name is Valentine—Val to my friends—of which you are certainly one, Haven."

Oh, she could've kissed him! As always, she *wanted* to kiss him—wanted to reach out, take hold of his coat lapels, pull him toward her, and kiss him square on the mouth! But she didn't dare, especially not in front of every citizen of Fletcher.

"Everyone partner up!" Old Mr. Crabtree hollered then. "Let's join the children in another round of the Virginia reel!"

Squeals of delight and gleeful laughter abounded as the parents and everyone else in Fletcher began to pair up. Haven watched as the children left the dance floor and chose partners who might not already have someone to dance with. She winked as she saw Andrew Henry and Johnny McGhee ask the Sandersan sisters to dance—watched Grover Lewis ask the widowed Catherine Bernard to be his partner.

"I suppose you taught them that too, hmmm?" Valentine quietly inquired.

Haven nodded. "Well, we must always be aware and care for those who might not be thought of as often as others."

"You got a partner yet, Miss Abernathy?" little Walter Crabtree asked.

"How kind, Walter—" Haven began to accept.

"But unfortunately she already *does* have a partner, Mr. Crabtree," Valentine kindly interjected.

"Very well," Walter said with a bow. "Another time perhaps, Miss Abernathy."

"Oh, I would be honored, Walter," Haven giggled.

As she looked back to Valentine—as he took her hand and started toward the dance boards—she thought she might faint dead away at being so thrilled. She was going to dance with Valentine Briscoe? It had to be a dream.

And yet it was not! As Sheriff Sterling and Arabella stepped onto the dance board—the sheriff across from and facing Arabella, as Valentine was Haven—Haven could see that Arabella's joy was just as at its zenith as hers was. Even in her wildest dreams of Valentine Briscoe, she'd never dreamt of dancing with him. Yet there she stood, facing him, ready to dance with him—listening to Jarvis McGhee begin playing "Turkey in the Straw" once more.

"And . . . forward and back," Old Mr. Crabtree called.

"Oh, what a lovely night!" Haven exclaimed— albeit softly, for she did not want her voice to frighten the crickets into shy silence. "I will admit to you, Mr. Briscoe," she continued, "I do not miss the heavy moisture of the southern air. I swear there were times I felt as if I were tryin' to inhale gravy!" She paused, drawing in a long breath of fresh, dry, Colorado zephyr.

"I'd bet everythin' on the fact that there aren't many nights so beautiful in all the world as these we have here," Valentine offered.

"I'm inclined to agree with you," Haven complied. "Why, just look at that moon up there! So bright and white—as if God hung a tremendous pearl in the sky . . . and a ribbon of diamond stars to complement it, hmmm?"

Valentine smiled, and Haven heard him chuckle a bit under his breath. She still could not believe he'd offered to see her home after the festival. Then again, she knew he held an aversion to ladies walking home alone after dark. He'd told her so that blissful night he'd kissed her in the cemetery. She even felt a twinge of guilt in her bosom at the knowledge she had walked home alone after dark the night they'd shared supper with the Sandersans. Still, as she strolled along beside him, she didn't care if he was simply being a gentleman. She'd hoped he'd accompanied her because he truly favored her.

"I never thought of it that way before," he commented, gazing up into the night sky. "I always just figured the moon was a big ol' round lantern God put up there for sailors and soldiers and cowboys to travel by . . . sleep peaceful under and just plain admire."

Haven smiled, pleased by Val's description of the moon. After all, lantern light was always preferable to jewels and gems. Lantern light was soothing, comforting, and warm.

Oh, what a night it had been! An apple-pie-scented night, full of golden firelight, good food, and handsome company. And then there had been the dancing! Like the sweet, confectionary icing that topped the Sandersan sisters' cinnamon rolls, the dancing had been the most wonderful part of the evening. Not only had the children performed perfectly, solidifying their parents' good faith in Haven's efforts, but she had also enjoyed so many dances with Valentine that she thought the butterflies in her stomach would never take their rest.

Haven had enjoyed dancing the Virginia reel with Valentine, and three other reels besides. Even so, it was the waltzes—the three warm, intimate, romantic waltzes with him—that even now left her breathless with bliss. Valentine had explained to her during their first waltz that his older sister, Alberta, had nearly driven him to running away from home with hounding him about learning to dance. Nonetheless, it wasn't because Valentine was a very capable dancer—which he was—that Haven was left so light-headed and awash in felicity. It was his touch—the sensation of his warm, strong hand at her waist—the way he caressed the back of her hand with the fingers of his other as he held it. It was moving in such proximity to him, gazing up into his handsome face. Dancing with Valentine had been euphoric.

"As for the stars," he continued, "my mama always said that each star was a person once—that the stars are a gatherin' of people who are angels of heaven now. And at night, the twinklin' we see—well, that's just the angels winkin' at us, lettin' us know they're watchin' over us."

Haven sighed with admiration. "That is possibly the most tender idea I've ever heard someone say out loud, Mr. Briscoe," she breathed. "I love that your mother told you about angels and stars . . . and that you see the moon as a lantern lightin' people's way."

Valentine grinned a little. Yet Haven noted that it seemed more a wistful grin of regret or sadness rather than of amusement or joy.

"I suppose those Henry boys of yours told you that I went home to visit with my folks last week?" he ventured.

Haven nodded, smiling. "Oh yes. Indeed, they

did. There isn't a whole lot of anythin' that gets past Robert and Ronald." Glancing over to him, wishing they weren't already so close to her home, she offered, "I'm sure it was wonderful to see your family again."

Valentine exhaled a heavy sigh. "Yep. It was good to see Daddy and Mama . . . good to know they're farin' just fine without me home."

Haven smiled, commenting, "Or at least it's good to know they keep up the appearance that they're farin' fine without you, hmmm?"

Valentine stopped in his tracks. Frowning, he reached out, taking hold of Haven's arm and staying her.

"What do you mean they're keepin' up the appearance that they're farin' fine without me?" he asked, a deep frown furrowing his brow. "You don't think they really are doin' all right alone?"

Horrified that she'd caused him doubt and obvious apprehension, Haven put a hand to her bosom and worriedly explained, "Oh no! No, no! I just meant that . . . well, if I'm ever blessed with children, of course I want them to grow up to be happy—to leave the nest, so to speak, just as they're meant to. But in the same breath, I can't imagine havin' to give them up. Do you know what I mean? Naturally, I would always appear as if I were just fine havin' to let them go, but in truth . . ." Haven shrugged. "I feel that my children, no matter how grown up they are . . . well, I'll always see them as my babies. Do you understand?"

Val exhaled a sigh of relief. For a brief moment, he'd wondered if Haven knew something about his parents that he did not, even though he knew it was an impossibility. Yet once she had explained herself, well, he did comprehend—knew that women never stopped being mothers, never stopped seeing their children as their babies, no matter what.

Smiling at her, he reached out, brushing a strand of hair from her cheek. "I do understand," he affirmed. "And I know my mama says those years when her babies were babies went by faster than a steam engine headed for a gold strike."

Valentine was delighted when Haven linked her arm with his as they began walking once more and said, "That's what Mipsie always said too. She says she always felt that one day she turned around and Arabella and I had aged two or three years at once, it seemed."

"You . . . uh . . . you have any luck coaxin' those folks to come on out here?" Val asked. He wouldn't push her about her relationship to this Mipsie and Joe—or mention that he suspected one or the other of them was a parent to Arabella. But he did hope she could convince them both to come west. He had no doubt the change would be difficult but beneficial for all concerned.

She shrugged. "I think they're gettin' closer to bein' convinced. We'll just have to keep tryin'."

Val liked the way it felt to have Haven's arm linked through his—liked the way her head would brush against his shoulder now and again. Part of him wanted to simply swoop her up in his arms, carry her home, and . . .

"Oh my," Haven sighed with disappointment. "We're home already? This has been such a wonderful evenin', I'm melancholy that it's over."

Haven was miserable in knowing her time with Valentine was at an end. He was nothing less than intoxicating, and Haven wished she could continue to bathe in the euphoric stupor he seemed to lure her into whenever he was near to her. Yet knowing it would not be at all proper to ask him in for a visit at such an hour, Haven did the only thing she could think to do. She offered him her hand and thanked him for seeing her home.

"Well, you're welcome, Miss Abernathy," Valentine began, taking her hand in a firm grip. "But it sure does seem a shame to say goodnight already," he continued, "not when there's a big ol' pearl hanging high in the sky, and angels winkin' at us to boot."

Haven blushed, thoroughgoingly thrilled that it appeared Valentine was not weary of her company. She certainly was not weary of his. In fact, she surmised such a thing as being tired of Valentine Briscoe's company did not exist.

"I suppose that would be a shame, wouldn't it?" Haven agreed. She felt her cheeks pink up with delight and hoped that the night, even for the full moon and stars above them, was dark enough to hide her blush from Val.

Valentine was still holding her hand, and his touch was far more than merely invigorating. In truth, Haven was so awash with enchanted warmth that she surmised her whole being must be as flushed with pink as were her cheeks.

"Though I suppose we could linger a bit here on the back porch . . . bein' that Arabella's not home at present," Haven pointed out. "I believe she and Sheriff Sterlin' will be strollin' this way on their own at some point in the evenin'."

It was then that she made her mistake—the mistake of glancing up into Valentine's bewitching, jade-green eyes. As their gazes locked, much like train cars being coupled—as Valentine's eyes narrowed and a grin of intent and pure misbehavior donned his lips—well, Haven's heart began to hammer just like a steam engine.

"Haven," he began. His voice was deep and rich, thoroughly beguiling.

Haven thought she might faint for the exhilaration that rinsed through her at the sound of her given name as he spoke it.

"Y-yes?" Haven stammered in a whisper.

"Well, if a man intends on letting the rascal in him get loose a while . . . it don't matter if it's the back porch, the parlor, or the cemetery for that matter," he said. "Any one will do for kindlin' that obvious spark between himself and a beautiful woman. Don't you agree?"

Haven bit her lip with delighted anticipation.

"Y-you like me enough to kindle that spark again, Mr. . . . Val?" Haven asked in a nervous whisper.

Val grinned, reached out, and took her chin in one warm, strong hand. "Do I like you enough?" he chuckled. "What do you think? That I have my way with every girl I stumble across havin' a bad night in the boneyard? Of course I like you, Haven Abernathy. I've liked you from the first moment I saw you chokin' on that damn lemon drop."

Haven giggled, humiliated at the memory yet delighted Val was admitting he'd liked her at once.

"And anyhow," he continued, moving closer to her—closer—until his body was flush with her own, "you know what they say . . . that the third time's the charm."

Already sinking into a sort of fervid intoxication as she allowed her hands to rest on his broad shoulders, Haven managed to whisper, "The third time's the charm? Wh-what do you mean?"

Val reached around her head, gently tugging at one of the long ringlets of hair hanging down her back. As he did so, his hand brushed her shoulder and the sensitive flesh at the nape of her neck, causing goose bumps to envelop the entire surface of her body.

"Well, I figure when a fella muddies up the first two opportunities he's got to prove himself to be worth kissin' . . . he better make up for it when the third chance comes around."

"Third time?" Haven asked, too delirious with wanting Val to kiss her to think clearly.

Val chuckled low in his throat. "The first time I kissed you," he answered, "out back here . . . just over there by your outhouse."

"Oh yes," Haven breathed, embarrassed by the memory. "The day you killed the spider and I gave you the . . . the . . ."

"The *Farmers' Almanac* as a token of your thanks," Val offered, his hands going to Haven's waist.

"Y-yes . . ." Haven continued to stammer. Oh, why did he rattle her so? She couldn't think one single coherent thought! Especially now that his hands held her firm at her waist, her senses filled with the light scents of leather and hay and apple butter that pervaded him.

"And then the second time?" he prodded.

363

"In the cem . . . cemetery," Haven breathed as she felt his strong hands leave her waist and move slowly, caressively, up over her back.

"These damn contraptions you ladies wear—it's like coverin' a woman in armor," Val mumbled as he pressed a warm kiss to her forehead. "Then again," he said, bending and placing a kiss to her neck just below her left ear, "I s'pose there's a reason for that . . . especially when a devil like me lives so close, hmmm."

Val had implied that Haven's corset was a sort of armor to protect her against him. And although Haven's upbringing, her fine finishing school education, and everything she taught to her etiquette and decorum students herself told her she should step away from him and deliver a hearty slap to his handsome, oh-so-intoxicatingly handsome face—or at least offer a powerful reprimand—her heart won over her mind, and she melted against him, her hands pressed against the solid contours of his chest, as he pulled her fully into his embrace and kissed her.

For a moment, Haven was certain she would plainly drop dead from the surge of rapturous sensations bathing her in dizzying delirium. For the kiss that Val was administering to her caused her knees to weaken, her toes to clench to curling inside her shoes. Even her palms, where they pressed against Val's chest, fisted—clutching the fabric of his vest with an odd desperation unfamiliar to Haven as she endeavored inefficaciously to draw herself closer against the strength of his powerful body. And although Haven had felt overcome with being timid when first his lips had pressed to hers again, as his mouth worked a bewitchment of passionate affection over hers, Haven found her reserve near instantly gave way to intense desire—to a craving, an appetite, an insatiable thirst to relish the moist flavor of his mouth with her own—not to merely receive the heavenly ambrosia of his exquisite kiss but to endeavor to rain as much pleasure over him as he was lavishing over her.

And it was when she felt the strength of his hands travel further up her back to take her shoulders—when she felt his fingers tenderly caress the bareness at the back of her neck, between her shoulders, when she felt the tips of his fingers slide beneath the hem of the top of her dress at the back, felt him gently tug on the fabric there, as if he wanted to tear the back of her dress away—*that* was when Haven Abernathy tossed all the propriety ever engrained in her into the dark of the beautiful autumn night as she slid her arms up and over Val's shoulders and let her hands move up the back of his neck and into his hair. That was when she kissed him as she'd imagined kissing him every day and night since their kisses in the cemetery—impulsively, passionately, hungrily.

Her abandonment to all things proper did not appear to dismay Val in the least. No, in fact, it seemed to have quite the opposing effect. No sooner had Haven begun to kiss Val with every brazen bone in her body as pure passionately as he kissed her then did he take hold of her waist, lifting her with ease and moving her back until her body was flush with the outer wall of the house, before continuing to plunder her kisses for his own.

Val was undone, and he knew it—but he didn't care. Haven had him right where so many other women had wanted him, tried to get him, and failed—bewitched and obsessed with her.

Of course, he knew Haven had no idea she held him wrapped around her little finger, especially in that moment. Fact was, he was certain she hadn't intended to put him there; she probably didn't even want him there. But he was there all the same. Oh, all the anger and hatred he owned in his soul were still there, even for his parents' counsel to let go of it, and Val feared nothing on earth could ever drive that from him, at least not completely. Still, his heart did not feel as callous, as cold and heavy as stone, as it had weeks before. Haven made him smile; she provoked laughter from him as well. Furthermore, it was true that visions of Haven Abernathy had been dominating his dreams since the day he'd first met her—since the day he'd turned her head over tail and shaken a lemon drop from her throat.

Truth was, if he was going to be honest with himself, her existence was beginning to soften him up. She didn't know that, of course. He knew she hadn't set out to weaken him—hadn't meant to dilute his resolve to remain the hateful, angry, vengeful, heartbroken man he had become. But she had managed to break through his determination somehow.

In an effort to regain his restraint, to keep his wits about him, Val forced his mouth to leave Haven's—growled a little as he tried to regain control of his labored breathing. But when he felt one of her graceful fingers twisting in his hair at the back of his head, his desire for everything beautiful and delectable that was Haven Abernathy further beat down the venomous malignancy that had been owning him for so long.

Taking her chin in one hand, he glared into the alluring emerald of her eyes.

"I am not the best of men, you know," he warned.

"I don't care," Haven breathed an instant before she raised herself on her tiptoes, took his face between her small, soft hands, and captured his mouth for her own once more.

Haven sighed as Val gathered her against him, binding his arms around her as their mouths blended in shared intimacy of affection. Every bright and beautiful color Haven had ever beheld in all her life flared brilliant and powerful in her mind as she and Val continued their impassioned exchange.

"Thank you for seein' me home, Sheriff Sterling."

Arabella's voice on the breeze wafting from the front of the house startled Haven, and she gasped as she broke the seal her lips had been sharing with Val's.

Val exhaled a sigh of obvious disappointment but grinned and winked as he said, "I'm guessin' you don't want to get caught sparkin' by the sheriff and his lady, hmmm?"

Haven shook her head. "That's not it at all," she whispered. "It's just that . . . well, I know Arabella and the sheriff will be discussin' . . . that it's important they have their privacy this evenin'."

Val grinned and gathered Haven in his arms again, however. "Well, I ain't finished makin' sure this third time is charmin' enough for you, you little Georgia peach. So close your ears, and give me your mouth."

Haven did not hear one word of the conversation between Arabella and Sheriff Sterling. The only thing she heard was the barrage of desire echoing through her being as Valentine Briscoe charmed her to rapture for the third time.

CHAPTER FOURTEEN

Val held the lines loosely in his hands. After all, he wasn't in any big hurry, so why rush the team? Of course, he wanted to get a good load of wood back to town and make sure Haven and Arabella had a sufficient pile to last them through the winter. Still, there was a sense of peace about the day, and Val hadn't noticed a peaceful day in a very long time.

He gazed up into the clear blue autumn sky for a time, thinking how rested he felt. The truth was, he'd expected to have a hell of a hard time getting to sleep after holding Haven in his arms, kissing her; he thought he'd be too wound up to get a good night's rest. Consequently, he was surprised when he woke up, having fallen asleep easily and slept the entire night through. He figured that maybe his mama had been right about the reason for his restlessness at night over the past months: that anger and hatred drive away peace of mind and keep a body wound too tight to find true respite. And now that he was attempting to let go of some of the fury and loathing he'd fed to his heart and soul for the past year—now that he had some true beauty in his life, compliments of Haven Abernathy—Val figured that, as she always seemed to, his mother owned a wisdom he did not.

Even as he passed the turn leading north, the venue he'd ridden so many times in searching, the tug at his conscience to search that way again was hardly discernable in him. And not just because he'd searched north before—but because his desire to make sure Haven had a stockpile of wood to warm her through the winter was stronger.

"Walk on," he said to the team as they began to slow too much in taking advantage of his easy mood. "We still got things to get done, no matter how nice the weather is, girls."

And the weather was indeed nice. The air was cool and crisp but not cold. An amiable breeze whispered through the parched gold of the quakies' leaves, and chipmunks and squirrels skittered hither and yon in making final preparations for the winter.

As the team pulled the wagon onward toward the area where Val had seen several dead trees that would be perfect for splitting for firewood, his musing lingered on Haven—as they had since the moment he'd awakened that morning. Oh, but she was beautiful! She was always beautiful, but the night before, dressed in her emerald party dress—the soft, smooth skin of her shoulders and neck revealed, the ringletted raven of her hair pendulating over her back—why, Val found his mouth had begun to water at the memory of the vision! And what fun he'd had dancing with her. Yes, fun! Something he hadn't experienced in a very long time—pure and utter merriment while dancing with her. And walking her home had been quite pleasurable, especially the kissing that went on between them once they'd reached their destination. Oh, the girl was under his skin! But contrary to how Val would've felt months before about it, he found he was now . . . well, hopeful—even happy.

Certainly, the pain had not left him, and the anger lingered. But he found he was able to consider other subjects when he had time to think—things that didn't have to do with loss, hatred, and fury. And he was surprised to find that there was something good and warm left in him after all—something unearthed by Haven.

The cry of a turkey vulture interrupted Val's daydreams of Haven, and he looked south to see a kettle of the scavenger birds circling about half a mile away. At first glance, he thought the kettle was simply gathering to leapfrog south for the winter months. Still, as he watched them, the hair on the back of his neck began to bristle. The birds were circling in a manner that indicated to Val they had found something dead—or something in the process of becoming dead.

He tried to shake the shuddersome sensation washing over him—tried to convince himself

371

that the birds were just ugly and that's why the feeling of dread was rising in him. But try as he might, something urged him to change his course—to ride over to where the buzzards were circling and make certain . . . well, make certain of something.

"Go on, girls," Val urged the team, pulling the lines to his right—south. "Let's see what them ugly gut-eaters are up to, hmmm."

It wasn't long before Val could see a horse lying on the ground near a group of young aspens. The horse wasn't moving, and by the way the turkey vultures were intermittently screeching, he figured the animal was dead—probably had been dead for hours. Yet he couldn't figure why the birds were still in flight. Why hadn't they landed, gathered in a wake to start tearing up the animal's flesh, to start feasting?

Again the hair on the back of Val's neck prickled. Goose bumps spurred by trepidation raced over his arms as he pulled the team to a halt and set the wagon brake. Retrieving his rifle from underneath the wagon bench, Val jumped down and started toward the dead horse. It was odd, finding a dead horse out in the middle of nowhere. Yet as he drew nearer—as he saw the hoofprints that had been painted on the horse to indicate it was taken in a raid, saw the coup feathers woven in its mane—Val leveled his rifle. Where there was an Indian horse, there was always an Indian. Furthermore, Val recognized the hoofmarks and other painted symbols on the horse: Comanche.

The Comanche had been the most brutal tribe to ever live; some renegade bands still were. No one knew the fact better than Valentine. If a Comanche were nearby, he knew he'd be better off just tucking his tail between his legs, running back to his wagon, and driving the team home as fast as he could.

But his curiosity and anger were piqued stronger than his fear. And so Val treaded closer to the dead horse, all the while his senses intently aware of his surroundings.

Yet the closer he drew to the dead animal, the less evidence of anyone else being nearby he saw. And in a matter of moments, he stood over the beast, realizing that it wasn't dead—not yet. Oh, it would give up the ghost any moment, but it still drew breath—very shallow breath.

Exhaling a sigh of discouragement at seeing the animal in pain—had been in pain for a long time, judging by the fractured cannon bone jutting out of its lower left leg—Val aimed his rifle square at the poor horse's head and fired.

The shrill scream that accompanied his shot startled him, and he spun around, aiming his rifle once more into the center of the small grove of quaking aspens at his back. Yet a frown furrowed his brow as he stared at what was hidden there. It wasn't a Comanche warrior or even a Comanche man who stood sobbing in the midst of the aspens. It was a Comanche woman! Dressed in a fringed deerskin dress, a woman of small stature stood among the trees.

"Please, sir. Please help me!" the woman called to Val—and in perfect English.

Val thought he'd taken leave of his senses, for not only did he understand what the woman was saying to him but also, for a moment, thought her voice sounded familiar.

"Who are you?" he growled. "And what the hell are you doin' out here all alone?"

The next words from the woman's mouth nearly knocked Val over the same as if someone had planted a fist to his jaw.

"Val? Valentine Briscoe? Is that really you, Val?" the woman with the familiar-sounding voice asked.

"Who are you? How do you know me?" Val demanded. He was surprised he was still able to level his rifle with a steady hand. He was confused, bewildered, and shaken up some.

"Val! It is you!" the woman cried out as she stumbled from the grove of aspens. "Help me, Val! You have to help me. You have to save my baby! Oh, Val!"

As the young woman reached him, collapsing at his feet, Val could finally see that she was with child. Furthermore, when she looked up to him—

even for all the dirt on her face and in her hair—he recognized her at once.

"Effie? Effie Grayson? Is that you?" he asked.

And as the young woman he'd known since childhood began to sob—as he saw the crimson of blood begin to pool near the place where she kneeled—all the hate and fury he'd carried for so long and all the anger and loathing he'd begun to bury over the last few weeks returned—tenfold.

"Yes! Help me, Val!" Effie Grayson sobbed. "You have to save my baby! You have to hide her! You have . . . have to . . ."

Effie collapsed then—collapsed into a weak, sobbing, bleeding heap at Val's feet.

❋ ❋ ❋ ❋ ❋

"What in all the world?" Haven exclaimed as she and Arabella both hurried through the kitchen toward the back door of the house.

"For pity's sake! It sounds like the Big Bad Wolf himself is tryin' to beat down the door!" Arabella added.

Haven turned the door handle with the intent of opening the door to see who was knocking so vigorously. In truth, she expected to find the Henry Buttons were up to their usual mischief and simply trying to startle her and Arabella. And if that was their strategy, they had been successful! Haven felt her heart would never recover from the jolt the unexpected and sudden pounding on the door had given it.

Yet as Haven opened the door, quite ready to lovingly scold Robert and Ronald for taking ten years off her life, the vision that met her was not only unfathomably unpredictable but also grisly.

Valentine Briscoe stood just beyond the threshold, cradling a young woman in his arms—a young woman who was covered in blood!

"Let me in," Valentine growled.

Without pause, Haven stood aside, watching in horrified, dumbfounded shock as Val stepped into the kitchen carrying the dirty, pale, frail young woman holding a newborn baby in her arms.

"Oh dear!" Arabella breathed in daunted dismay.

"Oh! Val! Follow me," Haven instructed without pause. "We have a spare bedroom."

Wordlessly Val followed Haven from the kitchen as she hurried toward the empty bedroom.

"I'll boil water and gather linens," Arabella called after them.

"V-Val . . . Val, my baby," the frail woman sobbed. "Don't let them take her, Val! Don't let them take her!"

"Lay her just here," Haven indicated, quickly gathering up the quilt that was spread over the bed in the empty bedroom and tossing it into one corner.

Val did, very gently, lay the woman and her baby down on the soft bed, and Haven winced with sympathetic pain as the clean white sheets seemed to imbibe the crimson of the woman's blood—for they were instantly saturated with it.

"I'm goin' for Doc Perkins and Dan," Val said. He looked to Haven, glaring with either threatening anger or panicked worry—Haven couldn't tell which. "Don't leave her," he added. "And if anyone else comes knockin' at your door, do *not* let them in. Do you hear me?"

Haven could only nod in pledging her obedience to his direction. She studied Val quickly from head to toe. He too was drenched in blood! His hands and forearms were covered in it; his shoulders bore small, bloody handprints; the entire front of his shirt, his waist, his thighs were soaked in blood. Blood covered his boots, as well, so that it was impossible to discern any longer whether they were brown or black. Yet she saw no injury about him—no lacerations or gunshot wounds. Val was unharmed. It was the young woman's blood saturating him. Feeling sinful for being thankful that Val appeared unharmed—that all the blood about him was from the pitiful woman—Haven nodded, and Val turned and strode out of the room.

"Val! Val! Don't leave me!" the young woman cried. "Please, Val!"

"Shh, hush," Haven soothed as she turned

and began to brush the woman's hair from her face. "There, there, now. He'll be right back, and with the doctor too," she said in her calmest voice. She smiled at the young woman as she reached into her skirt pocket and retrieved her own handkerchief. Tenderly she dabbed at the woman's forehead, streaked with dirt.

"Val!" the woman continued to sob. "Help me!"

"He is helpin' you, honey," Haven reassured. "He's gone to fetch Doc Perkins to tend to you and your sweet baby."

At last the woman's bright blue eyes turned their gaze to Haven. Haven smiled and dabbed the woman's tears from her temples. Though her hair was caked with blood and dirt, Haven could easily see that the young woman was blonde— and the question of what a blue-eyed, blonde, white woman was doing dressed in the deerskin garments of an Indian moved quickly through her mind.

"What a beautiful baby you have!" Haven cheerfully exclaimed, continuing to dab the woman's forehead. She hoped Arabella would be quick in bringing water, cold or heated.

"M-my daughter," the young woman managed. She looked down at her baby, stroking its tiny head with one blood-encrusted hand.

"Well, she's just as beautiful as the heavens," Haven sighed, feigning calm.

In truth, Haven was ready to burst into

hysterics. But the situation demanded calm, a level head, and compassion.

"I've always wanted a little girl," Haven remarked, attempting to distract the young woman from the fact that the sheets of the bed were drinking up more and more of her life's blood. Haven had assisted Mipsie and Arabella many, many times in helping women give birth, and she knew that the amount of blood the young mother was losing was likely to take her life if it couldn't be stopped. She knew that likely it already had.

"A little boy too," Haven added. "One that gets into the mischief little boys are meant to get into."

The young woman stared at Haven. Haven could see that the woman knew that she was in danger of meeting death. Yet something Haven had said or done had worked to becalm her a little.

"Here we are," Arabella said, entering the room with a washbasin and cloths. "Now let's get you washed up a bit, cool, and comfortable, shall we?"

"This is Arabella," Haven explained. "And I'm Haven. And we're goin' to take wonderful care of you and your baby. So no more worries, all right?"

The young woman nodded and attempted a grin. Still, she was weak, malnourished, and still bleeding.

"Oh, what a beautiful baby!" Arabella exclaimed. "Oh, she's just an angel—just a livin' doll!"

The young woman smiled. "Yes," she breathed.

"What have you named her?" Arabella asked as Haven soaked a clean cloth in cool water. She wrung it well and began to dab the young woman's forehead. Slowly and gently she turned her soft dabbing into tender bathing of the woman's face.

"Sadie Mae Prairie Flower," the young woman breathed. She smiled and kissed the tiny, dark-haired head of her baby. "We'll call her Sadie Flower, I think."

"Oh, what a lovely name!" Haven exclaimed. "And it fits her so perfectly, just as if she is a flower herself."

The young woman's weak smile broadened. "Yes. Wind Talker and I chose it weeks ago. And it does seem to suit her already."

Haven and Arabella exchanged glances, and Haven knew Arabella understood what was in her own mind: they needed to make sure the baby was well bathed and fed.

"Would you . . . would you allow me to hold her a moment, ma'am?" Arabella ventured. "Just for a moment. And . . . and I could bathe her for you quickly while Haven helps you to freshen a bit. It won't take long for me to bathe her. You'll both feel so much better, I promise."

The young woman's eyes narrowed as she studied Arabella and then Haven. Visibly her countenance turned from suspicion to trust, and Haven inwardly thanked God for it.

Kissing her baby's head once more, the young woman said, "I won't live to raise her—one way or the other I won't. I know that. Either God will take me now or . . . or . . ." Her voice trailed off a moment as new tears filled her eyes. "And it is better that God takes me from her now, so that she will be safe . . . my little Sadie Flower."

As the young woman wept, Haven felt tears fill her own eyes. Yet she knew she must remain strong—or at least appear to be strong, for the young woman's sake.

"My name is Effie Grayson," the young woman said. She looked to Arabella and seemed to struggle to find courage. "And if Valentine Briscoe has brought me to you"—she looked to Haven next—"then I am meant to trust you . . . and I know that I can."

With weak and trembling arms, Effie handed the tiny new baby girl to Arabella. Again Haven stared at Arabella and knew that her friend understood that she must make haste in bathing the baby—for the wee one's mother was at death's door.

"Thank you, Effie," Arabella softly said. "I will be quick as a bunny and have little Sadie Flower back in your arms in no time at all."

Effie nodded and brushed tears from her cheeks with one frail, bony hand.

"There now, peaches," Arabella cooed to the baby as she hurried out of the room. "Let's get you all cleaned up and comfortable for mama, all right?"

Haven knew that Arabella would not only bathe the baby but also replace the rough piece of twine someone (probably Val) had tied at her cord before severing her from her mother.

"Now, let's freshen you up a bit, shall we?" Haven said to Effie.

"I-I don't think I can stand," Effie said, tears streaming down her face.

"Oh, that's perfectly fine, sweetheart," Haven reassured. "I'll just turn you as I need to, hmm? All is well. Why, I've helped deliver more babies and wash up more new mamas than I can count. When I lived in Georgia—that's where I was born, you see—my Mipsie, Arabella, and I were always out and about midwifin'. So you have nothin' to worry over."

Haven knew that if she continued to talk about her life in Georgia, or anything else other than Effie's situation, Effie's mind would find a measure of distraction. It was necessary and one of the only comforts Haven could offer the woman.

Still, silently she prayed that Val would return

as quickly as possible, and with Doctor Perkins in tow.

"Oh, we picked so many peaches and pecans when we were little girls in Georgia!" Haven continued to babble as she reached into the drawer of the bedside table and retrieved a pair of scissors. "I remember one year when Arabella and I shelled so many pecans for pecan pies at Thanksgivin' we thought our hands would never stop achin'."

Haven continued to talk of tender yet light-hearted memories as she cut the deerskin dress from Effie's body. The deerskin was so soft and smooth. Even the buckskin fringe of the dress felt more like feathers than something that had once belonged to a male deer. Gently she removed Effie's knee-length moccasins and bunched up several cloths, placing them between Effie's legs to try and soak up some of the blood still escaping her frail body. It took a great effort, but Haven was able to roll Effie onto one side and then the other as she removed the bloody sheet, replacing it with the quilt she'd discarded from the bed earlier. The rolls of cloth between Effie's legs and the thicker quilt beneath her would make Effie more comfortable.

"And then there was the year that Ol' Joe let me and Arabella raise Orville. He was the turkey we were meant to have for Thanksgiving," Haven babbled as she placed a soft white sheet over Effie's fragile form. "Needless to say, *that* was a mistake! Arabella and I were so thoroughly attached to Orville that we ended up havin' ham for Thanksgivin' dinner that year. Goodness sakes! I do not to this day know what Ol' Joe was thinkin' lettin' us girls raise that turkey."

It was laborious work, bathing and turning Effie, even for her malnourished condition. Yet after a time, Effie lay clean and cool on the bed, her hair brushed back and rebraided, her face and body clean and ready to rest.

"And here she is," Arabella tenderly announced as she entered the room with little Sadie Flower swaddled up in a piece of a white sheet. Arabella set a glass of water on the bedside table as she continued. "And she thinks she's starvin'! Why, she's rootin' on me like a brand-new foal." She smiled as she placed the baby in Effie's arms.

"Here now, let's sit you up a bit so you can suckle her, hmm?" Haven suggested.

Haven and Arabella worked to help Effie to sit up, both wincing and exchanging worried glances as the movement caused the quilt beneath Effie to soak in more blood.

"There now," Arabella cooed. "Just let her latch on there. She'll get it."

The baby did indeed begin to suckle at her mother's breast, and Effie smiled as she gazed down at her precious daughter.

"Haven."

Haven turned to see Val, Sheriff Sterling, and Doctor Perkins standing in the doorway of the bedroom.

"Doc's here," Val mumbled.

Haven had not realized how much caring for Effie and the baby had affected her until that moment. But as she gazed at Val, tears filled her eyes, and she felt exactly as if she might burst into screaming with grief, fear, anger, and heartache.

She offered a quick smile to Effie and explained, "We'll just wait outside while you speak with the doctor, all right? We're just a step away if you need anything."

When Effie frowned with returning fear, Arabella soothed, "We'll be right back. It'll only be a moment."

Stepping out of the bedroom and into the hallway, Haven barely managed to cover her mouth to muffle the sobs that begged to be released. She braced herself, back against the wall, as Arabella also exited the room, bursting into tears.

"I'm sorry," Val whispered. "But . . . but I didn't know where else to bring her. Especially considerin' . . ." His voice trailed off, and Haven caught a glimpse of fury in his expression.

"Where on earth did you find her, Val?" Arabella asked, brushing tears from her cheeks with the back of her hand.

"She's not Indian, but she was wearin' a deerskin dress . . . moccasins," Haven pointed out. "And . . . and she seems to know you."

It was all so thoroughly, so overwhelmingly horrifying!

"I-I grew up with her . . . in Limon," Val answered, his voice low and filled with pain. "She was taken . . . a year ago. She and four other girls were taken by a band of renegade Comanches. I-I found her today . . . just south of town."

"Comanches?" Sheriff Sterling exclaimed in a lowered voice. "They will come lookin' for her."

"Someone is already lookin' for her . . . but not the Comanches," Val growled. "The Comanche sold her off to an outlaw, but she slipped away from him. And I have no doubt that he's already trackin' her."

"Then he'll track her here," Sheriff Sterling said, concern furrowing his brow as he looked to Arabella.

"Yes," Val agreed. "That's why I need to drive the wagon from here, over to my place, and then back into town and around a bit. I also need to get rid of any blood that might be on Haven's back steps and porch. I'm hopin' that, even though Cooley will track Effie to Fletcher, he won't be able to track her to any specific place."

"Val! Val!" Effie called in a weak voice. "Come quickly, Val . . . please!"

Sheriff Sterling placed a hand on Val's shoulder. "I'll take the wagon and drive it around town. I'll clean up the blood too. You just tend to your friend in there. From what you've told me already, I don't think she has long left in livin'."

"But I . . ." Val began to argue.

"Val, please . . ." Effie's weak voice pleaded.

Doctor Perkins stepped out of the room, looked to Val, and said, "There's nothin' I can do, Valentine. She's lost too much blood. She doesn't have long, and she's desperate to talk to you. You need to come in . . . now."

Looking to Haven and then to Arabella, Doc Perkins added, "She's askin' for you two ladies as well."

Haven nodded as Arabella said, "My paper and a pencil," and hurried into the bedroom she and Haven shared.

Haven already knew Arabella's thoughts—her plan. If Sadie Flower lived, then Arabella would make certain she knew what her mother looked like. Arabella meant to sketch Effie before she died.

"Val!" Effie sobbed.

"You need to hurry, Val," Doc Perkins instructed. "I'll head back to my office and fetch some bottles and rubber nipples for the baby. But her mother will be gone before I return, I'm afraid."

With one nod, Val strode back into the room where Effie Grayson would die.

Haven followed him, and Arabella was only a moment behind her.

Haven watched as Val knelt beside the bed, placing a strong, comforting hand on Effie's head. She smiled at him, and tears spilled from Haven's eyes.

She could hear Arabella's pencil strokes on the paper she'd placed on top of a wood slat she used for drawing.

"Wind Talker will come for me, Val," Effie said. Her voice was weak and breathy, and Haven barely restrained herself from sobbing—let only the tears streaming over her cheeks release her sorrow and anxiety.

"He will come for me, Val . . . for our baby," Effie said. "You'll know him for his kindness of countenance . . . and his blue eyes."

"And you want Wind Talker to have her . . . the baby," Val stated.

Effie nodded, swallowing hard. "Yes. He will love her and take her away where she can be safe." Effie swallowed once more, and Haven knew she was thirsting. Stepping forward, Haven picked up the glass of water Arabella had brought with her and offered it to Val. She watched as Val carefully drew the glass to Effie's lips and helped her to drink.

"But . . . but if Cooley finds her first . . . if

Cooley takes our Sadie Flower back to Wind Talker's father . . ." Effie began, weeping.

"He won't," Val growled. "I'll see she gets safely back to Limon with your family, Effie. You know I'll see to it. And I'll make sure none of them damn devils knows where she is."

Effie nodded, a smile of hope donning her thin, trembling lips.

Haven glanced to Arabella—watched a moment as her friend frantically sketched. She knew what was in Arabella's mind: that little Sadie must know her mother was happy in her last moments, knowing Valentine Briscoe would see that her baby was kept safe.

Effie Grayson raised one trembling, pale hand, placing it on Val's cheek. Val covered her hand with his own in sealing their promise.

"It was God sent you to find us, Val," Effie breathed. She smiled once more, her blue eyes sparkling as she gazed at Val a moment longer. "I always loved you, you know. Ever since I was a little girl. I used to think I would grow up and marry you, Valentine Briscoe." Effie giggled weakly. "I'm glad God sent you to me at the end."

"I'll see her safe, Effie," Val promised, his voice breaking with barely restrained emotion. "You know I will."

Effie closed her eyes for a moment, her delicate smile broadening. "I know, Val. I know. But if

Wind Talker finds her before you are able to take her home . . ."

"I will entrust the baby to him, Effie. I promise that too," Val assured her.

"He saved my life, Val," Effie said. Her voice was weaker, and Haven knew it would not be long before Sadie Flower's mother passed from one life to the next.

"Take her, Val," Effie said. She pressed a long, loving kiss to the baby's sweet head. "I don't want her last memory of me bein' of feelin' me go cold."

Haven could not keep her withheld sobs from breaking out into the air any longer. Although it was only a quick succession of gasps for air, Val looked up at her as he reached across Effie's body and drew Sadie Flower into the protection of his powerful arms.

Angry at herself for allowing Val to see her weakness, Haven quickly brushed at the rivulets of tears on her cheeks and glanced away from him.

"I'll see her safe, Effie," Val again promised to his childhood friend. "One way or the other, Cooley and the Comanches will never know she lived, let alone where she is. I swear it, Effie. I swear it."

"He can help you, Val," Effie breathed. "He can help with Lydia and Caroline; he can tell you where Alberta and Christine are restin', Val. Wind

Talker—when he returns and discovers what has happened to me—he will help you, Val. I know he will . . . for my sake . . . and his child's."

Haven looked to Val—watched a heavy, angry frown crush his brows together.

Effie opened her eyes, reached up, and weakly took hold of the front of Val's shirt, which was as crimson as the quilt beneath her own body.

"You can trust Wind Talker, Val. You must trust him," Effie whispered. "He was not involved in what happened to us. He saved *me,* Val. You must trust him when he comes. Give me your pledge. Promise me you'll trust him."

Haven could see the muscles of Val's strong jaw clenching, his still-furrowed brow indicating a struggle to accept what Effie was asking of him.

"Promise me, Val. You will trust Wind Talker when he comes. Promise me," Effie breathed.

Val nodded then, exhaled a heavy sigh of forfeiture, and said, "All right, Effie. I'll try."

"No, Val. You must promise me that you *will* trust him," Effie stated determinedly. "You *can* trust him, and you must. I won't rest until I know that you will trust him when he comes."

Val nodded once more, relinquishing his anger—at least a measure of it. "Very well, Effie. If he comes, I will trust him."

Effie exhaled a satisfied sigh and smiled once more. "My Wind Talker will come, Val. He will."

Effie looked past Val for a moment to Haven. "Thank you," she whispered. She looked then to Arabella. "Both of you. Thank you. God sent Val to me, and He sent Val to you two . . . I know it. With all my heart I know it. And I know you'll help Val keep my baby girl safe. Thank you."

Haven could only nod, brushing tears from her cheeks. But Arabella was stronger in that moment. Kneeling on the opposite side of the bed to where Val knelt, Arabella turned her sketch so that Effie could see it.

"This will be her last memory of you, Effie," Arabella said.

More tears flooded Haven's cheeks as she saw the quick yet beautiful sketch of mother and baby that Arabella had managed. A smiling Effie held her sweet Sadie Flower in her arms— an Effie that looked happy, healthy, and robust. Arabella had such a gift, and in that moment Haven was more admiring of it and more thankful for it than ever before.

Effie smiled as tears dripped from her own weak eyes.

"Thank you," she breathed, smiling at Arabella. "Thank you."

Haven nodded to Arabella in conveying her own thanks. Arabella had given the greatest gift that could've been given to Effie as she faced her own death—as she faced leaving her baby behind—and it was overwhelming to Haven.

"I'm so tired," Effie mumbled. "I-I think I'll just rest a moment . . . just for a moment."

Haven wept bitterly as she saw the stain of crimson beneath Effie suddenly spread farther and farther toward the borders of the bed.

"Just for a moment," Effie breathed. And it was her last breath.

CHAPTER FIFTEEN

Haven dabbed at her tears with the handkerchief she held. Yet the more tears she dried, the more tears her eyes seemed to spill onto her cheeks. It was all so awful, so heartbreaking! She watched as Doctor Perkins instructed Arabella on how often she and Haven needed to feed the baby and how to use the glass bottles and rubber nipples.

But when he had finished offering instruction—when Arabella had settled into the rocking chair to rock the newly motherless baby girl—it seemed Sheriff Sterling knew the time had come to discuss what had happened.

"Val," he began, "I . . . uh . . . I know you've been through a lot today and that . . . well, I can't imagine how you must feel. But I do need to know how all this came about. And I certainly need to know if some renegade Comanche warrior is gonna come to Fletcher in search of his wife and child." Sheriff Sterling raked a hand back through his hair, allowing his shoulders to slump where he sat in one of the kitchen chairs that had been brought into the parlor.

Valentine nodded. "I know," he mumbled.

He was pale; he looked faded, blanched with

grief and physical fatigue. Haven's heart ached in her chest—ached for the mother who did not live to raise her baby for any length of time at all, for the baby who would never know her mother's touch again, and for Valentine. It was clear from what Haven had discerned of Effie's brief conversation with him that there was oh so much she did not know about Valentine Briscoe.

Valentine stood up a moment and turned around the kitchen chair he'd been sitting on so that the back of it was facing Haven, Sheriff Sterling, Arabella, and Doc Perkins. Stepping over the seat, he straddled the chair, resting his folded arms on the back of it. He'd stripped himself of his shirt and boots, both so caked with Effie's blood that he hadn't wanted to risk soiling anything in the house—anything that wasn't already dark with evidence of the poor young woman's tragic and painful end.

Val cleared his throat before speaking. Yet his voice broke with emotion as he related how, while on his way to chop firewood, he had discovered first a fatally injured horse.

"As I got nearer," Val continued, "I saw the horse was painted with Comanche symbols. I was right unsettled, to tell the truth. You know how Comanches were back years ago, Dan— back when we were boys, right?"

"I do indeed," Sheriff Sterling affirmed with a nod. "Comanches used to be more brutal than any other tribe. Seemed they thrived on torture the way some folks thrive on pie and cake."

"Yep, they did," Valentine agreed. "And . . . well, I have my own experience with Comanches, so I was wary as I approached what I thought was an already dead horse. But when I reached it, I found it was still alive. It had a broken cannon bone and was lyin' there sufferin'. So since I hadn't seen anybody, I shot it—put it down so it wouldn't suffer any longer." Valentine paused, clearing his throat again. "That's when Effie called out to me. Of course, I didn't know it was Effie . . . not at first. But she recognized me soon enough, bein' that we've known each other since we were knee high to grasshoppers. You can imagine how surprised I was. I froze where I stood, wonderin' how on earth an Indian woman out in the middle of nowhere knew my name."

Val didn't speak for a long while. He visibly gulped, his eyes misting with excess moisture. No one pressed him, however. Haven knew he would tell them the rest when he was ready. Everyone else in the room knew it too.

"About a year back, my daddy and me were out huntin' north of our place in Limon," he began to recount. "My mama and my three sisters were home, puttin' up tomatoes and green beans, makin' up jams and jellies and such. Mama sent the girls to town for some more rubber gaskets for the jars." All the while he'd been talking,

Val had been staring at the floor. But now—now he looked up and straight at Haven. "My sisters never came home that day." He shook his head. "They never came home, ever. They were taken."

"Taken?" Doctor Perkins urged.

Val nodded. "My three sisters—Alberta, Caroline, and Lydia—were taken by a band of renegade Comanches. Effie Grayson and her sister, Christine, were taken too. We never found any of the girls. And believe me, we searched. Every man in town searched for weeks. My daddy and me, and Mr. Grayson and his two oldest boys, searched for months." Val shook his head. "But we never found a trace of them damn devils that took the girls."

"How do you know it was Comanches that took them, if you never found anything?" Haven asked before she could think better of it. Not that she didn't believe Val's terrible, tragic story; she just did not want to believe Indians were to blame.

Val's eyes narrowed as he looked at her. "Effie's little brother, Jay, was with his sisters and mine that day in town. But when they all started for home, Jay decided to cause trouble and run off. He was hidin' under some leaf litter in a grove of cottonwoods when the Comanches come. He watched the Comanches take the girls—knock all five of them unconscious, toss them over their horses, and ride off—evaporate like a silent, evil fog. Jay was so scared he stayed hidden 'til he heard his daddy callin' for him late that night." Val inhaled a breath of barely restrained anger. "What Jay witnessed, how he described the Indians and their horses—that and the fact we could tell from their tracks that their horses weren't shod—well, we knew it was Comanches even before two Texas Rangers who had been trackin' the band showed up in Limon the next day. They told us that this particular band of Comanches has been movin' for near to ten years, avoidin' bein' corralled on the reservation. They were once part of Black Horse's band that lit out for the Llano Estacado mesas. But after the Buffalo Hunter's mess, instead of headin' for Mexico the way the rest of them did, this band headed north into Colorado." Nodding with affirmation, Valentine added, "That's how we know it was Comanches that took my sisters . . . and the Grayson girls."

Haven brushed more tears from her cheeks, feeling sick. In truth, she was worried she might vomit. Indians had caused such misery to Valentine and his family—to the Graysons. And in that moment, she knew he could never know the truth about her lineage. Haven knew Valentine Briscoe might like her—might like her a lot—enough to dance with her, to spark with her. Nonetheless, if he were ever to find out that she was one-quarter Indian—Haven knew he would hate her for it.

"Tragedy," Doctor Perkins interjected, slowly shaking his head.

"Yes," Val said shortly. It did soothe Haven somewhat when he nodded at her with reassurance.

"All the searchin' we did . . . months and months . . . near to a year," Val continued. "And we never found anything—nothin' that would help lead us to where the Comanches were holed up, where the girls were . . . or even tell us whether they were alive. Comanches usually don't take prisoners. They didn't used to anyhow. They used to torture and murder captives that their women decided were too old to be assimilated into the band." His eyebrows arched in puzzlement. "So we had begun to think the girls were all dead, murdered, especially if they had refused to conform to the Comanche ways. Until today when I come upon Effie."

Valentine shook his head. "I could tell she was in a bad way when I got closer. She was so scrawny . . . so thin . . . bleedin'. But all she wanted was for me to make sure her baby lived and was safe."

"If you don't mind a question, Val," Sheriff Sterling tentatively ventured. "How on earth did she manage to get away from 'em? And how is it she came to be so close to Fletcher and on her own? Comanches don't let go of nothin'. They have to be lookin' for her."

Val nodded. "They will come lookin' for her, eventually. At least they'll come lookin' for that baby," he said, nodding to where Arabella sat rocking little Sadie Flower in the rocking chair.

Val sighed and rubbed the whiskers on his chin. "Effie told me the whole story while we were . . . while we were tryin' to get the baby birthed. What happened after she, her sister, and my sisters were kidnapped. The chief of the band had sent some men out to capture some women." He glanced from Haven to Arabella and back. "Women to use as slaves and such, I guess."

Haven knew Val was being careful—that he didn't want to refer to anything too shocking and horrible. Still, Haven well knew what he was implying, and her stomach wrenched at the visions that sprang into her mind.

"Comanches usually kill anybody over the age of three when they raid a home or town," Sheriff Sterling said, reiterating part of what Valentine had already told them.

"I know it," Val agreed. "But since the band has been disjointed and out on its own for so long, I guess some things have changed in the way they live.

"After the girls were kidnapped . . ." Valentine paused as he tried to regain control of his emotions. "Shortly after they were taken, Effie's sister, Christine, and my sister Alberta were killed . . . when they tried to escape. The chief—

who is the father of Effie's Comanche husband, this Wind Talker—refused to have the other three girls taken back to their homes."

More tears flooded Haven's cheeks, and she struggled with every ounce of strength in her not to burst into sobbing.

Val sniffled and then continued, "Well, Wind Talker had a wife that wasn't able to give him children. So the chief told Wind Talker to take one of the captive white women as another wife. He chose Effie. Seems Wind Talker ain't full Comanche after all, 'cause Effie said he's got eyes as blue as hers. Somethin' about his mother bein' a half-breed." Val sighed with obvious misery and, Haven guessed, pain.

"Effie said Wind Talker took care of her after he took her for a wife . . . protected her. He protected my sisters Lydia and Caroline too. He eventually convinced his father to let him have my sisters as wives as well, but Effie says he didn't . . ." Val's face grew crimson with barely restrained fury, his teeth clenched tightly together as he explained, "He didn't touch my sisters. Only Effie. He and Effie loved one another, or so she told me—so she swore to me."

"But if this chief's son was in love with her, how did she end up out in the middle of nowhere?" Doctor Perkins asked. "Seems he would've watched over her more careful."

A low rumble, almost like a growl, resonated

in Val's chest for a moment. "The chief sent Wind Talker and some others out hunting for the tribe. We killed the buffalo in order to break the Comanches' spirit, and we dang near cleaned them beasts off the face of the earth. With the buffalo gone, the band lives on deer and small animals, meanin' the huntin' parties have to go out more often.

"Wind Talker didn't want to go, Effie said. He was worried for her and the baby. But he did go, and no sooner was the man gone than Wind Talker's first wife, who Wind Talker had cast off, got hold of the chief's ear—talked him into gettin' rid of Effie and keepin' the baby for the band. I guess she convinced him that Effie would persuade Wind Talker to leave someday—to take her and the baby and make a different life for them apart from the tribe."

Again Val rubbed his temples. "I'm guessin' Wind Talker's father is a jackass, because he believed the old bi . . . the old witch. So the chief sold Effie to a devil of an outlaw name of Rattlesnake Cooley, on the condition that Cooley could do whatever he wanted with Effie, so long as he kept her safe long enough to have the baby. Once he brought the baby back to the tribe, Effie was his to let live, die . . . and worse."

"Rattlesnake Cooley!" Sheriff Sterling exclaimed. "Dammit to hell, Val! I know that name!"

Val nodded. "So do I. Ain't a man on earth that's as close to bein' the spawn of the devil as Cooley is."

"His name is Rattlesnake?" Arabella asked in a voice that revealed her fearful discomfort.

Sheriff Sterling looked to Arabella, explaining, "His name is Frank Cooley, but folks call him Rattlesnake. He's somewhat part Apache—at least he claims to be. He used to be a fur trader, but then he found there was more money to be made in outlawin'. But outlaws can't be trusted. Cooley tried to turn one of his gang—Big Boss Ikerd—into the law to collect the bounty on Ikerd's head. But Ikerd escaped and hunted Cooley down. Ikerd managed to get ahold of Cooley while he was drunk. Then he took a pair of hoof nippers to Cooley's tongue and slit it right in half. Cooley survived but had a forked tongue thereafter. He started makin' necklaces and such outta rattlesnake rattles and hangin' 'em from his neck and ears, around his wrists. Between his forked tongue and the rattlesnake rattles hangin' all over him . . . well, he became known as Rattlesnake Cooley. I seen a photograph of him once, and let me tell you . . . he truly looks like the spawn of hell." Sheriff Sterling shook his head. "How on earth did that girl get away from a man like that? I hear he runs with several Indians now too—an Apache, a couple of Comanche . . ."

Val nodded. "Yep. That's what Effie told me," he affirmed. "But when Cooley come to collect Effie . . ." Val's voice broke with emotion again, and he paused until he had it checked once more. "Seems one of the kinder Comanche women in the village gave some sort of herb paste or somethin' to my sister Lydia, and had Lydia give it to Effie. Then, when Effie heard Cooley say they were near to Fletcher, she fed the stuff to the men in the supper they forced her to cook for them. It didn't kill them, but it knocked them out cold. She took one of their horses, set the other horses to runnin' in different directions, and started ridin' west toward Fletcher. But she was so ripe with the baby that ridin' caused the baby to decide it was time to arrive. The horse threw her when she let out a holler at some point, and Effie hit the ground hard. The horse broke a leg comin' down after rearin' on her."

"Oh God above! Have mercy on her poor soul," Doctor Perkins quietly prayed.

Val swallowed hard, rubbing his whiskers. "Effie told me all this while we were . . . while we were tryin' to get the baby birthed. She told me that this Wind Talker is a good man—that he'll leave the Comanche to take care of the baby, that he'll search for Effie and the baby until he finds them, even if it takes him his whole life. I guess Wind Talker and the others were due back from hunting a couple of days after the chief sold Effie to Cooley. She made me swear to keep that baby away from Wind Talker's family . . . away from the band. She said he will come for her but that I'm to worry about the baby's safety first, above all else. And I promised her I would. I promised I wouldn't go lookin' for my sisters until that baby is safe."

Haven looked to Arabella—to the sleeping baby in her arms, the baby who would grow up never knowing her mother—and the flow of her tears increased tenfold.

"After I helped Effie birth the baby, I carried them both to my wagon, put them in as comfortable as I could, and headed back to Fletcher," Val said. "I-I knew Effie was . . . was gonna bleed out. She knew it too. I think we both knew she'd never live to be chased down by Cooley, to be found by this Wind Talker she loved, or to raise her little girl." As his eyes brimmed with moisture, Val added, "But I promised her I'd see that baby safe . . . and I mean to keep my promise."

"And we all mean to help you," Haven committed without even glancing to the others.

Val looked up to her, and her heart ached for the pain she could see in his beautiful green eyes.

"That's right," Sheriff Sterling said. "But Rattlesnake Cooley is one mean son of a . . . he's one mean bastard, and a hell of a tracker.

He'll track you to Fletcher, Val, even if it weren't the closest town to where you found Effie."

Val nodded. "Yes, he will. But I did have awhile to think about it, and I do have an idea—about how to keep the baby safe and out of Comanche hands." Val straightened in his chair. "And once Effie's baby is safe, if Cooley doesn't find me . . . I'm gonna find him. I'm gonna find him and beat the hell out of him until he tells me where to find my sisters. Lydia and Caroline are still alive . . . still slaves of the Comanche band."

"Maybe Wind Talker can retrieve them for you, Val," Haven offered suddenly.

Panic was rising in her like a bonfire. Comanches were brutal people—even still they were! And she could not even think of Valentine going after a renegade band by himself, even for the sake of his sisters. He'd be murdered—tortured and then murdered!

"Maybe when he comes lookin' for Effie, finds out what his father has done—what he did to her—maybe he can barter for your sisters and you won't have to go," Haven began to plead as tears rivuletted down her cheeks in desperate profusion.

Valentine didn't agree or disagree with Haven and her suggestion. He gazed at her a moment, his eyes narrowing, and she saw in them what she'd seen the first time she'd ever met him: hatred and fury.

It was Sheriff Sterling who spoke next. "I took your wagon out to your place, Val," he said. "But Rattlesnake Cooley, he'll track you here. Not just to Fletcher . . . but right here."

"I know," Valentine agreed. "But hear me out. Hear what I've got to say, and then tell me if you think there's a better way to keep everyone safe and get that baby outta town before Cooley shows up, all right?"

"Of course, Val," the sheriff said.

"I thought all the way home about what to do," Val began. "Thought more on it while Doc and the ladies here were seein' to Effie after she passed here a bit ago." Val rubbed at the whiskers on his jaw and chin. "The train to Limon don't run through Fletcher again until day after tomorrow. So we gotta keep this baby hidden and quiet until we can get her on that train—get her back to Effie's parents."

"But what about Wind Talker?" Haven interjected. "Effie swore he'd come for her . . . for the baby. I heard her tell you she wanted him to have the baby."

Val nodded. "I know. I know. But I ain't sure he'll make it here," Val said. "May be that his father will have him killed if Wind Talker tries to go up against him about it all. May be that it will take him weeks to get here. And we can't wait. I promised Effie I'd see that baby safe, and I mean to do it."

"Yes . . . yes, you're right," Haven agreed.

"So here's what I'm thinkin'," Val began again. "We go on and tell the town that I found a young woman and her baby out south of here—that she died . . . and that the baby died too. I'll dig Effie a grave. I'll do it now—today—and we'll bury her in the mornin', first thing. We'll wrap some rags or somethin', make it look like a swaddled baby . . . make sure folks see it in her arms before we nail the coffin shut. We tell the townsfolk that the baby died too . . . see?"

Sheriff Sterling nodded. "Then if Cooley does come lookin' for Effie and the baby, everyone in town can tell him the same thing: that they both died and were buried shortly after."

Haven exhaled a shallow sigh of relief. It was a good plan—a truly good plan. If Rattlesnake believed the baby was dead too, then Sadie Flower would be safe, regardless of whether Wind Talker ever reached Fletcher looking for her.

"But surely people will hear the baby cryin', Val," Doc Perkins put in. "This house is too close to town, and folks ride or stroll by every day. They'll hear the cryin'."

"Not if she's out stayin' with the Sandersan sisters," Val offered. "They live far enough out from town, and nobody walks out that way unless their purpose is to visit Wynifred and Merigold." Val gestured to Haven and then Arabella. "First thing in the mornin', Haven and Arabella can take little Sadie Flower out to the Sandersans, and she can stay with them. Maybe I can even get them two kind old ladies to take Sadie on the train to Limon to see her back to Effie's folks."

"But someone is bound to see Miss Abernathy and Miss Barnes totin' a baby through town, even early on in the mornin'," Doc Perkins suggested.

Haven gritted her teeth, wondering who on earth gave Doc Perkins the right to be so pessimistic.

"Not if we put her in a hatbox," Haven piped up. "I'm always carryin' hats out to Miss Wynifred and Miss Merigold," she said. "People won't think a thing of it—me carryin' another hatbox out their way. Bellie and I will just make certain little Sadie has a full tummy and is sound asleep before we leave."

Valentine grinned with approval, winking at Haven with one tired, misty, jade-green eye. "You're sharp as a whip, and I ain't lyin', Haven Abernathy," he said.

"Yeah . . . that oughta work," Sheriff Sterling agreed. "If we can get the baby to the Sandersans', get her poor mama buried tomorrow mornin', and then make sure she gets safely to Limon on the train day after tomorrow . . . yeah, that oughta work fine."

"And it won't matter that I brought Effie here," Valentine added. He winked at Haven once more.

"Cooley won't have any reason to come callin' if he's told Effie and the baby are both dead. Of course, we need to make sure one of us sees him comin' into town . . . so that he can be told." He smiled a little. "That will keep Miss Abernathy and Miss Barnes outta harm's way."

Haven's heart warmed and beat more quickly as Val continued to gaze at her. She knew he cared for her, truly. And that did not have to change—not if she kept her secret, kept it forever.

"Even so," Sheriff Sterling persisted, "you and me will be stayin' the night here, Val. I'll sleep at the front door, and you'll take the back door." The sheriff looked to Arabella, adoration mingled with worry evident in his bright blue eyes.

"Of course," Val agreed without pause.

"I'll be on my way then," the doctor said, rising from his chair and making ready to leave. Then wagging an index finger first at Arabella and then to Haven, he dictated, "But you ladies come fetch me if you need anything or have any worries, any problems feedin' that baby, you hear? Anything you might need, have someone fetch me."

"We will," Arabella promised.

"Thank you, Doctor Perkins," Haven added.

"Yes," Val said, rising from his chair and offering a hand to the doctor. "Thank you kindly, Doc."

"I only wish I could've done more to save that poor young woman, Val," Doctor Perkins said,

411

his countenance changing from determination to sadness. "Poor little thing."

As the doctor left the house by way of the kitchen door, Val exhaled a heavy sigh.

"I . . . uh . . . I suppose I oughta run home real quick and clean up before someone sees me and thinks I'm a murderin' lunatic," he mused aloud.

"You go on, Val," Sheriff Sterling encouraged. "I'll stay here with the girls, make sure nothin' or nobody comes in. And we'll set up here in the house tonight. We'll keep 'em safe."

"Yes, we will," Valentine affirmed with a strong nod. Looking to Haven, he told her, "I'll be back quick as I can, all right?"

"All right," Haven said, secretly wishing he didn't have to leave at all. She almost blurted out, *Can't I come with you?* but managed not to. She didn't want to be separated from him—not ever again. But she knew he had to wash Effie's blood from his body and put on clean clothes.

"Haven and I will see to Effie while you're gone, Val," Arabella offered. "Dan can hold the baby, and we'll make certain she's clean and fresh and dressed . . . as pretty as peach when she's laid in her coffin, all right?"

Val nodded, even as more moisture brimmed in his beautiful eyes.

"Thank you, Miss Barnes," he said.

Then Valentine strode to Haven, and she gasped as he bent, placing a warm, soft kiss to her lips—

right there in front of Arabella and the sheriff.

"Thank you, Haven," he said. "You were the first person I thought of when I knew I was in trouble."

"I'm glad," Haven breathed—her lips still tingling with bliss from his kiss.

As Valentine turned and strode toward the kitchen door, however, he paused. Looking back to Haven, Arabella, and Sheriff Sterling, he said, "I feel wretched . . . and sick to my stomach," he said. "It's gruesome—me goin' home to clean up, so I can dig a grave for a girl I knew all her life."

CHAPTER SIXTEEN

Haven was so tired. She and Arabella had not slept a wink during the night following Effie's death. Not only did Sadie Flower need to be fed, rocked, and changed every two hours, but also Haven's anxiety over what she and Arabella must do come morning kept her far too wound up to rest. Moreover, neither Haven nor Arabella could make herself leave little motherless Sadie Flower by herself for any length of time at all. Rather, they took turns holding her, talking to her, feeding her, and weeping over her for the sake of her great loss—her mother. It was a sleepless, heart-wrenching night, and Haven knew her eyes were red and puffy from crying intermittently the whole of it.

Yet as the sun rose, Haven found renewed strength and a determination to protect Sadie Flower that rejuvenated her. Thus, as she prepared a large, round hatbox—padding the inside bottom of it with soft cloth and even cutting small, decorative-looking holes and slits in the top and sides to make sure Sadie Flower would have enough air as she was carried to meet Wynifred and Merigold—Haven found she was not in the least bit sleepy.

Glancing out through the front parlor window,

Haven noted the freshly dug grave in Fletcher's little cemetery. Doc Perkins and Sheriff Sterling had carried Effie's coffin to the house early that morning, long before the sun had begun to rise. And after Val and the sheriff had placed Effie in it, Arabella had fashioned a bundle of cloth to look exactly like a swaddled baby, placing it in Sadie's arms. Of course, Arabella had been careful to position the bundle so that the baby's face, which would normally have been visible, was instead hidden against Effie's breast so as not to be seen by any townspeople attending her burial.

Val had suggested that the sheriff not place the lid to Effie's coffin until just before she was buried—suggested that they encourage folks in town to pay their respects to the poor woman who had died, even though they did not know her. That way, if anyone came looking for Effie, anyone in Fletcher who had seen her before she was buried could testify that she and her baby had died.

"She's very sleepy," Arabella said, entering the parlor with Sadie cradled in her arms.

"Oh, good," Haven whispered. "Lay her in the box, and we'll rock her in it a bit . . . make sure she's sound asleep before we leave."

Arabella nodded and nestled a tightly bundled Sadie Flower inside the hatbox.

Haven's eyes filled with new tears as she stared down at the little dark-haired angel. She saw Arabella brush tears from her own cheeks.

"Do you think it's strange that I'm feelin' desperate to keep her here with us, Havey?" Arabella asked.

Haven shook her head. "No—because I feel the same way. I feel sick in havin' to give her up. But I know we must . . . for her safety and her happiness," she admitted.

"I know," Arabella choked.

In no more than a few minutes, Sadie Flower was sleeping peacefully, and Haven secured the top to the hatbox over her.

"She'll be all right in here for the short time it will take us to get to the Sandersans'," Haven said, more to reassure herself than to convince Arabella.

"Well, let's be on our way then," Arabella sighed, "before I change my mind and decide I cannot give her up."

Haven nodded. "Yes. The sooner we have her safely tucked in with Miss Wynifred and Miss Merigold, the better . . . for her as well as for you and me."

Departing their house by way of the back kitchen door, Haven looked up and smiled, nodding to Val where he stood just a ways off. He would follow them to the Sandersans' as planned—at a distance, however, so as not to be seen by anyone Haven and Arabella might encounter on the way.

As Haven and Arabella made their way into town, keeping to the back of the buildings on the south side of the main thoroughfare, a rooster crowed somewhere nearby, startling them both.

"Why, I'm as jumpy as a cat in a room full of rockin' chairs!" Arabella quietly exclaimed.

"It's because we're on such an important mission . . . and because we haven't had a wink of sleep," Haven offered. "But we'll be there soon enough, and then Sadie Flower will be safe, and we can quit worryin' about runnin' into anyone and havin' to—"

"Mornin', Miss Abernathy!"

Seemingly out of nowhere, Robert and Ronald Henry popped out from the alley next to Mr. Griggs's livery.

Exchanging wide-eyed glances of concern with Arabella, Haven pasted on a smile as she nodded to the Henry Buttons and said, "Why, good mornin', Robert, Ronald. What has you two out and about so early this mornin'?"

Robert shrugged as Ronald answered, "We just woke up early this mornin' and figured we'd get out of the house and play while the weather is still good—you know, before the snow starts comin' in pretty soon."

"Well, that certainly does sound wise," Haven managed.

"What're you two ladies doin' out so early?" Robert inquired. He studied the box Haven was carrying—the box that held her precious secret—and then looked to the box Arabella was carrying—the box that secreted the diapers and bottles Doc Perkins had provided, as well as the drawing of Effie and Sadie Flower Arabella finished during the long, sleepless night. "Takin' new hats out to them Sandersan ladies?" he added, answering his own question.

"Yes indeed," Haven confirmed. "You know how Miss Wynifred and Miss Merigold enjoy receivin' new hats."

"But . . . it's awful early for deliverin' hats, ain't it?" Ronald posed.

"W-well, the two of us have so much work waitin' for us at the shop today, we thought we'd get these hats out to Miss Wynifred and Miss Merigold first thing," Arabella stammered. "That way we can get right to work in the shop."

Both Henry Buttons nodded, seeming to understand the wisdom in what Arabella had explained.

"Did you hear about the dead lady Mr. Briscoe found yesterday?" Robert unexpectedly asked.

Haven felt tears well up in her eyes and looked to Arabella for guidance. Arabella nodded, offering her encouragement that Haven should go ahead and answer the question with the response that she, Arabella, Val, and Sheriff Sterling had agreed upon.

"Yes," Haven answered. "Yes, we did. In fact,

the poor woman and her baby are in a coffin at our own house this mornin'.'"

"At *your* house? Why?" Ronald inquired.

"Because their house is closest to the cemetery, of course, silly," Robert answered, frowning at his brother. Robert looked back to Haven. "Mama says we're all goin' to go to her service this mornin', even though we don't know her."

"Yep," Ronald affirmed. "Mama says that even though we never knew the lady, it'll be nice for someone to send her to her grave with some tears and well-wishes that she and her baby will rest in peace."

"Your mother is wise . . . and very kind," Haven told them. "And I suppose she'll be wantin' you two home soon, so you can prepare for attending the service for the woman and her baby later this mornin', hmm?"

"Eventu'lly," Ronald shrugged. "But can we walk with you a ways farther, Miss Abernathy?"

"Yes, can we?" Robert inquired as well. "We really oughta make sure you ladies reach the Sandersan place safe and sound."

Haven smiled, winking at the boys. "You two are such gentlemen!" she complimented. "But are you sure you don't want to escort us just in case Miss Wynifred and Miss Merigold have some fresh cinnamon rolls bakin'?"

Robert and Ronald exchanged mischievous glances.

"Well, we really do just want to walk out there with you, Miss Abernathy," Ronald began. "But we won't say no if them Sandersan ladies offer us somethin' for bein' so gentlemanly."

Haven heard Arabella giggle a little with her. The Henry boys were too adorable for their own good.

"Very well," Haven agreed—even though she knew Arabella was as tentative to give permission as she. After all, what if Sadie Flower woke up and began crying? The plan to keep the town thinking that Effie's baby had died with her would be foiled entirely! Still, she couldn't just shrug off Robert and Ronald's kindness or their hopes that the Sandersans had been baking.

"But when we arrive, you need to promise me you'll run on home so your mother won't worry about you bein' late to the funeral, all right?"

"You bet, Miss Abernathy," the Henry Buttons chimed in unison.

Haven exchanged glances of deep concern with Arabella. It was a risk, allowing the boys to accompany them. But it was a risk Haven felt they should take. After all, maybe it would work to their benefit. If Robert and Ronald spread the news around town that they had seen Haven and Arabella out and about that morning, maybe any suspicion of things not being as regular as clockwork with them would be doused for good.

421

"Why, good mornin'!" Merigold exclaimed as she opened the door to see Haven, Arabella, and the Henry Buttons standing before her. "How wonderful! Haven Abernathy, is that a new hat you're carryin'? And you, Arabella Barnes?" she gasped.

"Um . . . yes," Haven stammered. "Arabella and I were wonderin' if we might come in and visit with you and Miss Wynifred a spell. We know it's very early and—"

"Why, of course you can come in for a visit," Merigold chirped. "You know we love to have you whenever we can." Looking to the Henry Buttons, Merigold added, "And we've got gentlemen callers too? What a delightful surprise indeed!"

"Thank you kindly, Miss Sandersan," Robert greeted. "But fact is, Ronald and me . . . we just escorted Miss Abernathy and Miss Barnes to see them safely here. We gotta be gettin' on home so we can get ready for the funeral."

Miss Merigold frowned. "What funeral? Who died?" she asked.

"A lady and her baby," Ronald explained. "Mr. Briscoe found them out a ways from town yesterday, so he brung them back to Fletcher so they could be buried proper."

Merigold frowned and looked to Haven with questioning suspicion, just as her sister appeared behind her, greeting, "Good mornin', all!" Yet as concern puckered her brow, Miss Wynifred added, "Did I hear you boys say someone has died?"

"A lady and her baby," Ronald repeated. "Mr. Briscoe found 'em yesterday."

"Yep. But we gotta be gettin' on home now," Robert reitcrated.

"Not without a cinnamon roll to add to whatever you already had for breakfast," Miss Merigold asserted. "I'll run get a couple for you. Haven and Arabella, you two come on into the parlor though, all right?"

"New hats?" Wynifred exclaimed as Haven and Arabella stepped into the house. The Henry boys stood at the threshold, smiling from ear to ear with anticipation of the treat Merigold was fetching for them.

"Um . . . yes," Haven said. "We . . . Arabella and I thought wc'd bring them by before our day gets too busy."

"Oh, I'm overjoyed!" Wynifred chimed. "But do tell me more about this woman Mr. Briscoe found . . . dead? Just outside of town?"

"Here you are, boys," Merigold announced as she returned, holding out a large cinnamon roll toward Ronald's and Robert's hands. "I've put them in a piece of muslin for you, so you have somethin' to keep you from gettin' too awful sticky."

"Thank you, Miss Sandersan," the boys chimed in unison, each accepting a cinnamon roll.

"I'm sorry we can't stay and visit," Ronald apologized, eyeing his cinnamon roll as if he were about to embark on the adventure of a lifetime. "But we do need to run on home. Mama will tan our hides if we're late again."

"Well, you best be gettin' there quick then," Wynifred encouraged with a smile.

Once the Henry Buttons had made their way down the porch steps, cinnamon rolls in hand, Wynifred closed the door, turned to face Haven and Arabella, and asked, "All right, you two, what on earth do you have in the box? Are you tryin' to trick us into takin' in a stray pup, a litter of kittens, or somethin'? And what is all this about a dead woman?"

"Yes," Merigold added. "You've never brought us a hatbox with holes cut in it. And anyway, you haven't said anything about making new hats for us. And who was she?"

Haven exchanged glances with Arabella as she carefully removed the lid from Sadie Flower's hatbox.

"My heavens!" Merigold exclaimed. "It's a baby!"

Without pause, Wynifred reached into the hatbox, gently lifting Sadie Flower and cradling her to her bosom as she smiled down at her.

• • •

"So that's where babies come from?" Ronald whispered to Robert as they both peered through one corner of the Sandersans' big parlor window. "I've always wondered where folks get their babies."

"Well, now you know," Robert whispered. He scowled, however, asking, "And no wonder Miss Abernathy was actin' so squirrely. But why would she and Miss Barnes bring a baby out here to two old ladies like the Sandersan sisters? They're too old to have babies, ain't they? And they don't even have husbands. And is that what hatmakers really do . . . deliver babies? I thought doctors did that. How does Miss Abernathy make 'em? Or maybe she gets them from somewhere else."

"Hush, Robert," Ronald scolded. "If we listen close, maybe we'll find out."

"Valentine found a woman south of town yesterday," Miss Abernathy explained as tears began streaming over her cheeks.

"That'd be the dead lady," Robert whispered.

"Seems so," Ronald agreed.

"She died shortly after givin' birth to her baby, and . . . and the whole town is bein' told that the baby died too. It's such a long, long story—which we will tell you the whole of, I promise. But first, no one else on earth can know little Sadie Flower lived . . . no one!

425

Everyone must believe she died with her mother."

"But why on earth for?" Miss Wynifred Sandersan inquired.

Robert and Ronald exchanged worried glances as Miss Barnes burst into tears then, as well.

"Oh, it's just awful, Miss Wynifred! Just so heartbreakin' and tragic. It's so awful!" Miss Abernathy sobbed.

"We better light out now, Robert," Ronald suggested to his brother. "There's somethin' goin' on we ain't supposed to know about."

But Robert frowned, took a bite of his cinnamon roll, and inquired, "Well, that's why we're listenin', ain't it? Because we ain't supposed to? We do it all the time. How else would we know that Mr. Briscoe and Miss Abernathy are lovers if we hadn't followed them home after the festival? It's how we know the sheriff is sweet on Miss Barnes too. That's the point of spyin', ain't it? To find out things you ain't supposed to?"

"Yeah," Ronald sighed. "But somethin' tells me this is different . . . like we really shouldn't be spyin' this time."

Exhaling a sigh of regret, Robert nodded. "You're right, Ronnie. You are." Brightening, however, he smiled, adding, "And anyway, we got what we really came for—one of them Sandersan cinnamon rolls."

Ronald brightened as well. "We sure did!" He

took a bite of his cinnamon roll, enjoying the perfect confection of it.

"Let's get on home," Robert said then, "before Mama really does want to tan our hides."

$$* * * * *$$

"Oh, my dear Lord! Please keep that poor young woman close to you now that she's passed," Merigold prayed aloud.

Wynifred sniffled as she gazed down into Sadie Flower's precious face—smoothed the thick, dark hair on the tiny head. "Poor little thing, motherless so early in life." She straightened then, however. "And of course Merigold and I will take her to Limon on the train tomorrow. And we'll make sure her grandma and grandpa Grayson have the drawin' too, Arabella."

Haven brushed the tears from her cheeks, bent over, and pressed a warm, loving kiss to Sadie Flower's tiny head. It had been difficult to recount the events surrounding Valentine's finding Effie, Effie and the others being captured by Comanches the year before, the danger Sadie Flower was in even yet. Nevertheless, it was helpful to share the burden of knowledge with the two older ladies she loved so dearly. It did indeed give Haven strength again.

"I'm just sick at havin' to leave her," Haven said, her voice breaking with emotion. "But we've got to. And we've got to get back home, make sure Effie's buried and that everyone thinks Sadie Flower died too."

"Yes, you do!" Merigold unexpectedly directed. "I've read about Rattlesnake Cooley, about the Comanche people and how brutal they used to be. Neither that devil outlaw nor those renegades can ever know Sadie Flower lived. Not ever!"

Merigold reached out, indicating she wanted to hold Sadie Flower for a time. Wynifred tenderly handed the precious baby to her sister.

"Yes," Wynifred said. "She must be spirited away as soon as possible. Were we younger women, we'd hitch up our wagon right now and . . . but we're not, and the train *is* the fastest way to get her home. Even leavin' on it tomorrow mornin' will get her there more quickly . . . and more comfortably."

"And more safely," Merigold added.

All at once, Arabella burst into sobbing.

"Bellie, she'll be fine," Haven reassured her friend, even as her own tears increased.

But Arabella shook her head. "It's not that. It's just . . . it's all so horrid! And it all began and ended so quickly. It seems like a nightmare . . . all of it! One moment we're dancin' at the Harvest Festival in town, havin' a wonderful evenin'. And all at once, Valentine is kickin' on our door and carryin' poor Effie and Sadie Flower in, with blood everywhere. And poor Effie is dead!"

"I know, honey," Wynifred soothed, gathering

Arabella into a comforting embrace. "I know. And it will haunt us all forever, especially you and Haven, the sheriff, and I'm sure most of all Mr. Briscoe. What a heartbreakin' thing for him—to find his friend, only to have her die and leave her baby in his care."

Merigold sighed with empathy. "That poor man. I can't imagine what his family has endured, what he's endured . . . and with this as the most recent part of it."

"Still, you girls best get back home," Wynifred encouraged. "Get on back home, and get that poor woman to restin' in peace. We'll see to Sadie Flower. You've given us the names of Effie's parents in Limon, and we'll let them know everythin'—includin' the danger the baby could still be in. I know it's hard to leave her, even to leave her with us, but you must. And I know you both know it."

Haven nodded. Arabella sniffled, straightened her posture, kissed Wynifred on the cheek, and wiped the tears from her cheeks.

"Thank you, Miss Wynifred," Arabella offered. "I'm sorry for havin' a weak moment."

"Weak moments are necessary if we hope to stand strong, sweet pea," Merigold said. "And in truth, they're not *weak* moments at all. They're emotional moments—moments that prove we are human, with carin' hearts. *Not* havin' those moments would be somethin' to apologize for."

"Merigold is right, Arabella," Wynifred agreed, "though you need to put on your false face for now so that no one will be the wiser as to why you visited us today. You go on and cry as often and as long as you need to when you get home. In fact, it's important that you do."

"Yes, ma'am," Arabella sniffled, straightening her posture once more, smoothing her hair and then her skirt.

"Thank you, Miss Wynifred, Miss Merigold," Haven said. She kissed Sadie Flower's sweet, soft forehead once more and then opened the front door of the Sandersans' home.

"She'll be fine," Wynifred assured Haven as Arabella placed a tender kiss to Sadie Flower's temple. "We'll keep her safe . . . with our own lives, if it's asked of us."

"I know you will," Haven breathed.

"Goodbye," Arabella said, closing the door behind them as she and Haven stepped out onto the front porch.

Haven glanced around in search of Valentine. But true to his word, she could not see him watching over them. She felt relief in knowing he was hidden—for if she couldn't see him, then neither could anyone else.

Linking arms with Arabella as they hurried back toward town and home, Haven exhaled a sigh of mingled sadness and hope.

"They'll see her safe to Limon and into her

grandmother's arms. I know they will," Haven said quietly.

"Yes," Arabella agreed. "She's safe now. And once we've seen Effie buried in her restin' place, I think I'll feel much calmer . . . even if that Rattlesnake Cooley and his men come lookin' for her and the baby. I'll be better once Effie's restin'."

"Me too," Haven sighed.

"But now . . . now I suppose it's time we started pretendin' that this is just an ordinary day," Arabella offered. "I mean, it won't do for folks to see us comin' into town with tear-streaked cheeks and red, puffy eyes. Let's pretend we're just out for a mornin' stroll, enjoyin' this brisk autumn day and all its loveliness."

"I think that's very wise, Arabella Barnes," Haven said. "And what happier thing in all the world is there to discuss on our mornin' stroll out in Mother Nature's loveliness than the fact that you will soon be Mrs. Dan Sterlin', hmm?"

Arabella smiled just a little yet shook her head. "Oh, for pity's sake, Havey. I didn't mean you should begin tellin' fairy tales."

"But I'm not!" Haven insisted.

Although Arabella had hardly had time to even begin to tell Haven about the conversation she'd had with Sheriff Sterling after the Harvest Festival, she had managed to tell Haven that she had found the courage to confess to Dan Sterling that she was a quadroon—that Mipsie was mulatto and her mother. Moreover, Arabella had had time to reveal to Haven that Sheriff Sterling didn't give a whit whether Arabella were all black, all white, half this, or half that—or, as he'd put it at the time, "as purple as a pansy." Sheriff Sterling had confessed his love to Arabella after the Harvest Festival—encouraged her to press Mipsie and Joe to move west to Fletcher. But just as Arabella had begun to reveal more to Haven, Valentine had kicked on the door—carried Effie and Sadie Flower into the bedroom. Everything else in all the world seemed to vanish after that. But Haven knew she and Arabella both needed something happy and wonderful to cling to, especially if they must put on the pretense that nothing more was amiss to them personally than the tragic death of an unknown woman and her new baby.

"Mark my words," Haven began, "Sheriff Dan Sterlin' will be proposin' soon enough—kneelin' down before you and askin' for your hand in marriage. You'll see."

Arabella smiled sincerely then. "Oh, I do hope so," she admitted. "And then, also soon enough, Mr. Valentine Briscoe himself will be askin' you to be his bride."

But Haven shook her head, even as tears caused from a different sort of sadness bored into her consciousness.

"I . . . I won't lie to you, Bellie," Haven whispered. "I've dreamt of just such a thing since the moment I first saw the man. But now . . . now I know that it's one thing for Dan Sterlin' to love you no matter what secret you hold . . . and quite another for Valentine Briscoe to love me—not after what that band of Comanches has done to his family, to his sisters, to his friends. He'll hate me if he ever finds out about me. And I'm no longer certain I could keep it from him forever . . . that I should keep it from him forever."

"Oh poppycock, Havey!" Arabella scolded. "I've seen the way that man looks at you. Even through all this horror, you put a spark in his eyes not to be denied. Why, he kissed you square on the mouth yesterday, right there in front of me and Dan, without takin' any pause. He loves you, Havey. And he'll love you no matter what."

"I'd like to think that he will love me one day, even for the fact I'm Indian—like the Indians that stole and murdered his sisters and the Grayson girls," Haven admitted.

"You are nothin' like those men, Haven! And you know it," Arabella declared. "Nothin' at all like them. Valentine does love you, and he will continue to love you. Mark my words, Haven Abernathy. You just mark my words."

Haven smiled at her friend, trying to appear as if she believed what Arabella claimed: that Val did love her and would love her no matter what he found out about her heritage.

As she and Arabella hurried home—home to make certain Effie was ready for burial, that Val's and Dan's accounts to be told to the people of Fletcher did not vary in any regard from their own—she and her sister-friend tried to talk of lighthearted things, tried to appear unruffled. Even as they met Mr. Griggs in town, they feigned calm.

And as they neared the cemetery and saw that Val and Dan had already moved Effie and her coffin to sit near her grave, Haven prayed in her heart—not to win the love of Valentine Briscoe or anything else pertaining to herself. In her heart, Haven prayed that Wynifred and Merigold would be successful in keeping Sadie Flower's existence a secret and that, once she arrived in Limon, the little baby girl who had had such a bitterly sorrowful welcome into the world would live a beautiful and happy life in impenetrable safety.

CHAPTER SEVENTEEN

As Haven lay in bed, she tried to concentrate on the beauty of the night—the warm glow of the embers in the hearth, the sound of the dry leaves of autumn as the cool breeze breathed through them outside the bedroom window. She thought she'd never felt safer in all her adult life as she felt in those moments, knowing Valentine slept inside the house in front of the kitchen door, Dan Sterling in front of the front door. And yet she could not rest. Indeed, thoughts of poor Effie plagued her. Haven wished she'd placed a warmer quilt over Effie before Val and Dan had nailed down the lid to her coffin—for wouldn't she be cold out there in the hard, dark ground, the autumn breeze wafting above? Haven thought about Sadie Flower—longed to hold, cuddle, and reassure her, longed to somehow let the little baby know what her mother had endured to try and ensure her safety—that she'd died in trying to do so.

And yet in the end, Haven knew that it was a great fear of losing Valentine's affections that kept her awake. After all, Effie wasn't out there in the cold ground, shivering and uncomfortable. She was in the arms of Heaven, warm, free from pain and fear. Haven knew that nobody in all the world would care for Sadie Flower more tenderly, more lovingly, and more perfectly than Wynifred and Merigold Sandersan. Sadie Flower was safe with them—would know even more safety by the next evening when the Sandersans arrived in Limon. And so Haven determined it was fear and guilt keeping her awake: fear of losing Valentine's caring for her, guilt as she considered keeping her secret from him forever.

As the clock on the mantel in the bedroom struck midnight, Haven knew she would never know another moment's peace if she didn't go to Valentine at once. She must tell him her secret, confess her lineage to him. Surely he would not despise her for it. If Dan Sterling loved Arabella all the more for who she was and what she'd endured in life, then surely Valentine Briscoe could see past Haven's bloodline. Couldn't he?

Haven listened intently for a moment. Yes, Arabella was asleep—deep asleep if the slow, even rhythm of her breath and the occasional quiet snore were any indication. Having made certain Arabella was peaceful in slumber, Haven quietly rose from her bed.

As she crept in pure silence down the hallway toward the kitchen, she wondered whether her grandmother Adair had been the one to bequeath her her light step. As long as she could remember, Haven, if she willed herself to do so, had been able to move without making a noise. Many were the times she had so silently approached Mipsie or Old Joe or even Arabella that each claimed to have been so surprised and so startled by her unexpected appearance to have nearly dropped dead where they stood. She had always known that it was a talent bestowed upon her—a gift—even if she could not fathom why it had been given to her. Yet in those moments, as she moved with such stealth—the stealth of a Cherokee warrior—she could not help but wonder if it was a gift given to her of her grandmother Adair's blood.

But as she stepped into the kitchen, having yet to make even the most inconceivable sound, she heard the click of a pistol hammer being cocked.

"Val?" she whispered into the darkness. "It's just me."

Haven gasped as Valentine stepped forward from the black of the kitchen at night. He'd been standing right in front of her.

"You about scared the hell out of me, woman," he whispered. "What in tarnation are you sneakin' in here for at this hour?"

"I . . . I-I need to speak with you," she answered. "I will never be able to rest another moment in my life until I have."

"Val? Everythin' all right over there?" came Dan's voice from the parlor.

"Yep," Val quietly called out. "Just Haven comin' in for a glass of water."

"All right," Dan said.

Taking hold of Haven's arm then, Val led her into the kitchen to stand before the kitchen window. The moonlight shining in cast a soft silver light over his face, and Haven's heart began to beat more quickly. He was so tall and handsome, so haunted, had endured such loss— and Haven loved him even more deeply for it all.

"What's wrong?" Val asked, a slight frown owning his brow.

"I-I . . . I need to . . . there's somethin' I need to confess to you, Val," Haven began, tears brimming in her eyes. "You . . . you may find you do not like me as much as you did before, but . . . but I have to be honest with you. I can't keep any secrets from you if I ever hope to . . ."

Haven could not finish her confession, however, for fear held her in its vice grip: fear of losing the only man she could ever love the way she loved Valentine Briscoe.

Holstering his pistol, Val grinned as he gazed down into her eyes, put his arms around her waist, and pulled her against him.

"You can tell me anything, Haven," he said in a lowered, coaxing voice that made Haven find it difficult to draw an even breath. "Anything. Nothin' could change my opinion of you . . . how I feel about you. Don't you know that?"

Gazing up into the mesmerizing moonlit jade of his eyes, Haven whispered, "Not this. Not this."

"Just tell me, Haven," Val urged. He leaned

438

forward, placing a lingering kiss on her forehead. "Just tell me."

Tears escaped her eyes then, and she glanced down and away from his smoldering, beguiling gaze.

"I . . . I thought it wouldn't matter," she began. "I thought you would . . . that you . . . that it wouldn't matter to you, the way Arabella's doesn't matter to Dan. But when . . . when you brought Effie to us, when I heard what had happened to your sisters . . . to Effie's . . . to Effie herself . . . I . . . I think your feelin's toward me . . ."

Val's lips pressing to hers silenced Haven, and in despair, for she knew it may well be the last kiss he ever offered her, Haven wrapped her arms around his neck, kissing him with a ravenous desperation.

Over and over Valentine kissed her, and she him! Such a passion blazed between them that Haven could have sworn her body was on fire— in the very least her nightgown.

And after minutes and minutes of such shared fervor, Val broke the seal of their lips, pressing his forehead to Haven's and asking, "Are you tryin' to tell me that you're part Indian, darlin'?"

"What?" Haven gasped, pulling back from him, staring at him in dumbfounded astonishment.

Val's eyes captured the moonlight as he smiled at her and put one warm, callused hand to her cheek. "Do you think I'm an ignoramus, pretty thing? No woman as beautiful as you is made up of just one plain ol' race or another. A woman like you has got to have somethin' stirred in to make her so uncommon to look at." Val reached out, combing his fingers through her hair. "And this here silk you got, I've never seen hair so pretty, so soft and lookin' like silk . . . never seen it on anybody, that is, except an Indian woman."

Taking her face between his hands and brushing the tears from her cheeks with his thumbs, he continued, "You thought I'd let you go because you got a little somethin' extra in your blood?" He shook his head. "Why, Miss Abernathy, I'm afraid you don't know me as well as I thought you did."

Haven's lower lip quivered with the powerful emotion moving through her. Was Valentine Briscoe truly standing there in her kitchen, standing there in the moonlight, caressing her face and telling her that he still cared for her? She wanted to believe it was truly happening—that it wasn't just a dream—but she was so tired from sleeplessness, from worry, fear, and mourning Effie, that she wasn't certain she was awake.

"Am I awake, Val?" she asked in a whisper. "Or am I dreamin' all of this?"

Grinning at her again, Val pressed his mouth to hers a moment before muttering, "You ain't dreamin', Miss Abernathy. You think a dream could make you feel like this?"

Val tossed any remaining inhibitions to the wind. Gathering Haven into his arms once more, he kissed her with such desire, with such demand that his desire be returned, he thought he might detonate and end up in pieces. Oh, how he loved the woman in his arms! How boundlessly he loved her! And as his arms banded around her, experienced the sensation of holding her without her soft body being all wrapped up in the hardness of a corset—absorbed the invigorating, provocative feel of her skin through her nightgown—Valentine felt the stone-cold of his heart begin to warm as well. In mere moments he knew again the Valentine Briscoe he once was—the caring, happy man, unscathed by harboring constant hate and the desire for vengeance. Certainly, the pain was still there; the determination was still mighty in him to one day see Lydia and Caroline returned to his parents. But he was different than he had been earlier in the evening. Before those moments of holding Haven, kissing her, Val had wanted to spill blood, kill the men who had taken his sisters. Part of him still did want that. But standing there with Haven's warm, curvaceous body against his own, he only wanted to find his sisters and return them to their home—find them and return them so he could hold Haven in his arms, kiss her, love her for the rest of his life.

As the clock in the parlor struck one, Haven sighed as Val broke the seal of their kiss. Laying her head against his shoulder as he held her there in the kitchen, a quiet giggle escaped her.

"And what's got you so amused at this hour? And after what we been enjoyin' together?" Val asked. His voice was deep but soft and comforting.

Haven exhaled a sigh of being awash with contentment and answered, "Oh, just Robert and Ronald Henry."

"Those Henry boys?" Val asked. "Here we are standin' in the kitchen—me makin' love to you like this—and you're thinkin' about Robert and Ronald Henry? Why, a man could be scarred for life by such a thing," he teased.

Haven giggled and pulled herself more snuggly against Val's muscular torso.

"I was thinkin' about how fortunate Arabella and I were this mornin'—that Sadie Flower didn't wake up and begin fussin' in her hatbox when the Henry Buttons joined us for our walk to the Sandersans' house," she explained.

Val chuckled, and Haven was lulled with further comfort and contentment as she listened to it resonate in his chest.

"Yep. I had my concerns too when they showed up outta nowhere," he admitted. "I was afraid they'd draw more attention to you two ladies than we could fend off too. Those two little towheads are about as inconspicuous as a tarantula sittin' on a slice of angel food cake."

Haven giggled, amused by the perfection of Val's comparison.

"Val!"

Dan Sterling's loud whisper startled Haven.

"Dan?" Val called in a whisper in return.

"There's someone movin' around out there by the cemetery," Dan said.

"Get on back to bed, darlin'," Val instructed Haven. "Wake up Arabella, and you two make sure you have them rifles ready to go, all right?"

"Val?" Haven asked as fear began to creep into her, dissipating the euphoria she'd been bathing in only moments before.

Gazing down into her eyes, Val winked, though he did not smile. "Go on. Do as I say. And have those rifles at the ready."

Haven nodded, raised herself on the tips of her toes, and kissed him quickly on the mouth before scurrying down the hall.

"It's a man, Val," Dan called. "He's comin' around to the back of the house."

Haven hurried into the bedroom, went to Arabella's bed, and shook her. "Bellie! Wake up, Bellie!" she whispered. When Arabella opened her eyes, Haven added, "Someone's comin' up to the house. Val says we should get the rifles."

Nodding and without saying a word, Arabella rose from her bed, and as Haven pulled the rifle out from under her bed, she prayed, "Oh, please, God . . . please keep us safe!"

"You see him, Val?" Dan asked in a whisper.

"Yep," Val affirmed as he watched the dark figure of a man silently creep up onto Haven's back porch. The man seemed to pause. He knelt down in the grass at the foot of the back porch steps. Pinching the grass, he drew his fingers to his nose.

"He's trackin' Effie," Val said. And although he knew he had spoken so quietly that he wasn't even sure Dan had heard him, the dark figure skulking at the back porch steps straightened, staring at the house. The man moved just a hair, but it was enough for Val to see his face and his long black hair, plaited on either side of his head with feathers woven in.

Instantly Val thought of Lydia and Caroline and of what Effie had told him. Effie had been adamant that Val believe Sadie Flower's father, Wind Talker, would come for her. Was this he? Was this the man who had saved Lydia, Caroline, and Effie from the same fate Alberta and Christine Grayson had suffered?

"Do you think it's him, Val?" Dan whispered. "This Wind Talker Effie told you about?"

Without waiting—without even thinking things through—Val called, "Wind Talker! Are you Wind Talker?"

He paused, looking toward the kitchen window through which Val and Dan stood watching him.

"If you're Wind Talker . . . we have information about Effie," Val called. "Are you Wind Talker?"

The man visibly inhaled a deep breath—nodded once.

"Effie told me to trust you," Val called. "But how can I trust a man whose people stole my sisters, Effie, and her sister? How do I know—"

"I know Lydia and Caroline Briscoe," the man's deep voice responded. "I took them as wives when my father gave me Effie. They live. I think Effie is dead."

"She is," Val affirmed. "I'm Valentine Briscoe. Lydia and Caroline are my sisters . . . and Effie was my friend. She told me to trust you."

"The baby?" Wind Talker asked.

"Can you be trusted?" Val called.

"That is a thing you will not know until you make a choice to trust me," Wind Talker answered.

Val looked to Dan and could see that he was as doubtful that they should trust a renegade Comanche as he was.

"Go back and stay with the girls, Dan," Val said. "I'll speak to this Wind Talker. But if you hear gunfire—"

"I know," Dan agreed. Then he turned and headed down the hallway toward the bedroom, where Val knew Haven and Arabella were most likely trembling with fear.

"I'm comin' out," he called to Wind Talker, "but I've got my pistol leveled at you all the same."

"I understand," the man said. "I will not move to make trouble with you, Valentine Briscoe."

Warily, Valentine opened the kitchen door and stepped through it onto the back porch.

"Let me see your eyes," he demanded of the stranger. Grateful that the moonlight was so bright, Valentine was glad that the man claiming to be Wind Talker raised his hands at his sides and tipped his head back so that Val could look into his eyes. Though Val was afraid that even the moonlight would not be enough to reveal the color of the man's eyes, it was. This man's eyes were, indeed, as blue as Effie Grayson's had been.

"She said you would come," Val spoke. "She said you would care more about her than you did your father . . . that you would leave him because of what he had done to Effie."

"And she spoke the truth to you, Valentine Briscoe," Wind Talker said.

Val frowned, uncertain whether to trust the emotion he saw in the man's eyes—the moisture heralding tears that were gathering in his eyes.

"She escaped Cooley," Wind Talker stated. "I found the horse . . . her blood near to it. You found her?"

446

"As God would have it, yes," Val confirmed.

"And . . . and the baby?" Wind Talker asked. "Did you find the baby with her?"

Val inhaled a deep breath. He was standing face to face with a man from the renegade tribe that had stolen his sisters and the Grayson girls. How would he ever find it in himself to trust the man? And yet he did—for he had promised Effie that he would.

"She had the baby after I found her," Val told him.

"Did the baby die?" Wind Talker asked, his voice cracking with emotion.

"She made me promise to trust you," Val said. "But . . . but your people have my sisters, Wind Talker."

"Did the baby die, Valentine Briscoe?" Wind Talker asked again.

"The baby lives . . . and she is safe in a place where no one will find her," Val answered.

"She?" Wind Talker whispered. "My daughter? I will take her with me."

Val gritted his teeth, willing himself to stay calm—to remember what he had promised Effie.

"That was Effie's wish," he admitted. "But I promised Effie . . . as she lay dyin', I promised Effie that her daughter, that your daughter, would never be returned to live with your people, Wind Talker."

Wind Talker's eyes narrowed, and he studied

Val intently. "I understand why you do not trust me. I understand why you will not tell me where my daughter is. My people have caused you pain . . . and great loss. I will prove to you that I am to be trusted . . . that I should have my daughter."

"How will you prove it?" Val asked.

Wind Talker inhaled another deep breath. Then straightening his posture, he said, "I will return to my people, to my father. I will tell my father that Effie is dead, that my baby is dead, that it is he who sent them to die. I will leave my people and take Lydia and Caroline with me. I will tell my father that I will do this, and he will allow it . . . or I will kill him. Then he will let me go. The band is weak now. Many of my people want to travel to join Quanah Parker in the Indian Territory. When I have said what my father has done, they will leave him. I will bring Lydia and Caroline to you here. Then you will know that Effie spoke the truth of me, and you will give me my daughter. Do you agree to this, Valentine Briscoe, brother of Lydia and Caroline . . . friend of my wife, Effie?"

Val clenched his jaw more tightly. Lydia and Caroline were alive; he knew that from both Effie and now Wind Talker. But how could he not go with Wind Talker to bring them home? Of course, he knew the answer; he didn't have to put the question to Wind Talker. A band of renegade Comanches would never barter with an angry white man, especially one who arrived to barter alone. But the son of their chief—the angry son of their chief, who had lost a wife and child because of their chief's evil greed? Val knew that his best chance at ever seeing Lydia and Caroline again was to trust Effie—to trust Wind Talker.

"What if your father won't let you take my sisters with you?" Val asked.

"Then I will kill him and take them anyway," Wind Talker answered.

Val sensed the man's sincerity. "You would be willin' to kill your own father for my sisters' sakes?" Val asked, disbelieving.

"No," Wind Talker said. "I am willing to kill my father for what he has done to Effie and to the child he stole from me. For that, he deserves to die."

Val nodded. He believed Wind Talker. He did.

"There's one more thing, before I agree to this," Val added. "Rattlesnake Cooley is trackin' Effie too. I have no doubt of it. Did you see him on your way here?"

"No," Wind Talker said. "One of my band—my brother Moon Eagle—found me and told me of my father's evil. I did not look for Cooley . . . not yet. I looked for Effie and the baby. But after I bring Lydia and Caroline to you, I will find him . . . and I will kill him."

Val nodded. "Well, just so you understand, if

Cooley and his men track Effie here, the whole town thinks your baby died with her. Anyone will tell Cooley that the baby is dead too. Your baby is safe, Wind Talker. But if you want her, you will bring Lydia and Caroline to me."

Wind Talker's eyes narrowed as he studied Val for a moment.

"Lydia and Caroline and Effie . . . all have told me of Valentine Briscoe," he said. "They claim you are a good man, a man of his word, a man who can be trusted. I will prove to you that I am a man who can be trusted, Valentine Briscoe. I will bring your sisters to you, and then you will tell me where my daughter is."

"I will," Valentine agreed at last. Though he was fearful, though he worried that he had lost any chance of saving Lydia and Caroline, he knew that Wind Talker was their best chance at freedom.

Offering his hand to Wind Talker, Val said, "We have an accord, Wind Talker."

Wind Talker reached forward, accepting Val's hand. "We have an accord, Valentine Briscoe."

"But if you do not keep your word, Wind Talker . . . you will never know your daughter," Val threatened.

"I understand," Wind Talker accepted. "I would ask you to know that it will take two days or more for me to return with Lydia and Caroline."

"Do you have a horse?" Val inquired.

"Yes. And I will ride hard. But I will be two days or three."

"Understood," Val said with a nod.

"Until we meet again, Valentine Briscoe," Wind Talker said. Then turning, the Comanche warrior sprinted off into the darkness, leaving Valentine awestruck that he had put his faith in a man whose people had kidnapped his sisters—a man whose people had killed his sister Alberta and Effie's sister, Christine.

Turning and entering the house once more, Val strode down the hallway straight toward the room where Haven, Arabella, and Dan were waiting.

"It was Wind Talker," he said before opening the door. Stepping into the room to see Dan, Haven, and Arabella all held rifles leveled his direction, he said, "I suppose I shoulda knocked first."

Haven placed her rifle on her bed as Dan and Arabella lowered theirs. She hurried across the room to him, throwing her arms around his neck as his arms enveloped her small, warm, soft body.

"Where is he?" Dan asked.

"He's gone to fetch Lydia and Caroline," Val said, pressing his face to the top of Haven's raven silk hair and inhaling deeply of her fragrance.

"Do you think he'll be able to bring them back?" Arabella asked him.

"I hope so," Val said into Haven's hair. "I can't

believe I've just laid my trust on a Comanche warrior."

He smiled as Haven took his face between her small, soft hands.

"Well, you might as well toss everythin' you ever thought you knew right out the window and lay your lips on those of a Cherokee—" Haven began.

But Val silenced her before she could finish her sentence—silenced her by claiming her warm, velvet mouth with his own.

CHAPTER EIGHTEEN

T his is a whole lot more difficult than even
I thought it would be," Val said as he and
Haven walked behind Dan and Arabella on the
way into town the next morning. Val shook his
head. "Just waitin' here, doin' nothin', puttin'
my sisters' lives in the hands of the son of the
Comanche chief who ordered his men to take
them? I must have lost my mind somewhere
along the way."

Haven frowned, her heart aching with sympathy
for Val. It would be hard enough for her to sit
back and allow someone else to try and save
Lydia and Caroline if they were her sisters, and
she knew it was all the more strenuous for a man
like Valentine to endure. Still, in her memory she
could hear Effie's telling Val over and over to
trust Wind Talker.

So she placed her hand on Val's arm, gazed
up at him, and said, "You're trustin' Effie.
Remember?"

"I know," Val said, winking at her. His eyes
still simmered with the pain and worry over his
sisters. But he grinned a little and nodded.

"Sheriff! Mornin' there, Sheriff!" Doctor
Perkins called as he hurriedly approached.

The man was pale as a cotton sheet and more

453

agitated than Haven had ever seen him before.

"Doc?" Dan called as Doctor Perkins reached them. "What's goin' on?"

Doctor Perkins stopped, bent over, and braced his hands on his knees as he panted for breath.

"There . . . there's a man in town," Doc puffed. "An Indian. Says he's here lookin' for his wife that was abducted by a group of outlaws."

"But Val talked to—" Dan began.

"Says his name is Wind Talker . . . and that his wife is a woman named Effie," Doc interrupted. "Thing is, Sheriff, the man's eyes are as black as night. And that sweet girl told us her husband's eyes were as blue as her own. Crabtree is talkin' to him in front of the general store now, tellin' him that the woman and the baby died here the day before yesterday and that he was at the funeral. But I thought if you could hurry on in and tell the story too . . . well, we might get rid of the fellow for good."

Dan exchanged worried glances with Val as he explained, "Doc, Val here spoke to Wind Talker last night—the Wind Talker with blue eyes. I'm sure this feller in town is ridin' with Rattlesnake Cooley." Dan lifted his hat from his head, raked a hand back through his hair, and set his jaw with determination. "If we're lucky, this feller will hear enough of the same story from enough people in town to set Cooley and his men to thinkin' they're out a woman and lost a Comanche chief's grandchild. I sure as hell would head for the hills if I had a renegade angry at me."

"Yep," Val agreed. "That oughta do it. I'll see the girls to the shop, and you go on ahead with Doc. I'll meet you at Crabtree's store."

"How about you head on back with the sheriff, Val," Doc Perkins huffed and puffed, "and let me see the ladies on to their shop? I don't think I can run all the way back just now, and I want the sheriff here to be quick."

Val frowned, however, and Haven could see he did not want to entrust her care, or Arabella's, to Doctor Perkins.

"We're nearly there already, Val," Haven told him, smiling with reassurance. "You go on with the sheriff. After all, wouldn't it be best to make sure this man knows Effie is dead? That he thinks the baby died too? That was the plan, after all—your plan."

"I know, but—" Val began.

"I'll see them there, Val," Doc promised. "I will."

Haven could see Val was still unconvinced. But Dan said, "Come on, Val. Let's take care of this business once and for all, so we can get back to livin' life, hmm?"

"All right," Val grumbled. "I suppose you girls are safer at the shop than you would be at home if Cooley is still trackin' me and Effie anyhow."

Val leveled an index finger at Doctor Perkins, adding, "Be sure to check inside the shop—make sure they're safe there—before you head back to your office, Doc."

"I will," Doc said, straightening his posture at last.

Val glanced over his shoulder to Haven as he and Dan started toward the general store.

Go on, Haven mouthed, smiling at him.

At that moment, she heard a train whistle. Knowing it would be the train leaving the station to take the Sandersans and Sadie Flower to Limon, Haven felt herself exhale a sigh of relief. Looking to Arabella again, she saw the same relief reflected in Arabella's eyes. Sadie Flower was on her way to Effie's family in Limon. That meant that at least Sadie Flower was safe from the man in town claiming to be her father, as well as any other of Rattlesnake Cooley's gang that might come looking for her.

"I do love the sound of a train whistle," Doctor Perkins remarked. "There's somethin' a mite reassurin' about them to me. Especially today."

Haven smiled as Doctor Perkins winked at her. She'd nearly forgotten that he knew that Sadie Flower was in the Sandersan sisters' capable care—that the train whistling meant the train and its passengers would be in Limon very soon, sealing the baby's exodus and delivering her to her sanctuary.

"I'm surprised Robert and Ronald aren't already out and about this mornin'," Arabella remarked as they walked. "They've usually had half a day of mischief and fun by now."

Haven giggled, nodding. "Those two just tickle me so. I never quite know what they're goin' to stumble into next."

As Doctor Perkins chuckled in agreement, Haven thought of the two Henry Buttons and her adoration of them. Yet in the next moment, a slight frown puckered her brow. Where *were* Robert and Ronald? Haven could not remember one single day since her arrival in Fletcher when Robert and Ronald hadn't been tearing up and down the street, escorting her to the shop, or prattling on to Mr. Griggs about the horses he stabled.

Haven glanced behind her, hoping to see the two little towheads sneaking along somewhere. But she didn't see them.

"Where on earth can they be?" she whispered to herself.

❋ ❋ ❋ ❋ ❋

Robert and Ronald Henry stayed very still. From their hiding place beneath the old rotted cottonwood stump, they had a perfect view of the three men who had been lingering in a thick grove of trees just outside of town.

"They're all as ugly as a handful of worms," Ronald whispered to his brother.

"And two of 'em look to be Indians," Robert added.

"That grisly white feller in the middle makes my blood crawl," Ronald remarked.

"He makes your skin crawl," Robert corrected. "Somethin' makes your blood boil when you're mad, and when somethin' ain't right, that's what makes your skin crawl. I told you that a hundred times."

"Shh," Ronald shushed as another man rode into the grove of trees.

"Rattlesnake," the man who had just ridden in began.

"Another Indian," Robert breathed.

"What'd you find out, boy?" the grisly white man asked.

"The woman and baby are dead," the newly arrived man announced. "The town buried them both in the ground yesterday."

"So you didn't see 'em for yourself?" the white man growled. "You just took the word of a bunch of townsfolk as truth?"

The Indian man shrugged, answering, "They took me to her grave. It is fresh. I could smell bodies under the soil."

Ronald and Robert both grimaced.

"Can Indians really smell dead folks in the ground?" Robert asked.

Ronald shrugged. How should he know? After all, only the day before he'd had a moment of thinking babies were delivered in hatboxes.

The ugly white man growled with frustration. "They're hidin' her somewhere in town," he gruffed. "Prob'ly hidin' that baby too. We gotta find out where she is!"

"I track the trail to a house," the scout Indian began, "then from the house to the grave. The woman and the baby are dead, Rattlesnake. There is no baby to take back to the chief. And when Wind Talker returns, when he is told what his father did to his wife and child . . ."

"Oh, to hell with Wind Talker!" Rattlesnake shouted. "I ain't afraid of one blue-eyed Comanche! There's four of us!" Rattlesnake leveled a dirty index finger at the scout. "They're hidin' that girl, and they're hidin' her baby. We gotta get 'em back."

"Robert?" Ronald asked in a whisper.

"For cryin' out loud, Ronnie!" Robert scolded. "Will you quit your talkin'?"

"But . . . but wasn't there three Indian men before?" Ronald asked. "I only see two now . . . and that's countin' the one that just rode in."

Robert narrowed his eyes as he studied the men. The ugly white fellow named Rattlesnake and two other Indian men stood there—but Ronald was right! They'd been so interested in the conversation, neither one of them had noticed that the third Indian man had slipped away.

Robert gasped as Ronald cried—as the Indian

grabbed him by his hair from behind them—took hold of the hair of Robert's head too.

"Rattlesnake!" the man shouted.

"Mama's gonna tan our hides good this time," Ronald sobbed as the other men hurried toward them.

"Well," the ugly white man named Rattlesnake said, "what have we here?" He smiled, and both Robert and Ronald grimaced at the sight of his tobacco-stained teeth.

"They were listening to us," the man who held them said.

"Is that so, boys?" Rattlesnake asked.

Robert and Ronald both gulped with horror as the man stuck his tongue out of his mouth. His tongue was forked like a snake's, and when he wiggled it, both boys let out a scream.

"Ah ha ha!" Rattlesnake laughed. "You see, boys? That's why folks call me Rattlesnake . . . 'cause I got a snake tongue." The man pulled back his dirty, long blond hair to reveal ears that had been pierced multiple times—each piercing having a rattlesnake's rattle dangling from it. The man had rattlesnake rattles at his wrists, around his neck, hanging from his belt.

"And you know the other reason I go by Rattlesnake?" he asked.

Robert and Ronald, so paralyzed with fear, just stared at the horrifying man.

" 'Cause I got poison in my teeth too, just like

a rattlesnake," Rattlesnake hissed. "Anybody I bite, anybody I get my venom into . . ." He snapped, and the action startled the Henry twins. "They drop dead within minutes. Do you boys want me to prove it?"

"N-no, sir," Ronald managed to respond.

Rattlesnake smiled—rubbed at the long, scraggly beard on his chin. "Well, I might be inclined to let you boys go. If'n you can tell me somethin'."

"Wh-what do you want to know, mister?" Robert bravely asked.

"Well, I'm lookin' for my sister, you see," the villain began. "Some Indians took her."

When Robert and Ronald exchanged glances of suspicion, their eyes darting to the Indian men that were Rattlesnake's company, Rattlesnake added, "Different Indians than these fellers here. Mean Indians. They took my sister with 'em, and she was gettin' ready to have a baby. And I just have to find her before she and her baby come to any harm."

"Valentine Briscoe . . . he found a lady out south of town day before yesterday," Ronald began.

"Hush, Ronald," Robert scolded. But as the man holding their hair in his fists jerked Robert's head backward, causing him pain, Ronald continued.

"Go on, boy," Rattlesnake said to Ronald. "I

promise no harm'll come to you . . . if you just tell me the truth."

"Ronnie, don't!" Robert cried out. This time the man holding the boys released Robert's hair, taking hold of his throat instead.

"The lady is dead," Ronald offered. "But her baby ain't. Th-the sheriff and Valentine Briscoe are hidin' the baby in town . . . i-in a back room at the jailhouse."

Robert's eyes narrowed as he studied his brother. Ronald knew as well as Robert did that the dead lady's baby was with the Sandersan sisters. At least that's where the baby had been the day before. Yet as Ronald stared at Robert, Robert began to understand. They needed a reason for Rattlesnake and his men to keep them alive.

"That's right, mister," Robert added. "We've sneaked into the jailhouse through the back door plenty of times. We can get that baby for you, mister. I'm sure your sister would want you to have her baby."

Rattlesnake's ugly gray eyes narrowed. He seemed to ponder whether he should believe the boys' story.

"We ain't got no reason to lie, mister," Ronald added.

"But if what you're tellin' me is true, boys," Rattlesnake began, "why're all the townsfolk sayin' the baby is dead along with her mother?

And how would you know different?"

"Because we were spyin' on the sheriff," Ronald said without hesitation. "We spy on folks all the time, mister."

"That's how we know about the baby," Robert added. "We seen Valentine Briscoe bring it into the sheriff after the baby's mama was buried yesterday mornin'."

"We see lots of things, mister," Ronald added. "It's how we know our et'kit teacher has a lover, how we know that Mr. Briscoe likes to sleep necked. We hear things when we're spyin'. And we see things too. We seen Valentine Briscoe bring that baby to the sheriff . . . and we seen the sheriff put it to sleep in the back room of the jailhouse."

Rattlesnake inhaled deeply, and when he exhaled, both Ronald and Robert gagged at the stench as the outlaw's breath hit them square in the faces.

"I'll cut your throats if you're lyin' to me, boys," Rattlesnake threatened. "I'll bleed you dry and leave your bodies on your mama's porch swing."

Robert shook his head. "We ain't lyin', mister," he affirmed. "And you know why we ain't lyin'?"

Rattlesnake chuckled, "Why?"

"Because we ain't stupid," Ronald answered.

All three Indian men smiled as Rattlesnake laughed.

"Well, we'll find out, won't we?" Rattlesnake asked. "We will indeed find out."

Robert and Ronald listened as Rattlesnake instructed his men. Rattlesnake and one of the Indian men named Iron Coat would ride into town. Rattlesnake figured that if the sheriff of Fletcher was hiding the baby, then the woman who died must've had time to tell him something about how she ended up in the middle of nowhere. He figured she'd told the sheriff about the Comanche chief giving her to Rattlesnake on the condition that the baby be brought back to the Comanche band when it was born. Therefore, Rattlesnake and Iron Coat would ride on into town. And while the sheriff and townsfolk were distracted by the presence of an outlaw, the other two Indian men, Forest Bear and Red Bird, would take Robert and Ronald to the back side of the jailhouse. Robert and Ronald would then show them the way into the jailhouse and to the baby.

Robert and Ronald both startled as Rattlesnake pointed a grimy index finger at them and said, "You boys better hope that baby is where you say it is. Otherwise, it's a painful death from a bite from me waitin' for you both!" Sticking his forked tongue out again, he slithered it up and down, making a slurping sound that sent Robert's and Ronald's stomachs to churning with disgust—and terror.

Haven looked up as the shop doorbell jingled.

"Good mornin', Mrs. Henry," Haven greeted with a smile. "What brings you into the shop today?"

Haven's smile faded, however, as she noted Claudine Henry's pallid complexion. The woman was always rosy-cheeked. Furthermore, she was nervously wringing her hands.

"H-have my boys been in to see you today, Miss Abernathy? My twins, that is?" Claudine asked.

At once, the hair on the back of Haven's neck prickled. Mrs. Henry let Robert and Ronald have the run of the town any day of the week except Sunday. Likewise, she had not forgotten her own concern when she hadn't seen the Henry Buttons on the way to the shop almost two hours earlier. Therefore, if Claudine Henry was out looking for Robert and Ronald, something was wrong.

"No, ma'am," Haven answered. Exchanging glances with Arabella, she added, "Have you told the sheriff they're missin'?"

"Oh, heavens no!" Claudine said as if it were unheard of to bother the sheriff with anything to do with her boys. "Why on earth would I tell Sheriff Sterlin' that I can't find the boys anywhere? It isn't his job to look after them. It's mine."

As trepidation leapt inside her, however, Haven linked her arm through Claudine's. "Come on," she said. "Let's the three of us find Sheriff Sterlin' and let him know the boys are missin'."

"Oh, they're not missin'," Claudine said, even as she walked with Haven out through the shop door. "They're just . . . I just can't find them anywhere."

As Haven and Arabella escorted Claudine along the boardwalk with the intention of heading to the jailhouse and Dan Sterling, Haven felt relief flutter in her bosom at the sight of Val and Dan standing not twenty feet away on the boardwalk.

"Sheriff! Oh, Sheriff!" Arabella called. "We have some concerns about Robert and Ronald Henry."

"Oh, surely I'm just bein' silly," Claudine said.

But as Val and Dan hurried to meet the woman, Haven was certain Claudine was not just being silly.

"What's the matter?" the sheriff asked.

"Well, it's just that . . . well, you know how my twins run off at times, Sheriff," Claudine stammered. "But they always, always, always come runnin' on home when I call. And the truth is, I've been callin' for them off and on for an hour now . . . and they haven't come home. And I'm worried, Sheriff. You know Peter is off to Denver today, and I . . . I . . ."

Haven looked to Val—watched his eyes

narrow—watched Dan and Val look to one another long and hard.

"Maybe that Indian this mornin' wasn't convinced after all," Val mumbled.

"Indian? What Indian?" Claudine exclaimed.

"Oh, that's another matter, Mrs. Henry," Sheriff Sterling countered. "We . . . uh . . . well, we'll just get everyone lookin' for Robert and Ronald. I'm sure they probably just found somethin' dead to poke at and didn't hear you callin'. But don't you worry. We'll find 'em. You bet we will."

"Val?" Haven breathed, however, as something beyond him caught her eye. "Val?" she breathed again.

"Dan!" Arabella gasped as she pointed to the two men riding into town from the east.

Val and Dan turned around to look at the riders.

"Wh-who are they?" Claudine asked in a whisper.

"Nobody we want ridin' into Fletcher," Sheriff Sterling said.

Val recognized Rattlesnake Cooley at once. Fact was, anybody who had ever heard of him or seen a newspaper with his likeness in it would have. The man was filthy dirty. Matted, long blond hair hung down his back and over his shoulders. He wore a deerskin shirt and buckskin britches—and appeared to have rattlesnake rattles hanging from every part of his body he could viably hang them from.

"Damn," Dan breathed. "That's the Indian was here earlier."

"Looks like Cooley didn't believe what he was told about Effie and the baby both bein' dead," Val said. "And where are those two Henry Buttons? Seems a mite too coincidental they're missin' at the same time Cooley is ridin' into town."

"Yes, it does," Dan agreed.

Val felt fury rising in him. The man riding into town was responsible for Effie's death. Who knew how many other deaths he was responsible for?

Furthermore, Val was sickened by the way the outlaw simply rode up to the sheriff, smiled, and said, "Mornin' there, folks. Any one of you happen to see my sister and her baby round these parts of late?"

"Your sister?" Val asked.

"Yep. My sister. And this here's her husband too . . . Wind Talker," Rattlesnake answered. "See, she was kidnapped awhile back, kidnapped by a band of renegade Comanche. But I hear tell she managed to escape and make it here. That's why Wind Talker rode in earlier." Rattlesnake's eyes narrowed accusingly as he added, "But it seems you folks didn't have the hearts to trust an Indian was tellin' the truth."

"It might be your sister I found a couple days back," Val said, ignoring the villain's implication that prejudice was the reason they had turned the man with him away. "I'm sorry to say, she died. The baby died too."

Val saw the Indian with Rattlesnake look past him to where Haven stood. It infuriated him that he had looked at Haven, and Val took a threatening step forward.

"Fact is, we buried the woman and her baby yesterday mornin'," Dan said. "We saw that they had a right nice restin' place."

"Is that so?" Rattlesnake asked.

"Yep," Val said. "That's so."

Rattlesnake straightened in his saddle. "Well, you see . . . that ain't what the two little towheaded boys we found spyin' on us said."

Claudine gasped, bursting into tears. "My boys!"

Haven felt dizzy—like she might faint at the horror of knowing Robert and Ronald had been found by such men.

"Where are my boys, you monster?" Claudine shrieked.

"Why, ma'am," Rattlesnake said, feigning offense, "your boys are just fine. We sent 'em runnin' on home to you the moment we realized they was lost. Seems to me they oughta be home by now. So why don't you run on and greet 'em, hmmm?"

Tears spilled from Haven's eyes. She knew that a man who was willing to buy a woman, take her baby away, and give it to a band of renegades would have no trouble killing—killing children. As Claudine ran down the boardwalk, past the outlaws, and toward home, Haven reached out, taking Arabella's hand.

Rattlesnake dismounted and walked closer to Sheriff Sterling.

"Not another step, Cooley," Val said.

Haven hadn't even seen Val draw his pistol, but he had—and he had it aimed right at Rattlesnake Cooley's forehead.

"Simmer down there, boy," Rattlesnake said. "I'm just lookin' for my sister's baby, that's all."

"She wasn't your sister," Val growled. "I know . . . because I knew her before she was taken by the Comanches."

"Is that so?" Rattlesnake asked, his face growing red with fury.

"Yes," Val answered.

"Get on your horse and ride outta town, Cooley," Sheriff Sterling ordered. "But know this: if them boys ain't home where you said you sent 'em—"

"Sheriff! Sheriff! Help!" Ronald Henry screamed as he came running out from an alley between the jailhouse and the livery.

Distracted by Ronald's cry, Haven hadn't seen Rattlesnake pull his own pistol from its holster at his hip—knew Val and Dan had been distracted as well—for as the shot rang out, Ronald Henry cried out once more and then hit the dirt, lying still.

Val instantly aimed his pistol at Rattlesnake's forehead again, even as Haven screamed, "No!"

"Hang on there, slick," Rattlesnake said. "Remember, I still got the other one."

"You dirty sons of . . ." Dan began, leveling his pistol at the man who had ridden in with Rattlesnake.

"Boys! Boys!" Rattlesnake hollered. "You still got hold of the other towhead?"

A sound like a shrill birdcall Haven had never heard before echoed through the air. And as people began to appear on the boardwalk—Mr. Griggs, Mr. Crabtree, and others—Rattlesnake Cooley shouted, "Then bring him on out! Bring that nosy brat out here now!"

Gasping as two Indian men appeared from the alley from which Ronald had run out, Haven's heart nearly stopped as she saw one of the men held Robert Henry by the throat. Her heart hammering like a steam engine, Haven released Arabella's hand and silently took a step backward.

She had to do something—she had to! Her first thought was that maybe she could manage to slip away—to somehow cross the street and sneak up behind the man holding Robert by the throat. Still, her way wasn't clear. Even if she could slip away unnoticed, there was no way to cross the street without being seen—not without backtracking far enough out of the way that it would take much too long. Furthermore, she did not have a weapon—not a knife and certainly not a gun. She quickly determined there and then that she would take to wearing an ankle sheath under her dress and petticoats the way her mother had once mentioned her grandmother Adair had done. Haven vowed never to be found feeling so helpless and ill prepared to assist ever again.

"Give him to me!" Rattlesnake demanded as he walked to meet the two men.

"Ronnie? Ronald!" Robert cried when he saw his brother lying in the middle of the street, motionless.

"Shut your piehole, boy," Rattlesnake growled, taking hold of the front of Robert's shirt. The outlaw turned the boy around so that he faced Val and Dan while he holstered his pistol, pulled a bowie knife from a sheath at his waist, and held it to Robert's throat.

"I'll gut him like a fish," Rattlesnake threatened. "I'll cut him ear to ear if you don't give me that baby you been hidin' in the jailhouse."

"What?" Dan asked.

"We had to tell him, Sheriff," Robert sobbed. "We had to tell him about the baby the dead lady had—had to tell him where you hid the baby—or he would've killed us both right then and there!"

"How did they know about that baby?" Val muttered.

As Arabella glanced back at her, Haven and Arabella exchanged understanding glances. Haven knew how the Henry Buttons knew about Sadie Flower, and she could tell Arabella did too.

"They didn't go right home yesterday," Haven whispered.

"No, they did not," Arabella agreed.

"I want what's mine, Sheriff," Rattlesnake shouted. "And I want it now."

"Get this one here, near to us, Dan," Val mumbled quietly. "I can get the other three—Rattlesnake first, before he hurts Robert. We can't risk that he won't hurt the boy just for spite . . . even if he thinks he'll die."

"Now none of that, boys," Rattlesnake chuckled. "Just give me what I come for, and I'll be on my way. And your little town here will only have one less grubby little devil instead of two less."

"Robert? Robert?" Claudine Henry called.

Haven looked to see Claudine starting toward where Rattlesnake held Robert with a knife at his throat.

"Claudine, no!" Haven called.

"Ronald? Ronald!" Claudine screamed.

And all at once, Haven thought again of her Cherokee grandmother—of Amadahy Adair, whose name so beautifully translated to Forest Water, her courage and the painful self-sacrifice her grandmother had made for Haven's mother's sake. In those moments, she knew that her grandmother Adair's decision to leave her child with those who could give her a better and safer life was not only heartbreaking but also brave beyond measure. The Henry Buttons weren't Haven's babies—of course they weren't. But she loved them almost as much as she could imagine loving her own.

"Stop!" Haven shouted. "I moved the baby. The boys don't know where the baby is because I took her from the jailhouse just this mornin'. I was worried you would come for her the way Effie feared."

"Haven!" Val growled.

But Haven stepped into the street and began walking toward Rattlesnake Cooley—toward Robert Henry.

"You're lyin', woman," Rattlesnake growled.

"No," Haven countered firmly. "I took the baby. I couldn't stand the thought of her cold and alone in a jailhouse cell. So if you want her . . . you're goin' to let that boy go."

"I ain't lettin' him go," Rattlesnake chuckled. "What? Do you think I ain't got brains in my skull, woman? I know you're just tryin' to save this boy."

"I am tryin' to save him," Haven said as she

slowly drew closer to the villain. "And if you kill him, you'll have to kill me too. Because if you harm a hair on his head, I'll never tell you where I've hidden Effie's baby girl."

"Haven!" Val shouted—and she could hear the fear in his voice.

"I'll slit his throat, girl!" Rattlesnake hollered. Then removing the knife from near Robert's throat, Rattlesnake pointed the long, thick blade threateningly at Haven. "And then I'll slit yours!"

Haven covered her ears and dropped to her knees as the shots rang out—as in less than a second a bullet hit Rattlesnake Cooley between the eyes, causing his body to go limp and release Robert. In less than another second, another shot—then two more. Haven watched as the men who had been standing on either side of Rattlesnake dropped like sacks of grain—each man owning a bullet hole in his forehead the way Rattlesnake Cooley did.

"Mama!" Robert Henry sobbed as he ran to meet his mother. "Mama! I'm so sorry! I'm so sorry!"

Haven watched as Claudine and Robert Henry kneeled in the dirt, sobbing as they held tightly to one another.

Crawling to him, Haven gently turned over Ronald's lifeless body.

"Oh, Ronald!" she cried.

Arabella was next to her at once, and they both

gasped when Ronald's eyes fluttered open—when he looked directly at Haven and asked, "Babies don't really come from hatboxes, do they, Miss Abernathy?"

"Ronald! My Ronald!" Claudine laughed and cried with hysteria. "My baby!"

"Let me see," Doctor Perkins asked. "I saw everythin' from my office window. Let me see the boy."

"I been shot, Doc," Ronald mumbled.

Doctor Perkins breathed a heavy sigh—smiled as he inspected the wound at Ronald's shoulder. "You surely have, Mr. Henry. Shot through and through right here in your shoulder. It might pain you awhile, but I don't think the bullet hit a bone, so we'll just clean the wound thoroughly, and you'll be just fine."

"Oh, my baby!" Claudine sobbed, gathering Ronald into her arms.

"Ow, Mama," Ronald weakly whined. "Be careful. I been shot, remember?"

Haven sat back on her heels, buried her face in her hands, and began to sob. It wasn't in her to scold the Henry Buttons for spying on the Sandersan sisters, Arabella, and her. All she could do in that moment was offer silent prayers of gratitude that the boys hadn't been killed, that Val and Dan had saved their lives, and that Effie Grayson could rest in peace, knowing that her Sadie Flower would be safe.

It wasn't until she felt Val's arms around her—felt him lift her to her feet, turn her around, and bind her in his powerful arms—that Haven was able to take a deep breath.

"I oughta tan your hide, girl!" Val lovingly scolded. "But it's over, darlin'," his rich, reassuring voice said. He pressed his lips to her ear and whispered, "It's over. Everythin's all right now. The devil and his backscratchers are dead. And Effie's baby is safe in Limon. It's over. But I still oughta paddle your pretty little fanny."

"This part is over, Val," Haven wept, however. "This part is over. But it won't truly be over until Lydia and Caroline are back with you."

Val took Haven's face between his warm hands, gazing down into her eyes with the moisture of emotion glistening in his.

"But you bein' in danger, Haven," he said, "*that* is over. I was so afraid Cooley would track me and Effie to your doorstep, darlin'. You don't know how anxious and sick I've been about it. And then you go waltzin' out there like you did. I nearly dropped dead of my heart stoppin'!" Val inhaled a deep breath of relief, however, adding, "But he's dead, and he won't be trackin' anybody any more. You're safe . . . and that's what matters most to me. God forgive me, Haven . . . but that matters more to me even than my sisters' bein' found and—"

"Shh," Haven said, pressing her fingers to his mouth to hush him. "Don't say that, Val."

"But it's true," he mumbled against her fingers. "I couldn't live without you, Haven Abernathy. I love you . . . so much more than you realize."

"I love you, Valentine Briscoe," Haven wept, "ever since that first day when—"

But Valentine interrupted her confession— interrupted her by pressing his mouth to hers in such a kiss as to send even Merigold Sandersan to gasping in astonishment.

"You see, Mama?" Haven heard Ronald Henry say. "Me and Robert told you Mr. Briscoe and Miss Abernathy was lovers."

CHAPTER NINETEEN

W ell, as it turned out, them filthy ol' outlaws was all dumber than a sack of hammers," Haven heard Robert say as she stepped out of the general store and onto the boardwalk. "They believed me and Ronald, that we knew where the baby was."

"And it was a good thing too," Ronald interjected. "Otherwise we'd both be dead for sure and for certain."

She smiled, amused to see Robert and Ronald sitting on the boardwalk with little Walter Crabtree and Cleveland Lewis. If anything on earth was for sure and for certain, it was that the Henry Buttons were not tired of telling the harrowing story of how they helped rid the world of four malevolent outlaws.

"I still can't believe you was gunshot, Ronald," Cleveland awed, eyeing the sling Robert's arm was cradled in.

"Yep," Ronald affirmed with pride. "Shot through and through. Doc Perkins says I only have to wear this here sling another day or two. Then the bullet hole will have had a week to heal, and I don't have to be so careful."

"Still tellin' their tale, huh?" Val chuckled

quietly as he stepped out of the general store to stand next to Haven.

"Yes indeed," Haven answered. "And I'm sure they'll continue to tell it for as long as someone is willin' to listen."

Haven glanced to Val, noting the way he looked out toward the east—the way a slight frown wrinkled his handsome brow.

"I'm sure he'll bring them soon, Val," she encouraged. "It probably just took him longer than he thought it would to barter with his father or . . . or to get the girls ready to travel."

Val's frown had been nearly perpetual since the third day after Wind Talker's leaving with the promise of bringing Lydia and Caroline home. Once the fourth day dawned, he'd begun to doubt he'd done the right thing in trusting Wind Talker at all. And now it was day six since Wind Talker had vowed he would bring Val's sisters home, and she could see the worry, the doubt, even the fear in his beautiful eyes.

"Maybe," Val sighed—though Haven knew he wasn't convinced. He gazed down at her, grinning, even for the worry in his eyes. "But at least we know the Sandersans are on their way back to town."

Haven smiled as she remembered the telegram Wynifred and Merigold had sent to her and Arabella the day before. "Yes, they are," she said, relieved. "Although I cannot understand why they lingered in Limon an entire week. They missed all the frightful, horrifyin' happenin's. And you know how they hate to miss anything that goes on in Fletcher."

"Indeed I do," Val affirmed. Then, winking at Haven, he asked, "Are you ready to head out to the train station to meet 'em when the train arrives? Dan and Arabella left a bit ago."

"Of course," Haven answered. "I cannot wait to give Miss Wynifred and Miss Merigold a hug, tell them all about what they missed, and thank them for seein' Sadie Flower safely to her grandparents."

Again worry puckered Val's brow. "Yep. And it looks like she may be stayin' there, 'cause if Wind Talker don't bring—"

"He will," Haven interrupted. "I know he will."

Val exhaled a breath in attempting to believe the fact himself. "All right then. Let's go greet them two nice ol' ladies, hmmm?"

Haven nodded, sighing with bliss as Val took hold of her hand as they began walking.

"See, Cleve," Haven heard Ronald say. "We told you Mr. Briscoe and Miss Haven are lovers."

Val chuckled, leaned closer to Haven, and whispered, "Oh, that boy don't know the half of it."

Giggling, Haven wrapped her free arm around Val's that held her hand. "Don't be so sure, Mr. Briscoe. Almost gettin' murdered by outlaws hasn't kept those Henry Buttons from continuin' to spy on folks, you know."

Chuckling again, Val agreed, "I expect not."

❋ ❋ ❋ ❋ ❋

The day was flawless, exquisite in its splendid artistry. The sky was azure and clear. The aspens' transformation was complete, and they had begun to drop their gold leaves so that each tree seemed to have a pile of pirate's booty scattered beneath it. The breeze was crisp and filled with the fragrance of harvest, woodsmoke, the cool mint of Jack Frost's breath. And yet, to Haven, the most wonderful, delicious morsel of the day was the warmth of Val's body, the feel of his touch, the knowledge that he loved her.

It was true that with all that had transpired over the past week—Effie's death, the need to spirit Sadie away to Limon, Rattlesnake Cooley and his men taking the Henry boys, and the shootings that left Ronald Henry wounded but alive while purging a measure of evil from the world—there had been very little time for Haven and Val to simply bathe in the wonder of having found one another. After all, there were outlaws to be buried, other lawmen to be notified. Most of all, there had been the ever-present anxiety over whether, after all that had been endured, Wind Talker would keep his word. Would he even be able to keep his word?

At Val's insistence, Miss Wynifred and Miss Merigold did not breathe a word of hope to Valentine's parents regarding Lydia and Caroline's possible return, though Haven and Arabella had told Wynifred and Merigold the story of what had happened to his sisters. All concerned knew it was inevitable that the Sandersans would meet the Briscoe family. After all, they were bringing not only Sadie Flower to Effie's parents but also the tragic, heart-wrenching news that both Effie and her sister, Christine, were dead. Following the execution of Rattlesnake Cooley and his men, Val sent a telegram to his mother and father, explaining that, although the fates of Christine and Effie had been certain, there was no news of Alberta, Lydia, and Caroline. Haven knew that Wynifred and Merigold would've told Val's family exactly what he'd asked them to—or rather asked them not to. Furthermore, she agreed with Val's decision to keep what was known about his sisters from his parents, at least for the time being—at least until enough time had passed to allow Wind Talker to return with them.

Of course, Haven saw with each passing day Val's fears multiply—fear that he may have to tell his parents he'd put his faith in a man who rode with the band who had taken his sisters, that he may have to tell them he had made a mistake, and that he alone had sealed Lydia and Caroline's horrifying fate. Oh, he didn't constantly speak of it to her, but Haven knew. She could see it in his eyes, and it was why she so often encouraged him to keep his faith and hope in Effie's confidence in Wind Talker.

"What're you thinkin' about?" Val asked, drawing Haven from her musings.

"Oh, just how excited Robert and Ronald will be that Miss Wynifred and Miss Merigold are returnin'," she lovingly fibbed.

Val smiled. "So that they can get back to bakin' their cinnamon rolls?" he asked.

"Exactly," Haven giggled, "though I do like to think the Henry Buttons are fond of the ladies, as well."

"I'm certain they are," Val assured her.

The sound of the train whistle urged Val and Haven to hurry their pace. And as they stepped up onto the train station platform to see Arabella and Dan standing there waiting for them, the train, not so far off now, began to slow. Steam exhaled from the engine as it slugged to a stop to position the passenger car directly in front of the platform.

No sooner had the conductor stepped off the passenger train, calling, "Fletcher!" than Miss Wynifred and Miss Merigold appeared.

"Yoo hoo!" Merigold called, waving to Haven and the others. "We're home at last!"

Her instant pleasure at knowing her friends

had returned caused Haven to giggle with delight.

"They can see that for themselves," Wynifred said to Merigold as the conductor helped each woman step down onto the platform.

"Oh, our angels!" Merigold exclaimed, throwing her arms around Haven's neck as Wynifred did the same to Arabella. "I feel like we've been gone for simply eons!"

"It does feel that way," Wynifred agreed. "Even if it was less than a week." Turning to Dan, she offered a hand. "Good mornin', Sheriff. Why, I certainly didn't expect to be greeted by the law."

"Well, I wanted to be here to thank you for your heroism, Miss Wynifred . . . Miss Merigold," Dan said, smiling as he squeezed Wynifred's hand in greeting and then Merigold's.

"Oh, fiddle-faddle, Sheriff," Wynifred said, blushing. "We just had us a little holiday in Limon, that's all." She winked at Dan before turning to Val, offering her hand and saying, "And Mr. Briscoe! What a pleasure to see you here."

"Thank you, ma'am," Val said, smiling as he accepted the woman's hand.

"I see you left your quilt at home this mornin'," Merigold added with a wink as she clasped his hand in greeting.

Val chuckled, "Yes, ma'am," and winked at Haven.

"You were gone so long, Miss Wynifred, Miss Merigold," Haven offered. "I'm sure the expense was . . . I feel badly that . . ."

"Oh, nonsense," Merigold interrupted, however. "Fact is, Wynnie and I have plenty of money to our names. For one thing, our father taught us to squeeze a nickel 'til the buffalo dropped a meadow muffin."

"Merigold!" Wynifred scolded. "Don't be so indelicate."

"Well, it's true," Merigold stated. "And besides, I don't want Haven worryin' over our expenses."

Clearing her throat, as if it would vanquish the image Merigold had placed in everyone's mind concerning a defecating buffalo, Wynifred said, "Well, I'm certain you've all got news for us, and we certainly have tales to tell about our adventures. But before we all start chattin' like hens in a henhouse, Merigold and I have a surprise for Haven and Arabella." Wynifred's face pinked up with the anticipation of delight.

"Oh, we certainly do!" Merigold confirmed. She looked as perky as a hummingbird. "Go on, Wynifred. Tell them."

"Well, it's one reason we lingered in Limon longer than you all expected," she began. "You see, Merigold and I have been usin' telegrams to communicate with some folks these past couple weeks. And wouldn't you know it, while we were in Limon, everything we'd been correspondin' with others about . . . well, I suppose there's nothin' to be explained but to . . ."

Having turned their backs to the train after Wynifred and Merigold had exited the passenger car, and having been enraptured by the rather gregarious reunion, neither Haven nor Val, Arabella nor Dan, had taken notice of anyone else who may have departed the passenger train in Fletcher.

"Go on, you four! Turn around and see who we've brought with us!" Merigold exclaimed.

When Haven turned to see Mipsie and Old Joe standing on the train platform behind them, she burst into tears of joyful astonishment!

"Mama!" Arabella cried as she rushed forward, throwing herself into her mother's loving embrace.

"Papa Joe," Haven wept as Old Joe enveloped her in the familiar, protective strength of his arms.

"I told you they'd be surprised, Wynifred Sandersan," Haven was aware of Merigold saying.

Old Joe stroked her hair and whispered, "Dere, dere, darlin'. We's come out to be wi'ch you. We ain't never any of us goin' to be apart a'gin."

The smell of home still clung to Joe's shirt— the smell of thick green grass, horses, and fresh-chopped wood—and Haven inhaled the familiar aroma deeply. Visions of her mother and father lingered in her mind as her tears soaked the front of Joe's shirt, and although she was joyful that the rest of her family was now with her, the pain in her heart in knowing she would never see her mother and father again in this life returned, and it was bitter in its excruciation.

"Daddy!" Arabella sobbed as she released Mipsie and opened her arms to Old Joe.

Turning to face Mipsie, more tears flooded Haven's cheeks. Throwing herself into Mipsie's maternal embrace, Haven sobbed, "Mipsie! Oh, Mama Mipsie! How I've missed you!"

"And I missed you, my baby girl," Mipsie wept.

After a long time of lingering in Mipsie's embrace, weeping for the pain of what she had lost, and rejoicing in what had been returned to her, Haven sniffled and released Mipsie, saying, "Why, I'm as weepy as a summer willow! I'm so sorry. It's just that . . . oh, so much has happened since we've been apart, and Arabella and I have missed you two so much, and . . ."

Haven's thoughts were scattered—lost—as she glanced behind Mipsie to see someone else standing there: a woman—an elderly woman with long dark hair in two plaits, wearing a simple blue gingham day dress—a woman she had seen in the photographs she'd found after her mother and father had died.

"Grandma?" Haven breathed. "Grandma Adair?"

The beautiful, dark-skinned woman smiled as tears spilled from her eyes.

"Yes," she said in a soft voice that remineed Haven of her mother's. "Yes, granddaughter. I am your grandmother . . . the mother of your mother."

Haven nearly swooned! If it hadn't been for Val stepping up behind her to steady her, she would surely have toppled over from the shock of seeing her grandmother Adair standing before her on the Fletcher train station platform.

"I hope you are not angry with me for coming," her grandmother said. "When I received the telegram from your kind friends, they said I should come, and I—"

Now it was Forest Water Adair's turn to lose her thoughts of what she had meant to say, for as Haven wrapped the woman in her arms, sobbing with joy, so her grandmother began to weep as well.

"I know we did the right thing, Wynnie," Merigold sobbed.

"So did I, Meri," Wynifred wept. "So did I."

✳ ✳ ✳ ✳ ✳

Haven sat on a bench at the back of the station platform with her grandmother, holding her hand as they conversed, and Arabella sat on the bench as well, between Mipsie and Old Joe. Val stood before them, watching over them like a powerful sentinel, as Dan headed back to town to fetch a wagon and team from Mr. Griggs to carry them all into Fletcher.

"It's my grandmother, Val," Haven said, as she had already said several times before. Gazing at him, momentarily wondering if she were only dreaming it all—Val's love, her grandmother's appearance, Old Joe and Mipsie's arrival—her heart swelled with joy, with hope, and in knowing her happiness was complete in that moment.

Yet even though Val smiled at her, winked, and said, "I know, darlin'. I know," Haven again sensed his deep anxiety—his own pain that would not be vanquished by the arrival of unexpected loved ones at the train station.

"Excuse me for a moment, Grandma," Haven said. "Do you mind?"

Her grandmother smiled, fresh tears brimming in her green eyes—her eyes the same shade of Haven's mother's and of her own.

"Not at all, my dearest," her grandmother said. "I can see that you love him very much and that he loves you in return. And I can see there is pain in him. I am here now. See to your man."

"Thank you," Haven whispered, leaning forward and placing a loving kiss to her grandmother's cheek.

Rising from the bench, Haven walked to where Val stood, his legs straight and his strong arms folded across his chest.

"I-I'm sorry for all this, Val," Haven began. "That I should be feelin' so much joy, when I know your poor heart is miserable, is simply—"

"Is simply wonderful, Haven," Val interrupted. And he was sincere. As he reached out, taking her hands in his, drawing one hand to his lips and kissing the back of it, he smiled. "Your joy is my joy, darlin'," he said. "Just as I know my sorrow is in you too. But don't feel like you can't be happy, Haven . . . because I am. No matter what happens from here on, you are my happiness, Haven. You're everything to me. Everything."

Haven nodded, trying to believe him. Yet his pain, his worry, now joined by the guilt he felt at having allowed Wind Talker to go for his sisters instead of going himself, weighed heavily on his handsome countenance.

"Mr. Briscoe?" Wynifred asked from her seat on the bench behind Haven.

"Yes, ma'am?" Val answered, looking over Haven's head to Wynifred.

"Is your pistol fully loaded?" Wynifred asked.

Haven turned around, discomfited by Wynifred's unexpected question.

"Yes, ma'am," Val assured her, frowning. "Why?"

Pointing across the now-empty train tracks to the open space beyond, Wynifred said, "Because I think we might be in trouble here in a moment or two."

Turning with Val to look in the direction Wynifred was pointing, Haven's heart nearly stopped as she saw five horses approaching in the distance, three of them carrying riders.

"It's him!" she breathed. "It's Wind Talker."

"Or it's someone else lookin' for Effie," Val mumbled.

"No, no—it has to be him," Haven countered.

"One Indian, two women," Haven's grandmother said as she came to stand next to Haven. "No paint on the horses."

Haven looked to her grandmother quickly, wondering how it was possible that such an elderly woman could distinguish horses and riders from such a distance.

"Is it him?" Arabella asked, moving to stand next to Val.

"Is it who?" Wynifred asked as she and Merigold joined the others.

Val held his breath as the riders and horses drew nearer. Yes—he was certain the man riding in front was Wind Talker. But he was too afraid to hope that the other two riders were indeed Lydia and Caroline. Everyone stood on the platform, silent. Haven released Val's hand she'd been holding as he placed his other hand on his pistol grip at his hip.

"Is it Wind Talker, Val?" Haven whispered.

"Yes," Val answered, still afraid to hope.

Yet as Wind Talker led the horses and other riders closer to the train tracks, Val heard a woman's voice call, "Val! Oh, Val!"

"It's Lydia," Val breathed.

Jumping down from the train platform, he ran toward Wind Talker, Lydia, and Caroline.

Both Caroline and Lydia had dismounted by the time Val reached them, and the three reunited siblings collapsed to their knees, in desperate embraces.

Haven gasped and burst into more tears of joy as she watched Val hug and kiss his sisters. His nightmare—though it would haunt him the rest of his life—was no longer in the present but the past. There would be mourning—mourning Alberta, mourning the loss of Lydia and Caroline's ever feeling entirely safe again. But actually living the nightmare was over, and Haven's heart swelled with thankfulness to Heaven—with joy for the man she loved.

Everyone standing on the train platform watched as Val and his sisters walked toward them— as Wind Talker rode toward them, leading the riderless horses in his wake.

"These are my sisters, Lydia and Caroline," Val said as he helped the girls step up onto the platform.

"Hello," Haven offered in a whisper.

The Briscoe girls were dirty. They were dressed in deerskin dresses and moccasins the way Effie had been. They were thin and frail looking, but their bright green eyes glistened with hope.

"I'm Haven," Haven said, offering a hand to one of the young women.

"I'm Lydia," the young woman said, weeping as she accepted Haven's hand.

"I'm Caroline," Caroline said as she accepted Haven's hand next.

"Now, Valentine Briscoe," Wind Talker said as he sat astride his horse, "I have kept my word. I have left my people, killed my father, and brought your sisters to you. You will tell me where my daughter is now."

Val brushed tears from the corners of his eyes. He nodded. "Thank you, Wind Talker. Effie was right to tell me to trust you. And she wanted me to see that your daughter was with you. Your baby is in Limon, with Effie's parents. Do you know Limon?"

Wind Talker nodded. "I do."

"The baby is there," Val confirmed. "I sent her to be safe. And it was good that I did because Rattlesnake Cooley and his men came for her six days ago."

Wind Talker frowned. "Does the devil Rattlesnake know my daughter is in Limon?" he asked.

Val shook his head. "No. Rattlesnake is dead. I

shot him. His men are dead too. Sadie Flower is safe."

Wind Talker's eyes misted. "Sadie Flower?"

"Sadie Mae Prairie Flower," Haven blurted. "It was Effie's wish that she be named so. We all call her Sadie Flower."

Wind Talker glanced away from the group for long moments. And when he did look back to them, he asked, "Valentine Briscoe . . . will Effie's people love my daughter? Will they teach her, educate her in the white man's world, so that she may live free and well cared for?"

"Of course they will, sir," Merigold answered.

Wind Talker scowled at Merigold, but she seemed undeterred. "My sister and I, we are the ones who took Sadie Flower to her grandparents in Limon. And oh, how they love her, sir! She is their daughter's child as well as yours, and they will care for her as if she were their own daughter."

"I know what is in your mind, Wind Talker," Lydia said. "You mean to let Effie's people raise Sadie Flower. You think she will be happier, better cared for with them . . . especially since you have left your people."

Though Wind Talker did not confirm or deny Lydia's claims, he did straighten. "I have no people. I will need to find work for wages. I cannot care for a baby when I must find work . . . when I have no people."

"Stay here," Lydia begged unexpectedly. "Stay with us. Stay with me, Wind Talker. I will be your people. If you believe Sadie Flower will be safer, happier with Effie's parents, then that is well and good. But please, stay with me."

"Lydia?" Val began.

Lydia looked to her brother. "We owe our lives to him, Val. We—me, Caroline, Effie—none of us would have survived if not for him. He saved us, Val. And he brought us to you."

Haven watched as Val inhaled a deep breath, rubbing his face with his hands a moment as if struggling with confusion mingled with anger.

"Wait," he said. "Just wait a minute."

Taking Haven by the hand, Val led her aside.

"What should I do, Haven?" he asked.

Haven could see the conflict in her lover's mind and heart. His sister—the sister he'd worried about for a year, the sister he'd searched for, bartered for—she was asking one of her captors to stay with her. It was, in truth, inconceivable to Haven—but perhaps not so inconceivable as it was to Val.

"She is young, Val," Haven began. "Young and . . . and has experienced horrors neither you nor I can imagine. What her fear must've been when she was taken, when she saw Alberta and Christine murdered—I can't imagine it, Val! And that's why . . . it's why . . . I don't know what you should do. But I think that if Lydia feels somethin' for Wind Talker, if what she feels is simply safe when she's with him and nothin' more, it may be that Lydia and Caroline both will need . . . I don't know what they'll need, Val. All I can tell you is . . . Lydia looks terrified at the thought of Wind Talker leavin'. Furthermore, you and I both know that Sadie Flower will have a much more normal existence if she's allowed to stay with Effie's parents . . . at least for now. I . . . I . . ."

But her stammering was silenced when Val gathered her into his arms and ground his mouth to hers as if he thought kissing her would give him strength and wisdom.

"I see a lot has happened since we left for Limon," Haven heard Merigold say.

Breaking the seal of their kiss, Val gazed into Haven's eyes.

"There's a lot that's gonna transpire here in a bit, darlin'," he said. "I can't even fathom the tornado of emotion and decisions that are gonna come crashin' down on the both of us once I let you go—whether Wind Talker will stay or go, whether he wants to take Sadie Flower away from Effie's parents. Your folks are here, your grandmother. Two of my sisters have been returned." He reached out, brushing a stray strand of hair from Haven's cheek. "And that's why I'm not gonna wait another minute to ask you to marry me, Haven Abernathy."

Haven gasped, new tears springing to her eyes as Val lightly pressed his lips to hers and mumbled, "Will you marry me, darlin'? Will you?"

"Yes, my love! Yes!" Haven wept.

Valentine kissed her and then held her face between his hands, smiling down at her with so much love visible in his eyes that Haven's knees turned to mush.

"Oh, I'm glad," Val said. "I'm so glad. After all, it's like Ronald Henry's been tellin' folks of late . . ."

Haven giggled as she and Val simultaneously said, "I told you they was lovers!"

EPILOGUE

"Oh, these will be so pretty come spring, Grandma," Haven said as she patted the soil over the newly divided iris rhizomes. "I'm so glad you brought them with you from the territory. I had no idea that Mama's butter iris were some you'd left with Grandma and Grandpa Adair."

Haven's grandmother laughed where she sat planting more iris near Mr. and Mrs. Latham's headstones.

"I am glad I brought them, as well," she said. "My mother tended them, and so did my grandmother." She smiled at Haven lovingly. "And now my granddaughter tends them."

Haven sighed as she stared in admiring awe at her beautiful grandmother. It was true, Forest Water Adair was growing older by the day. And Haven knew that in the not-too-distant future, she would have to endure the loss of the woman she loved so deeply. But Haven chose not to worry about impending loss in that moment. In that moment, there in the small Fletcher cemetery, she would simply enjoy the time she had and still enjoyed in her grandmother's loving company.

"Mama," little Effie began as she sat next to Haven, playing with a long foxtail.

"Yes, sweetie?" Haven asked.

As her daughter looked up to her, Haven was awestruck by how much she resembled her father, Val. Effie had his jade-green eyes and dark lashes. And even though it was Haven's long raven hair that hung in two plaits on either side of her head, Haven still thought she was her father's daughter over and over.

"Is Sadie Flower ever gonna get here today?" Effie sighed with impatience.

"Yes, honey," Haven giggled. "You just have to be patient. We heard the train whistle a while ago, didn't we?"

"Yes," Effie whined. "But why is it takin' Daddy so long to drive the Graysons here in the wagon?"

Forest Water laughed a little, amused by her great-granddaughter's restlessness.

"Oh, I'm afraid many things take much longer to arrive than we'd like," Haven explained. "That's why we need to learn to be as patient as we possibly can."

"You mean like Aunt Lydia's baby takin' two weeks too long to get here last summer?" Effie asked.

"That's exactly what I mean," Haven confirmed. "Just imagine how anxious Aunt Lydia and Wind Talker were! Why, they wanted to see baby Albert more than even the rest of us did. But when Albert finally came, weren't we all just too happy to have him to worry about him tryin' our patience?"

"Yes," Effie sighed. "But I'm so excited,

Mama!" she exclaimed, turning on a dime. "I can't wait to see Sadie Flower." Effie lowered her voice, adding, "And I can't wait for Wind Talker to see her either."

"Shhh," Haven gently hushed, glancing back over her shoulder to where Wind Talker and Lydia were planting iris at Effie Grayson's headstone. "We don't want Wind Talker to hear us, remember."

Haven smiled as she watched Lydia and Wind Talker for a moment. She remembered the day Wind Talker had brought Caroline and Lydia to Fletcher—to Val—and remembered the way Lydia had pleaded with Wind Talker to stay. At the time, Haven didn't realize that Lydia already loved the man who was now her husband. And although Caroline had chosen to return home to Limon, Lydia stayed in Fletcher—near Wind Talker. Two years later, for Wind Talker had bitterly mourned the loss of Effie, his heart was healed enough to see Lydia for who she was—a beautiful young woman who loved him unconditionally. Before long, Lydia had won his heart for her own. And now there they sat, planning iris rhizomes at Effie's grave—their darling son, Albert, by their sides.

"But, Mama," Effie began, attempting to whisper, something that was still hard for her, even though she was nearly five years old, "why does Wind Talker think it will be a bad thing for

Sadie Flower to see him? She already knows what he looks like because of the drawin' Auntie Arabella gave to her. I don't understand why we can't tell him that today is the day Sadie Flower is comin' and not tomorrow."

Smiling at her beautiful baby girl, Haven leaned over, planting an affectionate kiss on her forehead. "Oh, someday it'll make more sense, sweetheart, I promise. But for now . . . well, Wind Talker is afraid, I think."

"Afraid of what, Mama?"

"Afraid that Sadie Flower won't love him . . . or maybe that once he's seen her, it will break his heart to let her go."

"Eww wee!" Old Joe exclaimed as he hurried over from the direction of the house. "Havey, that boy of yo's is muddier dan da Miss'ssippi and twice as ripe!"

"Oh no!" Haven laughed. Removing her gloves, she laid them on the ground and stood, intending to head to the house. "I better run on in and—"

"No, you just stay where's you is," Joe instructed, shaking his head. "Mipsie dun changed his mess already. You just stay dere and do what you was doin'. I just want a breaf of fresh air is all. Lo'd almighty," Joe exclaimed as something toward town caught his attention. "Looks to be dem Sandersans is trottin' on ovuh disa way. I best run my raggedy bottom back to da hose."

Haven laughed. "Why, Papa Joe!" she exclaimed.

"Why do you run off like you do every time Miss Wynifred and Miss Merigold come callin'?"

Lowering his voice, Joe answered, "Why, them two is da huggin'ess, kissin'ess two women I ever did know, Havey. And I mean to skedaddle fo' they start in on me 'gin."

As Joe turned and awkwardly hurried back toward the house, Haven, Effie, and Forest Water exchanged amused glances and giggled.

"I like Miss Merigold and Miss Wynifred," Effie chirped.

"You like their cinnamon rolls too, I think," Forest Water remarked with a wink.

"Oh my!" Merigold chimed as she entered the cemetery. "Why, our little cemetery is bound to be the prettiest place in Colorado come spring and summer!"

"Yes indeed!" Wynifred added, gasping with dramatics.

"Good mornin', ladies," Haven greeted as Effie hopped up, running to the Sandersan sisters and hugging them both.

"We heard the train whistle," Merigold said in a lowered voice. "We didn't miss anything, did we?"

"Not at all," Haven answered in a loud whisper. Everyone turned and looked to where Wind Talker and Lydia were planting iris rhizomes. Baby Albert whimpered a bit in the cradle Val had made for him, and Lydia cooed at him and rocked his cradle where it sat in the grass close by.

"Mama! Mama!" little Effie exclaimed in a whisper. "I know why it took Daddy so long to bring 'em. Look! Everyone is walkin' this way. There's Daddy and little Val, Aunt Arabella and Uncle Dan, and oh! Mama! There's—"

Haven giggled as Miss Wynifred managed to gently clamp a hand over Effie's mouth to keep her from drawing Wind Talker's attention.

Haven watched as Val picked up little Valentine and hefted him up to ride on his daddy's shoulders. The sight caused her heart to flutter and butterflies to take to flight in her stomach. Her husband never failed to send goose bumps racing over her arms when he appeared. And to see her little dark-haired, green-eyed son giggling as his father carried him on his shoulders brought tears to her eyes.

Her life was more wonderful, more filled with love and rich companionship, than she had ever imagined it could be. She thought back on the day she had arrived in Fletcher nearly six years before, remembering the way Wynifred and Merigold Sandersan had helped and encouraged her, offering her unconditional love and friendship. Val had burst into her life by way of her instruction room door only a few months later, and that was the moment she'd known she'd never be the same—that Valentine Briscoe would be her life forevermore in one way or the other. And oh, how thankful she was every minute of every day for him—for he was her life! Val had saved her, shown her what true love, what passion and safe security was.

Then Arabella had come and found love with Dan Sterling. Haven turned and looked when she heard the screen door of the house Mipsie and Joe shared slam closed—watched them cross the very front porch that she and Arabella used to sit on in those early autumn days years ago, sharing daydreams of Valentine Briscoe and Dan Sterling. Mipsie carried Johnny on her hip, and Haven smiled, overwhelmed with joy in knowing that her youngest child was being loved by the woman who had loved her her whole life. Old Joe rather tumbled out of the house with Arabella and Dan's boys in tow—three little Sterling Buttons who were as darling and almost as mischievous as the Henry Buttons had once been. Haven smiled when she thought of Robert and Ronald Henry—of what fine young men they were. Hard workers too—which had rather surprised many in Fletcher. They still stopped in to see her and Val and the children three or four times a week, between helping their daddy with chores and working for Old Joe and Wind Talker in training horses.

In that moment, Haven's happiness was complete. Everyone she loved was there—including her grandmother Adair, who had taught her so much about her Cherokee ancestry, taught her so much about so many things. She smiled at her grandmother, saying, "I love you so much, Grandma."

"I love you, Haven," Forest Water said. Tears brimmed in her eyes as if she'd been thinking beautiful thoughts of gratitude and love as well.

"Mornin', all," Val greeted as he lifted little Val from his shoulders and set him to standing on the ground just inside the cemetery gate.

"Mornin', Val," Old Joe greeted. Everyone else greeted Val as well—though Wind Talker did not turn to look at him but simply called "hello" over his shoulder as he continued to work.

"Hey there, pretty little hatmaker of mine," Val said, stepping into the cemetery and taking Haven's hand in helping her to her feet.

"Hello, darlin'," Haven said.

She kissed her husband square on the mouth, giggling when she heard Arabella's boys simultaneously grumble, "Yuck!"

Val stepped aside, and Mr. and Mrs. Grayson smiled and nodded silently to Haven.

Hello, Haven mouthed. She noted the way Mrs. Grayson held tight to Sadie Flower's hand—as if she were afraid of somehow losing her. Haven felt tears gather in her eyes at how perfectly Mrs. Grayson resembled her daughter Effie. It made her think for a moment on Effie's tragic death and the fact Sadie Flower was growing up without knowing her mother. And yet the little girl was obviously very happy.

"Go on, Pearl," Mr. Grayson said, placing a comforting arm around his wife's shoulders. "Let her go. It'll be all right."

Everyone fell silent. Even Robert and Ronald Henry seemed not to make a sound as they suddenly appeared, having apparently been spying again and discovering that this would be the day that the baby whose birth had sent them on an adventure of a lifetime would finally meet her father.

"Go on, Sadie honey," Mrs. Grayson breathed, letting go of her granddaughter's hand. With a smile that Haven knew was more pain than joy, Mrs. Grayson nodded at her granddaughter. "You go on, baby. You go meet your daddy."

Everyone watched as Sadie Flower, now nearly six years old, stepped through the gate of the Fletcher cemetery. Oh, she was a beautiful child! Her dark hair complemented her bright blue eyes in much the same way that Arabella's always had.

"Daddy?" Sadie Flower quietly called.

Everyone watched—held their breath as Wind Talker suddenly became very still.

"Daddy? It's me, Sadie Flower, Daddy," Sadie said, a bit louder.

Haven was certain tears were brimming in everyone's eyes, just as they were in hers. Everyone there knew what had transpired all those years ago—the tragedy, the loss, the heartache. Haven glanced to the Henry Buttons, noting the way

Ronald Henry's right hand moved to press his left shoulder, to rest at the place that Rattlesnake Cooley's bullet had passed through him. Everyone there felt the joy mingled with sorrow as they watched Sadie Flower move toward Wind Talker—move toward her father.

At last, Wind Talker—the brave, powerful, heroic Comanche warrior—turned.

As tears spilled from his eyes, Sadie Flower asked, "Do you love me, Daddy?"

Haven put her hand over her mouth to stifle the sobbing that wanted to escape. And as Sadie Flower drew closer to Wind Talker—as Wind Talker reached out to her, gently gathering her into his arms—Haven was not the only one in Fletcher who could no longer restrain the deep emotion.

"I love you, my Sadie Flower," Wind Talker wept as everyone in attendance either wept or sobbed.

Haven looked up to see Val brush a tear from the corner of each eye, and she knew how deeply emotional the moment was for him.

"I love you, Daddy," Sadie Flower said, bursting into tears as she flung her arms around her father's neck and sobbed into his shirt.

"There they go—Mama and Aunt Haven, bawlin' like always," Arabella and Dan's oldest son, Joe, moaned.

Haven smiled, amused as Arabella snapped her

fingers at her son, wagging a reprimanding index finger at him.

"Come on, little Joe," Ronald Henry said, reaching and taking Joe by the hand. "Me and Robert will show you Sterlin' Buttons an old dead coyote we found this mornin'." Ronald looked to Dan and Arabella. "Is that all right, Sheriff? Mrs. Sterlin'?"

Dan nodded, as did Arabella. And Haven thought it very fitting as she watched Dan and Arabella's three boys run off, seeking adventure at the hands of the Henry Buttons.

"We've decided to come to Fletcher permanent," Mr. Grayson said to Val and Haven. He looked to his wife, pulled a handkerchief from his pocket, and handed it to her as he saw the tears streaming over her face. "Pearl and I agree that Sadie needs to be near her father . . . and her new baby brother," he explained. "And there's nothin' left for us in Limon." He glanced over to the grave where Wind Talker and Lydia had been planting iris—to Effie's grave. "We need to be here with Effie. And we need to be here with Sadie, so she can be with Wind Talker."

More tears escaped Haven's eyes—Val's too, as he nodded and said, "I think it's what Effie would want. I do."

"I do too," Mrs. Grayson sniffled.

Then, helping Grandma Adair to her feet, Val asked, "Grandma? Would you mind takin' Effie and the boys out to your place with you and Miss Wynifred and Miss Merigold for a bit? I'd like for Haven and I to spend some time with Wind Talker and Lydia . . . and the children. If you don't mind."

"I would never mind having my grandchildren at my knee, Valentine," Forest Water said.

"Oh my! No, we don't mind at all," Merigold said.

"But I want to play with Sadie Flower," Effie began to whine.

"Oh, you'll get to play with her soon enough, honey," Wynifred said, taking Effie's hand as Merigold took Val's.

"I'll bring Johnny on out to yo' place in a bit, ladies," Old Joe said.

"Thank you, Joe," Merigold cooed. "And we've got cinnamon rolls waitin' when you do bring him."

Merigold winked at Old Joe, and he exhaled a sigh, sending Mipsie into amused giggles.

Everyone began to go their own way, for they'd seen what they'd come to see. The baby girl who was born in secret and spirited away to keep her safe had been reunited with her father. And Haven couldn't help but think of her grandmother, for she had made the same sort of sacrifice Wind Talker had. She'd given up the thing she loved most in the world, Haven's mother, in order that her daughter and granddaughter would not have to endure the atrocities she was forced to endure. And although Haven admired her grandmother all the more for the sacrifice she'd made so long ago—although she admired Wind Talker for his kind sacrifice—Haven's heart was happy in knowing that Sadie Flower and Wind Talker would be separated no more.

"I love you, Haven Briscoe."

Haven looked to Valentine, seeing that new tears lingered in his eyes.

"Well, I love you too, Valentine Briscoe," she said, reaching up to lay one hand against his handsome, whiskery cheek.

As Valentine continued to stare at her—as his eyes smoldered with love, desire, and gratitude— he whispered, "It's all because of you, you know—all this joy."

Haven shook her head. "Oh, fiddle-faddle, Val," she said, rolling her eyes. "What are you talkin' about?"

Val shrugged. "All of it. If you hadn't come to Fletcher before me, if you hadn't choked on that damn lemon drop from hell, I mighta just gone on lookin' to murder the men who took my sisters and the Grayson girls. I woulda wasted my life in hatred and anger and never found Effie and Sadie Flower, never trusted Wind Talker . . ." Val's voice cracked with emotion, and he reached out, taking Haven's face between his hands. "You saved me. You saved me and Sadie Flower, Wind

Talker and Grandma Adair, not to mention Robert Henry. You saved us all."

"I didn't save you, Val," she whispered. Haven smiled, teasing, "Though I probably did save your behind when I gave you that silly *Farmers' Almanac*." She shook her head, "Good gravy, Valentine Briscoe. Corncobs?"

Val smiled. "That *Farmers' Almanac*," he chuckled. Caressing her lower lip with one thumb, he added, "I love you so much, woman."

"I love you, Val," Haven said, tears of joy spilling from her eyes to trickle over her cheeks. "Thank you for savin' my life . . . in so very many ways."

"Any time, darlin'," Val mumbled. "Any time and always."

And as he kissed her, Haven heard Sadie Flower squeal with delight at finally knowing her father. Haven thought of all the people she loved and cherished—wondered what she had ever done to be blessed with having them surround her, linger in her life. Most of all, she thought of Valentine Briscoe, whose heart had once been so cold—but who now warmed hers to the very core forever with his infinite, impassioned love and his masterful lover's kiss.

AUTHOR'S NOTE

I've got a plethora of snippets waiting for you in this author's note! Therefore, I won't ramble on too terribly long before them. I'll simply thank you for reading this book and hope that it entertained you or touched you in some way. I hope the Henry Buttons made you giggle—that every time you see a *Farmers' Almanac* at the checkout stand at the grocery store, you'll smile and maybe buy one for your husband/boyfriend/ significant other as a gift. (Just leave it with the other reading material on the back of the toilet there.)

This book was written during a very difficult time of my life. While writing this book, Kevin and I lost a nephew. Twenty-three days later, I lost one of the greatest loves of my life—my mother. Fourteen days later, our little granddaughter was born, spending two weeks in the NICU and enduring a life-saving surgery. And those are just the three most heart-wrenching things I thought of first. It has been a rough decade, a summer that caused my heart to ache so badly I was many times certain I was going to have a heart attack—that my body wouldn't live through the excruciating pain of losing my mother and the other stresses life was throwing at us. And that's why I really hope you liked *The Stone-Cold Heart of Valentine Briscoe*—because I know everyone has years like the one we've had this year. Everyone needs a little distraction from it all.

Still, I want you to know that I poured my heart and soul into this book in a way I haven't done in years and years. I wrote this book for me and my closest friends—for you—the way I used to write, before I began to worry so much about making sure everyone in the world was happy with what I'd written. I love this book, even its sad parts, because it makes me feel so deeply. And I so hope it makes you feel deeply, as well.

Moving onto brighter things, *The Stone-Cold Heart of Valentine Briscoe* is one of the books I've written that started out with just a title. Like *A Crimson Frost*, I was just driving along one day, and I thought, "You know what would be a good title for a book? *The Stone-Cold Heart of Valentine Briscoe*!" I'm weird that way. I mean, who comes up with a title and *then* figures out what the book is going to entail? Ha ha, right? But I'll admit to you that I secretly like to come up with a book in that way—title first, content later. So I'm glad this one came to me the way it did.

And now, I'll let you hop on down to the snippets! Snippets are fun for me. In reading my books into audiobooks, I cannot believe how many real-life things are in each and every one of them. I could write a book of just snippets! So many readers have written to me letting me know that they hope I never stop including snippets at the end of my books—because they love the insight into my writing process. And here's hoping you feel that way too. So enjoy the snippets, and thank you for all you do for me!

Yours,
Marcia Lynn McClure

Snippet #1—Anybody else out there ever heard the old song, "Little Bitty Bilbo Abernathy Nathan Allen Quincy Jones"? When I was little, I had a 45-rpm record of "Little Bitty Bilbo Abernathy Nathan Allen Quincy Jones," performed by Sheb Wooley. On the flipside was a sad, heart-wrenching song about a sick little girl, entitled, "Daddy Kiss and Make it Well" (a happy-ending story that used to cause my little three- to seven-year-old self to sob through the entire thing). "Little Bitty Bilbo Abernathy Nathan Allen Quincy Jones," however, was a bouncy, happy song with a catchy tune, and I loved it! It still runs through my head very often, and one day while it was playing in my mind, "Abernathy" just struck me as the perfect surname for Haven!

Snippet #2—My mother had an "Aunt Alice," her father's sister, Alice States. I was blessed with the opportunity to meet Aunt Alice twice before she passed away. "The kids used to call me Alice United States," she told my daughter on one occasion. Though I never knew her well, I've always had a soft spot for Aunt Alice. Thus, you know whence came the inspiration for Haven's Aunt Alice.

Snippet #3—You may have noticed that I have a soft spot for "Turkey in the Straw." Although "Turkey in the Straw" made its debut in my books in *Dusty Britches*, it is a tune that has echoed through my mind for over forty-six years! That's right, forty-six years! One reason I love it is because it was the tune played during the opening credits of an old Tom Sawyer TV series back in the late '60s—the series wherein my love for Huckleberry Finn was solidified for eternity! However, the most vivid memory I have of "Turkey in the Straw" takes place in Grace, Idaho, during my first grade school year. I can't remember if our little class learning the Virginia reel was during PE time (although I think it may well have been) or just as an extracurricular activity during school. But what I do very vividly remember is the song we reeled to—"Turkey in the Straw"! I also remember Tony Spencer, a first-grade classmate—a boy who was always smiling, always teasing, and just plain fun! He used to pick me up and carry me around all the time, as I playfully kicked my feet and demanded he put me down. He was my partner for the Virginia reel and added so much flirtation to my day that it was really quite romantic! "Turkey in the Straw," learning the Virginia reel, and Tony Spencer carrying me around is still one of my most vivid memories of that time.

During the course of writing *The Stone-Cold Heart of Valentine Briscoe*, I was blessed with reconnecting with my BFF from those early years of my life spent in Grace, Idaho (and I literally mean blessed)! Renae found me via an Author's Note in one of my books and contacted me—and boy, oh, boy, has that meant so much to me, buoyed me up so often, and just plain made me gleeful! One day, while discussing old classmates with Renae, I mentioned Tony, and she gently let me know that Tony had passed away almost ten years ago; cancer took him. It's funny how someone you only knew for a little while, as I did Tony—someone you never saw again after first grade—could brand themselves so permanently into your mind and heart. Sadly, I also discovered the passing of two other friends from that time of my life— two boys who, like Tony, still continue to inspire me because of the memories I cherish of them.

Eric Rudd was one, my sweet little towheaded friend with whom I used to play house and pick huckleberries. The other loss to my heart was a boy named Bennie Thornock—the boy I had a crush on and shared a seat with on a school field trip to see *Willy Wonka and the Chocolate Factory*. Memories of Bennie have tugged at my heart nearly my whole life, and when I discovered that he too had passed away (nearly twenty years ago), an awful melancholy settled in my chest for several days. This isn't the perkiest, happiest snippet for you, I know, but I do have a reason for sharing it—my own personal proof that each of us touches the lives of others. We may not know them for a long time, may not even know they remember us and how we treated them, but we all brand hearts with our interaction. It's something I ponder quite often—whose hearts have I branded with good memories and feelings and whose have I scarred, you know? Anyway, it probably isn't the last time you'll get to hear "Turkey in the Straw" in your mind while reading my books. And after all, it's a catchy tune!

Snippet #4—The Lemon Drop. Herein lies an excerpt from something my mom jotted down in 1992. You won't understand why it's relevant to this book unless you read this entire snippet (wink wink!).

We lived with Grandma and Grandpa States for about a year and then moved into a little cabin on "the Knapp place" and later into one owned by a man named Pop Curtis. It was during this time of my life that my mom says I would have starved to death if she hadn't been able to nurse me until I was eighteen months old because all they had to eat was beans and rice; that I put my rubber dolly in the oven to keep her warm, and Mom, not knowing she was in there, shut the oven door, and my dolly burned; that the little pigs would knock me down and get my freshly baked, buttered bread if I wandered outside to eat it; that I choked on a lemon drop, and my mom picked me up by my feet and shook me, and the lemon drop shot out of my throat and went rolling across the ole wooden floor. I can still see it by the dim light of the kerosene lamp as it bounced across the floor.

Snippet #5—For those of you who are wondering—yes! Haven's use of "fiddle-dee-dee" *is* my nod to Margaret Mitchell and Scarlett O'Hara!

Snippet #6—For those of you who are also wondering—yes! Wynifred and Merigold Sandersan are my nod to my favorite movie to watch in autumn, *Hocus Pocus*!

Snippet #7—For those of you who are wondering about Valentine's first name—why yes, it is! Val is my homage to Kevin Bacon's character in the original, epic movie, *Tremors*!

Snippet #8—If you've never read the children's book *Andrew Henry's Meadow* by Doris Burns, you must! It was the favorite storybook of my childhood and still is my favorite storybook as an adult. My daughter and oldest grandson name *Andrew Henry's Meadow* as one of their favorites too. Thus the names of Andrew Henry, his brothers, Robert and Ronald, and his sisters are my tribute to Doris Burns and that beloved book I enjoy to this day.

Snippet #9—If you've read a few of my books, by now you should be somewhat familiar with my decades-long friend, Barbara (a.k.a. Baa Baa and Babs). She's my friend to whom my book *Divine Deception* is dedicated. You also know her from *Indebted Deliverance*—from the Author's Note therein, at least. She's the palzie-wowlzie who not only challenged me to somehow incorporate the word *emasculate* into one of my books (I did so, just for *her,* in *Indebted Deliverance*) but also once uttered the word *multisyllabic* during the course of a conversation she and I were having. I loved the rhythm of that word—multisyllabic—and it became one of my favorite words to say forever thereafter. Ha ha! My point is this: during the course of reading *The Stone-Cold Heart of Valentine Briscoe,* you may or may not have had to slow the pace of your reading whenst you happened upon the word *pulchritudinous.* Whether it gave you pause or not, I do want Barbara to know that "pulchritudinous" was incorporated just for her! So was *exhibitionistic*—for it seemed a good companion to *emasculate.* There are a few other nods hidden here and there throughout the text and just for Barbara's sake (should she ever read the book). I miss Barbara so much, miss having her friendship close at hand and her contagious, hysterical laughter! Love you forever, Babs!

Snippet #10—Robert and Ronald Henry being referred to as "the Henry Buttons" was inspired by stories my dad tells about some brothers he knew during the Great Depression, the Taylor Buttons. When my dad was a child, the Taylor Buttons were already grown men. Bob, Hank, and Terril were friends with my dad's parents, and Dad has wonderful, very fond memories of the three brothers, the Taylor Buttons. I asked Dad once why everyone called them the Taylor Buttons. Why didn't he just call them the Taylor kids or something? He explained that everyone called them the Taylor Buttons—that groups of little boy brothers were often called "buttons" when they were all together, simply because they were just cute as buttons. It was a popular part of the 1920s and 1930s vernacular that I've always adored. Maybe someday I'll write a children's book with that title—*The Taylor Buttons*, or something. But for now—well, it's obvious that Robert and Ronald Henry are as cute as they are mischievous. Thus, Haven called them the Henry Buttons!

Snippet #11—When I write historical fiction—a book meant to be very historically accurate like *The Fragrance of Her Name*, *A Crimson Frost*, or *Beneath the Honeysuckle Vine*—I really do try to be very accurate with the history mentioned throughout the book. I've had some questions before—some doubting Thomases who try to call me on the carpet about certain things. And so I thought it would be fun to mention something I learned while writing *The Stone-Cold Heart of Valentine Briscoe*. The two poems we have all heard that begin with, "What are little boys made of?" and "What are little girls made of?" are much older than even I realized! The first appearance of these two nursery rhymes in print is in a manuscript by English poet Robert Southey. Southey was born in 1774 and died in

1843. It is generally believed that the poems owe their origin to him.

His version is thus:
What are little boys made of?
What are little boys made of?
Snips and snails and puppy dogs tails
And such are little boys made of.

What are young women made of?
Sugar and spice and all things nice.

The more modern version we are familiar with is:
What are little boys made of?
What are little boys made of?
Snips and snails
And puppy-dogs' tails
That's what little boys are made of

What are little girls made of?
What are little girls made of?
Sugar and spice
And everything nice
That's what little girls are made of.

Fun, huh?

Snippet #12—The Outhouse Fire in the Hole and *Farmers' Almanac*. My mom told me many horror stories about using the outhouse when she was growing up. I even have my own tales to tell about having to use one when our plumbing went caput when I was little and our family lived on a dairy farm. However, it was this past summer—when my Uncle Wayne was telling me about watching my mom and her sister, Sharon, light pieces of paper on fire and drop them down into the outhouse hole to scare the black widows away from the seat—that I knew Haven and Arabella would do the same thing! Consequently, as I was talking to Uncle Wayne and asking him outhouse usage questions, he mentioned that their family used the Sears and Roebuck catalog as toilet paper. Now, although I knew that the Sears and Roebuck catalog was America's choice for toilet hygiene, I didn't know that rural folks still used it into the '50s! Well, instantly I knew that, although most people in rural Colorado during the 1880s used corncobs to clean themselves after a visit to the outhouse, Haven and Arabella were far too dainty and ladylike to use corncobs. But when I started doing research and discovered that the first Sears and Roebuck catalog wasn't printed until 1888, and knowing Haven moved to Fletcher in 1885, I had to find an alternate periodical that would be readily available. Of course, my first thought was the *Farmers' Almanac*! It's been around since 1792 and is just the right size for usage by two Georgia peaches transplanted out west, don't you think?

Snippet #13—Sugar Flower/Sugar Teat. My own dad inspired the "sugar flower" conversation between Haven and Val—only my dad and his family referred to the proxy pacifier as a "sugar t-t" or "sugar t-tty." All my life I've heard the story of how grandmother once gave my dad a sugar t-tty when he was a little boy. Everyone made fun of him—being that he was no longer a baby—but my dad didn't care. After all, he got to suck on that sweet "sugar flower," and it was yummy! My dad came for a visit during the time I was working on *The Stone-Cold Heart of Valentine Briscoe*, and while he was here, he said something about a sugar-you-know-what, and my daughter asked him what one was. As I listened to Dad describing it to his granddaughter, I got to thinking about it and decided to do a little historical research and . . . voilà! A sugar flower or sugar t-t was referenced as far back as 1802. Of course, the more decorous name for it was a sugar flower—being that the visible folded fabric looked something like the baby had a flower sticking out of its mouth. Still, as you know, I am driven to immortalize vanishing aspects of history—especially of my own family's history. Therefore, I decided that I needed to incorporate the item in the story. Yet I knew I couldn't flat out refer to it as a sugar t-t the way my family had always done. So, I came up with referring to it as exactly what it is—a sugar teat. I considered dubbing it sugar nipple when Haven and Val were talking about it—but you know how difficult it is for me to type out words like navel, nipple, and things. And besides, I didn't think Haven or Val would be comfortable using the word "nipple" in front of one another so soon after their acquaintance. So I went the route of my dairy farm upbringing and settled on sugar teat. Besides, further research proved that "sugar teat" was in use by 1847—so I felt validated.

Snippet #14—Dotted Swiss. Whilst I was in the midst of writing Chapter Eight (where Val appears at his front door with a quilt wrapped around his waist), I was at lunch with a few intimate friends. In the course of explaining the chapter to my friends over a delicious meal of Panera Bread broccoli cheddar soup with bread and a piping-hot mug of hot chocolate, I mentioned the opening scene of that chapter, and the fact that Val had been so groggy, he'd simply gotten out of bed (having slept in the n-de) and grabbed something to wrap around his waist and thereby provide him with modesty.

In the very next instant, my cherished friend "Jane Doe," with eyes wide as saucers and a smile that could charm the Ghost of Christmas Yet to Come himself, giggled, "I hope it wasn't dotted swiss!"

Through my gasping laughter, I breathed, "I HAVE to put that in there! I have to! That's hysterical, 'Jane'!"

"Jane" has provided so many inspirational comments to me in the past—not just for use in my books but more for my own wisdom-building benefit and amusement—that I just could *not* let the dotted swiss comment go by without immortalizing it and "Jane" in fiction! As I've told you so many times before, if I didn't live the life I live and have lived, I would never be able to write.

P.S. For historical correctness's sake: dotted swiss is thought to have first appeared in Switzerland in 1750. So there could have, indeed, been a length of dotted swiss lying around Mrs. Vickers's old sewing room in Val's farm in 1885!

Snippet #15—Cinnamon Rolls. Did I mention that I was craving cinnamon rolls (specifically Cinnabon's) the entire time I was writing this book? Thus, the incorporation of the Sandersan sisters' cinnamon rolls. (FYI—my cinnamon roll craving was *so* much worse after Wynifred and Merigold showed up with that first batch!)

Snippet #16—Adair. My great-grandmother's grandmother was Sara Ann Adair. She was born in Georgia in 1834 and traveled the Trail of Tears with her family in 1838. I know that at least

Sara, her mother, and her father lived to reach the Oklahoma Indian Territory. They were left near a property owned by Philemon Guthrie, and Sara grew up to marry his son, Calvin. Sara Ann Adair's father was Edward Adair, and he passed away in 1864 in the Cherokee Nation, Indian Territory. Edward's father was John Adair, born in Scotland in 1738. Sara Ann Adair's great-granddaughter was my grandmother, Opal Edith Switzler States, and the inspiration for Sweet Cherry Ray's character. My grandmother Opal had many siblings, but Carthel, Loren (Jack), and twin boys Herbert and Hubert (Rusty) are, as you noticed, remembered in this book. Finally, my youngest son's middle name is Adair. Maybe a little too much information, but I do like to share with you from whence certain elements of my books are conceived. So I hope you enjoy the Adair stuff just a little.

Snippet #17—The Cherokee driven from Georgia really did own African slaves! Horrifying, I know! In fact, many historians calculate that ten percent or more of all people on the Cherokee Trail of Tears were Africans that were either slaves or freed people who had married Cherokee people. Even after the Civil War, as a freed people, former slaves remained in the Indian Territory, having married Cherokees after the Trail of Tears.

Snippet #18—Haven's *gorgeous* hair is actually inspired by the gorgeous, raven, silk-like hair I see here in my home state so very often! The Navajo people of New Mexico have hair like you've never seen before. It's always long and perfect—I mean perfect! It truly does look like strands of silk, and I am awed every time I see a woman or man of that tribe wearing their hair down or even braided. It's incredible! If any of my Cherokee ancestors had hair like the Navajo people here do, none of us inherited it, that's for sure!

Snippet #19—Some may think that Val's tendency to answer the front door while wearing only a quilt is just far too risqué—although I hope everyone has a good enough sense of humor to giggle about it. For as my friend Amy "Aimes" W. once said to me, "It's always funny to catch someone naked!" And it's not just Amy's timeless quote that inspired Val's impish delight in nearly flashing Haven and the Henry Buttons when they called on him to ask him to judge the apple butter contest. It was also the impish delight my own husband, Kevin, relishes by doing similar things to try and astonish me that lent inspiration to Val's mischievous nekked-ness! During the first few months we were married (back when young married couples were penniless and almost always living in apartments void of furniture), Kevin and I owned exactly two pieces of furniture: a used waterbed and the cedar chest my parents had given me the Christmas I was sixteen. Now the waterbed was in our bedroom, of course. But the cedar chest was against the long wall in our front room that was to your right when you walked into our apartment—you know, where the couch would've been had we owned one yet. Well, one day (on one of Kevin's few days off from work) I arrived home from work, pushed my key into the outside doorknob of our apartment, unlocked the door, and pushed it open. As I closed the door behind me, I glanced to my right, and there, standing on my cedar chest, butt-naked, was Kevin, performing his male stripper impersonation! Ah ha ha! Yep, truth is often stranger than and more amusing than fiction! (P.S. Something the rest of the world will never know is that Kevin does a profoundly impressive male stripper impersonation!)

Snippet #20—And now we come to the Comanche people. Before I give you this historical truth, I do want to reiterate that many scholars, historians, and documents theorize or reveal that the Spaniards were brutal to the Comanches—torturing, murdering, and everything sickening that travels with evil men doing evil deeds. It is thought that the Spaniards' treatment of the Comanches is what led to the

Comanche being the most brutal Native American tribe in the past. From what I've read and researched, the Comanches made the Apaches' brutality seem kind in comparison. Thus, the old adage—murder begets murder, evil begets evil—seems to ring true in the Comanches' experience at the hands of the Spaniards. The only historical discrepancy that I took creative license with in this book would be in reference to the renegade band of Comanches that took the Briscoe and Grayson girls. The last Comanches were driven to the reservation in 1879. However, *The Stone-Cold Heart of Valentine Briscoe* takes place in 1885, which was necessary for me to be able to incorporate the Trail of Tears timeline and the millinery fashions of that day. Therefore, the Comanche band needed to be renegades. In truth, there was a Renegade period with the Apache people between 1879 and 1886. But because of the location of Fletcher, and the fact that Comanche people were more violent even than Apache, I tweaked the history a little.

Snippet #21—Truth be told, Wind Talker was not my first attempt at naming Effie's heroic Comanche husband. My first try was Stream Dancer. I wanted Wind Talker to have a more unique name than his fellow warriors in the renegade Comanche band. However, the more I thought about it—the more I said it out loud to myself—I just wasn't sure about the word, "Stream." I sometimes get really, really hung up on historical correctness (and sometimes I don't, obviously), and I wasn't sure "Stream" would be the name of a Comanche warrior. It sounded a little too soft—and also caused one of my favorite childhood songs, "Give, Said the Little Stream," to rivulet through my brain for days on end, which further spurred my feelings of Stream Dancer being just a little too soft for a Comanche warrior of Wind Talker's character. Initially I wanted to stick with the "Dancer" part of the name and decided to try out a different first-name option—something other than Stream. Naturally, the first body of water I thought of that may have been of importance to the Comanche band was "River." But then I said it out loud: "River Dancer." Ah ha ha ha! Yep! As visions of Michael Flatley "Irish dancing" across a stage— his curly, blond mullet bouncing in time with the downy-white billowing sleeves of his silky shirt—began to leap through my mind, I knew that a complete name change for Stream Dancer/ River Dancer was in need. Upon doing a bit more research on Comanche names, I immediately thought of Wind Talker. Now, Wind Talker is a more exceptional name for Wind Talker than you may realize. Having a mom who was not only of Native American Cherokee descent but also a die-hard World War II historian and a true patriot in every regard, I grew up hearing stories of and learning to deeply appreciate and respect the Navajo Code Talkers. Although the Cherokee and Choctaw tribes were the pioneers of code talking during World War I, it was the Navajo code talkers of the second world war that I knew had been an invaluable force in saving thousands of lives during that time. I even had the privilege of meeting a few of the remaining twenty-nine Navajo code talkers a few years back. And I am so grateful for that opportunity, especially since Chester Nez, the last of those original Navajo code talkers, died in 2014. To this day, the Navajo Code is the only spoken military code that has never been deciphered. Thus, though Wind Talker is of Comanche origin, his name pays tribute to a group of men and military veterans I have admired all my life. (River Dancer? Seriously? Ha ha ha!)

Snippet #22—My mom was what my two sons referred to as "stealth!" She ascended or descended a flight of stairs, walked through an entire house, or appeared in a room without anyone hearing her at *all!* Many were the times when one of us would be watching TV late at night, thinking we were very aware of our surroundings, when all at once, a voice from behind us would ask, "Whatcha watchin'?" Furthermore, no matter how hard any of us tried, we could never sneak up as silently as my mother could. I think it was that she always worried about bothering someone, interrupting, and not wanting to inconvenience people. It was an incredible skill she had, and the romantic in me likes to believe that, like Haven, my mother inherited her "stealth" from her Cherokee ancestors. (I'm not exaggerating. You could never hear my mom coming if she didn't want you to! Ask those of us who nearly jumped out of our skins on more than one occasion!)

Snippet #23—In my backyard there is one corner that is precious to me. Every late spring, a space of very pastel yellow iris thrives. (My grandma and mom call them flags, but all I can find about "yellow flag iris" is that it's a noxious weed that's poisonous to cattle and can irritate the skin. Mine do resemble the description but don't irritate the skin and are beautiful! So I'm not sure what to think!) Anyway, they may not be vibrant like the purple bearded iris I love, but I love these little flags/iris all the more because, as with so many things I treasure in life, there's a story here!

In a recent comment I read on one site concerning my books, someone said, "She [meaning me] seems to always be longing for the past." And you know what, I do long for the past! Anyone with any age, wisdom, and experience tends to miss the past and long for simpler, happier times at one point or another. And I admit that I really do! I miss the times when kids played outside all summer long, using their imaginations or running through sprinklers! I miss when we had an intelligent man in the White House who deserved to be there and deserved our respect. I miss my grandparents and feeding calves formula from a great big bottle. I could go on forever (as you well know), but suffice it to say that the story of my plain little flags/iris is another prompt from the past that I love. Therefore, I thought I'd share it with you!

My great-grandma Edna Mae Guthrie Hutchens Switzler Howell is the first person to have cared for the rhizomes from whence my yellow flags spring. Edna Mae kept the flags in her flower garden, and at one point, my grandmother (her daughter) Opal Edith Switzler States dug up a bunch of the flag rhizomes and planted them on the place she and my grandpa owned in Canyon City, Colorado. Sometime after Edna Mae passed away, Opal Edith and my grandpa left Canyon City and moved to Colorado Springs, taking some of the flag rhizomes with them and planting them in their backyard.

Both Opal Edith and my grandpa (Wayne States—you know him as helping to inspire Brevan in *The Heavenly Surrender*) had passed away by 1993, when my uncle decided to move from their home in Colorado Springs. Before he moved, in the summer of 1993, my mother, Patsy, and I dug up a clump of Edna Mae's yellow flags and moved them to my mom and dad's house in Albuquerque, New Mexico.

In 1997 Kevin and I moved our little family to Ferndale, Washington, and in 1999 my dad dug up some of Edna Mae's rhizomes and sent them to me. I planted them in Washington, and they thrived like never before. And then in 2005, Kevin and I moved again. In an effort to get back to New Mexico, Kevin accepted a job in Colorado. Before our house in Ferndale sold, my dear friend Amy W. (Yes, "It's always funny to catch someone naked!" Amy) did me a great service; she went to our little butter-yellow house, dug up a clump of Edna Mae's iris rhizomes, and plopped them into her own garden. Then that fall she dug up the majority of the rhizomes and shipped them to me in Monument, Colorado. Knowing that we wouldn't be in Monument forever, instead of putting great-grandma's flag rhizomes in the ground, I plopped them in a whiskey barrel half with a bunch of potting soil and dirt. They thrived in Monument at 7,400 feet above sea level, even though they'd come from 300 feet above sea level in Ferndale. They also bloomed a lot later than they had in Washington. But they survived and thrived.

In 2009 Kevin and I were finally able to move back to New Mexico. The move was crazy and rushed and stressful, being that it was in the middle of winter—and in Colorado, that's precarious! I was so thankful when Kevin opened the back of the moving truck to reveal that he'd managed to pull the whiskey barrel half out of the snow pack in Monument and, with my son Mitchel's help, heft it up into the moving van and bring Edna Mae's flags back to New Mexico once more!

I left the rhizomes in that same whiskey barrel half until 2013. I'd noticed that there weren't as many shoots coming up from my great-grandmother's, grandmother's, and mother's rhizomes, and I knew it was because they were long past needing to be divided. And so Kevin and I busted them out of the barrel, separated them, and plopped them in a spot in one corner of our backyard.

I was worried that first year, because the iris did not bloom. I knew it was because of the trauma of being transplanted and also because we'd moved them in the spring instead of waiting until fall. However, the very next summer, Edna Mae's flags were blooming beautifully!

Four years later, they've tripled, and I divided them last fall for my own daughter, Sandy, to plant in her own backyard! Now my daughter has her great-great-grandma Edna Mae's flags in her yard, and I know that every time she looks at them—every time she tends to them, every time they bloom—she'll know that they have sprung from the efforts, love, and care of five generations of women in her family!

Snippet #24—Special Acknowledgments. I usually don't include "acknowledgments" in my books, simply for the fact that I would literally have to thank everyone I've ever known, seen, talked to, or passed on the street—at least it seems that way to me whenever I sit down and start to make of list of those who have inspired me and helped me get to where I am today as an author—as a person even! However, so much transpired during the time that I was working on *The Stone-Cold Heart of Valentine Briscoe* that I did want to take a moment to thank a very, very, very few people who, to be quite frank, helped me make it through to the end of this book—not to mention several months of enduring heartache, loss, and overwhelming stress.

Mom: You are undeniably the most wonderful woman to ever walk the earth! My heart has been breaking for years as you began to slip away and continues to break without you here. I miss you every millisecond of every moment of every day and long for the time when I can be with you again, give you the hugs you never got enough of here on earth, and remind you how much I love you and how grateful I am to you for loving me more than yourself! Thank you for continuing to inspire me as you always have, Mom. I love you!

Dad: Thank you for giving me the gifts of insight and discerning souls! Thank you for my sense of humor and for the gallons of Maalox you drank while raising me—never complaining, just taking swig after swig right out of the bottle. Thank you for the love of my ancestry you and Mom gifted to me and for telling me stories and making sure those who went before were never forgotten. Thank you for my brown hair and hazel eyes, for nicknaming me "Skeeter," and for my ability to laugh no matter what life throws at me. I love you so much, Dad!

Uncle Wayne: I know you won't believe it, but I've admired and loved you since the day I was born! You always seemed like a mythical man to me—so smart, so interested in the same things as I was and am. You will never know what your influence, love, and attention has meant to my life as a whole and to the person that I am. I love you, Uncle Wayne! Thank you so much for letting me pick your brain during the writing of this book!

Sandy: My Roni Pony. You have given me such strength, my sweet, wonderful, caring daughter! I truly do not know how I would've made it through these past months, and this book, without your constant encouragement, unconditional and patient love, and the things/events you've arranged for us to do together. You will never know the strength you are to me! I love you so much, my perfect baby girl!

Brette J.: For hanging in there with me as I fall so far behind on everything over and over and over again! For being my cheerleader, my confidant, and professional ALL! I loved you as a baby, and I love you now! Thank you!

Renae H.: Thank you for finding me, my long-lost but never forgotten Bestie! It was divine intervention that you found me, especially finding me when you did. I had missed you for forty-six years, thought of you during all of that time apart. Reconnecting with you, being able to talk to you, and most of all hearing you call me "Skeeter" and give me hugs meant more to me than you will ever know! I love you forever!

Bennie Thornock, Eric Rudd, and Tony Spencer—Three little boys that I have cherished nearly my whole life. You inspired me without ever knowing it, and I wish you all the happiness Heaven has to offer! Thank you, boys! I love you!

Kevin, Sandy, Mitch, Trent, Soren, Mallory, Karli, Sandy, Deb, June, Weezy, Stace, Lisa, Shannon, Andrea, Nate, Leilani, Melody, Jean, Barbara, Dixie, Karen, Gina, Amy L., Amy W., Bobbie, Uncle Russell, Auntie, Luanna, Brice, Grandpa, Grandma, Grandma Hutchens, Aunt Alice, Sara Ann Adair, and to any and all who have touched my life: You have inspired me, built me up, given me strength, and made me who I am today.

ABOUT THE AUTHOR

Marcia Lynn McClure's intoxicating succession of novels, novellas, and e-books—including *Shackles of Honor*, *The Windswept Flame*, *A Crimson Frost*, and *The Bewitching of Amoretta Ipswich*—has established her as one of the most favored and engaging authors of true romance. Her unprecedented forte in weaving captivating stories of western, medieval, regency, and contemporary amour void of brusque intimacy has earned her the title "The Queen of Kissing."

Marcia, who was born in Albuquerque, New Mexico, has spent her life intrigued with people, history, love, and romance. A wife, mother, grandmother, family historian, poet, and author, Marcia Lynn McClure spins her tales of splendor for the sake of offering respite through the beauty, mirth, and delight of a worthwhile and wonderful story.

Books are produced in the United States using U.S.-based materials

Books are printed using a revolutionary new process called THINKtech™ that lowers energy usage by 70% and increases overall quality

Books are durable and flexible because of smythe-sewing

Paper is sourced using environmentally responsible foresting methods and the paper is acid-free

Center Point Large Print

600 Brooks Road / PO Box 1
Thorndike, ME 04986-0001 USA

(207) 568-3717

US & Canada:
1 800 929-9108
www.centerpointlargeprint.com

BOOK "MARKS"

If you wish to keep a record that you have read this book, you may use this space to mark a private code. Please do not mark the book in any other way.
